AF264647

HURRICANE

JUSTICE

Patricia Watkins

Published by Down Design Publications
All rights reserved
© Patricia Watkins, 15th November, 2017
ISBN 978-0-9572104-93
www.downdesignpublications.com

All characters in this publication are fictional, and any resemblance to real persons, living or dead, is purely coincidental.

Cover illustration by
www.goodcoverdesign.co.uk

OTHER BOOKS BY PATRICIA WATKINS

TRICK OF FATE: Connell O'Keeffe & The Pen Caer
Legacy

DYFED ODYSSEY: Connell O'Keeffe & The
Spider's Web
(Sequel to TRICK OF FATE)

THE WAYWARD GENTLEMAN: John Theophilus
Potter & The Town of Haverfordwest

THE WAYWARD GENTLEMAN: John Theophilus
Potter & The Smock Alley Theatre
"A spirited historical novel marked by humor, intrigue
and entertainment." – *Kirkus Reviews*
(Prequel to THE WAYWARD GENTLEMAN: John
Theophilus Potter & The Town of Haverfordwest)

VOYAGE INTO LIMBO
(One of our top ten self-published books of 2014*)
*The Bookbag (www.thebookbag.co.uk)

CHAPTER 1

Finn Westlake's battered WWII jeep's sudden, sliding halt almost catapulted him out into the churning river, and he stared at the woman, eyebrows raised, questioning what he was seeing, but there she was, clad only in dripping bra and undies, leaping up and down in the middle of the lane, waving her arms at him. He leaned forward, rested his elbows on the steering wheel, slid his aging Tilley hat to the back of his head, and gave her a wide grin. He was ready to accompany the grin with some witty comment appropriate to the occasion, when he realized her face was streaked with tears mingling with the ochre dust his screeching tires had thrown up and now covered them both.

He leapt out over the door, leaving the jeep's ancient engine dieseling noisily after having stalled itself so dramatically. "What's wrong? What's happened?"

"It's my father! He's out there!" She waved

her arms towards the center of the river. "I'm sure he has to be dead or drowning already! I can't see him anywhere!" Her voice rose to a hysterical pitch. "He has to be trapped! See it? See it? Look! Right there! It's his plane… out there, in the river, and… and… he's in it. I… I don't know what to do. It was crazy…! Just crazy… I wouldn't have come out jogging if I'd thought he would go…" Still jumping up and down in agitation, she pointed down at the river bank and the tangled mass of reeds along the edge. "I tried to go out there, but it, it… There was no…"

Finn held up his hand. "Whoa. Hold it a minute. You're saying your father's plane did a nosedive into the river right in front of you? Just like that?"

"Yes, yes, I'm telling you, I was out jogging, and he…"

He shook his head. "No. Forget the details for now; if he *is* trapped, then we need to get him out of there asap. How long since it crashed?" He peered out towards the center of the river, where the light aircraft's tailfin was barely visible in the early-morning mist swirling around it.

"Three… Maybe five minutes, I…" She grabbed his arm. "Please, please…"

"Okay, okay. Let's calm down a bit here. Have you called for help already?"

"No. I couldn't… I… I don't have my phone."

"And the battery's flat on mine."

"I did try, but… but… it's so wild out there…" She grabbed hold of him again. "Please, please! You must help me. I don't know what… We must *do* something."

Finn glanced up and down the road. It was empty. "The best thing I can think of is…"

"Oh, do please hurry. We must do something. Oh, I do wish he hadn't…"

Finn pointed towards his jeep. "Think you can drive that?"

"I… I guess so. Why? What are you going to do? I… I still can't see him… He *has* to be still inside… And if he can't get out… Oh! Oh! I wish he hadn't… I'm sure he must be… Can *you* reach him? What can we…?"

He took hold of her arms, forcing her to stand still. "Okay, I'll see if I can reach the plane, but you're going to have to take the jeep and drive to the callbox up at the next crossroads. You know where it is?"

"Yes, but…"

"But nothing… Look at me. You need to calm down and listen to me. Come on now. What's your name?"

"Diana."

"Right Diana. You're way too distracted here, and you'll need to calm down and think clearly if you want to help. Look at me, will you? You understand what I'm telling you?"

She looked up at him, and he smiled at her, letting go her arms. "That's better. Okay, now listen. The key's in the ignition. Call 911 first, and explain what's happened, then phone this number." He rummaged in his pocket, found his wallet, and thrust his business card and some change into her hand. "Whoever answers, tell them Finn needs them both here pronto, and to bring their scuba gear with them.

Got that?"

"Yes." She nodded tentatively. "Yes, I... I think so. But what about...? I can't just drive off and...and..."

"Look! You want to help, or not? Because right now, me swimming out there is the only hope he's got, and I'm going to need help, and you're the only one who can get it. Right? So, go! Now! Come on! Don't stand there, dithering! We're wasting precious time here."

Diana nodded again, went over to the Jeep, and climbed aboard. "Yes... yes, you're right, of course."

Finn watched nervously as she sat down in what was left of the bucket seat, moved it forward a few notches, fired up the engine, found the gears, and set the vehicle in motion. Then, satisfied that she knew what she was doing, he bent down quickly, snatched up her jogging clothes and shoes from the grass verge, and tossed them into the back of the retreating jeep. "Better take these with you."

He pulled off his boots, khaki shirt and socks, and by the time she was on her way, they lay in a heap on the still dew-covered grass, his hat and boots perched on top. For a few moments, he watched her and his jeep lurch unsteadily up the dusty Florida road, his brain struggling to adjust to one minute driving to his office, working on the logistics of inspecting the damage to a freighter sunk in sixty feet of shark-infested water, to the next minute being faced with the task of rescuing someone from a sunken light plane, the nose of which was resting in about eight or nine feet of wildly churning river. He blinked, pushed the contents of his jeans' pockets under his hat, and dived in.

The strong current seized him at once, drawing him downriver. He struggled against it, aiming for the plane's still visible tailfin, then noticed a man's head bobbing around near it, but he too was being dragged downstream, and before Finn could reach him, the head had vanished. Both being swept along by the river, he may not be able to catch up with him, but took a deep breath anyway, put his head down, and swam towards the spot where he judged him to be.

After a couple of minutes, he raised his head and looked about, but there was nothing to see but roiling water and broken tree branches being carried along by it. The plane was way behind now too, and he was no nearer to saving the man or anyone else who might still be in the wreck. He dived down and opened his eyes, but the turgid water hid everything. He came up for air again, and this time saw the head bobbing on the surface barely a few feet away, so reached out and grabbed hold of a coat lapel.

The man's outstretched hands seized the leather belt on Finn's jeans, dragging them both under. He was heavily-built and very strong too, and, now in a violent panic as well, was pressing down on Finn's shoulders, grabbing his hair, pushing him deeper, using his body as a means to reach the surface, threatening to drown them both.

Finn pulled at the grasping fingers, prizing himself free, and together they rose to the surface. "Relax!" he yelled, but frantic eyes stared at him, and white-knuckled hands gripped him, nails ripping at his face, drawing blood.

He managed to wrench himself away again, but the man's adrenalin-fuelled terror was giving him phenomenal strength, thwarting all Finn's efforts to rescue him, so he reached out and punched him as hard as he could on his unshaven chin, knocking him out. A few moments later, his arm around the man's chest, he was able to tow him to shore.

It took much of his remaining energy to drag him up onto the embankment, and he looked around, but the road was still deserted, so once he got his breath back, he left the man lying on the verge, then ran back up the road to where the plane's fin was still visible out in the middle of the river, but there was no-one there either.

Diana had not mentioned anyone else, but, afraid others could still be trapped, he dived in once more, and headed out towards the wreck again. The water stung his face where the man had scratched him, and the soles of his feet burned where gravel and stones from the road had cut into them, but he kept aiming for the plane, eyes constantly on the tailfin, fighting the current all the way so as not to be swept downstream.

He hoped his partners and their scuba gear would come soon as his strength was beginning to fail now. If others were inside the wreck, trying to save them on his own without diving equipment would be difficult, if not impossible, risky for him too, and the minutes were passing.

He grabbed hold of the tailfin, treading water, catching his breath, then dived down, feeling his way along the sloping side of the fuselage to the cockpit. The door was open, but, unable to see anything in the cloudy water, and afraid to climb inside for fear of becoming trapped himself, he stretched his arms inside, feeling around, and wishing that he had thought to ask Diana if she knew how many people were on board. Maybe her father had been alone. He needed to make sure though, and within seconds his groping fingers found a man's arm. He tugged at it, but there was no response.

Out of breath, he clawed his way back to the surface, lungs straining, then dived down again, leaning further into the fuselage this time. The man's seat-belt buckle was jammed, and, needing to breathe again, he had to give up struggling with it.

There was no other way; if he was going to get the man out, he would have to climb right into the fuselage, and he began backing away from the cabin door, needing to fill his lungs again before venturing inside, but then the belt on his jeans snagged on something, trapping him. Desperate for air now, he tore at the buckle until it gave way, then ripped the belt through all the loops, before fighting his way to the surface yet again.

For several minutes he trod water, drinking in the welcome oxygen in deep gulps, then glanced towards the shore -- still no sign of anyone. Perhaps his old jeep's idiosyncrasies had stopped Diana from ever reaching the callbox; somebody, at least, should be here by now, and he could not go on much longer without help.

"It's this time, or not at all, Finn Westlake," he told himself. He filled his lungs once more, dived down, climbed inside the fuselage, and, finding the man's seatbelt again, wrestled with it until it snapped open with a jerk, and with him now free, Finn dragged his body out of the plane, and hauled this second victim to the riverbank.

He had lost all sense of time, so had no idea how long it was since he had first jumped into the water, but now a police cruiser, rescue truck and several cars were lined up along the grass verge. The first man he had brought to shore was being loaded into an ambulance, and two men were reaching out to take the other one from him.

Diana ran up to the edge of the river, and stretched out her arms towards him. "What can I say? Thank you so very, very much. You've been absolutely terrific!" She glanced back towards the ambulance, where a paramedic was calling her. "Oh dear! They need me… Sorry… Must go… Dad's unconscious… He must have taken a turn for the worse…" She turned to leave. "Oh dear… do have to go… I hope he's going to be okay… So sorry to have to leave you like this…" She started running back towards the ambulance. "I'll be in touch as soon as I can," she called back to him. "Thank you properly… Hopefully have good news for you."

"Wait! Wait a sec. Are there any others on board? There's room for more than two." Finn held onto the reeds, treading water, fighting the current, his breathing labored.

"I'm sorry," she called over her shoulder. "Don't know. Oh dear! They're still beckoning me… Do hope Dad's not…"

"My workmates? Are they coming?"

She climbed into the ambulance, and turned briefly. "Yes," she shouted to him. "But don't go out again without them. Don't put your own life…" The door slammed shut, and she was gone, siren wailing, leaving him still grasping hold of the reeds at the edge of the river, fighting the current doing its best to drag him downstream.

Diana had been right in urging him not to risk going out again without help. He was now feeling not only the effect of the whole stressful situation, but that of fighting against the river, and dragging two large men to shore. That struggle with the first one had sapped much of his strength right from the start. There was still no sign of his fellow divers either, but he knew that if there were any chance at all of rescuing anyone else who might still be alive, but trapped in the plane, he would need to go out there again right now, without them. He thought about the risk, but what if someone drowned because he had been afraid to make that extra effort? And he set out one more time.

The plane, it turned out, was empty, but, suspecting that someone might have made his way out of the fuselage, but then become entangled somehow before reaching the surface, he dived down to take a look around the outside of the wreck.

He was very cold now, and his jeans, waterlogged, stiff and heavy, clung to his legs like plaster casts. He had been in dangerous situations before, but never felt as exhausted as this. He was losing the feeling in his arms and legs as well, and his muscles seemed to have lost all their strength. Then his shoulder bumped against the long, vertical edge of the submerged propeller blade, and a great weight slammed into his back. It drove him downwards, trapping him against the slimy river bottom.

"… have visitors."

Finn opened his eyes and blinked, trying to focus his attention, and looked towards the door, recognizing her immediately; it was the woman whose name he remembered as being Diana, the one who had been standing in the middle of the road that day -- dancing around like a cat on a hot tin roof, had been his first impression, before realizing the severity of the situation -- and now she had with her the large man he last remembered as having left lying unconscious on the riverbank. He had to be her father. He *did* survive after all, so all the pain and suffering he himself had endured ever since, after damaging his chest and lungs so severely, had at least been worth it. He wondered about the other man. Had he been able to rescue him too? No-one had told him anything.

"Hello Finn! You don't mind if I call you Finn, do you?" Diana was saying. "We get to see you at last!" She pointed to herself. "I'm Diana, Diana McGuire, and this…" She turned towards the man. "This is my father, Chester McGuire, whose life you saved. We've tried to visit you several times already, but they told us 'no visitors allowed'. Today, though, they've finally agreed to let us come to see you for just a few minutes. We've been so anxious about you, you know, and wanting to be able to thank you so very much for what you did for us."

"Yes indeed! Yes indeed." Her father accentuated his words with vigorous nods of his head. He was standing, hands behind his back, raising his bushy eyebrows like a surprised bear, Finn thought, and obviously feeling extremely awkward about having to face his rescuer in this situation.

"You can't feel any more awkward than I do, lying here like a zombie," he wanted to tell him. "I must look a complete ghoul with all these tubes sticking out of me."

"Yes indeed! Yes indeed," the father repeated, his head continuing to bob up and down like a nodding car-decoration. He sounded like an old-fashioned stuck record too, and Finn wished he could have helped him out of his quandary.

"What makes us feel so particularly guilty about what's happened to you…"

Diana was talking to him, and he looked back at her -- much more satisfying than having to watch her father's embarrassed struggles to express himself. Lovely hair and eyes. He liked what she was wearing too -- fashionably casual. Very becoming. Her voice too: clear, confident, but with a seductive, almost husky tone to it. And her earrings, he liked them as well; they were funky -- a miniature silver fork in one ear, a matching knife in the other. So, she even had a sense of humor! He liked her already! How very different from when he first saw her that morning, wet, frantic and bedraggled, and all but naked too.

"… all totally unnecessary," she was telling

him. "I couldn't believe it when I saw Dad's plane flying overhead, dipping its wings at me in a salute like that, especially when he'd said only the previous day that he needed to get a mechanic to check it out before flying it!" She turned to face her father, and shook her head. "It should never, ever have happened in the first place!"

"I know, my dear, but as I keep saying, it was only for a quick checking over. It wasn't as if I'd noticed anything wrong with it, so how could I have possibly turned down someone like Sandy Moseley that day?" McGuire turned to face Finn. "I should explain to you, Mr. Westlake. Mr. Moseley, in case no-one has told you yet, is the other man who's indebted to you for rescuing him -- and quite an important person you saved too, he being no less than the Director of the State Department of Transportation back in our home state in New England. Not only that, he's also brother-in-law to our state governor, Governor Silas Brigham, with whom I'm also very well acquainted; we frequently play golf together at the Country Club, and..."

Finn looked back at Diana, who appeared to be studying the wall, but then she turned and smiled at him, and he was glad that she must have felt him looking at her as it was his only way of communicating with her, or anyone right now. He wished, though, that he could also tell her what a beautiful smile she had. He looked back towards McGuire, who was still explaining.

"You see, Mr. Westlake; it was like this. Mr. Moseley, who was visiting with us at the time as our guest at our second home here in Sarasota, had specifically asked to be taken up for a spin that morning, and, as he had to return home to New England the following day, I felt I couldn't refuse him. The thing is; he's thrown a great deal of business my way over the years, and when he asks a favor, well, he's not the sort of person I can afford to refuse, if you see what I mean." He gave Finn an encouraging smile, and patted the rail at the bottom of the bed. "No, indeed! I don't know where I'd be if you hadn't managed to save him as well."

Diana smiled at Finn again. "Dad, I'm sure Finn must be tired already. We are his first visitors after all, and he's been through so much. As I said, we've been most anxious to visit you, Finn, so that we could let you know how very grateful we are for what you did, but we mustn't end up by leaving you exhausted now as a result, though, must we?"

McGuire gave his head some vigorous nods. "You're right, my dear, and I'm sure Mr. Westlake doesn't want to lie there listening to us arguing about whether I should have taken the plane up or not either." He turned his attention back to Finn again, bushy eyebrows coming together in a deep furrow. "I must say, nevertheless, that the end result, regardless, is that I'm the cause of your current dilemma, young man, and I'm simply overwhelmed." He gave a big sigh, and shook his head. "Yes, there's no other word for it, overwhelmed." His eyebrows sagged. "I find it hard to know what to say… That you should be suffering like this on my account." He shook his head again. "It's too much. How can I possibly ever thank you for what you did?"

He stared at Finn, then slapped his hand on

the bed rail, eyebrows shooting up again into inverted Vs, head nodding vigorously. "No, no! I'm wrong. Yes indeed! There *is* a way! Well... a small way. Listen, now. Although I have this second home here, where I like to play host to some of my more important business associates, such as Mr. Moseley, our main home is in New England where I own a pretty sizeable waterfront estate, and I insist that as soon as you're able, you must come to visit us. Yes indeed." His head gave another series of vigorous nods. "We'll be only too happy to show you around our neck of the woods, take you sailing, fishing, visit all the sights... And Diana here is a wonderful cook too, and there's nothing anywhere like New England seafood, you know." He gave Finn yet another encouraging nod. "Yes, indeed, I insist. You *must* allow us to repay you in some small measure, although, as I said, I'll never be able to thank you enough."

"Anyway," Finn heard Diana saying. "We're so happy and relieved to learn you're well on your way to getting better. And yes, I second my father's invitation. Florida gets way too hot in the summer anyway, so once you're up to it, it would be..."

But Finn had fallen asleep.

CHAPTER 2

Diana was sitting out on the bamboo sofa on the porch, hands wrapped around her mug of early morning coffee, gazing across the bay, and looking forward to meeting up with her best friend, Janice, in town later in the day. Barely seventy-five feet away, at the edge of the lawn, was the water, pale at this early hour with shades of pink and mourning-dove grey, and the windows of the homes across the water on the mainland flashed fiery orange against the fading indigo of the western sky, reflecting the rising sun.

"Good morning, my dear." McGuire, newly shaved, and already dressed in his business suit, came to sit beside her. "You know, it's so good to see you getting back to being your old self again, sweetheart. Having to watch my lovely daughter go through that dreadful experience of being let down so very drastically by the man she loved was something no father should ever have to witness. Believe me, if that guy Eric were to ever show his face around here again, I don't think I could vouch for what I'd do to him."

Diana leaned over and gave her father a kiss. "I know, Dad, and thank you for being so understanding, putting up with me being so glum all the time. Anyway, I think I can finally say he's all in the past now. It's sad, though, because the one thing it *has* done to me is to make me not want to enter into another relationship in the foreseeable future for fear of it happening again. I don't ever want to go through such emotional turmoil again. Talk about love being blind! How can I ever trust my own judgment again? Janice has been encouraging me to start going out again, but I... Oh! I can hear your office phone. Would you like me to get it?"

McGuire patted his daughter on the knee, and stood up. "No, you sit here, my dear, and enjoy your coffee." He laughed. "It's probably Louise Lillacray, reminding me yet again that she's going to be holding a re-election fund-raiser for Governor Brigham at her mansion in the fall. Anyone would think it was next week, not five months away!"

Diana finished her coffee, and was deciding what to have for breakfast, when her father returned. "Well, that was a surprise. Guess who that was. It was Finn Westlake."

"What!"

"Yes, he's decided to take us up on that offer to come to visit, so naturally, I've told him, fine; we'll be delighted to have him come to stay. I suggested a whole week, but he says he's on the way home to the UK to visit family, so can't stay more than a few days."

"Oh, my goodness! I'm so relieved to hear he's alright, and well enough finally to visit! The last I heard was that he'd been released from hospital, but he's never replied to any of my emails since, so I'd begun to think we were never going to hear from him again. When's he coming then?"

"The second week in June… the tenth to be exact."

"Oh no! Not then! You'll be away!"

"Oh yes, so I will, won't I? Totally forgot about that, but not to worry; I'm sure you'll do a great job of entertaining him for just a few days, my dear. You're always the perfect hostess, just as your mother used to be. Anyway, it'll do you good… get you out of yourself."

"Get me out of myself? Yes, but here we were just a few minutes ago, Dad, with me telling you how nervous I am about the thought of getting involved again anytime soon, and there I am now, suddenly faced with the immediate prospect of playing hostess on my own, right here, in our own home, and for several days, to what I remember as being a very attractive young man! Obviously, nobody wants more than I do to have the chance to thank him for what he did for us, especially as he almost died in the doing, but given what I can only describe as my current fragile mental state regarding men, I know for sure that I'm not at all ready for this. Is there any way we can arrange it so that you're here for support, Dad?

"No, not really. He said he hasn't been able to come sooner because he hasn't been fit enough to travel, and, with him going to the UK, there's no knowing when he might return. Besides, as you point out, after him nearly losing his life like that on my account, I wouldn't feel right putting him off; it would look like I really wasn't keen on having him come to stay after all. No, I'm not going to call him back, my dear, so we'll have to leave things as they are, I'm afraid. Anyway, I'm sure that, when he does arrive, your natural friendliness and common sense will prevail, and everything will go smoothly, don't you think?"

"There's one thing I could do, I suppose. I could ask Janice to come to stay too. Yes, I'll do that. She'd be perfect."

Her father nodded. "Yes, by all means. An excellent idea, my dear. I ask only one thing, and I'm sure you wouldn't do this anyway: please don't take it out on this poor guy for the way Eric treated you. Not all men are bastards, you know."

"No, of course I know that, Dad. Besides, after what Finn Westlake did for you and that weasel Sandy Moseley, I wouldn't dream of giving him the cold shoulder."

He kissed the top of her head. "No, as I said, I'm sure you wouldn't, my dear… By the way, I don't like to have to ask you, but can you please be more careful not to spread around about your personal opinion of some of my friends and associates? Friends like Sandy Moseley are very important to me, and it wouldn't do for word to get around what you happen to think of them.

"Anyway, I'm off. Got to catch the 10:15 plane. Pick me up at the airport on Friday, will you, love? Plane's due in at 5:30." He gave his daughter another quick kiss, and laughed. "Heh! Who knows? Maybe Westlake'll turn out to be your Mr. Right after all! Wouldn't that be something? It's about time I got you off my hands."

"Oh Dad!"

Diana and her friend, Janice, sat in the corner of the Starbuck's coffee shop in Davenport, overlooking the bay.

"Oh no, Jan! Of course, I'm delighted for you that you've landed this great new job in France, but from a purely selfish point of view, I *do* wish you didn't have to leave so soon… Just three days before he gets here, yet! And the thought of entertaining him all on my own terrifies me! I'm sure I'm going to end up being all stilted and awkward, and he's going to think I'm a complete bore."

Janice laughed. "Nonsense. Actually, if you think about it, you're both going to be off to a great start."

"What do you mean? Because he saved Dad's life? That'll make me feel even more awkward."

"No. Surely you're not forgetting, Diana; he's already seen you in what amounted to a wet T-shirt show, along with wet see-through briefs to match!"

"Oh Jan! You're bad! Oh, I do wish you weren't going away quite so soon. It would be so much easier with the two of us, and I'm going to miss you so much anyway."

"Yes, I can just see us both here with him; if

this young man is anything like the looker you've described him to be, we'd both end up falling for him, then you'd be wishing like mad that you *hadn't* asked me to come and help entertain him."

"Well, one thing I *have* promised myself, and that is that I am *not* going to allow myself to fall for him; As I keep saying, I'm just not ready to enter into any sort of relationship again yet, and that's that."

Janice laughed. "Oh yeah? Wanna bet?"

CHAPTER 3

Finn stretched out his legs as far as he could in the cramped quarters of the plane, put his seat back, and shut his eyes. He was heading for Logan airport, in Boston, and thinking back over the long struggle to get his health back after being almost crushed to death that day.

As his partners had explained it to him later, rescuing him had been dramatic too -- more so even than his own efforts -- and it had almost ended in failure. Apparently, they had arrived on the scene just in time to see the tailfin suddenly jerk downwards, and, having been told he was out there on his own, and seeing no sign of him, had had no time to put on their scuba gear, before diving in and swimming out to the plane to see what had happened to him. They had found him trapped on the river bed, beneath the fuselage, the only thing preventing it from crushing him completely being one of the propellers, which had snapped in half, allowing the plane to collapse part way, but leaving it still supported tenuously by the remaining half.

Getting him out had been very dangerous; the remaining part of the propeller could have given way at any moment, not only killing him, but them as well. Even moving his body at all could have caused it to shift, with similar results, but it was a risk they had been willing to take to save him, a risk made even more difficult because, like Finn, they too had to rely on whatever air they had in their lungs, needing them to balance being quick, with being as gentle and careful as possible so as not to damage him even further.

They had had to dig into the silt beneath him so as to create a space through which to extricate him, and by the time they had brought him to the surface, they were not only gasping themselves, but at the same time had to hold onto Finn, who, in a desperate effort to draw air into his damaged lungs, was writhing about frantically and in danger of breaking free from their grasp.

He gave a shudder, reliving as he had done so many times since that morning the horrendous experience of fighting to breathe during their struggle to get him back to shore. After that, the paramedics had given him a shot that put him out, so he had no memory of the ventilator being put down his throat, nor of anything else until he had woken up in hospital.

Their big fear, they told him, was that because he had been without air for so long, he might have suffered permanent brain damage. He smiled; it was something they had teased him about ever since, telling him that was definitely the case.

He opened his eyes, and stared down at the

fair-weather, cotton-ball clouds beneath. It had been a long, painful and sometimes depressing time since that day, but his partners had been as supportive as they could, helping to boost his morale and struggling to finish, without him, the contract regarding that sunken freighter that they had been working on together.

He thought about them again now, and how fortunate he had been in hiring such well-qualified and competent men, who had not only saved his life while putting their own at risk, but had simply taken over everything, leaving him with no worries about what was going to happen to the business while he was incapacitated; and when they had said goodbye to him this morning after driving him to the airport, he could relax, knowing it was in safe hands.

It was because of this trust he had in his partners that, now he had more or less recovered, although still a long way from being able to pass the stringent physical tests that would allow him to return to work, he had decided to take the McGuires up on their invitation to visit them.

He was a bit concerned that he barely knew them, although he had received several emails from Diana, wishing him well and repeating her father's invitation to visit – emails that he felt a bit guilty about for not having replied -- but even so he was not sure at all what to expect, anymore than they were, which is why he had told them he was on his way to the UK to visit family, so would be staying just a few days with them. He shrugged; they were coming into Boston now, so he would soon find out.

Not being the sort of man to carry more

baggage than necessary, he had brought along only the minimum in the way of clothing, all of which was rolled up in his small and rather dilapidated old canvas hold-all, and with this he strode out into the large arrivals area, ready to meet Diana's father, but the first person he saw instead was Diana.

He was very pleased, of course, that she had chosen to come to collect him, but immediately began to feel a bit shabby, dressed as he was in his usual casual clothes: well-worn jeans, open-necked shirt, Timberland boots and old Tilley hat, while she, by contrast, looked elegant and trim in a pretty, pale-yellow shift and high heels, showing off her figure in a way he found most attractive. He consoled himself, knowing that what he was wearing was at least all freshly laundered, although an iron was not among any of his household possessions. He went up to her, smiling.

Diana shook his outstretched hand. "You're looking so well, Finn! This is great! I have to admit I've been sitting here worrying that I was going to see someone permanently disabled by what you went through that awful day. Instead, I see you looking really well. Fantastic!"

"Can't complain. Good to see you again too, Diana… Right, how about we get out of here then?" he suggested when she hesitated.

"Oh, I was thinking you needed to collect the rest of your baggage first."

"Nope. All in here." He held up his hold-all. "I'm what you might call a light traveler."

"Yes, very light, I should say, if that's all you've got. Okay. Let's get going then, shall we?"

They walked towards the huge parking area, before finally stopping beside a small red Mercedes sports car with the top down. He dumped his hold-all on the floor on the passenger's side, then climbed in, but even with the seat as far back as it would go, his knees were almost under his chin. He patted the dashboard. "Hmm... The sort of car you have to put on, rather than get into. Very neat... I like it. A bit different from driving my old jeep, eh?"

"You can say that again! I'd certainly never driven anything like that before... Has quite a mind of its own, hasn't it? Or should I call it 'she', like a ship?"

"Believe me, it/she gets called a lot of things, most of them not repeatable in polite company."

They waited in line to pay the parking fee. "I don't know about you, Diana, but I could do with something to eat. I'm hungry, and they didn't offer anything much on the plane. How about you? Would you like to eat now as well?" He leaned behind her and put some notes in the man's outstretched hand.

"Oh! I didn't mean for you to have to..."

"My pleasure. So, how about I take you out for a meal here in Boston first, before we head back to your place? That's if it's okay with you, that is."

"I'd thought to fix us some supper back home, but your plane was late, so yes, I wouldn't say no to a bite to eat either now. Anyway, you look as though you've already made up your mind."

"Well, yes. Can't have you driving all the way home, then have to start cooking, can we?"

"There's a nice place down on the wharf we could go to, if you like. They serve good steak and seafood there."

"Sounds good to me. Let's go then."

"Well," Diana commented, once they were settled in the old converted warehouse, and had a chance to study each other over their martinis. "You certainly look a whole lot better than when I saw you last, Finn, I must say."

"And you'll have to admit you look a bit different too from the first time I saw you... Too bad about the circumstances." He gave her a wide grin.

"Hmm. Yes. Come to think of it, I imagine that driving around the corner that morning, and coming face to face with a woman in her underwear probably did come as a bit of a shock... Not something that happens to you every day, I would think... Anyway, what have you been doing recently? Lying in the sun? That's quite a tan."

He laughed, and bent over in mock agony.

"No, seriously, Finn. It's over three months now since the accident, isn't it? I assume you haven't been working, and you said you're now taking time off to visit your folks, so presumably you aren't well..."

"Just wanted an excuse to see you again, that's all..."

"Come on, Finn. Admit it. You're not well enough to go back to work yet. That's really it, isn't it? And you won't say so. Please tell me what's going on. I'd really like to know... Please? After all, we..."

"All right. I'm out of work for quite a few months yet, I'm afraid... Diving and bad lungs, and all that. I do get to see you again though, don't I?"

"Now don't go changing the subject on me, Finn. What about your business if you can't work?"

"Determined to be serious, aren't you?"

"What's wrong with that? As I started to say: After all ..."

"Okay. It's not going to fall apart if I'm not there for a while, if that's what you mean."

"I'm sorry to push you like this, but you must understand, we're the cause of..."

"I know. I know. You feel it's your fault, or rather, your father's fault, but I assure you; I don't want you to feel that way. It was one of those things, and I'm just glad I happened to be there. Now, can we lay the subject to rest, please? All these guilt and gratitude complexes are getting in the way."

"Okay, I guess you're right."

"Yes, I am. By the way, I'm looking forward to meeting your father too. Neither of our two earlier encounters exactly made for the ideal introduction, did they?"

"Oh Yes! I should have told you. Sorry. My father forgot he'd be away while you're here. Left just last week, so I'm afraid you've just got me to show you around."

"Oh! I can see it's going to be a tough few days for me then," he laughed. "You're sure, by the way, you don't mind me coming to stay then, especially with your father being away? I don't want to impose."

"Not at all! I'll be happy to show you around our corner of New England."

"Good." Maybe it was his imagination, but although her words said one thing, he thought the tone in which she expressed them sounded more as though she were trying to make polite conversation with a client, rather than open up a friendship. Perhaps she was not that happy having him come to stay despite what she said.

They savored the excellent New England black chowder and baked, stuffed flounder, and chatted mostly about what he did for a living and about his family.

"They must have been very worried about your accident, especially when they arrived to find you in such a critical state."

"Uh, well, I haven't actually told them about it yet… Haven't told them about going home to see them either."

"You didn't tell them? Why ever not?"

"Didn't want to worry them. My mother would probably have had a heart attack if she'd seen me like that, and now, if she knew I was coming home, she'd start organizing lots of parties to which all the 'right' young ladies would be invited. She's still trying to get me married off." He laughed. "And I'm not ready for that. No way! I scarper like a jet when things start to get serious." He shot his arm out like a plane taking off.

"I need to tell you, Finn; I was worried when you didn't reply to my emails asking how you were. I imagined the worst."

"Back to that again, are we? Well, sorry about that… about not replying to your emails, that is. I meant to, but kept putting it off until I knew I'd be able to come to visit you and give you a date. But then the time went by, and, in the end, I thought I might as well just phone instead. I'm not a very good correspondent anyway, I'm afraid. My family's always complaining I don't get in touch often enough, but in their case, I don't do that regularly on purpose."

"You don't contact them on purpose!"

"Oh, it's not for the wrong reasons. If I wrote to them on a regular basis, then missed writing for a while, they'd get into a panic, thinking something terrible had happened to me. This way, when they don't hear from me, they assume I'm just being me, a bad correspondent."

"Sounds like a rationale for not doing what you should do."

"Now, don't *you* start!"

She was looking into his face, and he returned her gaze. "Am I being inspected?"

Diana blushed. "Oh, I'm sorry."

"No, don't turn away. I like it."

"It's just that I haven't seen you before, properly, that is," she explained.

He nodded. "Well I suppose I owe you that much."

"You do? How come?"

"Well, when you last saw me, all I could do was lie there and inspect you, so now it's your turn."

Diana smiled. "Not too much of a trial, I hope."

Finn raised his glass. "On the contrary."

It was after midnight by the time they arrived at the McGuire home, where Diana left him in the guest room after wishing him goodnight, and it was early morning when he woke. He lay there for a few minutes, then climbed out of bed, yawning and stretching his way over to the window for his first daylight look at this part of New England. It was impressive.

Close by, at the end of the lawn, a heavy wooden dock reached about fifty feet into the water, and not far from it, the McGuire sailboat sat motionless, reflected in the bay, its limp mooring-line lying on the water. He read the name '*Moonglow*' on the transom -- a pretty boat with her white hull and rich-red sail covers.

Out on the bay, an early quahogger was already at work, raking the bottom for clams, and his small skiff, with its odd, one-man cabin at the stern, rocked back and forth as he worked the seabed, sending ripples out across the flat water.

Off to the north he could see the high arch of a bridge, presumably the one they had crossed on their way home last night. He remembered Diana mentioning they lived on an island... Yes, Cautuxet Island. That was it.

The bridge, spanning the whole distance between the mainland and the island -- over a mile long, he judged -- rose from a series of immense piers set in the water, the roadway itself cutting straight through a latticed-iron arch in its center. This morning, and from this distance, the sturdy, triangular, gray-metal trusses looked as delicate as a filigree necklace, and just as beautiful. It was going to be a beautiful day, from a weather point of view, at least. Diana, he was not so sure about. She had seemed rather tense the whole time last night, despite his own attempt to look at ease and make her feel comfortable with him. He liked her, and was sure that if she would only relax, his visit would turn out to be a most pleasurable one.

They were sitting out on the porch, eating breakfast. Myriads of miniature suns bounced around on the bay, and, in the distance, traffic was already beginning to build on the bridge. Now, though, his brief visit was over, and tomorrow he would be leaving, despite Mr. McGuire's insistence previously that he stay at least a full week.

He looked out over the water. Not many had the chance to enjoy the luxury of waking up every day to look out over such an idyllic, but ever-changing scene, and he thought about the past three days in which Diana had taken him to sample everything her part of New England had to offer. They had driven to Provincetown, on Cape Cod, and spent a day on a whale-watching cruise; gone to Newport, in Rhode Island, and wandered around Bannister's Wharf and Thames Street, and spent a few hours looking at the *Marble House* and *The Breakers*. They had visited Fall River, where they went over the battleship, *Massachusetts*, and looked around the *Whaling Museum*, and had eaten at fine restaurants – all meticulously organized as though she were determined to keep them fully occupied with a carefully planned and pre-arranged timetable of activities, allowing no spare time in which they could casually lounge around, doing nothing other than simply enjoying each other's company and developing a friendship.

Yes, of course he had appreciated the sight-seeing excursions, and Diana had been consistently charming and solicitous, but she had nevertheless never really opened up and let her hair down, as it were, keeping up instead what he considered to be an unnecessary level of formality that he had found disappointing.

Maybe, he thought, it was because he had not been able to hide his attraction towards her that she had acted in such a way as to ensure he did not try to lead them into a relationship it was obvious she did not want. It was a shame, though. It was not that he felt compelled to sleep with her, but if only she had relaxed enough to allow them to become friends, it would have made his stay so much more pleasurable. But she had not, and as a result of exploring nothing deeper than polite conversation permitted, they knew each other almost no more now than when they first met, and, as a result, he was now ready to say goodbye.

It was too bad, he thought, because every now and then he had had glimpses of what he imagined was the real Diana, and what he saw he found so very attractive, leaving him longing to get to know her better, and yes, of course, to make love with her. He sighed. Oh well, it was simply one of those things, and there was nothing he could do about it, so it was just as well he would be leaving the next day.

"… interested you are in all things underwater," she was saying, "I think the perfect way to spend your last day would be to go to *Mystic Aquarium*, in Connecticut. It's not that far… Finn?"

"Oh! I'm sorry. Yes, Mystic would be fine. Yes, it *is* my last day here, isn't it?"

Diana placed her knife and fork down on the plate with careful precision, and surprised Finn with a genuinely friendly smile. "You know, Finn, that offer to stay longer still stands. Just because you said you would be staying only a few days, doesn't mean you are duty-bound to leave because of that, so, you are still welcome to stay on longer, if you'd like to."

Finn's raised eyebrows showed his surprise. "Stay longer? You're sure? I mean, I've had a great time visiting with you, of course, but you've spent so much of your time ferrying me around, showing me everywhere and everything, I'm sure you must be looking forward to getting back to doing whatever it is you normally do."

Diana was still giving him that friendly smile. "Not at all, Finn. I've enjoyed ferrying you around, as you put it. Yes, it's true I was nervous at first, not knowing you at all, and not knowing if you'd have recovered well enough from your injuries to do all the things I'd planned, but you've been a great guest, and that's made showing you around a pleasure. So, as I said, you're welcome to stay on. That's if you'd like to, of course, and aren't in a hurry to see your family."

"You weren't the only one who was a bit nervous, you know, when I found out that it was just you who'd be doing the entertaining. Anyway, I have to say you stepped up to the plate magnificently. You've been the perfect hostess."

"You'd like to stay on then?"

"Well, I have to admit I'm a bit surprised that you're inviting me to stay longer as I've had the strong impression that despite being, as I said, the perfect hostess, you've really not felt comfortable at all having me here on your own like this, even to the extent of not allowing us to really get to know each other, if you see what I mean, and because of that, I've assumed you'd be more than ready now to see me go… Oh dear, I think I'm getting bogged down here. Anyway, what I'm trying to say is that I guess it's been a bit difficult for both of us. Am I right?"

"Yes, you *are* right, Finn, although from my side at least, there's a bit more to it than that."

"Oh? And you still want me to stay on anyway?"

She nodded. "Yes, I would like that, Finn."

"Well, I certainly don't want to pry when you say, 'there's a bit more to it than that,' but if you really would be happy to have me to stay on, then, yes, thank you. I'd like that too, Diana."

CHAPTER 4

Diana held the phone under the sheets, not wanting Finn, who was in the guest bedroom next to her, to overhear, although, with the phone clamped between her ear and the pillow, nobody, other than she herself, could possibly have heard what the person on the receiving end was saying.

"Oh Jan! I *do* wish you weren't so far away!...

"What!" She exclaimed in a loud whisper. "You've met up with some guy already, Jan? Well, I suppose you *are* in Paris after all...

"He is? Well, all that sounds great, and I'm so glad you're having such a good time, and enjoying your new job as well, especially as you know so much about the wine industry. I'm amazed how you can even tell which vineyard a wine comes from! I can't even tell which country they come from...

"How am I getting along with my visitor? Well, that's the main reason I'm calling you, Jan." Diana pulled the blanket further over her head. "Right now, I'm thinking I may have made a huge mistake. It's like this: I've been taking Finn around all the places I can think of, and, as I promised myself, I've managed not to get involved in any way. The trouble is that, having spent so much time with him like this, and knowing too how he almost lost his life saving two complete strangers, the *old* me would believe he's a genuinely honorable man…

"I know, Jan; you're right; there really is no reason why he wouldn't be. It's just that, after the way Eric led me on so outrageously, then abandoned me the way he did, I've lost my confidence in my ability to judge men. It's made me so I'm afraid to trust any of them anymore, which is why I've not allowed myself to behave naturally with Finn at all… The old me keeps telling me I've no reason at all not to trust him, and I do like him a lot; he's so laid back, amiable and easy-going. He makes me feel as though if I *were* to let myself go and allow a relationship to develop – and I can tell he would like that too -- I could feel so comfortable and at ease with him.

"Ah Jan! You should have seen him the day of the accident. I'd lost it completely, and yet he was able to calm me right down. He has such gentle eyes too. Then, of course, as I told you," Diana laughed quietly. "On top of everything, he's so very attractive as well. I do wish you could meet him. Well, perhaps not. The way you are, my dear Jan, I don't think I could trust you not to make off with him before I could get a look in!...

"Oh yes… So, what's the huge mistake I think I've made? Well, I was looking at him at breakfast this morning, knowing that, in all probability, when he would be leaving tomorrow as planned, I would never, ever see him again; and the thought of that, and that we would be parting company without ever having got to really know each other -- become friends even -- suddenly seemed unthinkable, and, despite all my promises, I found myself telling him he was welcome to stay longer if he'd like to, and, amazingly, he said 'yes'!"

"What do you mean, you had a bet that I would fall for him?

"Well, yes, I suppose you could say I do, well, you know… Oh what have I done though, Jan? To be honest, the way I've been with him, I'm surprised he did say 'yes', because although I've been polite, of course, I haven't given him any encouragement at all, but now he's going to be staying on anyway… Oh Jan! Yes! I really do like this guy; I find him so *very* attractive, and, yes, I would so much like for him to get to know the real me, not the standoffish prig I'm sure I've been!...

"Am I regretting what I've done? No, I don't think so, but, as you can imagine, I *am* sort of scared and thrilled at the same time. One thing's for sure, I can't un-invite him, so I'm going to do my best to relax and show him my old and friendly me -- whatever that used to be. I do hope it works out okay. I don't know what I'd do if he were to let me down too, and be another Eric after all…

"Oh, how very different you and I are, Jan! Perhaps that's why we're such close friends. You take such a different view on relationships, or what you happily call your 'flings'…

"Yes, I know I'm probably a bit old-fashioned in my outlook when it comes to men, and your attitude certainly seems to work for you. 'Enjoy it while it lasts,' you're always telling me, 'and don't let it get serious emotionally. That way you don't get hurt.' But it seems I can't help myself falling for them. That's the trouble, and you're right; that's when you leave yourself open to getting hurt…

"Yes, I know we *are* in the twenty-first century. Perhaps that's where I went wrong with Eric. Because we became like partners in every way, I took that as being a long-term commitment on both our sides. Anyway, for good or bad, as I said, I can't un-invite him now, so wish me luck.

"Oh Jan, what would I do without having you to unload on? And yes, I guess you won your bet, okay?"

The guest room was hot; the humidity was making the air as suffocating as in Florida even though the window was open, and Finn lay on the bed, sweating. The gentle slap, slap of the waves on the shingle beach, and the light scraping of the small stones and seashells retreating or advancing with each wavelet should have helped lull him to sleep, but his brain was far too preoccupied to allow that to happen.

He punched the pillow. "Dammit! You idiot. What the hell made you agree to stay on when it's obvious she isn't the slightest bit interested in you?"

He turned over and lay on his back, putting his arms behind his head, and thought back to the moment when Diana had made that invitation. What had there been about it that had made him agree so readily to stay, especially given that she had seemed so uncomfortable about having him visit at all?

He sat up. That was it! It was the smile she had given him when she asked him. It had been real, genuine -- one of those glimpses of the real Diana that he had witnessed so rarely during his stay. That smile had told him she really did not want him to leave! She was not being simply polite. And that was the reason he had said 'yes'.

He lay down again. So, she really did want him to stay, but what had she meant by saying too that from her side there was "more to it than that"? What was that all about? And her mixed message now made him wonder what he might have brought upon himself by agreeing to stay on? He sighed. Perhaps he *should* leave in the morning after all. There had to be some reasonable excuse he could come up with. But another part of him did not want to leave. He *wanted* to see more smiles like that one –the real Diana – and he did not want to never see her again, and that would be what would happen if he did leave in the morning.

He turned over and punched the pillow again. "Aargh!" His thoughts were circling like roundabout horses, going nowhere. Maybe by the morning his brain would have sorted it all out.

It was almost nine o'clock when he woke.

CHAPTER 5

It was now nearly two weeks since Finn had first arrived, and that side of Diana which had caused him to accept her invitation to stay on, had become more and more visible as she began to relax and open up to him. She was, he mused, rather like a beautiful blossom opening up, and he found it exciting and erotic, almost more so than if she had been like this with him from the beginning, and he put his arm around her, giving her a gentle hug.

They were standing on a low, rocky promontory, overlooking the ocean. The Mercedes, top down, was parked some yards behind them at the side of the narrow lane. The wind was just strong enough to whip up small whitecaps on the waves, and below, a black cormorant stood on a rock, wings outstretched, drying itself in the sun.

Diana looked up at him, and smiled. "I thought we could take our picnic, and walk over the cliffs to a small cove I know. We can leave the car here. It'll be quite safe. By the way, you *are* all right for walking here, are you, Finn? It's quite steep in places."

Finn sighed. "Do I still look that bad?"

She reached up and gave him a light kiss, laughing. "No, of course you don't, Finn. You look great! It's just that I do have at the back of my mind the knowledge that, no matter how good you look, you aren't completely recovered from what happened to you, so I'm afraid you'll just have to put up with me being what you consider over-solicitous about your welfare, okay?" She took his hand and squeezed it.

He nodded, and smiled. "Okay, Nurse McGuire, I guess I can live with that." He pulled the basket from behind the seat and followed her along the cliff edge, ignoring the clown-spotted bodies of the monarch butterflies and the pungent smell of bayberry, and mesmerized by the rhythmic swaying of her hips along the narrow path ahead of him. It aroused him, and he looked away, stopping to divert his attention by looking at the scenery. Apart from themselves and the wildlife, the place was deserted.

Diana looked back at him. "People hardly ever come to my little beach. It's a good half mile from the surfaced road, so most don't even know it's here... You're *sure* you're all right, Finn? You stopped, that's all, and I thought maybe..."

He caught up with her, and pulled her towards him. "Right. I think you and I are going to have to come to an agreement here, Madam. Tell you what; if I think I'm about to collapse at your feet with a heart attack, or whatever, I'll let you know. Okay? Otherwise, you can rest assured that I'm just fine. Agreed?"

Diana nodded, and laughed. "Agreed, Mr. Westlake, Sir… Come on then." She took his hand again and walked ahead. "And me holding your hand, doesn't mean I'm thinking you need my help to walk along this path either, okay?"

They eventually came to the end of the path, which opened onto a tiny, crescent-shaped cove. It was, once reached, not particularly inviting, consisting mostly of seaweed-covered rocks and pebbles, the high tide mark littered with a thick, smelly layer of slipper-shells, piles of loose seaweed and oddments of civilization thrown back to land by the sea.

Diana led the way to a sunny spot on a high, flat rock, where she set out their lunch of cold ham sandwiches, cheese, apples and a bottle of chilled wine. "I know it's not much of a beach, but I still like it here. It's what I like to think of as my own, special place, and I wanted to share it with you, because I consider you special too. It's called Bass Cove, and it's always peaceful here."

It was, as she had said, very quiet, and apart from themselves, some seagulls, and a small freighter making its way around the distant sand bar to Davenport, there was no other living creature to be seen.

"You don't happen to have another of those sandwiches in that picnic basket do you? I do have to say; one of your many attractions is that you do make one helluva good ham sandwich, and I like your taste in wine too." He smiled and raised his glass to her, while casually tugging at a rusted iron ring set into the rock on which they were sitting.

"The Army Corps of Engineers put that thing

there during World War II" Diana told him. "It's amazing that it's lasted this long, isn't it?"

He gave it another, hard tug. "Yes. Still solidly fixed in there too."

They finished off everything in the hamper that was either edible or drinkable, and for a while sat in comfortable silence, their arms around each other, her head on his shoulder, just gazing out across the bay and the sunshine glittering on the water.

Finn leaned over and kissed her. "You know, Diana, I'm so very glad that you asked me to stay on. I've been enjoying our time together so much this last week, sharing your company and getting to know you like this. I wouldn't have missed it for anything."

"And I'm so very glad that you agreed to stay on, Finn." She jumped down off the rock. "Come on. There's a nice, sandy place nearby where we can lie in the sun, and be comfortable. It's just around this corner."

The sand, warmed by the sun, was soft and inviting, and they lay down on their backs, side by side, Finn taking her hand, and holding it to his chest. She could feel his heart beating. It was strong and comfortably steady -- just like the rest of him, she thought.

After a few minutes, he turned on his side, and looked at her. "You know what I'm thinking right now?" He put his hand up and stroked her hair. "Having you lying here like this, so close to me, the sun shining through your hair. It's so beautiful. How I ache to hold you close to me, Diana… how much I..." He caressed her face gently.

Diana leaned over and gave him a cheeky

smile. "I'm not saying you can't, Finn."

CHAPTER 6

Sebastian 'Sandy' Moseley smoothed thin strands of hair across the large bald patch on his head. Physically, he had recovered from his near-drowning experience in Florida, but the frightening memory of the plane crash still continued to wake him up at night and, in addition, seemed to make him worry over matters that he would have previously considered trivial. "I don't know how we..."

Governor Silas Brigham tapped his fingers on the table. "Sandy, my dear brother-in-law, let me remind you once again: I have obligations... debts. I'm being leaned on... being reminded I've not pushed hard enough for a new bridge across the bay to Cautuxet Island. You and I both know failure to get a new bridge approved won't simply be a case of me not getting re-elected as governor next term. My... my uh... supporters..." He sighed. "Very, um, influential. They expect a return on their invest... uh... contributions to my re-election, and if the start of that new bridge isn't constructed right there on the Honeydale Farms land, they… um… the consortium… owns, they stand to lose a fortune on it, and'll hold me responsible. Politically, that'll be the end of me… financially too."

Moseley was very much aware his own future was entwined with that of Brigham. His position as Director of the State Department of Transportation was dependent on him, and if Brigham failed to get re-elected, his only claim to importance would be as brother of an ex-governor's wife; he would be out of a job, a nothing. He had grown used to the benefits brought about by his position, the perks, and had even benefitted personally from some of that election-contribution cash. Yet how could an unwilling electorate be convinced of the need for a brand-new, over-a-mile-long bridge, without some forceful promotion? They were complaining of their heavy tax burden already.

"… it's going to be a tough one, I realize," Brigham was saying.

"How do you mean?"

"I was merely referring to my problem of getting the public to go for a multi-million-dollar new bridge while pushing my re-election stance of fiscal responsibility and restraint at the same time… Not insurmountable though. I've been thinking a lot about it. Damn that '*Save our Bridge*' lot. Who'd have thought a group of old women on Cautuxet island would suddenly decide their old bridge was worth saving, and then go and form a lobby to protect it?"

"They're not all old women, Silas. It's those island people in general, and they… Besides, we're talking big money here. A bridge like that isn't going to cost peanuts as you've pointed out, and federal money isn't being handed out like it used... Well, to put it simply: federal money has simply dried up, as you know, so there's no hope from that quarter."

"Okay, Sandy. Look at it this way. I've given a lot of thought to this, and this is how we're going to handle it: you're going to have to issue a notice to the press at once, stating reasons why you, as Director of Transportation, are convinced it's essential for a *new* bridge to be built in this *new* location at the southern end of the island -- one that will replace the old island bridge -- and don't forget to emphasize that the new location is essential. That way the Honeydale Farms land will rocket in value, because, as I said, that's where the new bridge will have to start, and the consortium can make a killing on its investment by selling it to the state for that purpose. We're talking big bucks here too, and that's why I need to..."

Moseley waved his hand in dismissal. "Yeah, yeah. I know. I get the picture. Even so, how am I to...?"

Brigham placed the flat of his hands on the table. "No problem. Listen. I'll just play it cool. Once your declaration is published, stating that the new bridge is essential, I'll make my response by brushing the whole thing off, saying that I don't think a new bridge is called for at all at this time, and don't want to burden the taxpayers, etcetera, etcetera, but that if you, as Director of Transportation, insist it's absolutely necessary, then I'll feel obliged, naturally, to set up a commission to study the issue... public safety... boost to the state's economy... create jobs. You know... the usual spiel. By being against it for fiscal reasons, but for it for other, popular reasons, I stand to gain a lot of votes. What I'm saying is, we could make it work for me rather than against me. What do you think, eh Sandy?"

"Hope you're right, Silas. We'll have to play it very carefully though. And what reasons am I supposed to find for declaring this new bridge to be essential anyway, let alone move it to a new location?"

"Oh. the island population has increased considerably more than was foreseen when the old bridge was last repaired, and it's now subjected to traffic loads beyond its structural capabilities. You know… health and safety… could endanger people's lives, or whatever."

"You mean functionally obsolete."

"Yeah, whatever… On the other hand, it's too bad that, apart from a few very minor repairs called for on this spring's inspection report, it states that the wretched bridge is as solid as a rock -- safe as houses. But then, no-one, least of all the public, ever reads these reports."

"You can bet your life those '*Save our Bridge*' people, or whatever they call themselves, will read it. They'll make it front-page news! What else can you think of?"

"Come on, Sandy. *You* think of something. Maybe you could say it doesn't conform to new federal guidelines."

"*What* new federal guidelines? Anyway, it should be grandfathered in under the old ones."

"Oh, come on, Sandy, surely you can find something amongst all those regulations! You're going to have to, or losing the election won't be our only worry. If that Honeydale Farms land isn't used for the new bridge, it'll be useless for anything else because of all the toxic waste under it. I dread to think what'll happen to me if that land becomes worthless. My contributors… the consortium… one way or another a new bridge just *has* to be built, and built starting right there on that land."

"Okay. So what else have we got in the way of plausible reasons for this?"

"I think we have an excellent case for creating a viable seaway up the bay, so Davenport can become a major commercial port again. I'm certainly not the first to point out that, in these days of containerized shipping and supertankers, Davenport has lost a tremendous amount of its former importance in world trade. It simply can't compete with other major ports on the eastern seaboard anymore. None of the new stuff can negotiate its way under the present island bridge."

"Boy! The sailing community's going to hate that one! Tankers coming up the sound! It'll ruin their playground… and they've got mighty deep pockets too. I don't know, Silas."

"One thing though, we're going to have to move fast if we want this thing settled before the November elections. Once I've conceded to your stance about needing a new bridge, Sandy, I'll have to come up with a commission and a report and everything. Damn. It's a tough one… a tough one."

"No problem coming up with a commission, though, Silas. Right off the top of my head I can think of several who'll be willing to produce a report for us declaring the bridge is unsafe. After all, choosing the commission members is the governor's prerogative. All we need to do is to choose those that owe you a favor."

"Ah, but don't forget those '*Save our Bridge*' people, Sandy. They'll be sure to check to see to it that the survey is independent, and it's not as if they're known exactly for trusting us up here in the State House, is it?"

Moseley stood up. "Well, we're just going to have to work on that one, I guess. I don't know. This had better all work out, hadn't it?" The enormity of the problem struck him, as well as the knowledge that more than elections and positions were involved here. His whole future depended on it as did that of Brigham who -- as Moseley had already learnt via the grapevine -- was himself a part of the consortium, and stood to lose financially as well if the Honeydale land deal went down the tubes. He made his way towards the front door, where his brother-on-law patted him on the back, before sending him on his way.

Several days later, the *Davenport Daily News* published a report issued by the Director of the Department of Transportation, Sebastian Moseley, stating that recent studies showed the time had come to replace the Cautuxet Island Bridge. The report cited various reasons for the Department's conclusions. The *Daily News* also noted that, when contacted by reporters, Governor Silas Brigham had reacted negatively to the report, quoting him as saying that while he respected the Director's concern for public safety, he was convinced nevertheless, that, in these times of financial hardship for so many in the state, every possible avenue must be explored before taxpayers were burdened with paying out any more of their hard-earned money. Governor Brigham was also quoted as stating he would meet with the Director of Transportation at the earliest opportunity to discuss the matter, and, depending upon the outcome of their meeting, would decide whether or not to set up a commission to study it. If indeed public safety were really at stake, he would certainly waste no time in securing an early report. "Public safety and fiscal responsibility," he was quoted as saying, "absolutely have to be our number one priority."

CHAPTER 7

Diana had risen early, leaving Finn still asleep in her bed, which they now shared, the guest room having been abandoned and left to serve no other purpose than as a somewhat untidy place in which to scatter the few clothes he had brought with him, along with his overflowing duffle bag. Now, an hour or more after she had already showered, dressed and eaten her breakfast, he appeared at the door leading out onto the porch, where he was surprised to see McGuire as well; he had not expected him back so soon.

As soon as he saw Finn, his host leapt up and rushed forward to greet him, giving him a jovial slap on the back, and guiding him back to the table. "Well, well! This is a more auspicious meeting than the last, I must say. Yes indeed! Yes indeed! Don't you agree Diana?" He waved his hand towards the kitchen. "Go along, then, my dear. Bring the guy some breakfast, then. Don't let the poor man starve. Can't tell you how glad I am you decided to stay on a while, Finn. I wouldn't have wanted to miss seeing you, and I do hope you've been enjoying your time here in our neck of the woods. Diana says you'll be staying a while longer yet too, so I hope we'll have time to really get to know each other finally."

Finn answered with something appropriate to the occasion, then watched as his host continued to demolish his breakfast, eventually wiping the plate clean with a piece of toast, before running his napkin over his face, pushing his plate away, and leaning back in his chair.

"So… You're a professional engineer diver then, as well as being a structural and civil engineer, and you make your living at it. You must do something pretty special with all those qualifications then?" McGuire raised his bushy, sandy eyebrows, revealing sharp blue eyes.

"Well, yes, I suppose you could say that. I specialize in underwater structures: bridges, pilings, wrecks, oil rigs, that sort of thing, mostly in places where using a towfish with a video camera isn't feasible, and mostly inspecting other people's or Mother Nature's work." He laughed. "I'm not much for sitting at a drawing board."

Finn, urged on by McGuire, then continued by regaling his host with some of his more exciting experiences, pleased with the older man's interest in what he did for a living, their conversation lingering long after he had eaten his breakfast, and Diana had cleared the table and left them alone.

"Finn." McGuire waved his mug of coffee at his guest. "I owe you."

Finn shook his head. "Uh-uh, no, Mr.

McGuire, Sir. Please. You don't owe me anything." He stood up and began walking away.

"No, don't go walking off now, Finn. At least hear me out. Come on back here now, and sit down a bit while I explain what I've got in mind… Right. That's better. Now… You know the bridge that connects us to the mainland? Well, it's a long story, but the long and the short of it is that Governor Brigham is going to be setting up a commission to study the question of replacing it, and one important component of that commission is an inspection team to investigate the underwater section of the supporting piers." McGuire grabbed hold of Finn's arm, and started hustling him out of the porch and down the lawn to the end of his private dock. "Here, come with me."

Finn looked out over the bay, glittering today in the bright sunlight. He would have preferred to stand there, watching the fleet of large sailboats sailing past, colorful spinnakers set, but McGuire was pointing in the opposite direction, towards the bridge.

"… those piers," he was saying.

"What's wrong with hiring a local company?" Finn interrupted.

McGuire slapped him on the back for the second time that morning. "Ah, I see you've read the newspaper article then, and have guessed where I'm going with this. Well, that's just it. There's a lot of opposition to having a new bridge, and Governor Brigham's going to have to make sure the people who want the old bridge to stay where it is -- they call themselves, *'Save our Bridge,'* by the way -- are convinced the company he's chosen to inspect it is, shall we say, independent of state ties, if you see what I mean." He winked at Finn. "And the thing is, well… the island people here… Let's just say I know they'd trust anyone I myself would propose, like you, for instance. My position in the community, you understand. I'm well thought of here, I'm proud to say, and of course, it'd mean a nice bit of change for you too, young man."

Finn shook his head for the second time. "Uh-uh! No thank you, Mr. McGuire. I appreciate your offer, but apart from anything else, it'll be a quite a while before I can dive again anyway, and obviously that's the only way I could carry out any sort of inspection. Besides, my Underwater-Diver-Inspector Certificate has been suspended until I get back my diver's medical certificate, and without that, I'm not allowed to work anyway."

"Not to worry, son." McGuire gave Finn's shoulder a fatherly squeeze. "It'll be a while too, before the commission meets anyway, so I'm sure you'll be fine by that time. I'll have a word with my friend Sandy Moseley about it. I've a feeling we can arrange this thing to our mutual benefit. There are ways, you know…" He tapped the side of his nose. "By the way, I don't know if you recognize the name, but Moseley's the other guy you pulled from the plane, so *he* owes you too, if it comes to that."

They had arrived back on the porch, and Finn, in no way wanting to embark on a business relationship with his host, was relieved to see Diana coming out to greet them.

She smiled. "I'm so happy to see the two of you getting on so well together." She held Finn's hand, and they all trooped back into the house, where McGuire gave his daughter a quick kiss on the cheek, snatched his hat off a chair, and prepared to leave. "Sorry to have to go, but I've got to see a couple of people up at the State House this morning." He gave Finn another wink, at which Finn simply looked down at his boots.

"Then tonight I've got a meeting at the yacht club. When you're commodore, you have to turn up to these things, you know. Screening new members tonight. We have to be careful, you understand."

Finn continued to study his boots.

"By the way, you *are* coming to our yacht club ball on Friday night, I hope." McGuire raised his enormous eyebrows in expectation.

Finn looked up and opened his mouth to say he had not heard about it.

"Good, good." McGuire removed his hat, used it to wave farewell and strode off through the hallway.

Diana stood on her toes and kissed Finn. "Dad really seems to like you… I mean, apart from the fact that he owes his life to you, that is. What were the two of you talking about out there?"

"Oh, just something to do with replacing that bridge up there."

"Oh that! Yes, there's quite a bit of a fuss about it here on the island."

CHAPTER 8

Diana was in the kitchen, preparing supper; McGuire, sitting in his favourite armchair, was savoring his second bourbon on the rocks, and Finn was idly flipping through the supplement to the Sunday edition of the Davenport Daily News, when the house phone rang in the library. McGuire stood up and, glass in hand, went to answer it, leaving the doors to both rooms open.

"Frederick! How are you? How's Louise?" Finn heard him say, and, sometime later: "Well, Frederick, just so as I can plead your case with all the facts in front of me, let me go over your problem here... Yes, I know which piece of land you're referring to. It adjoins your own twenty-five-acre plot, right?

"Can't you alter the architectural plans for the house you want to build on it, so as to comply with the zoning regulations?...

"Ah, yes, I understand. So, what you need then is a variance that'll allow you to build closer to the edges of the property than regulations allow. I forget for the moment, but how much extra footage on either side do you need?...

"Another ten feet? Hmm, that's quite a bit over the limit, but let me see what I can do for you, Frederick. I know Jack Walker well. He's the chairman of the board, so I have a good chance of persuading him to bend the rules, seeing that you're a good friend of mine. Everything else checks out, does it? Perc test? Setback from the waterfront, etc.?...

"Okay, let me talk to Jack then, and I think you can rest assured you'll be receiving your building permit, no questions asked...

"No, no problem at all, Frederick. As you know, I'm always happy to help out my friends. Right, give my best to Louise. We'll be seeing you at the Yacht Club Ball, yes?...

"Excellent! See you there then. Goodbye."

McGuire returned and sat down, pointing his glass towards what Finn was reading. "You know, Finn, there was an article in there just a few weeks ago about this island, pointing out how the value of waterfront real estate here is rising rapidly." He took a sip of his bourbon. "Yes, and I'm proud to say that I myself was able to foresee that potential and to act upon it by snapping up this particular thirty-acre estate that I call home, right before people began to cotton onto its value." He took another sip. "I'm now seriously considering investing in some more waterfront property here as well, before it gets out of reach even for people with substantial financial assets such as my own."

Glass empty, he stood up, and went to the

liqueur cabinet, where he poured himself another bourbon. "Can I get you another one, Finn?"

Finn held up his still half-full glass. "No thank you, Sir. I'm fine."

McGuire, new drink in hand, settled himself back down in his armchair. "Yes, the property I'm thinking of purchasing belongs to the Lillacrays -- they're from a fine old Philadelphia family -- class written all over them. Frederick Lillacray -- the man just on the phone to me -- is due to retire soon. He's head of Lillacray Life Insurance, with offices in Manhattan, and scattered elsewhere around the globe, and as they have no-one to inherit the property, he's been making noises about selling it and using a small, ten-acre plot he has adjacent to it for building a retirement cottage for himself and his wife, Louise. In fact, that was just what he was calling me about. That lot, although it's ten acres, is long and thin, and he wants to take advantage of all the width so as to make the best possible use of the view of the bay. Trouble is that his plans, which include a modest five en-suite bedrooms, among other amenities you'd expect to find for someone of his social status, are too wide to conform to the zoning regulations regarding distance from the property boundaries on either side, so he's asked me -- and this is just between you and me, of course -- to put in a word for him so that the Zoning Review Board will give him a variance. This is the type of little favor that I, knowing the right people to talk to, as I do, am usually in a position to wangle for my friends, I'm happy to say, and they're always very appreciative, of course." He winked, and raised his glass to Finn.

Diana's face appeared around the kitchen door. "Finn? Would you mind setting the table for me, please? Supper's almost ready."

Finn leapt up. "Of course, I wouldn't mind. I'll get right to it," and, hoping to deter McGuire from continuing to make him privy to affairs he felt were none of his business, he made as much noise as possible, clattering cutlery, but McGuire was not to be put off.

"Yes," he continued, "as a close friend, I'm well in with the Lillacrays and all their other friends who move in the same social circle, so naturally I'm invited to all their society dos, Fred aware too, of course, that, as a graduate of the Harvard Business School, I know what I'm talking about when it comes to financial affairs.

"Yes, I'm thinking that, providing the market doesn't suddenly go through the roof in the very near future, I can get him to let his current home go for a couple or so million, which wouldn't make too big a hole in my pocket, you might say... "You're sure you wouldn't like another drink, Finn? No? My thoughts are to turn it into a luxury hotel. It'll need another million or so spending on it, of course, but I reckon I'll start making a profit on my investment within about three years. I've never misjudged the market yet, and am happy to say that I can thank my astuteness for the comfort in which I've been able to afford to live for a number of years now." He leaned back in his chair, holding his glass out in front of him, and waving it slightly towards Finn. "As you can gather from what I'm telling you, Finn, I have no need to work, of course, but I do think it's important to keep one's hand in, don't you? So, I've held onto my lumber mill up in Maine. I guess that brings in roughly a quarter mil a year, which always comes in useful of course. Socially, I'm also Vice-chairman of our prestigious State Country Club, as well as Commodore of our Cautuxet Island Yacht Club, you know, and, as I mentioned, am happy to use my considerable influence to help my friends whenever possible – as with old Fred Lillacray, and you with the bridge-inspection job, of course. So, what with one thing and another, I do manage to keep myself busy as you can see." He laughed, and raised his glass to Finn again.

Finn finished setting the table. "I think I should offer Diana a hand in the kitchen, don't you? I don't like the idea of her slaving away there while we enjoy ourselves here, drinking and chatting."

"Oh? Sure, sure, go ahead." His voice followed Finn's retreat into the kitchen. "Remind me to tell you sometime about the hundred-acre patch of waterfront I snatched up in the Caribbean a few years back. The big, international luxury hotels have been after me to sell it, but I'm holding off; that market hasn't peaked yet, so there's plenty of time..."

CHAPTER 9

McGuire had left early for the yacht club ball, leaving Diana and Finn to finish getting themselves ready, something that required Finn's shirt and his tux to be pressed after having remained all this time rolled up in his old canvas holdall.

Diana set up the board, and plugged in the iron. "Dad takes his obligations as commodore of the yacht club very seriously. I sometimes think he overdoes his role a bit, but he's forever worrying that someone will make some sort of complaint that'll reflect badly on him and his office."

"I get the impression that his social status means quite a lot to him."

"Yes," Diana nodded. "Yes, it does." She handed Finn his shirt, and he went upstairs, returning later, dressed in his newly-pressed tux, ironed shirt, bow tie and polished shoes. He found Diana seated at the table, making some last-minute alteration to her dress, and bent over to kiss her.

"Thank you for pressing my clothes for me."

"If I hadn't, I have to say you'd have been a sorry sight indeed. Come to think of it, I don't even know how you managed to cram all your clothes into that old hold-all in the first place, although I'm glad you thought to bring your tux with you."

"Well, I didn't know what to expect from my visit, so reckoned I should be prepared… Okay if I get us a drink while I'm waiting?" He poured them a glass of wine each, then settled himself, feet up, in McGuire's big, La-Z-Boy armchair.

"When do…?" he began, but was interrupted by the front door bell.

Diana pushed back her chair. "Who on earth can that be at this time?"

"Stay there. I'll get it."

The woman at the door looked up at him. "I don't know you, do I?" Her voice was strident, and had that pseudo-English accent peculiar to some Bostonians. She stepped inside without being asked, and he stood aside to let her pass.

"No. We've not met before. My name's Finn Westlake, and I'm a friend of Miss McGuire's."

"Oh Diana, you mean. I'm Louise Lillacray." She smiled, revealing a large set of aging, yellowing teeth… rather like a horse, he thought.

"Please come in, Mrs. Lillacray." He stood back again, this time to allow her to sweep into the living room.

"Can Finn get you a drink, Mrs. Lillacray?"

"No, no! Can't stop, my dear. Thank you anyway. I've only come to collect for the Heart Fund. I really can't stay. Do you happen to have a contribution?"

"Yes, of course." Diana handed her a note from her purse, and Finn rummaged in his pocket and found something to contribute as well.

"Thank you so much." Mrs. Lillacray headed back towards the door. "By the way, my dear, you *will* come to my fundraising dinner for Governor Brigham's re-election campaign, won't you? I know it's a bit early to ask, but I *do* want to be sure I've as many people committed as possible. A governor who runs on a platform of fiscal restraint is exactly what we need, and Brigham, as you know, is against all this new bridge nonsense too, so as president of the *Save our Bridge* group, I intend to do everything I can to help him get re-elected."

"Thank you Mrs. Lillacray. I'll be delighted to come, as I'm sure my father will."

"Excellent. Well, I must be on my way... off to the yacht club ball later," and Finn wished Mrs. Lillacray 'goodbye', allowing Diana to show her out, after which she disappeared upstairs to get ready.

He sat down again and waited, and waited, and when he finally heard her footsteps coming down the stairs, went to meet her. She pranced past him, head high, a hint of elegant legs teasing him, and pausing to reach up to give him a quick kiss on the cheek on her way.

"You look terrific, Diana. What on earth were you doing up there though? You were almost an hour."

"You look pretty good too, Finn... Won't be a minute." She put down her beaded purse and handkerchief, opened up her lipstick, and turned to face the big oval mirror above the fireplace.

"Women!" he sighed, and settled down in the chair yet again, his legs stretched out on the raised foot, looking at the back of Diana's head. She really did have beautiful hair; it was the first thing he had noticed that day when she had come to visit him in hospital. His eyes moved down over her trim waist and sexy hips… yes, definitely sexy hips. Her dress, a simple, silky dress of soft dove-grey, hugged her elegant figure in such an alluring way. And her legs too, really…

"Finn!"

Finn jumped forward in the chair. "*What*? What's wrong?"

"Your shoe! There's a big hole right through the bottom. I can even see your sock!"

He sat back again. "Oh that?"

"It must be terribly uncomfortable. How can you wear it like that?"

"I've been meaning to get it mended, or throw them out. They're pretty old, and I don't wear them often. Polished them up nicely though, didn't I?"

"They're beautiful, simply beautiful. Oh well, just be sure to keep your feet firmly on the floor tonight."

"What did you expect me to do? Stand on my head?"

CHAPTER 10

Finn drove them to the yacht club, remembering its location from the day they had made a tour of the island, and on the way Diana described what they could probably expect the evening to be like: no doubt a bit stuffy and old-fashioned, with lots of older people engaged in social one-upmanship, and later, so crowded, it would be difficult to move.

Tonight, there were cars parked everywhere, even lined up half way down the road, and this is where they left the little Mercedes. Finn had the tickets, and Diana introduced him to the people sitting at the checking-in table near the entrance, then stopped.

"One minute, Finn. I just need to go to the ladies' room."

"What! Already?"

"It's your fault. You shouldn't have insisted on trying to kiss me and drive at the same time. My hair must look like a scarecrow's."

He wandered into the big main room and

waited for her near the door. The view from the windows overlooking the Atlantic was spectacular, with small islands and rocky outcrops that stretched away into the ocean, and he leaned back against one of the tubular iron support-pillars, looking off to one side, where small cliques had commandeered their places for the evening at collapsible wood tables already scattered with plastic mugs, paper napkins and dishes of store-bought hors d'oeuvres. Looking out of place amid the surprisingly utilitarian surroundings, haute-couture evening purses gleamed or glittered in the harsh, fluorescent light.

Bored already, he watched new arrivals greeting one another -- the men with hearty handshakes and business-like claps on the back, the women reaching across, pursing their lips, then brushing cheeks, careful not to disturb their makeup.

Diana re-appeared. "Come on. Dad's saved us a table."

"You've been ages. Surely, I didn't make that much of a mess of things, did I?"

She put her hand on his shoulder. "Oh! Sorry to have to leave you again, Finn, but I've just seen a someone I need to talk to about something. Be right back."

Finn sat down at the reserved table, and looked around. Not far away was McGuire. He was huddled in a corner, within earshot, and deep in conversation with another man, their backs to Finn, so did not notice him sitting nearby.

The other man turned to face McGuire. "I saw Diana come in with a young man, Chester. Who's he then? She certainly knows how to go for the classy stuff, doesn't she?"

Finn raised his eyebrows.

"Well, I suppose you wouldn't recognize him, Sandy, given the state you were in at the time, but he's the one who dragged you out of the plane that day."

So, this was Moseley!

"*He is*! You're having me on, Chet! No, I didn't recognize him, I'm afraid."

"Yes, he's the one, and I invited him to come to stay as a sort of thank you. By the way, did you know he actually almost lost his life on our account?"

"Nope. Didn't know that either. Having to fly back here the next day, of course, I wouldn't have known anything about what happened after I got knocked out in the crash. No harm done, thank goodness. Just a bump on the head that knocked me out… Don't even know his name, come to think of it, so never got around to thanking him, I'm afraid… You know how it is. With one thing and another…"

"Well, now you *do* have your chance to say thank you to him, Sandy, and I've been thinking; you might like to thank the guy in a more tangible way as well," and McGuire went on to explain about Finn's qualifications, and how he would be ideally suited to carry out the bridge-inspection part of the upcoming commission. "… and as you and I both know, Sandy, people aren't too trusting of the powers-that-be up there at the State House when it comes to impartiality, but these island people, especially this '*Save our Bridge*' group, they trust me, so if you were to hire Westlake to do the job, based on my recommendation, that would satisfy them that all's fair and square in that regard."

"I don't know, Chet. You say he has all the right qualifications to carry out the inspection, but how is he otherwise?" Moseley lowered his voice, but not enough to prevent Finn from hearing it. "I mean, can he be trusted? Know which side his bread is buttered, if you see what I'm getting at? He'll have to understand that, regardless of what he finds, he'll still be working for us up at the State House, and we have to be sure he'd..."

Someone let out a loud guffaw, causing Finn to miss what about him they would have to be sure about.

"Well, although he hasn't popped the question yet, the way things are going, I fully expect to welcome him as my son-in-law very soon. If he has an eye for opportunity, and he's no fool, you can bet on it that, like anyone else, he'll quickly cotton on to the fact that, if he plays his cards right, there could be a whole lot more contracts where that one comes from, and'll have the sense to..."

Moseley coughed. "I'd hate for anything to jeopardize your own future with the party, Chet."

"Come now, Sandy; when have I ever let you down, eh?"

"Well, let me talk it over with Governor Brigham then. Is there anything else you have that I can put on the plate as an incentive for him to go along with your recommendation?"

"How about if I hold a fund-raising party for Brigham at my place, right before the election? With my social standing in this community here, I'm well placed to bring in the island vote as you know, and my mansion would be the ideal place for such a fundraiser. In fact, it'll be a two-way street: help Governor Brigham get re-elected, and consolidate my own position in the party and the community at the same time. What better combination, eh, Sandy?"

"A generous offer, Chet. I don't see how he can refuse."

Finn, shocked to find himself the object up for grabs in some political deal, turned to see McGuire and Moseley slap each other on the back and go their separate ways, unaware that, regardless of any proposed agreements on their part, there was no way this young man would ever accept any offer to work for them.

Diana now back at Finn's side again, they made their way to the dance-floor, but before they could even get started, McGuire hailed them from the bar. "Over here," he mouthed, beckoning lustily with his whole arm, his face glowing even more than usual from the several bourbons Finn had watched him down already. His duties as commodore no longer appeared to weigh on him, and he put his arms around the two of them, leading them towards his group of friends.

"Come with me." He introduced his house-guest all round, including to the vice commodore and the club sailing champion, as well as other island dignitaries. "And this is Sebastian Moseley, Finn..." He turned to Moseley. "And at last you get to meet the man who saved your life, Sandy."

And with that he drew Diana away, asking his daughter to dance with him, leaving Finn marooned in a small circle composed of the newly-introduced group, and to receive Moseley's belated thanks for his rescue, followed by a lull in the conversation.

The vice commodore broke the silence. "Well then. You're here, visiting us, I hear?"

"Yes, for a while. Then I'm off to visit my family back in England."

"England!" Moseley's face brightened. "I spent a couple of days there about five years ago… a place called Stockport. You know it?"

"Only that it's near Manchester."

"Which part do you come from then?" Moseley began drawing him away from the others, giving the appearance of being delighted to have the opportunity to discuss his visit to England.

They chatted for a while, or rather, Moseley did the chatting, until Finn noticed Diana looking in his direction, beckoning to him, pleading, so he made his excuses, and went back to her.

"I'm sorry; I couldn't seem to get loose from the man. The minute he found out what I do for a living, he started in about that bridge. I think if anyone asks me again about what I do for a living, I'm going to say I'm a mattress salesman. All people want to talk to me about is that bridge of yours."

"Well, he *is* the Director of the Department of Transportation, so I suppose a job such as yours might be of interest to him. He…"

"This is *amazing*! I've not seen you since high school, but I'd recognize you anywhere, Diana. Where have you been?"

Finn looked up to see a man advancing on them, hand held out.

Diana gave him a welcoming smile. "Right

here all the time, Ben."

"Of course! You live on the island, don't you? I only wish I did. I'm thinking about moving here though. In fact, that's why I'm here tonight. The vice commodore invited me along to meet some of the local people… I got divorced recently."

"Oh? I'm so sorry to hear that, Ben… Ben, I'd like you to meet a friend of mine, Finn Westlake. Finn, Ben's an old high-school acquaintance of mine, Ben Bradley."

The two men shook hands, making the usual appropriate greetings, after which Bradley headed for the bar, having insisted on getting them drinks.

Diana held her hand out across the table, and Finn took it and squeezed it. "Not getting to see much of each other tonight, are we?" she commented.

"Seems that way."

Bradley returned with the drinks, and out of politeness they invited him to join them.

"Thanks. Don't mind if I do." He grabbed one of the chairs, swung it around, and sat down facing the back of it, arms folded across the top rung. "Yes. We were married a couple of years. No kids though, thank goodness."

"So where do you live now, Ben?" Diana asked.

"Well, I have a small apartment in Davenport, but it's a bit pokey, so I spend most of my time living at my aunt and uncle's."

"Oh! You mean with Governor Brigham, then? Ben here is our state governor's nephew, Finn."

Bradley nodded. "Yes, they pretty much raised me anyway, so I feel right at home there. It's nice because I can come and go as I please; they treat me like the son they never had, really," he continued, his eyes fixed on Diana, while Finn tried to decide what sort of man he was.

Physically, he was tall and muscular. His hair was black and curly, and he was good looking, with pale-blue eyes, so why had he already taken a dislike to him? "Come on Westlake. Face it," he told himself. "You're just jealous because you can see him setting his sights on Diana... and with him being recently divorced..."

Bradley turned towards him. "Anyway, Finn, that's enough about me. What are you doing in this neck of the woods then, eh?"

And once again Finn found himself explaining what he did for a living, relieved finally when the subject changed to spear-fishing.

Bradley slapped his hand on the back of his chair. "You like spear-fishing? That's great! Maybe you and I could go out together sometime before you leave, Finn. What do you say? Yes?"

"Finn can't go diving for several months, Ben. He was in a bad accident, and severely damaged his chest and lungs."

"Really! Oh wow! That's bad! How long then before you can go down again?"

"I don't think a bit of snorkeling and spear-fishing would hurt, but, to answer your question, it'll be another few months at least before I can go back to work. That's why I've had the chance to visit Diana."

Bradley furrowed his eyebrows, and grabbed hold of the back of his chair again, his pale eyes staring at Finn. "You're out of operation for the duration then? That's too bad, man." He peered into Finn's face. "Tell me. What happened?"

"Oh, I was doing some underwater rescue work, and got pinned down, that's all. So yes, I'm afraid I am 'out of operation' as you put it."

Diana opened her mouth to say something, but Finn shook his head. He was fed up discussing his work and his health, and, as the music had conveniently started up again, he leapt up. "Ah! Time for a dance. Excuse us please, Ben, if you don't mind." He grabbed Diana's hand, and pulled her to her feet.

Bradley stood up as well. "I must be off too, I guess… Time I joined my host anyway. It's been great to meet you Finn, and to see you again too, Diana. Finn, you and I must definitely go spear-fishing then some time, okay? I'll give you a call. Bye."

"A good-looking guy."

"You think so?"

"Yes, of course he is, and he knows it too. I saw the way he was looking at you."

"Finn. I do believe you're jealous!"

"Do I need to be?"

"Don't be ridiculous. Of course not, you silly." She reached up and kissed him.

They danced together and chatted with other club members until eleven o'clock, when Diana suggested they leave. "It's getting too crowded in here."

"Will your father mind if we take off?"

She looked over to where McGuire, bourbon in hand, was deep in conversation with Moseley again, and smiled. "No. Dad's fine. He's in his element at…"

"Oops! Sorry." A tipsy woman, holding her drink aloft in one hand, and a tomato-colored hors d'oeuvre in the other, tripped in front of Finn. He grabbed her arm to steady her, but failed to stop the red concoction from painting a greasy smear down his jacket, shirt and pants.

"Oh gee! So sorry, honey! Now look what I've done! How could I have done that? Here, let me wipe you down a bit, see if…" She reached towards him with a paper napkin, and stumbled against him, the hors d'oeuvre wedged between their chests, her drink spilling over both of them.

"Sorry about that." Her partner took her arm and led her away.

Finn acknowledged the apology with a nod, and he and Diana continued their way to the exit, during which he took a look down at himself and surveyed the damage.

Once outside, Diana turned to look at him. "O dear, Finn! That woman couldn't have made a worse mess of you if she'd tried, could she?"

Finn sighed. "Well, look at it this way: my old tux was ready to be thrown out anyway, I guess, so I suppose you could call it a good excuse to ditch it. It can join my holey old shoes in the garbage. My shirt has pretty much had it too. I can't see all that mustard and ketchup coming off anytime soon, can you?" He took her hand. "Come on. Let's forget about it and go for a walk along the beach. The fresh air feels great, doesn't it?"

They took off their shoes, and walked barefoot across the cold, wet sand. There was no wind at all, and the waves barely lapped against the shore.

"Tomorrow's Saturday. What shall we do, Finn? They're forecasting thundery rain for the afternoon."

Finn skittered a stone across the water. "Then the morning would be a good time to go fishing. How about taking the boat, and, now that Bradley's mentioned it, do a bit of spear-fishing on our own? Just the two of us?"

"Great idea, but I'll let you do the fishing. I'll take a book and relax on board instead."

"You wouldn't mind? You wouldn't be bored?"

"No, not at all. I'd like that."

Finn picked up another stone. "Come to think of it though, I don't have any snorkeling equipment; it's not something I'd normally ever use, and wouldn't have thought to bring it with me anyway."

"I think we may have some up in the studio. In fact, I'm sure we have, because I remember seeing it there somewhere. We'll pick it up in the morning. What'll you fish for?"

"I don't know. What's good around here?" He watched the second stone as it skittered across the water.

"This time of year, you can find some nice tautog around the bridge piers. They're delicious baked in foil with some butter."

"I don't seem to be able to get away from that bridge, do I? Ah! Maybe the fate of Finn Westlake is locked up in the island bridge." He clutched his chest and feigned a suitable voice of doom.

"A fine actor *you*'d make." Diana ran away

from him into the water, pulling her dress high above her knees, and he followed her.

"Ah well, so what? This is all going into the garbage tonight anyway," he muttered.

Sometime later they were driving home. "That Ben does seem an okay sort of guy," Finn remarked.

"Well! That damns him with faint praise, doesn't it?"

One hand on the steering wheel, and one arm around Diana, he leaned over and kissed her. "And I'm not jealous of him either."

She returned his kiss. "And I assure you, Finn; you have no reason to be."

They drove in silence for a few minutes. "You know," Finn commented. "I've been thinking, and I know there were lots of pleasant and genuine people there tonight, but, and perhaps I shouldn't say this, I somehow got the impression from a few of those I met or overheard in conversation, that much of their camaraderie was a bit phony, with all the jovial backslapping and loud laughter with heads thrown back in merry mirth. I like people who are open, what-you-see-is-what-you-get kind of people, if you understand what I'm getting at. Those I'm talking about gave me the impression somehow that they each had some hidden agenda of their own. I can't describe it exactly, but I got the feeling that if their own interests were somehow threatened, they'd sell you down the river as soon as look at you."

"Yes, I do know what you mean. I'll introduce you to my own friends sometime. They're the sort of people you'd get along with really well, I know. You'd find them totally different. We have good times together, and politics and business rarely enter our conversations, let alone play any role in our friendship."

"I'll look forward to that."

She leaned over and kissed him on the cheek. "It's just that I've been enjoying keeping you all to myself, Finn."

CHAPTER 11

It was the morning after the yacht club ball, and Finn followed Diana through the dew-covered grass leading to what she referred to as 'the studio'.

"Here we are. I'm afraid it's in need of some repairs and a good coat of paint, but it serves its purpose." The latch lifted, rust grating on rust, and they went in.

Finn looked around the small room. It was more a gardener's shed than a studio. It had no ceiling, just the bare rafters, and some time, long ago, someone had painted the walls white. A single light bulb hung from a long cord from the ridge pole, and Diana pulled the attached string to switch it on. The only furniture was a bare wood table and a kitchen chair.

Regretting now his enthusiasm of the previous evening, and wishing that they could have enjoyed a lie-in after the ball instead of going out fishing so early, he sat down at the table and rested his head between his hands while Diana started poking around amongst the shelves.

He watched her. "Thank you for your company at the ball last night, Diana. I was so proud to be with you; you were by far the most attractive woman in the room, you know." Dust went up his nose, and he sneezed, making her laugh.

She turned around and planted a kiss on top of his head. "And I was proud to be with the most attractive man in the room too, Finn… so much more so than Ben Bradley." She grabbed his hand. "Come on, now; we need to get going before the tide turns. Don't just sit there, looking gorgeous. Give me some help here, yes?"

He stood up, yawned, then joined her in the search for the snorkeling equipment which, she told him, had to be somewhere in one of the various containers scattered around the shelves projecting from the open studs of one wall. There were pickling jars, dried-out cans of paint and old beer-crates full of oddments scattered around. On another wall, a collection of tools and other equipment hung from nails long-since rusted, each leaving a brown streak down the once-white paint. There was only one window, and it was draped with dusty cobweb-remains dotted with the long-time desiccated shells of flies, beetles and other insects. He got up and helped her rummage among the boxes, and, eventually finding the snorkeling equipment they were looking for, they set off.

There was not enough wind for sailing this early, so were using the outboard motor. Finn, in charge of the tiller, looked towards the bridge, its massive piers starting to loom over them, less and less like filigree, and more and more like the sinister bastions of a medieval fortress.

"Would you believe me if I said I've never let on to any other woman how much I'm attracted to her?"

"Why? *Shouldn't* I believe you?"

"Yes, because it's true."

He looked up at the now immense concrete and steel structure soon to be towering above them. "Where am I aiming for here?"

Diana pointed towards the nearest pier. "I imagine around there would be as good a place as any... At your age Finn, and you've never been attracted to another woman before? That's hard to believe."

"I didn't say I hadn't been attracted to another woman before; I said I'd never before *let on to* another woman that I was attracted to her."

"What makes this time different?"

"I think it's probably because on the one other occasion I was going to say it, by the time I'd plucked up the courage to do it, she'd already dumped me."

"Dumped you! That doesn't sound very auspicious. I know I've known you only a short while, but you don't strike me as the sort of man a woman would want to dump, Finn. What on earth did you do to turn her off? Don't tell me the perfect Finn Westlake has hidden vices."

"Oh, so at least I come as far as being perfect in your eyes, do I?"

"Not if you caused a woman to flee from

you."

"Nope. Nothing hidden. What you see is what you get, warts an' all."

"I haven't seen any warts as yet."

"There, so I'm perfect after all, you see. No. As far as that other young lady was concerned, I think I wasn't anything more objectionable than being myself, and any woman looking for a partner with a humungous income, membership at all the right clubs, and plays golf on weekends, isn't going to find it in me, I'm afraid. I suppose I'm a bit unpredictable in a way too. I get bored easily. I'm what you might call 'project-oriented'; I love new projects. That's why I love my work; each new contract is a new project."

He turned and killed the motor. "I think that lobster-pot float there would make a good mooring, don't you? Besides, I can't see anything else to tie up to, and our anchor line won't reach the bottom here. Can you grab the hook there, and catch hold of it before the tide sweeps us past it?... Great, thanks."

He let go of the tiller, and made his way for'ard to where Diana was clutching the seaweed-slimy float, and took it from her. "No, I hate the monotony of maintaining something, doing the same thing day in, day out, that's all. It's not that I'm irresponsible; I'm not, and I always finish what I start, and take pride in what I do, but other than that, I can be in one place one day, the next decide I'm bored, and then I'm gone. That's what used to annoy my parents too. Anyway, I clearly didn't offer that woman what she was looking for, and that was that."

"Poor Finn."

"Not really. It obviously wouldn't have

worked out."

"And what exactly was it that you did to annoy your parents then?"

"My father expected me to enter the financial world, like him, instead of which, when I left school, I joined a luxury travel company that took people on scuba-diving holidays, and that, as far as my father was concerned, was the last straw. 'Well, if you think I'm going to support you for the rest of your life, messing about like that, you've got another thing coming'." He imitated his father's rather upper-crust accent. "And then he pretty much wiped his hands of me... I don't know about you, but I need to go in now. It's getting pretty hot here already. You're sure you don't want to come in with me? You're going to get roasted."

"No, I'm fine here with my book. I'll smother myself in suntan lotion, and I've got my big hat here. Really, I'm fine. You go ahead."

She took off her sweatshirt and hauled some faded, green-canvas cushions out of the locker. "I'll be perfectly happy here while you go fishing." She set out the cushions and lay down with her hands behind her head, looking up at him, and smiling.

"What's that smile about?"

"Oh, I don't know. I'm just thinking about how none of this would be happening if I'd known there were only two people in that plane that day...You do have lovely eyes, you know, Finn. They're gentle and honest-looking, not shifty like some I get to see."

He grinned at her, and bent down and kissed her on the cheek.

"I like that too, Finn."

"Which, the grin or the kiss?"

"Both. You're such a good-natured guy too, Finn. You know that?"

"Flattery, flattery, it'll get you everywhere, my dear Diana." And he kissed her again.

"Well, just don't get too full of yourself… speaking of which, that old high-school colleague of mine, Ben Bradley, it's odd, but until last night I'd never set eyes on him since we left school. It was nice to see him again, though. He seemed genuinely interested in what you do for a living too, and in making friends, didn't he? I think he really liked you."

"You mean he *pretended* to be interested in me and my job. I watched him; he couldn't take his eyes off you."

"No. You're wrong; he hardly looked at me. Has a really nice smile though, doesn't he?" she teased him.

He stood up and stamped his feet, working them into the clumsy fins, and shook his head. "Uh, uh, it was obviously you he was interested in, not me… And yes, regarding that charming smile of his: my dear granny would have said he was 'all teeth and trousers'… Oh, what I'd give for my scuba gear right now. This silly thing..." He held up the snorkel.

"Finn! I do believe you're jealous after all."

"No way!" He picked up the spear and jumped over the side just as Diana aimed a cushion at him.

"Go on. Get us some tautog for supper."

It was still slack tide, and the water was flat and almost still. Not the slightest wind caused even a ruffle, giving the water an almost oily-looking sheen, and the floats stood upright at their moorings. The only noise was the rumble of an occasional car crossing the iron-grids forming the road high above them, and the sudden 'plop' as a fish jumped. Even the gulls, perched one to a lamppost high above the bridge, were silent. The sky too, a monotone of gray, seemed to act as a muffler to all sound.

It was good to be in the sea again, and with the slack tide, Finn found it effortless to swim. The water was warm and clear, and Diana's suggestion that the fishing would be best around the huge piers was a good one; there were fish everywhere. Small scaup and pilot fish darted in and out of the long streamers of green and brown seaweed growing out from the pier, and here and there shoals of baby bluefish chased after minnows that broke the surface in a shower of droplets.

"Hi there! How's that?" He held up a big tautog impaled on the spear "Want to take it off for me, please?"

He waited while she unscrewed the head off the spear. She was right; he *was* jealous of that fellow Bradley, and he still did not like him; maybe it was that odd, blank look about his eyes. He shrugged -- not worth wasting time thinking about, anyway.

The black fish flopped onto the deck, and Diana handed the bloodied spear back to him, holding it delicately and with obvious distaste between her thumb and forefinger.

Now the tide was beginning to turn, and he could feel the current pulling. Soon it would be too strong for him. He was running out of steam already, and it annoyed him. A scallop, with its necklace of brilliant blue 'eyes' inside the open valves, propelled itself along in front of him, and then he saw the tail of a large tautog burrowing in the seaweed for small shellfish. He aimed the spear, but the big fish caught his movement, and slipped away, swimming down into deeper water.

He dived down after it, but the fish, after swimming back and forth a few times, preventing him from taking proper aim at it, disappeared into the marine growth around the pier.

"Come on then, where are you? You're much too big to think you can hide from me in there."

He began pulling away the seaweed, but instead of finding the fish, found something that shocked him. He surfaced, then dived down again. It was probably something he should not be doing, given his state of health right now, and having to hold his breath so long, but even so, he began pulling away the seaweed at random, taking a closer look as he made his way around the pier. What he found disturbed him greatly, and despite his now labored breathing and warning pains in his chest, he continued to surface and dive down again and again to make sure of what he was seeing, until his lack of stamina forced him to give up.

He began to make his way back to the *Moonglow*, and was glad of Diana's hand to help him back on board.

"I know you don't like me asking, but are you all right, Finn? You don't look good."

He nodded, and slumped down on one of the seats, too out of breath to remove the fins, then stretched out on the cushion, where he lay and watched Diana set out the lunch she had prepared, his mind on what he had just seen.

She offered him a sandwich. "To get back to you, how did you end up getting your degree in structural engineering then?"

Finn propped himself up on his elbow, trying not to think about what it was that had alarmed him down there. "Uh, well, what I was doing wasn't really enough to live on comfortably, so it suddenly occurred to me one day that if I could combine the diving with the necessary bits of paper I could show people, namely qualifications, I could earn a very good living and enjoy doing it, so that's what I did. And there you have it... Finn Westlake in a nutshell... Thank you." He accepted the mug of homemade lemonade. "Oh! Now that's *really* good." He drained it, and held it out for a refill, still worrying, not only about what he had discovered, but that he should also tell Diana about it. If he did, though, it would spoil not only their morning, but could even affect their comfortable relationship by his having to suddenly become all professional and business-like, and report it to the authorities. It was something he did not want to face right now, and tried to shut his mind to it, at least until he could concentrate properly on the problem. "Now it's your turn. What are you doing, spending your life looking after your father, acting as his chief cook and bottle-washer, elegant hostess and general dogs-body?"

"Oh Finn! That sounds awful, the way you put it."

"I'm sorry, but I have to say I don't think

your father appreciates what he has in you."

"I'm actually a qualified primary-school teacher."

"You are? What a waste! I think you'd make a wonderful teacher."

"Yes, well, when my mother became ill four years ago, it seemed to make sense that I stay at home to help out. Then, when she died a year later, my father kept pressuring me not to go back to work. There was always 'one more thing' he wanted me to do, one more party he wanted me to put on and to act as his hostess. Now I don't know what he'd do if I weren't at home. He relies on me."

"I think that's a bit selfish of him."

"Maybe, and time is going on too, and soon I'll probably need to take some remedial classes to get employed again. It's a shame really, I suppose, but I'm afraid I can't find it in me to go against him. He'd be lost without me."

Finn got up and went over to her side, sat down next to her and kissed her. "He doesn't know how lucky he is. What do you do then, when you're *not* looking after him… other than entertaining me, that is?"

"I've always been interested in painting, and if I'm not out with my friends, I like to go off on my own and paint pictures, landscapes mostly. I particularly like skies, and here is a great place for skies, especially first thing in the morning, or in the evening."

"So those are your paintings I've seen around the house! They're excellent, and I've been admiring them. I didn't realize they were yours, because you haven't signed them. You should. Do you sell them as well?"

"No. I hadn't thought to do that."

"Well, *I* think you should do that too." He leaned over and kissed her again.

"Finn?"

He wished they *had* chosen to have a lie-in this morning, and that he had never seen the wretched bridge. "Hmm?"

"You remember how I was when you first came to visit? I wasn't very nice, was I?"

"Well, I can't say you weren't nice; you were very polite and hospitable, but now you mention it, no, you weren't particularly friendly. That doesn't mean I didn't still find you attractive enough to be glad you asked me to stay on, though."

As often happens when it is too sunny first thing in the morning, the sky had clouded over, and it was starting to rain, a fine, soaking drizzle. It matched Finn's spirits, and he unhooked the boat from the mooring. The wind had come up now, so he hoisted the sails, brought the boat about, and headed for home.

"And remember how you said it had probably been awkward for both of us," Diana was reminding him. "And I remarked that in my case there was more to it than that?"

Finn, holding the tiller in one hand, and the mainsheet in the other, looked up at the mainsail, adjusting the tiller till the boat was making the best possible use of the available wind. "Yes, and I thought it an odd thing for you to say, but didn't want to pry by asking you what you meant."

Diana put her hand on his knee. "It wasn't

fair of me to have even mentioned it, without explaining what I meant by it, but I do owe it to you to tell you what I *did* mean, and why I held you at arms' distance all that time." And she told him all about Eric, and how the experience had affected her. "I'm sorry. I do hope you understand now why I behaved as I did."

"Given how you felt, then, why did you ask me if I'd like to stay on?"

"I'd been awake much of that night in such an emotional dilemma, on the one side thinking about my fear of getting involved in a relationship, and on the other, about how much I'd come to like and respect you during our brief time together. It brought home to me the reality that, as things stood, if you did leave that morning, I'd never see you again, because you'd be going away with such a negative opinion of me, you'd never want to see me again. It was that that made decide to ask you if you would like to stay… something that would give me the chance to show you the real me, and to hope you would like what you saw… and… and find me as attractive as I found you." She took his hand, and kissed it. "Once I'd made that decision, I couldn't wait for the morning to come, dreading that you'd say 'no', which wouldn't have surprised me at all, given the way I'd behaved towards you… Why *did* you say 'yes', Finn?"

"Because I was equally attracted to you, and hoped that, if I did stay on, you'd come to feel the same way about me, and open up." He reached across, and kissed her. "And you did, and here we are, aren't we?"

with his handkerchief, and looked down at himself. "Not too bad, I suppose… What's that? Yes, a bourbon and water sounds fine."

Finn ignored the misunderstanding, poured him a drink, and handed it to him. "Sir, I have to talk to you."

McGuire sat down heavily, downed a mouthful of bourbon, and smacked his lips. "Ah! That's good! What was that you said, Finn?"

Finn drew up a chair and sat down. "I have to talk to you about the bridge."

McGuire smiled, and waved his hand in dismissal. "I knew you'd come around to my way of thinking, Finn. Don't give it another thought. As I promised, I've had a whisper in the right ears, and you'll be getting that contract; you wait and see."

"No Sir, it's not about any contract. It's about what I discovered while fishing around one of the piers of that bridge this morning, and it wasn't good. In fact, it was extremely bad." He took a deep breath. "The concrete casing around the reinforcement steel rods of the pier I looked at is so eaten away by the salt water and other corrosive chemicals in the sea, that large areas of the core are exposed, and obviously have been that way for some time, because I could even see the rods! Because they're open to corrosion as well now, they're disintegrating, rusting right through, something that's well on its way, making the bridge's supports dangerously fragile. I know I haven't seen the worst of it either, but I saw enough to know right now that not only is that bridge definitely unsafe, but to hazard a guess that its sufficiency rating is absolute zero! Any big storm or too heavy a load of traffic, even a big accident up there, and I don't mind betting the whole thing's going to come down; it's that bad."

He stood up and began walking around the room. "With all those cars, buses and eighteen-wheelers pounding constantly over it, I'm surprised it *is* still standing, and it's essential that we let the authorities know about this at once, Sir."

McGuire set his drink down on the coffee table beside him and waved his arms in a downward, calming motion. "Heh! Heh! Hold your horses here a minute, Finn. Let's get this straight. You go fishing with a mask and snorkel, and see a few holes in one of the piers, and now you want to rush to the authorities and tell them, I suppose, to close the bridge immediately?"

"Yes. That's exactly what I want to do."

"Just like that! Come now, Finn. Let's think about this sensibly now, shall we? I don't mean for you to take this the wrong way, but surely to rush off and create a turmoil like that on such flimsy evidence would be quite irresponsible, don't you agree? Have you thought what the media would make of this?"

"I don't care what..."

"Now, I can tell you this: I happen to know not only the person responsible for keeping that bridge in a good state of repair -- his name's Rollo Devine, and he's a very close friend of mine -- but I also know for a fact that it's inspected on a regular basis by qualified and competent people. So, think about it, Finn. Don't you think if anything untoward had been found, it would have been reported and fixed? It *has* to be safe, or it would have been closed already.

"All this business about a special, independent inspection, the one I'm setting up for you to do, that's purely to satisfy the public. Heaven knows why Moseley even decided to announce it needed to be replaced in the first place, given that the inspection reports show it to be perfectly sound. Between you and me, though, the man hasn't a clue about what he's doing, but he happens to be Governor Brigham's brother-in-law, so... Sure, the bridge has some age to it, but..." He stood up and went over to Finn, giving him a fatherly squeeze on his shoulder.

Finn shook his hand off. "Then something's not as it should be! I tell you there's no way that bridge could be certified safe! Some people are either not doing the job they've been paid to do, or else they're covering something up."

"Those are pretty harsh accusations."

"With people's lives at stake? Yes, they *are* harsh accusations, and I intended making them. It's strange, isn't it? One minute you're ready to recommend me as being qualified to fill a state contract by inspecting the state of the bridge, the next you're telling me I'm an irresponsible fool."

"Oh, come along now, Finn. Don't take it that way. I've only now this minute come in through the door. I'm wet and tired, and you greet me with this... And I do have to say, I've not witnessed *this* Finn Westlake before. Can get quite feisty with an old man, can't you? All right. Now, let's be reasonable here. Before I let you rush off and virtually shout 'fire' in a crowded theater, let's think this thing out. I'm sorry, but, for myself, I have to say I think you must be very much mistaken, but if you feel so positive, let me talk to my friend Devine first; there has to be a simple explanation for all this.”

“Mr. McGuire, Sir. This is my profession, and I know what I saw, even from the brief look I had. There certainly *is* a simple explanation, and it isn’t good, and my integrity and concern for the public’s safety are not about to let me keep my mouth shut while I fly out of here without saying a word to anyone. That bridge should *never* be being used the way it is, in its condition.”

“All right. All right. Can I at least finish my drink here? Then I’ll call Devine for you, and we’ll have a logical and satisfactory answer, I’m sure. I certainly don’t intend to rush off, or let you, my house guest, rush off half-cocked, causing a public outcry, because you happen to think you see something while out fishing, okay? I’d be the laughing stock of the whole community.”

There was silence while Finn struggled to hold onto his temper. The last thing he wanted was a fight with Diana’s father. He would let him call this Rollo Devine man, then wait for the outcome of that.

Shortly afterwards, McGuire left the room. Finn heard the door to his office close, and went back to the window. The thunderstorm had moved off into the distance, and the flashes of sheet lightning were silent. Water dripped from the eaves, and a mist was rising from the lawn. In the distance, the diamond necklace of lights above the bridge winked against a pewter sky.

He was still standing there when Diana finally appeared, just as her father emerged from his office. She had showered and washed her hair, and was dressed in a plain, but attractive turquoise dress. "Hi, Dad! Ready for supper? Baked fresh tautog tonight."

McGuire grunted, headed for his favourite chair, sat down, and reached for his drink; the glass was empty.

Diana turned on the table lamps and looked at the two glum faces. "Come on; cheer up everyone. The thunderstorm affected the two of you too? I'll begin to wish I'd stayed upstairs. How about an aperitif? Then I'll go put the fish in the oven."

"Sorry, Diana, but I forgot all about gutting it for you. It's still lying on the counter in the kitchen. You want me to do it for you now? It'll take only a couple of minutes."

"No. Don't bother now. You just sit there and relax, and I'll find something else. We can have the fish tomorrow."

"Yes, I'll have a drink please Diana… another bourbon, that is." McGuire handed her his glass.

"You want a drink as well, Finn?"

"No… No thank you."

Diana gave her father his bourbon, then sat down on the edge of the ottoman, looking from one to the other. "Would anyone care to let me know what's going on?"

"Oh, it's not much at all, my dear. This… uh… young man of yours here was concerned because he thought he saw signs this morning that our bridge is about to collapse."

"Collapse! Finn! And you said nothing to me!

Why didn't you tell me about it?"

"I didn't want to…"

"Before you go any further, Finn, let me say that I've just finished talking with Rollo Devine, who is, as I already told you, the very person to know exactly what state the bridge is in, and he assures me there's absolutely nothing to worry about at all. So now let's have a pleasant evening, shall we, and forget all about it?" He stood up and walked over to where Finn had sat down, his expression blank, and gave the young man's shoulder another paternal squeeze. "Quit worrying, Finn. Everything's just fine, I assure you."

Diana looked across at Finn. "And you have nothing to say in answer to this, Finn? Please, what exactly happened out at the bridge this morning? I knew you didn't look well when you came back on board, but you don't like me worrying about your health, so I didn't say anything. As I said, though, you should have told me. Why didn't you?"

Finn took a deep breath, ready to explain his reason, but again McGuire pre-empted him, relating to his daughter in a light and offhand manner the details of what he referred to as Finn's "alleged discovery".

At the end, Diana stood up and went behind Finn's chair, putting her arms around his neck, and bending over to kiss his cheek. "Oh Finn! Come on. Of course, no-one would allow people's lives to be put in jeopardy like that. It simply couldn't happen. It's not that I doubt your professionalism in any way, but as I said, you weren't exactly well when you got back to the boat this morning. I'm thinking that any sort of heavy exertion is too much for you yet, especially under water like that. I'm convinced it has to have affected your normally good judgment, don't you agree? I do wish you'd told me, though." She kissed him again and smoothed his hair.

Not knowing what more he could do, Finn took her hand and kissed it, offering her a half-hearted smile.

That evening the air was hot, humid and mosquito-laden after the storm. Moths fluttered against the porch screen, and large June-beetles rattled their wings on the fine mesh wire. For Diana's sake, Finn made every effort to take his mind off the bridge and to be sociable, but kept finding himself imagining, with quick intakes of breath, the scene if the bridge were to collapse. Maybe a heavily-loaded truck, or maybe a school bus could be the cause, or even a summer traffic jam, or an accident. The most probable one though, he thought, would be a high wind combined with a strong tide.

"I'm sorry, I can't do it, Mr. McGuire, Sir. That friend you spoke to, that Mr. Devine. I'm sorry, but he's wrong. I know he is, and I can't ignore what I saw, and, as I said earlier, I can't fly out of here without doing anything about it; it would be criminal of me. I'm sorry."

"Now look, Finn," McGuire sighed. "I'm sure Diana's right. You're still recovering from that horrendous accident, and you over-exerted yourself today, no question. It obviously affected your normally good judgment, as Diana said, and if it weren't that I feared you might do yourself severe harm if you were to go down again, I'd insist that that's what you should do, appropriately equipped this time, so you could get an accurate picture of what you think you saw, before going off and creating a scandal of monumental proportions."

"Yes, I have to agree with Dad, Finn. You can't rush off and report anything until you're a hundred percent sure of your facts, and as I agree too that you'd be taking far too great a risk going down again in your present condition, you'll just have to trust Mr. Devine's word, and let the matter go; it's the only way."

Finn slapped his hands on the arms of the chair in frustration. "No, I'm sorry, but I *can't* let the matter go, and I'm even willing to take the risk of going down properly equipped, using scuba gear, to prove I'm right; and I'll agree too to take someone with me as a diving buddy if that's what it'll take to satisfy you as far as my safety's concerned."

"But Finn, you aren't..."

"No. I know I'm right, but if neither of you can trust me enough to understand the significance of what I did, for a fact, actually see this morning, then that's what I'm going to have to do."

McGuire sighed. "I gather, then, that nothing is going to stop you going off on this wild goose chase, even though you've been assured there's absolutely nothing wrong with the bridge?"

"No, nothing. And for your information, I'm not the sort of idiot who's prone to going off on wild goose chases, as you call it."

"Well, on your head be it. And yes, if you insist on doing this, then I agree; you must take a diving buddy with you, but who on earth you're going to find, God knows, and I'm certainly not going to let you go down without one, and that's flat. It's too much of a responsibility."

"I have to say, Finn, that I think Dad's arguing most reasonably under the circumstances. Like him I'm very concerned about you going down like this too, but taking a buddy with you does seem the only way out, doesn't it, if you insist on going ahead? And you certainly do need to be sure of everything, before reporting it, don't you?"

Finn held up his hands. "Okay, okay. I'm *already* sure of everything, but as you insist on my confirming..." He shrugged. "So... Can you suggest anyone who'd come down with me? It'll have to be soon, like tomorrow. I want this thing settled... And we'll need all the appropriate gear too."

McGuire nodded. "I don't like this at all, but yes, I agree; the sooner this thing is sorted out, the better."

"What about Ben Bradley?" It was Diana's idea.

"Bradley? He's Governor Brigham's nephew, isn't he? No! We definitely don't want anyone with that type of connection involved. The quieter we keep this, the better. The last thing we want is him rushing off and telling his uncle about this. Brigham would be bullshit, and I can't afford that; it'd ruin me politically. You'll have to find someone else, someone with no connections with the state government, and wouldn't know how the bridge piers are supposed to look anyhow -- some Joe who just knows about scuba diving, and can act as a buddy for you, that's all... What about that man one of your friends used to go diving with? You know, back when you thought you'd like to learn to scuba dive too, Diana. Lives over on the mainland somewhere." McGuire snapped his fingers, trying to recall the name.

"Oh yes! I do remember vaguely. Let me see; I'd remember the name if I heard it. Wait a minute! I might even have jotted it down in the back of the old phone book. I'll see if I can find it." She disappeared and returned with the torn-off page from an old White Pages. She ran her finger down the sheet. "Right. I've found him. His name's Dave Harvey. Shall I call him for you, Finn?"

"No thanks. I'll need to talk to him myself, but as I can't give him the real reason for going down, what on earth am I going to use as an excuse for asking him to do this, eh?"

"How about you tell him you've unexpectedly found you've got to leave first thing Monday morning," Diana suggested. "And that you'd heard how great the spear fishing is around our bridge, so had been really looking forward to checking it out before you left, and tomorrow's the only day you've got?"

"Hmm. Pretty flimsy. There are plenty of places I can do some serious spear fishing any old time."

"But he's not to know that. Just make out that this is something you're really anxious to do, and had heard he'd be just the right person to have with you, or something. I don't know; I'm sure you'll think of something."

Finn sighed and gave a shrug, then left the room, returning a few minutes later. "Well, I gave him my spiel, sounding as gung ho as I could about it. The guy must think I'm a complete dolt, so no surprise that he wasn't too keen on coming at first, but then he put me on hold while he called someone -- something about having to cancel some other plan -- and finally agreed, so that's settled. We've arranged to go very early tomorrow morning to catch the slack tide, so he'll pick me up at the end of the driveway at five. He's also got gear he can lend me. I should really have a waterproof video camera too, but obviously that wouldn't make sense if I'm supposed to be going spear fishing."

"You didn't tell him the reason, did you? The fewer people involved, the better."

"Of course not, Sir. You don't have to worry. I won't let on."

Things settled down again, but the atmosphere was uneasy, and not long after, McGuire got up. "You'll have to excuse me; I have to make a phone call, then I'm going to bed, so I'll say goodnight."

Finn stretched himself out on the sofa while Diana disappeared into the kitchen to put a load of laundry into the washer. Even the washing machine, however, refused to cooperate tonight, for it stopped right in the middle of the wash cycle, and nothing would make it start up again. After suggesting all possible solutions, he got up to help her carry all the soaking things to the kitchen sink.

"You know, Diana, I have to say I'm really disappointed that your father, and you especially, don't feel you can trust my professional judgment. I would have hoped that by now you knew me better. I know I wasn't carrying out an official inspection this morning, but that didn't mean I wasn't able to form a professional opinion as to what I saw even from that brief look. It makes me feel you can't trust me any which way." He stood back from the sink to avoid the splash of soaking sheets being dumped into it.

"That's not fair, Finn, and you know it. This is different, and it's not a matter of trust anyway; you have to admit that professionally you're what you might call 'compromised' right now; it's the reason you don't even have a license to work."

"For heaven's sake, Diana! Just because my lungs aren't up to snuff, doesn't mean my brain and all the expertise in it aren't either!"

"That's not what I'm trying to say, Finn. Look at it from our point of view; on one side we have a well-respected contractor responsible for the state of the bridge, adamant that it's safe, and even has the annual reports to back it up, and on the other side we have you who, as Dad says, goes fishing with a snorkel, happens to see something that you believe is amiss with one of the piers supporting the bridge, and is intent on rushing off immediately to report it to the authorities, who will know nothing at all about you, except that you don't even have a license to back you up; and then you go on to even accuse their contractor and bridge inspectors of hiding something, basically calling them crooks. Which of you do you think they're going to believe?"

"Well, I've got to do as my conscience tells me, and I've agreed to go down again now to prove what I say, so what more do you want?"

Diana dragged the last sheet from the machine, but dropped it on the way to the sink. It landed with a loud splat onto the kitchen floor, splashing them both with soapy water.

He was bending down to help her clear up the mess when McGuire re-appeared. "After everything that's happened this evening," he said, "I decided I should call Devine again to discuss the situation. As you can imagine, he wasn't at all pleased that, as he put it, 'some know-it-all breezes in' and questions his integrity. He was so annoyed, in fact, that he told me to inform you, Finn, that if you tarnish his reputation by going to the authorities and falsely accusing him of not doing his job properly, he'll sue you for every cent you've got.

"Look Finn, this is turning out to be pretty unpleasant all round and emotionally draining for everyone. Why don't you calm down a bit, take an early night, and by the morning, I'm sure you'll realize that it's simply not worth putting your own life and professional reputation on the line to try to prove something that is…"

Finn picked up the sheet and turned to face McGuire. "When I go to the authorities, I won't be *falsely* accusing him; I'll be *rightly* accusing him, and I'll tell you something else: right now, no-one wishes more than I do that I'd never set eyes on the wretched bridge! But you're right with one suggestion at least: I *am* going to bed. Goodnight." He dumped the sheet in the sink and strode out of the kitchen.

They heard the door of the guest room slam shut, and Diana dried her hands. "I'd better go after him. Poor Finn. He's got himself into a right old state, probably because he's not only not well, but exhausted too."

McGuire put out his hand to stop her. "I don't think that's a good idea, Diana. Finn's in no mood to think straight at all right now, and with nothing more you can do to help resolve the problem tonight, it's better that you leave him to it. Let him have a good night's sleep, and, in the event that he does insist on going with this guy tomorrow, just let him go and get it over with. Then, when he gets back having discovered he was mistaken after all, you can get together both of you, and hopefully smooth things over. I'm right, aren't I?"

Diana sighed. "Yes, I suppose so. At least, I hope so; until he's got this sorted out to his satisfaction, I guess there'll be no use trying to reason with him." She sat down and put her head in her hands. "Oh! It's such a shame! And everything was going so well too."

CHAPTER 13

Finn looked at his watch. It was just gone four o'clock. He got off the bed, where he had lain awake all night, and, for several minutes, stood at the window looking out to where the stone-gray of the early dawn sky was reflected in the water of the bay. "Oh, damn it all to hell!"

He turned and took a piece of paper and a pen from the drawer of the small cabinet beneath the window. The cabinet, being wobbly, caused a ceramic vase sitting on top to topple off onto the carpet. He swore again, but it had not broken, so he picked it up, put it back on the top of the cabinet, pulled up a chair and sat down.

"*My darling Diana,*" he wrote. "*I'm so sorry about what has happened. Please, please forgive me, but this is something I have to do, otherwise it will haunt me, especially if something terrible were to happen because of the state of the bridge, and I had done nothing to try to prevent it. I can't wait for us to be in each others' arms again, hopefully in just a few hours. Finn. xxxxxxxxxxxxx "*

He folded the note and put it in his shirt pocket, ready to slip under her bedroom door when he left, then went into the bathroom and took a cold shower and a shave, hoping to wash away the weariness. The blade of his only remaining instant razor was blunt, and the can of shaving cream empty, so he gave up on that, and tossed them both into the waste basket.

Dressed again, he looked at his watch and found there was still quite a bit of time left before he was due at the gate, so he sank down onto the bed, realizing how tired he was, which was not surprising considering all that had happened since yesterday morning, as well as not having slept for almost twenty-four hours. He was starting out on an empty stomach too, but did not feel like eating -- not exactly ideal circumstances in which to go diving, especially after he had not been down for so long, and was physically out of shape.

He made a half-hearted effort to tidy up the room, not that there was anything much to tidy up. His old ketchup-stained tux and holey shoes had already been thrown away, as had his ruined dress shirt, and whatever else he had brought with him was all stuffed in his hold-all.

He looked at his watch again -- still another twenty minutes before he needed to be at the gate, and as there was no point in going early, only to be molested by swarms of mosquitoes while waiting at the end of the driveway for his diving buddy, he flopped down on the bed, and tried to relax.

He lay there, hands behind his head, staring at the ceiling, and trying not to think about what had caused him to lose his temper and storm out. That Diana had not trusted him had hurt, but had not changed how he felt about her. He just hoped she would have realized how stressed out he was too about the whole situation, and would forgive him for it.

At one time in the night he thought to go to her, but with nothing having changed, and unable to convince her he was right, he decided it would be better to wait until he came back home, by which time he would have proved himself right, and she would have read his note as well, so would know how he felt about her.

He woke with a start, and leapt up. He was late already, and dashed out of the door only to remember that his wallet, complete with credit cards, driver's license and passport, were all in his back pocket, along with his cell phone. He should leave them behind for safety's sake; he was not going to need them anyway for the next few hours, and after a quick look around, dropped them into the ceramic vase standing on the cabinet beneath the window, keeping enough change in his pocket to be able to take this man Harvey out for a thank-you meal once they were back on land again. He then grabbed up his hold-all, which held anything else he might need in the way of a change of clothes for the occasion. and made his way out of the house as quickly and quietly as he could.

It was already quite hot, and the low, white mist smelled of wet earth and vegetation after the storm. He ran up the long avenue of trees, but then had to wait for a couple of minutes to allow a skunk to shuffle its way across the driveway to its daytime hideout. A loud honking like the horn of an old Model T Ford came from the woods opposite -- a pheasant greeting the new day. And he was right about the mosquitoes; squadrons of them were dive-bombing him, even as he ran.

Harvey was already waiting for him, and leaned across to open the door. The two men greeted each other, and, tossing his hold-all onto the back seat, Finn apologized for keeping him waiting.

"No problem, Finn. I'm Dave Harvey."

"Good to meet you." And they shook hands.

The car crawled along the road, Harvey keeping it in its path with the forefinger of his left hand, his other arm lying along the back of the passenger seat, and Finn was grateful that the man kept up his side of the conversation along the way, without asking him any awkward questions.

"I have to tell you, Finn, you heard right; these piers here are a great place for fish… very popular. Me and my friend, Gus, we often go after tautog there. Have you tried tautog? A great eating fish… nice firm flesh."

"No, but with luck, I'll get to try it tonight."

"Wrap it in tinfoil; add some butter and rosemary, and bake it. It's great that way."

"Yes, I think that's how my partner planned on cooking it, assuming I'm lucky, and catch one."

He glanced at the speedometer. At this rate, though, the tide would have long-since turned before they ever got to Harvey's boat, let alone out to the bridge. Had the man forgotten the reason he had given him last night for insisting that they come out so early? That he was still recovering from an accident, and would have trouble coping with the tide once it was running?

"Littlenecks too," Harvey was saying. "Have you tried littlenecks? What about steamers? If you're in New England, you've got to have steamers… Nothing in the world as sweet as steamers."

As a result of Harvey crawling along, the sun was already well above the horizon by the time they stowed their gear aboard his boat, the *Brandy X*, and made their way out of Brickton harbor. Finn could see by the way the boats were lying that the tide had already turned as well, but there was nothing he could do about that now, although the current would be racing under the bridge in another hour or so.

He looked around for something to sit on, but there was nothing, not even a lobster pot, so he squatted down, cross-legged on the boards, his back against the hull. It was beginning to get hot now, and he pulled off his sweater, tossing it down through the open companionway door onto one of the bunks below. He caught a whiff of the particularly foul-smelling air wafting upwards, and pulled the door shut, grimacing, glad he would not be having to spend any time down there.

The engine was making too much noise to allow much in the way of conversation, so he looked around at the *Brandy X*. At one time, she had been a pretty fishing craft, functional, sturdy and simple, but with an elegance that told she had been built with pride. She was about thirty feet long by eight feet across the beam, he estimated, and she sat quite low in the water. A good eighteen feet of the stern section consisted of a simple, flat deck of white-painted planks on which he was now sitting. Forward of this, a bulkhead came to about chest height, and above this a divided windshield stretched from one side of the boat to the other. A narrow roof above the windshield protected the helmsman from the weather.

He looked across at Harvey standing at the wheel set into the starboard side of the bulkhead. He was a small, wiry-built guy with thin, sandy hair and sharp features, his face covered with freckles. He turned when he noticed his passenger looking at him, and Finn gave him a smile, glad that he had made the decision to take him out for a good meal somewhere after the dive was over, then resumed his survey of the boat.

Next to him, on the port side, was the small white, two-paneled companionway door leading to the cabin below. He stood up, stretched, and peered through the salt-covered windshield. For'ard, and almost level with the base of it, another deck reached right to the bows, forming the roof of the cabin. Beyond it, a bowsprit added another good nine feet to her length. The *Brandy X* also had a short wooden mast with a diminutive crow's nest, and a heavy boom reached back almost to her stern, so presumably she had originally been a sailing vessel. At one time, her hull had been painted green, but much of the original color had rubbed or flaked off now, leaving her dappled with a variety of faded undercoats, like an army camouflage.

With nothing better to do, the *Brandy X*

barely making three knots against the now ebbing high tide, and the sun becoming brighter and hotter, he sat down again and pulled his sunglasses out of his shirt pocket. A piece of paper dropped out at the same time, and settled on the deck.

"Oh damn!" It was his note to Diana. In his hurry this morning, he had forgotten to slip it under her bedroom door.

Harvey turned. "Something wrong?"

Finn held up the note. "I meant to leave this message for my partner before I left, and forgot."

"Nothing too important, I hope."

"Well, let's just say I wish I hadn't forgotten."

Once within swimming distance of one of the piers, Finn helped Harvey tie the boat up to a lobster float, then nodded in the direction from which they had come. It was a long way behind them, but a small motor boat with two men on board was heading towards the bridge as well. "Someone else out early today too," he remarked.

Harvey glanced in the direction of the boat. "Probably looking to catch some tautog around the piers, same as you. I told you this place was popular, didn't I?"

Finn turned his attention back to Harvey, and watched him untangle the anchor line, then push the heavy Danforth anchor overboard to act as an extra hold, or drag, as the water was quite deep here.

"Can I help with anything, Dave?"

"No, no problem. Easier if I do it myself... Know where everything is. Thanks anyway."

Relieved that he did not have to breathe in the stench down there in the cabin, he watched Harvey wading through a collection of junk, finally emerging with a red and white 'DIVERS BELOW' flag, which he fastened to a slot in the stern.

That done, he sorted through the diving gear, inspecting each item minutely before handing any of it over to Finn, so it was yet another half hour before they were swimming towards the nearest pier. It was not the one he had looked at the previous day, but this was probably just as well as it was most likely to be in the same condition as the other, and this would strengthen his case.

He dived down, and began probing around with his spear gun, as though looking for fish. Knowing that most of the damage would be near the surface, where salt-water corrosion of the cement surrounding the rods normally takes place, he had no need to go very deep, and was able to find plenty of evidence to confirm what he had found the day before. Nearby, he could see Harvey, swimming around casually, and was glad to have him, doing what he had been asked to do, which was to act as a diving buddy, and to be there to help if needed.

At last, with enough information to satisfy himself, he began searching for a tautog or two, as proof of his claimed reason for being there, but today they seemed to elude him, and with only one to show for his efforts, and most of his energy used up, he was ready to quit and surface.

He looked around for Harvey, ready to signal his intention, but could not see him. Wondering where he was, he turned to look behind him and breathed in, but instead of air from his tank, inhaled seawater.

115

CHAPTER 14

Diana went out again to the porch, and looked through the screen window. Nothing had changed from the last time, or the time before that. She had been down to the end of the dock several times with the binoculars, but apart from a fishing boat and a Boston Whaler that had hung around near the bridge for a while earlier in the day, she had not seen anything, and after a few minutes, had turned back towards the kitchen, and began putting together the ingredients to make a lemon meringue pie for supper. Finn would like that. She set everything out on the table, but then changed her mind and put it all away again; she was not in the mood for baking, or anything else right now, so she went outside again instead, and wandered around the estate, picking a few dead heads off the rhododendrons, and going over in her mind how and why her happy relationship with Finn had received such an unpleasant jolt.

For most of the night she had lain awake on top of the covers, every now and then getting out of bed, intending to go to him, but then deciding that her father had been right; nothing had changed since Finn had stormed out of the kitchen, and as she could think of nothing new to say that would make the problem disappear, they would still be left at odds with each other, so it was better to let him do what he wanted, especially as she was convinced he would discover he had made an honest error after all. That all behind them, they could then go back to the relationship they had both been enjoying so very much, because none of this had changed how she felt about him, and she couldn't wait for them to get back together again.

Believing it to be the best thing to do, when she had heard him go past her bedroom door early in the morning, she had let him go. After a few minutes, though, she had changed her mind, deciding instead to run after him, and to give him a big hug and to kiss him. She had jumped out of bed and thrown on some clothes, but by the time she arrived at the end of the driveway, he was already gone. She had then tried calling him on his cell phone, but it was switched off, so had wandered back to the house and into bed again. She had fallen asleep finally, and woke well after nine o'clock. She was alone, her father having already left for a day's golfing at the country club.

Now the hours were passing so slowly, and she continued to wander around the grounds, absentmindedly plucking the dead flower-heads off the rhododendrons as she went. "Please, Finn, please hurry up, and come back home. I want so much for us to make up and return to how we were before. Our argument last night was so unnecessary. My fault entirely for pushing you, knowing how tired and stressed out you were. I'm so sorry, my dear. Oh, do hurry up and come back, please, please." And another rhododendron flower lost its head.

The afternoon passed, and as Finn had still not returned, Diana once again wandered down to the end of the dock and watched the *Moonglow* pulling at her mooring. They should be out sailing now, not quarreling over the wretched bridge. She checked her phone for messages as she had done several times already, but no-one had called, so once again she tried calling him, but his phone was still switched off. Not feeling like accomplishing anything, she climbed back up the path to the house, made a sandwich, put on her swimsuit, and then went out to lie on the lawn in the sunshine, trying to relax, but now becoming increasingly anxious for him to return.

"Oh Finn! Where on earth are you? You should have been home ages ago. Surely it can't have taken you all this time. I do hope nothing's gone wrong, and you've had another accident. No, if something like that has happened, someone would have called me to let me know." And she checked her phone yet again to see if she had missed any calls, but there were no messages. Apart from the two calls she made to him earlier, she had not called him again, not wanting to appear like some fusspot girlfriend, but now she did, but his phone was still switched off, so this time she did leave a message, asking him to please call her as she was getting worried about him.

Yet another hour went by, and she got dressed and went out to the end of the driveway again, but the road was empty. It was already past six in the evening now, and with the sun getting lower in the western sky, worry turned to panic. She went upstairs to the guest room; perhaps it would help to just touch his things -- convince her that everything was all right. Maybe he had even taken this Harvey guy out to a meal somewhere, and they had spent the afternoon chatting. Yes, that had to be it. He should have called to let her know, though. But maybe he had not called, and had switched off his phone because he was still annoyed with her, and this made her even more anxious for him to come home so they could make up.

She looked around the room and smoothed the un-slept-in bed with her hand. "Ah, Finn, you didn't even go to bed last night! You must have been so tired this morning, and that now makes me worry about you even more. You were in no condition to go diving at all, let alone like that!"

She glanced round the door into the bathroom, then went over to the bed and sat down, wondering, waiting for him to arrive, or call, and looking around the room until it finally dawned on her there was nothing of Finn's to be seen anywhere.

He was not normally tidy, his clothes for the most part left lying on a chair. Not today. She checked the closet. It was empty, as were all the drawers. She looked under the bed. Nothing, not even his hold-all was there. Everything was gone! She pushed open the bathroom door again, slamming it back against the wall, but all that was there was an empty can of shaving cream and a discarded razor. She went back into the bedroom, and for a moment stood in the middle of the room, then lay down on the bed, pulling the pillow towards her, crushing it in her arms and pressing her face into it. It smelled of Finn, and she began to cry. He had taken all his things! He was not coming back!

CHAPTER 15

Diana stood, staring out of her open bedroom window. The outside world was silent, and apart from a sliver of setting new moon, the only lights were those from the bridge, from the mainland the other side of the bay, and from her cell phone.

"Jan? Oh, there you are! I was so afraid I was going to get your answer machine. Is this a bad time? I know it's late evening where you are, but not too late though, I hope…

"Not a bad time at all? Oh, that's a relief. I do so want to be able to unload on you…

"Well, yes, I might sound relatively calm, considering what's happened, but I'm going through so many different emotions right now, that I've reached the stage where I'm feeling almost numb.

"Remember when you called me last week to tell me that you and Pierre had decided to call it quits, because you had both decided your relationship had 'run its course', I think was the way you put it. Well, I wish so very much I could feel as cheerful about what's happened to Finn's and my relationship. To put it bluntly, he's walked out on me! Just like Eric did!...

"Yes, you may well ask what happened, given how well I thought things were going! I can tell you, though: this time it's going to be very different. This time, I'm not going to let it devastate me. No, this time I'm just plain furious, and not just with Finn, but with myself too for being so stupid. How on earth, Jan, could I have been so trusting like that, twice in a row yet? And there I was, as you know, so afraid of letting myself fall for him, and promising myself not to let it happen. But no, when it came down to it, I just couldn't help myself, could I? Just plain stupid.

"How could I possibly have misjudged yet another man so completely, like this! There has to be something wrong with me. And just like with Eric, there was I, thinking we had a great relationship. Yes, we did have a bit of a tiff last night, but I find it hard to believe it was serious enough for him to simply pack his bags, as he did early this morning, and walk out without a word. There has to be more to it than that...

"What was our row about? Well, it was over what he considered to be a serious problem he thought he'd found with our bridge. We got into an argument over what he wanted to do about it, and he ended up storming off to bed on his own after insisting on going to recheck it this morning. I didn't see him again before he left at dawn, and that was that! He never came back. Then, when I checked, he'd taken all his things -- scarpered.

"Even so, as I said, there must have been

other reasons as well for him dumping me like that, and I've been thinking about signals I should have picked up on, such as right at the beginning, when I went to Logan Airport that evening to pick him up, and we went out to dinner. I remember him saying then that he wasn't ready for serious relationships, and him shooting out his arm like a jet taking off if he thought things were getting too serious. He had to have been actually putting me on notice right then at the very beginning, not to get serious, don't you think? Then, just yesterday morning, while we were out on the boat together, he made a point of telling me he gets bored easily, and actually described himself as unpredictable, 'here today, gone tomorrow', was how he phrased it, so that's probably what's really happened; while I'm happily thinking our relationship was great, he was bored with it, and decided to use our row last night as an excuse to end it! Stupid, stupid me, for being so blind, but I'll tell you one thing, Jan: I'm going to make sure it never, ever happens to me again. Never…

"What? Yes, I know; I said that the last time, but this time I've made another decision: I *do* want to go out with other men, and I *will* go out with other men, and I'll enjoy myself too, but it'll never allow myself to fall for one again, I swear it, and this time I really mean it! Blast Finn Westlake for what he's done…

"Write to him? Call him to find out exactly why he did leave? No way! I'll never chase after him the way I chased after Eric. No, as far as I'm concerned, I just have to accept that I'm a lousy judge of character, and close the book on him. The sooner I get him out of my mind, the better, is the way I feel right now…

"Well, I'm sure you've heard enough of me for tonight, so I should let you go. I'm sorry for being so negative, but thank you so much for listening to me and all my woes, Jan, and for offering consolation like this. It's helped me so much, and I do feel a lot better now than when I picked up the phone to call you. You're such a good friend, you know, and always manage to say all the right things… I hope it's the same for you when you call me, and are down in the dumps about something…

"That's good to know – that it's not all one-sided, that is… So, you've got a wine tasting organized for tomorrow? Lucky you! I wish I could join you. Anyway, drink to my success in living up to my promises this time, will you? Oh, and say 'hi' to your new date for me. Bye."

CHAPTER 16

White-painted planking over Finn's head erupted with oozing blisters of amber gum. On either side, three symmetrical discs undulated rhythmically up and down, up and down, alternating from light blue to dark, and back to light as first the sky, then the sea appeared through the portholes of the gently rocking boat. That, and the dreadful stench made him nauseated, and he shut his eyes, then opened them again when he heard snoring.

Across from him, on the other bunk, a shirtless, fat-bellied man with a profusion of partially graying hair and beard lay on his back, asleep, his equally hairy chest rising and falling, his breathing almost in unison with the boat.

Finn, sure that he would feel better if he could reach fresh air, raised his head, but immediately everything started to turn black, and he fell back. Chills crawled over his muscles, and every hair on his head prickled. He was very thirsty too, but no sound came out when he tried to call to the sleeping man, and, except for the snoring, an empty soda can clattering its way across the floor from one bunk to the other and back again as the boat rocked, and the rhythmical sloshing of water in the bilges, there were no sounds at all. He drifted off.

When he woke up, he was alone, and it was dark. Men were talking up on deck, and someone asked if he was alright.

"Still breathing anyway."

He watched as a figure appeared at the top of the companionway steps, wearing an LED head-flashlight which was so bright it prevented Finn from even seeing whether it was a man or a woman, let alone who it was. All he *could* tell was that whoever it was then came down into the cabin, and started emptying the contents of a bag out onto the empty bunk, after which he heard something being poured from a container into a mug, which was then offered to him. The light, shining directly into his face, was so dazzling, Finn had to close his eyes, and, too weak to handle the mug himself, he had to accept help, and swallowed what turned out to be lukewarm water.

He lay back, and kept his eyes closed against the light while the person started to remove a bandage from his arm. He was glad whoever it was did not start asking him questions or try to engage him in conversation; he felt too sick and too much in pain to talk, and flinched when some strong-smelling antiseptic bit into his arm, after which it was re-bandaged. His head was then held up again while some pills were put into his mouth, followed by an injection in his arm, the whole operation carried out in silence.

Whatever he had been given sent him to sleep immediately, because he had no recollection of anyone leaving, and when he woke up this time, still feeling distressingly ill, it was daylight.

There must have been a swell now as the boat was rocking more, making him even more nauseated, and although he tried to concentrate, his brain was so befuddled, it refused to cooperate, and because every time he tried to raise his head, everything started to turn black, he wondered if there was something else wrong with him as well, other than whatever the injury was to his arm.

The last memory he had before waking up in this stinking cabin was of struggling to fight off some creature, a shark perhaps, and being bitten on his arm. It still hurt like hell, and he touched it with his other hand, but the bandage covered the damage. Someone had to have rescued him, though, but how long ago was that? How long had he been unconscious? And why was he on a boat that was obviously moored, not racing to get him to a hospital? He gazed up at the blistered white boards above his head, and drifted off again.

Finn had lost track of time, and was sleeping or unconscious most of it, but, during the brief periods when he *was* awake, was desperate to get off this foul-smelling bunk, but his limbs were too heavy to lift, his arm too painful to move, and he could not keep awake long enough anyway to accomplish anything, either physical or mental. He tried to concentrate. What had attacked him? What was happening to him now? Why was he still on this moored boat, and why had Diana not yet come to see him? But his brain kept playing tricks on him, confusing him, blurring everything, and he fell asleep yet again.

This time, when he opened his eyes, he realized the boat he was on was Harvey's boat, the *Brandy* X, and managed finally to sit up without blacking out. He then concentrated on trying to get off the bunk…

The next thing he was aware of was that he was lying face down on the wooden floor planking of the cabin, the smell of putrid bilge water filling his nostrils, making him sick to his stomach. Frightened and still confused, he lay there and wondered what could possibly be wrong with him. Why was he so weak and suffering from vertigo and blackouts like this? Was it because he had lost so much blood from whatever had happened to his arm? The pain in it now was even more excruciating, so bad that even trying to move it at all made him want to cry out, let alone use it to try to get up from where he lay on the floor. How long had he been on the boat? Why was he not getting better, stronger? If only he could think clearly, but every time he tried to concentrate, his mind went off at a tangent. Why did he keep falling asleep? Maybe if he could stay awake for longer than a few minutes at a time, he could…

Someone was standing over him. It was the hairy man he had seen lying asleep, snoring on the other bunk that time. The big man hauled him carefully back onto the bunk. "You'd better not try anything like that again, buddy." His voice was gentle, concerned. "What did you do? Try to get up? You're not ready for that yet. You haven't eaten anything proper yet either. Do you think you could get something down if I help you with it? I've been giving you liquid stuff the medic gave me, though, when you've been with it enough to swallow it." He sat on the edge of the bunk, and pushed Finn's hair back from his eyes.

Finn blinked up at him. "Why am I…? Who are you?" His speech was slurred, his voice hoarse, and the cabin was rotating. It was as though he had been on a bender. "Why here…? need to… dying… weak... why…?"

"I'm Gus Tucker, a friend of Dave Harvey's. You remember Dave Harvey? Do you remember at all what happened?"

"… tried to kill me."

"Yes, we know that, but don't you remember *what* tried to kill you? You talked about it enough when you came down with that fever. Had us really worried there for a while."

"Dave… attacked too?"

"Yes, but he's alright now. Managed to get away relatively unscathed. Only a minor injury. Very lucky. Had quite a bit of a shock though. He said he'd be coming to see you later." He stood up, and gave Finn a friendly slap on the knee. "Is there anything I can get you? Something to drink, or anything?"

"No… thanks…" and Finn fell asleep again.

CHAPTER 17

Diana heard the garage door opening, and put down the book she had been trying to read. In the last half hour, she had turned over only three pages, and even at that pace, had no idea what she had read. No matter how hard she tried to concentrate on other things and drive Finn Westlake out of her mind, she was finding it impossible. Worse still, her first thoughts were always the positive memories she had of him: how much he had meant to her, how happy she thought they had been together, and how much, despite everything, she still yearned for him and the way they had made love together. These were then interrupted by what he had done to her by dumping her like that, and the anger that brought with it, and the constant flood of contradictory thoughts was leaving her stranded in an emotional maelstrom in which she found it difficult to concentrate on anything else, so she was glad when her father strode in and dropped the evening newspaper on the coffee table.

"Hello, my dear." He rubbed his hands, and

stood poised over the liquor cabinet like a pianist preparing to play. "A little before-dinner pick-me-up?"

"No, not tonight, thanks."

"Oh! By the way, I've been meaning to let you know about the fund-raising dinner I've agreed to hold here in late fall for Governor Brigham, after Louise Lillacray's affair. I've already spoken to Sandy Moseley to let him know that the man I felt sure was going to be my son-in-law won't be able to carry out the bridge inspection after all. I told him Westlake had to leave on account of an emergency back home. It was the best excuse I could come up with under the circumstances. Uh… I guess you're not in the mood to listen to the details of my fundraiser right now then, eh? No news today then? No letter or anything? I have to say I'm very surprised he scarpered quite the way he did. Somehow it didn't seem like the sort of thing he'd do, but then, people do funny things sometimes. I remember when I…"

"Dad, I don't want to talk about it, okay?"

"Well, if that's the way you want it." McGuire sat down, clutching his drink in one hand, and picked up his newspaper.

Diana slapped her book down onto the glass-topped coffee table, and jumped up. "I've changed my mind. I will have that drink after all." She dropped some ice cubes in a glass, and slopped some vodka on top of it. "Get out of my mind, will you, Finn Westlake! You're driving me crazy."

"What was that you were saying, my dear?"

"Nothing, nothing at all. Cheers!" She was raising her glass when the front door bell rang.

"Ben! What a surprise! Come in, won't you?" Diana led Ben Bradley into the living room, and introduced him to her father, her tone sounding unnaturally upbeat to her.

McGuire leapt to his feet, and gave Bradley's hand a hearty shake. "Ah yes! Mr. Bradley! It's so good to meet you. I know your uncle, Governor Brigham, and his wife, Mary-Sue, very, very well, of course, and shall be holding a fund-raising party here in the fall for what I'm sure will be his re-election. An excellent governor he's been too, I must say, so I'm only too pleased to be able to use all my considerable influence among the island people here to make sure he *is* re-elected." He nodded his head vigorously, and beamed again. "Yes indeed!"

Diana held her hand out towards the sofa. "Do sit down Ben. You're just in time for a drink. What can I get you?"

"Scotch would be fine, thanks."

Diana handed him his whisky. "Well, what brings you this way then, Ben?"

"Diana, you sounded so depressed when I phoned the other night to ask Finn to go out fishing with me. I have to say I'm not at all surprised you're so upset under the circumstances; it had to have been a huge shock for you to have him leave like that... A huge shock, which is one reason why I'm here. What I'm trying to say is that I do hope you don't think it... uh... obtrusive of me coming round to visit like this."

McGuire beamed yet again at the visitor. "Not obtrusive at all, Mr. Bradley, not obtrusive at all. We're only too delighted to welcome Governor Brigham's nephew into our home, aren't we Diana?

Your drink all right? Would you like Diana to add some ice to that?"

Bradley held up his glass, and looked at Diana. "No, no, not at all. This is just perfect, thank you. As I was saying, Diana, sadly I too know what it's like to have that happen; my wife walked out of my life as well. Takes some getting used to, I know. Well, what I'm getting at is, uh… I came over to ask if you'd perhaps like to come out tomorrow evening and have some dinner with me."

"That's really very kind of you, Ben, but I don't think..."

McGuire shook his head, and waved his glass at her. "Oh, come on now, Diana. It'd do you good to get out. You've been such a misery since Westlake left, and you do keep going on about how you're hell bent on getting the guy out of your mind, so here you are. Now's your chance. You have to admit, Diana, it's very thoughtful of Mr. Bradley, so why don't you accept, and go have a nice dinner with him somewhere?"

"I… I just thought maybe you'd like someone to talk to," Bradley went on when Diana said nothing. "Make you feel a bit better perhaps,"

"I'm not sure I'm ready yet, Ben. I need more time. I know it sounds ridiculous, given what Finn did, but despite everything… I can't explain it exactly, but I feel somehow as though I'd be being disloyal."

"Disloyal! How can you possibly feel disloyal after he dumped you like that? The way I understand it, the bastard -- excuse the language -- didn't even stop to say 'goodbye'. You don't owe him a thing, Diana."

"I'm sorry, Ben. I shouldn't have unloaded on you like that when you phoned the other evening. You just happened to catch me at a particularly bad moment I'm afraid, and I can't help it, even though I'm utterly furious with him, I still feel uncomfortable when you talk about him like that. I…"

"Oh! I'm so sorry, Diana, if I spoke out of turn. But please, do come out to dinner with me tomorrow. Please?"

"Oh, come on, Diana!" McGuire urged her. "I can't see why you're hesitating like this. Westlake's history. Forget about him, and accept Mr. Bradley's invitation, why don't you?"

"O dear. You're both right, I guess. My own judgment seems to be all wrong lately, so perhaps it's time I trusted someone else's." She smiled at Bradley. "So, yes, thank you very much for inviting me, Ben. I should like that."

Since the night of their first dinner together Bradley had phoned Diana a number of times to ask her out again, but she had accepted only twice, offering up various excuses for refusing him on other occasions, including his latest invitation, so today he had arrived at her home bearing a bunch of roses, and, finding her sitting out on the lawn, was now kneeling beside her clutching them in front of him – very much as though he was getting ready to recite a love poem to her, she thought.

"I'm so sorry, Ben. I really am. You must think me terribly ungrateful. I know you've been trying really hard to help me get Finn out of my mind, and I do appreciate it, you know. It's so kind of you."

Bradley pushed the roses towards her, dropping them in her lap, and clutched her hand. "Well yes, I have to say I've made every effort to do just that, but every time I call you, you keep coming up with some reason not to come out with me. Why? Is it something I've said, or done? I need to know. Is... is it because I came on too strong? I promise not to again if I have. It's... uh, as I said, I thought you needed someone right now, and I'm really a very considerate and caring person, you know."

"Yes, I can see that, Ben, but that's not it; you've done absolutely nothing wrong. Far from it. Exactly the opposite, in fact... Oh, I don't know." She released her hand from his grip, got up and began walking down towards the dock. He tried to put his arm round her, but she evaded it. "None of it makes any sense to me at all. I keep thinking about how sure I was that I knew Finn, which made his going off the way he did seem so... so out of character."

They stood together on the dock, and she tossed a pebble into the bay, watching it sink in the clear water. "Ah well. It just goes to show I didn't know him at all, I guess. But then, I thought I knew Eric too, and I was just as wrong about that. It's all made me lose faith completely in my own judgment, and I feel right now that I'll never risk trusting any man ever again. I'm sorry, Ben, but that's how I feel right now, I'm afraid, and I know it's not fair of me to… well, basically, use you like this, especially as you've continued to be so kind and thoughtful despite the way I've acted. I must be an utter bore."

She turned, and started walking back up to the house. "It has to be awful for you, listening to a woman talking about another man all the time, and it's because I don't think I'm being fair to you that I usually say 'no' when you invite me to come out with you, and because I still feel... Oh, I don't know. What's the use?"

He took her hand again. "Have you tried writing to him? Maybe he's back in England or Florida by now."

"Absolutely not! I do have *some* pride, you know."

"Diana, please, please come out with me again. I do understand what you're going through. That's why I want to be near you, to help you, and to be a good listener. Let me take you to the very best restaurant in town -- the *Poulet Noir*."

Diana laughed. "I must admit you don't give up easily, Ben, although what you want with a wet blanket like me, I can't imagine."

"It's because I like you, Diana. I like you a lot. I'm so sorry about what happened, and want to... to make amends."

"Amends? For what? None of this is your fault."

"But I saw the way you were looking at him that night at the yacht club, and though I suppose I shouldn't say this right now, but I can't help it, I... I want more than anything for... for you to feel the same way about me. At least, I hope... Besides, you can't not go out for ever, can you?"

"Well..."

"Then you'll come to the *Poulet Noir* with me? I booked a table already."

"Then it would be very ungrateful for me to refuse yet again, wouldn't it? Thank you. And thank you too for the roses, Ben. They're beautiful."

CHAPTER 18

"Hi, Finn! How are you coming along, man?" Dave Harvey looked down on the still prostrate Finn as he set down a bag of black grapes next to him. "Didn't know what to bring you. Gus said he didn't think you were up to having a beer yet, given all the medication you're on at the moment. He's been looking after you well, has he?" He slapped Tucker on the shoulder. "Good man, our Gus here, aren't you, Gus? He says you'd got some proper food down you at last. We've been worried about you, and thinking that perhaps we should have taken you to hospital after all."

Finn stared at up at him, recognizing Harvey's sharp, sandy-haired features and freckled face. "Not getting better... why...? Can't... can't think straight... So weak... Sound like a... like a drunk..."

"Well, you did lose an awful lot of blood, and maybe you're also feeling extra groggy because the medic's been giving you sedatives and painkillers to make it easier for you."

"Sed...?"

"Yes, sedatives, and painkillers for your arm."

"When...How?"

"When you're asleep. Shots."

"No!... Mustn't!... uh... kill me... need to..." Finn stopped, unable to go on. "... Don't feel..." he added after a long pause.

Tucker looked at his watch. "The medic's late coming over tonight, Finn. He has a regular shift, you see, so can't come till that's over, and I guess the last dose you had must be wearing off."

"I have to say you're certainly more with it than when I came to see you last. You didn't even recognize me that time, but the medic definitely said it was better for you to be kept quiet right now, though." Harvey patted him on the knee. "Don't worry, Finn; you'll start to feel much better soon, I'm sure." He turned to leave.

"...heard anything?"

"Heard anything? You mean about the shark that attacked us both that day? No, not yet. Whichever one it was, though, meant business, that's for sure, and, of the two of us, you took the brunt of it, unfortunately for you. Well, I guess I'd better be taking off now. Hope you start feeling..."

Finn raised his hand slowly, and pointed at Harvey's neck. "That where...?"

Harvey turned back and smiled. "Where it got me too? Yes, I meant to show you. Look." He came up close so Finn could look at the damage. "I guess you could say I was considerably more than just lucky; it could have bitten my head off. It seemed more interested in getting you, though, for some reason -- must have found your blood more tasty! I'm only sorry I couldn't come to help you out, though, but by that time I wasn't in a fit enough state myself to do anything."

He turned again to leave, giving Finn a friendly tap on his foot. "Well you look after yourself now, man, you hear? And get better soon. Gus and I, we can't have you taking up permanent residence on our old fishing boat now, can we?"

CHAPTER 19

Diana and Bradley sat side by side, French style, in the *Poulet Noir* restaurant. This was their third or fourth visit; she had forgotten which, and the waiter, now recognizing the couple, had led them to a secluded corner where a small candle scattered romantic flutters of thin light onto the white tablecloth. Bradley had his hand on Diana's thigh, and every now and then he had tried to slide his fingers upwards, sliding her dress higher, but whenever he reached a certain point she pushed him away, so he had to be content with pressing gently, massaging her leg lightly with his thumb.

"Diana, I've tried to do… to behave the way you want me to, but please, do me this one favor at least: please, please don't mention Westlake's name to me again. I can't stand to hear about him anymore. I really can't. I've even reached the stage now where I wake up from this wonderful dream in the middle of the night: you and I are making love, but then he comes and places himself in between us, and you turn away from me, and go to him. It's really getting to me; I can't go back to sleep afterwards. So, as I said, can you at least stop talking about him now? Please? Besides, I'm having trouble getting over the idea that you're obviously a lot more than simply attracted to this man. You have to be, despite all your so-called efforts to eradicate him from your mind. You're not behaving like anyone would expect you to towards a man who's dumped you as brutally as he did. Where's the woman scorned? 'Hell hath no fury', and all that? You should be hating him. I don't get it."

"I've been through that, Ben. I'm *still* going through it. I *do* feel scorned, and I *do* hate him, and I hate him not only because of the way he dumped me, but because, despite all my efforts, I can't get rid of the affection I still have for him, and it's stifling me. O dear, I'm really sorry, Ben. I do want you to know, though, that I do appreciate your efforts to raise my spirits and to try to get me to forget him. I'm only sorry I can't bring myself to be any sort of company at all these days. I am trying, but, as you say, the way I'm behaving, obviously doesn't give that impression, and, as I keep telling you, I don't know why you go on asking me out! Any other man would have given up long ago."

Bradley took her hand and kissed it. "It's as I said, Diana, it's because I like you. I like you a whole lot more than I'm sure you realize, and, as you've discovered, I'm not one to take 'no' for an answer."

She laughed. "Yes, I must admit, Ben, your staying power is nothing short of phenomenal!"

"Let's dance, shall we." And they danced on the small square of parquet in the center of the floor, and he held her close. Someone at a nearby table remarked on what a handsome couple they made, and Bradley smiled at Diana. "There. Someone else thinks we go well together too."

She returned his smile, and allowed his body to caress hers for a few moments, before pulling away. "No," she told herself. "You can stop that right now, Diana McGuire! You're confused enough as it is, without allowing yourself to fall for yet another man! Given your track record anyway, he too will abandon you. No, you're just not going to let it happen again, do you hear? And that's that!"

"You're particularly quiet this evening, Diana, and why did you pull away from me like that when we were dancing? For the first time, I felt you beginning to warm to me too. Is it because I asked you not to talk about Westlake anymore? Maybe I shouldn't have said that. I'm sorry. Perhaps the more you can express your thoughts about him, the easier it'll be for you to come to accept that he was, after all, a right bastard. And I'm sorry if you don't like me saying that, but it's true."

"No, Ben, it's not that at all. You were right, anyway, asking me to stop talking about him. As I keep saying, I can't believe you still want me to go out with you!"

He kissed her cheek. "Like I said, Diana; it's because I'm so very fond of you. I really am."

Diana looked around the restaurant. "Ben, I'm sorry to change the subject rather abruptly like this, but it's getting late, and I can see the waiters are beginning to get restless, so maybe we should go, don't you think? We're the only ones here now, so it's not fair to make them wait for us to leave.”

“Uh… yes, well… I guess so.” He settled up with the waiter, and they went out to the lobby, where she waited while he picked up their coats. It had started raining earlier in the evening, and was now pouring. The parking attendant was nowhere to be found, so he left her while he fetched the car from the far end of the parking lot.

She took shelter under the canopied walkway at the entrance, and waited, pulling her coat about her, and went back to thinking about her odd relationship with Bradley. She was not much company for him that she could see, but she had been particularly careful to be honest with him too, so it was impossible for him to have any illusions about how she felt about him. She shook her head. No, there was absolutely no way he could think she was leading him on. She stepped back as the car drew up, scattering muddy water over her legs and shoes.

Bradley reached over and opened the door for her to get in. “Must have walked into a branch or something. Feels like most of it’s still in my eye.”

“Ouch! Don’t rub it like that, Ben. Here, let me see. Put the light on.”

He leaned back while Diana took a handkerchief out of her purse. It was white, with very fine crochet work round the edge. She had admired it at an antique store one day, and Finn had bought it for her.

“I can’t see anything in there. Whatever was there may have scratched you a bit, but it seems to be gone now.”

“Can I have a look for myself, please.”

Bradley took the handkerchief, and leaned forward, peering into the rear-view mirror. A horn sounded behind them.

"I think we're blocking the entrance, Ben."

"Okay, okay." The horn sounded again. "All right already. I'm going." He put the car into gear, and drove off.

"I think you were right. Whatever it was, it's gone now." He blinked several times. "Yes, it's much better now."

They drove back to Diana's home, and after offering him no more than a perfunctory kiss on the cheek, she thanked him again, got out and ran to the house, pausing only to turn and give him a brief wave before closing the door.

CHAPTER 20

Beers in hand, Gus Tucker and Finn sat one on each side of the cabin's two bunks, facing each other, Tucker, his big, hairy beer-belly hanging out over his chinos, describing at length the details of his last holiday.

Tucker was the only one to have spent all his time on the *Brandy X* looking after Finn, who had not seen Harvey since that one visit. Now that the medic had stopped giving him sedatives, having told Tucker the patient was well enough to do without them, Finn had improved daily, although was still incredibly weak. At least his brain was functioning properly again, though, allowing him to think, and his speech was no longer slurred.

The weather had been becoming warmer too, and that was the reason, Tucker told him, they had blacked over the portholes -- to stop the sun making the temperature in the cabin too hot -- so, except for the dim glow of a small hurricane lantern at night, he had been in the dark ever since. Finn had suggested several times that he would be better off on deck, in the fresh air, but was told that the medic had instructed that he stay put until the next visit, which was not expected to be any time soon, now that he no longer was receiving the daily shots.

Tucker had been most attentive to him all this time, changing the bandage on his arm for him every day, and making sure he was well fed. He was, Finn decided, what people like to call 'a good old boy'. He had this permanently bemused look on his round face, not sharp and business-like, like Harvey's, and Finn was beginning to wonder how it was that he was able to spend all this time looking after him, and what's more, why. The man liked to chat to him too about anything that came into his head, from his tank of prized fantail goldfish, to gossipy tidbits about local politicians, none of whom Finn knew, or cared about. Even so, he appreciated Tucker's company; still feeling nowhere near his normal self, and his arm still very painful, it was good to have someone take an interest in how he was feeling, and make the effort to see he was as comfortable as possible.

On this day, their chat had turned to discussing the pros and cons of buying and selling stuff on eBay. At least, it was Tucker who did the discussing, leaving it hard for Finn to get a word in, even if he had wanted to, which he did not, his mind on trying to figure out how to broach tactfully the subject of why he was here on his and Harvey's fishing boat, without sounding ungrateful for all Tucker had been doing to help him.

"I know this guy," Tucker was telling him, "who makes a fortune on it. He buys up stuff cheaply that the seller doesn't have a clue about, and doesn't describe properly, then puts it back on with a proper description, and makes a killing."

"Is that right?" Finn had done that once himself with a piece of WWII militaria, but right now he did not feel like continuing the conversation by giving Tucker a blow by blow account of the deal, this because he had now decided that, whether he sounded ungrateful, or not, he had reached the point where he needed to have answers to the questions that his brain was now clear enough to start asking. All he wanted, therefore, was for Tucker to stop prattling on, and give him a chance to ask them.

"Yep, that reminds me of a story I heard about Brigham," Tucker went on. "You know, our current State Governor? Silas Brigham? Well, perhaps I shouldn't be telling you this, but I happen to know that Brigham has this really fancy antique gun collection, see? I don't know much about guns myself -- not my thing -- but I guess he has some really rare and unusual ones. Anyway, he always amuses himself by telling everyone that they're all repros, and that he picked up the whole lot for a song, fancy glass display-case and all, on eBay, and that he only bought them because they went with the décor. Puts anyone off wanting to nick them, I guess. As I said, though, I guess I shouldn't be blabbing about…"

"Gus, I'm sorry to interrupt you, but we need to have a proper talk here. I have questions I need to ask you."

"You do? Like what?"

"I know you've been doing a great job of looking after me since I was attacked, and don't misunderstand me, I do appreciate all you've done for me, but what am I still doing here? In fact, why am I here in the first place, and not in a hospital, which would seem to be where I should have been all this time? It's taken me a long while to come to my senses, and there's a lot I don't understand, and I need you to do some explaining. I need to get my life back, and I don't see any reason why you didn't just take me back to my partner's place once I was well enough to be moved. I need to see a specialist about my arm too. I don't know whether any permanent damage has been done, or if something more can be done to hasten the healing process, like physiotherapy, or something. As you can see, I can't use it at all yet."

"Well, at the time, we obviously couldn't move you in the state you were in, and look at you; you can barely stand up even now. That's why we got a medic to come here to you instead."

"Yes, but it's also obvious that I've been pretty ill, and you should have had me taken me to a hospital. Surely that wasn't an impossibility; injured people are taken safely off boats all the time. I could have died from blood loss or infection."

"You're saying the medic we found for you hasn't done a good job?"

"That's not the point, Gus. There's a whole lot more I don't understand either. For starters, I don't understand why no-one's been here to ask me any questions. Surely, it's of interest to the authorities that Dave and I were attacked so badly! Why haven't we heard from them? Shark attacks can't be an everyday occurrence in this area. Doesn't it matter to anyone what happened? I have to believe it does. Also, and most important from my own point of view, I can't understand why I haven't heard from my partner yet. Dave has to have told her what happened to me, but if he didn't for some reason, then she must be thinking by now that I've dumped her, and that worries me more than anything, especially as we'd had a bit of a bust-up right before I left. Come to think of it, Gus, why don't you just lend me your phone right now, and I'll call her myself, and let her know where I am? She must be worried sick."

"Wow! You've been so out of it since we saved you, you're certainly making up for it now, aren't you!"

"So how about some answers then, eh Gus? I can't stay cooped up here in the dark on this boat for the rest of my life. I'm well enough now, so we need to make arrangements to get me out of here. So, to start with, how about letting me have your phone, please. I know the number, and I'm sure my partner will be only too happy to come and fetch me on her sailboat. That's if we're not too far from the island. Like I said, I can't understand why I haven't heard from her."

Tucker popped the top of a can of beer and pinched the sides, causing it to overflow, then made a big point of wiping it off his pants. "Damn! These are my new chinos too."

"Gus, forget your chinos for the moment, will you?" He held out his hand. "Your phone, yes?"

Gus continued to wipe the liquid from his pants. "I'm sorry, Finn. I'm as pissed off about this as you are, but I was talking to Dave on it last evening, and leaned out over the side, and it dropped overboard into the water, so it'll have to wait till I can get another one."

"Right. Well, I guess I'll have to pass on that then for now, but I still need answers to my other questions, the first and foremost being why my partner hasn't contacted me. Do you have any idea why she hasn't? Has Dave said anything to you about that?"

Tucker, who was still studying his lap, looked up at him, his face glum. "I have to admit, in your ramblings while you were ill, you kept calling out for her. It seemed obvious you really had a thing for this woman, so Dave did actually call her, but she told him you two had had a row, and you'd walked out on her, and as far as she was concerned, that was that, and she put the phone down on him, so he didn't bother to call her again. We assumed you were calling out for her just because you were delirious."

"Oh no! I was afraid she'd think I'd dumped her. Please, Gus, we need to call her again to let her know where I really am. Poor Diana! Gus, I'm really close to this woman, and would never, ever have done that to her!" He put his head in his hands. "We've *got* to call her and let her know I didn't run out on her!"

"To be honest, Finn, I don't think that would do much good at this stage. I happen to know for a fact that she's dating someone else now."

"*What*! No! I can't believe that, especially after what happened to her once before."

"What are you talking about?"

"Oh nothing. Something between her and me, that's all. Anyway, how come you know so much about what she's doing? That she's dating someone else now? You know the family, or something?"

"No, not personally, but her dad's pretty much a big wig on the island, and he'd been spouting off about you going to marry his daughter, so when you dumped her, it... well, people starting gossiping. You know how it is, and word just started getting around, that's all."

"I still don't understand, though. When Harvey called her, didn't he explain to her that she was wrong? That I hadn't run off, and was right here on this boat?"

"I dunno. I don't think she gave him time to explain anything. As I told you, she put the phone down on him. Either way, Dave said she made it clear she didn't want to have anything more to do with you."

Finn sank back down onto the bunk.

Tucker stood up and patted him on the shoulder. "I'm sorry, pal." He climbed the companionway steps, and disappeared out into the sunshine.

A short while later Finn got up and made his way onto the deck for the first time. Once there, he stood, blinking into the bright light, and clinging onto the side rail, his legs unsteady. When his eyes had adjusted to the glare, he looked around for Tucker, but he was gone. He then peered out across the glittering water, and could make out someone in a small dinghy disappearing out of the salt-marsh bay they were in. It could only be Tucker.

He slid down onto the deck, his back against the side of the boat. There were so many other questions he needed answered as well, but all he could think about now was Diana. Surely their row had not been so bad that she would end up thinking he had walked out on her because of it! What side of himself could he have possibly shown to her that would have led her to think he was even capable of behaving like that? He tried to go over in his mind the night of their row and the whole day leading up to it.

Was it that he had questioned her father's judgment, and suggested that his friends were crooks? Yes, he had been in a temper at the time. And yes, he had stormed off to bed. Maybe he *had* gone too far, and he began torturing himself with the thought that he had driven Diana away by leading her to believe that he was just like that guy Eric. He missed her so much, and needed more than anything to see her, to take her in his arms and make love to her, and prove that he had not just run away.

He pulled himself to his feet, and looked around. The cove in which the *Brandy X* was moored, was deserted. The air smelt terrible, but that, he could tell, came from the pungent natural gases rising from the marsh some several hundred yards away. That was the closest land. Where was this cove, though? He could be miles away from Diana, and even if he made it to shore, there were no houses that he could see anywhere, so where could he go for help? He looked down at the water. If he jumped in, could he swim to shore? The answer to that, he already knew, was 'no'. It had been as much as he could do to get where he was now, on the deck. Even climbing over the rail would be impossible, let alone swimming to shore.

He sank back down onto the boards again, his head in his hands. He was in the middle of nowhere, with no means of calling or finding Diana, and no way to tell her how much he wanted her and how he longed to have her close to him again.

He lay down on the deck, and as he lay there, forced his thoughts away from her and towards his reason for being kept on this boat for so long. His brain, not fully capable till now to recall properly what had happened that morning, was now willing to concentrate and give serious thought to what had occurred from the moment he had been attacked. He closed his eyes, and tried to visualize everything that had happened.

He remembered breathing in that lungful of seawater instead of air, and reaching out towards the surface, but something had seized hold of his foot, keeping him underwater. He had looked down, but with his visor filled with seawater, could see nothing but a dark shape below.

He remembered kicking out at it with his other foot, but the unwieldy fin had had no effect, so he had unhooked his heavy weight belt, and swung it at his attacker. At the second try, it had let go, and he had managed to reach the surface, retching, coughing up seawater, and gulping air.

He remembered seeing the *Brandy X* not far away, and struggling to reach the boarding ladder on her far side, but then the tide had swept him to the nearside, away from it. He had reached up to grasp the gunwales, but they were beyond his reach, and it was then that his attacker had struck again, jerking him under, and he vaguely remembered seizing hold of it, gripping it with all his remaining strength, until it bit deep into his arm, causing a film of blood to pass in front of him. And that was it; he remembered nothing after that, until he had woken up on the bunk in this filthy cabin.

Finn shut his eyes, and went over the whole scene again, concentrating on the details. What had caused him to breathe in seawater in the first place? And what about that shark? He had dealt with sharks before, in Florida, seen them attack, and looking back now, had second thoughts about what it was that had attacked him. Its behavior had not been consistent at all with what he knew about shark attacks. But if it was not a shark, what *did* attack him? He looked at his arm. Though he had certainly felt the pain it had inflicted, and was still feeling it, he had not yet seen the damage, and he began to remove the bandage, using his teeth to help undo the knot. The sight was unpleasant -- a long, ugly gash that was still wide open, lacking any stitches to pull it together. No wonder he had lost so much blood! He studied it. One thing he could tell immediately was that this was no shark bite. A shark would have removed a chunk of his arm. This was a deep cut, crude, but still a cut – a cut that had not even been stitched together! This was a knife wound!

He bandaged it up again, then spent the rest of the afternoon trying to work out who, not what, had attacked him, and why. It could not have been Dave Harvey; he had been attacked as well, but then he thought back to when Harvey had shown him his neck the day he had come down to the cabin and given him the grapes. Now that he could concentrate, and take another, mind's-eye look at Harvey's neck, he realized that was not anything a shark could have achieved either. It had been bruised rather than bitten.

He went over the scene yet again. Was there anything unusual that he may have noticed at the time, but dismissed? There was that other boat with two men in it that had followed them out. They had assumed they were just fishermen going after tautog. Had they not been fishermen after all? Were they the ones who had attacked them? With two of them, they could easily have killed both him and Harvey. What had stopped them from completing the job? Did Harvey and Tucker know something he did not? Was this why he had never been taken to hospital? Given proper treatment?

The more he thought about it now, the more he began to suspect the motives of those who were supposedly caring for him. It made him look at the caring Gus Tucker in a new light, and find that all the man's light-hearted cheeriness and help now irritated him; it no longer seemed genuine, and he was determined to get to the truth if, and when, he came back.

CHAPTER 21

It was dark when Tucker returned to find Finn still sitting on the deck. He was in a jovial mood. "Hi! So, you've made it up on deck, I see. Well done. We'll have you out of here yet."

He tied the dinghy to the stern of the *Brandy X*, and climbed aboard carrying some bags of groceries, which he dumped down on top of a lobster pot. "Thought that after all that business with having to tell you about your partner this morning, we both deserved some cheering up, so I decided to treat us this evening. Got us a bottle of vino and a couple of everything-pizzas. The wine's in a cooler, and the pizza's in the opposite," he laughed. "Are you hungry? You ought to be; I've been gone all day, and we were out of grub here on board."

Finn studied him. Now that Tucker had come back, and he himself was sitting there on the deck, looking up him, his determination to get to the truth wavered. He wondered what would happen if he were to put Tucker on the spot, and corner him. Would he turn on him? He was a big man, and Finn, although also big and normally strong, but in a muscular way, not fat like Tucker, was anything but strong after all he had gone through. "Not that hungry, actually."

Tucker handed him a Styrofoam cup of white wine. "Come on, pal. Forget about her. There's plenty more fish in the sea, and if she doesn't want you… Heh! What you going to do, eh?"

"Gus, I've remembered something. We've all been assuming it was a shark that attacked Dave and me. Maybe it wasn't. After all, neither of us saw it; we just assumed it had to be, but now I'm beginning to wonder. The day Dave and I were attacked, there was a boat coming towards where we were moored next to the bridge. It had two men in it. At the time, we thought they were there to go fishing like us, but now I'm thinking they could have been the ones who attacked us. In fact, it couldn't have been anyone else, unless it *was* a shark; they were the only other people out on the water at all."

"Come on, Finn. Eat it while it's hot. Great pizza, this. This place makes the best pizza out. Never go anyplace else."

"Has anyone found these men, Gus? Questioned them? Even if it wasn't them, they must have seen something."

Tucker, his mouth full of pizza held out the bottle of wine.

Finn shook his head. "No thanks. Well?"

Tucker finished his mouthful. "Well what?"

"For heaven's sake, Gus, answer me, will you, and quit avoiding my questions! What's the problem? Why do you keep on stalling?"

"Finn. Everything we're doing, we're doing for your own protection, so why don't you just leave it at that until we've sorted everything out for you."

"What do you mean: 'doing for my protection'? Why do you need to do anything for my protection? I haven't done anything wrong! So why do you need to sort anything out for me? Come on, man. Spit it out, and stop trying to fool me. I'm not an idiot!"

After a silence in which Tucker continued to munch away, he placed a half-eaten slice of pizza back down in the box, and licked his fingers. "Okay, okay. I'll tell you, but there's really nothing to it. You're just getting paranoid with nothing else to think about."

"All right then. Tell me, so I won't continue to be paranoid, as you call it."

"Wait a minute, then, and I'll tell you." He picked up the remains of the pizza. "Shame to let this go cold."

"Come on, Gus! Forget the pizza, will you!"

Tucker pointed to his mouth; it was full. "Well," he continued at last. "As I said, there's really nothing to it. You were so convinced a shark had got you, we decided not to upset you by telling you what really happened."

"Well, I've finally figured out for myself that it wasn't a shark, so what, or who was it? I took a look at my arm as well, this afternoon, and discovered that that certainly wasn't a shark bite, and when I thought again about Dave's injury, I realized that that wasn't done by a shark either. So, in what way am I going to be upset to find out that it wasn't a shark?"

"It was you."

"What do you mean, it was me?"

"It was you who left the mark on Dave's neck. You nearly strangled him!"

"*I* nearly strangled him! Why?"

"Well, what happened was this: first of all, you caught your air hose on a piece of rusty iron sticking out from the pier. It's a good job it wasn't your eye it got. Anyway, you panicked when you breathed in seawater, and managed to get your foot jammed in a cleft in the piling. Dave went to help you, but you obviously thought you'd been attacked by a shark, and clouted him with your weight belt, just as he got your foot free." He crammed the remains of the pizza into his mouth, and emptied his cup of wine.

"Okay. Then what happened?"

Tucker pointed to his mouth; it was full of pizza again. He munched away, then swallowed. "Well, by the time you made it to the surface, you were drowning, so Dave then tried to save you, but you grabbed him by the throat, throttling him."

"So, *I* made that mark on his neck! But why didn't you tell me all this before? What's all the secrecy?"

"Well, in hindsight I suppose we should have done, but, as I said, you seemed happy with the shark attack idea, and we thought you'd be upset to think you'd nearly killed Dave, not intentionally, of course, so it wouldn't have done to get the police involved, and have you accused of trying to murder him."

"Well, of course, I'm very glad I didn't, and that he managed to break free of me, although I don't see why the police wouldn't have believed your story.

That still leaves my arm though. Who decided to try to cut it off?"

"Heh! Go easy on the accusations here, Finn! Nobody did that. Dave was hauling you back on board, and you caught it on a shard of broken glass. I suppose you could say that was my fault. The glass above the companionway door had broken a couple of weeks before, and I'd moved it to one side, meaning to take it back to the mainland with me, but kept forgetting. And that's it. I told you there wasn't anything sinister about it."

"All right, but there's still the question as to why I'm still here. I suppose I can understand perhaps why you didn't want to get the police involved, or take me back to the McGuires', given how Diana's feeling about me right now, but I can easily prove to her that I *didn't* dump her. All I need to do is to get her to look where I put my passport, credit cards, cell phone, everything, and she'll realize at once that there was no way I abandoned her. After all, I can't go anywhere without them, so there's absolutely no need to keep me on the this tub any longer. Just take me back there."

"Finn! As I said before, have you seen yourself? You're not fit to go anywhere yet. At least in our opinion, you're not, but if you're not happy to stay here with us until you *are* well enough… We've been doing our best for you, pal, but if you don't feel we're doing a good enough job of looking after you, then I'll be only too happy to drop you off outside McGuire's, and you can take it from there. There! Satisfied now?" He picked up the bottle of wine, and held it out. "Are you sure you don't want some more?"

“Yes.”

“Well, if you’re not going to have it, I’ll finish that as well, if you don’t mind.”

CHAPTER 22

"You love sailing, Diana. What's wrong with you?" her father complained. "Yet you never go out anymore. The boat's just sitting there, and if you're not going to sail the thing, then I might as well sell it."

"You know why I don't want to go out, Dad. I've told you before; it reminds me too much of Finn and that miserable argument we had the day we last went out on the *Moonglow*."

"Well, to my way of thinking, you need to get back up on the horse, as they say. If you'd take Mr. Bradley out with you a few times, you'd create some new, positive memories." He made this last suggestion in front of Bradley, who had backed up her father, so she had relented, and this was now their third venture out onto the bay.

"So, which way would you like to go today, Ben? I know! You've managed to get me to sail under the bridge finally, and we've been down the bay as well, so how about we sail around the whole island? We've got time, and the wind is good either way."

"Whichever way you want to go. It makes no difference; it's all new to me. Don't know the area at all."

"Okay, then today we'll sail round the whole island. How about that?"

"Fine."

"You want to sail her then, Ben?"

"Sure. Why not?" And he took the tiller, and headed the *Moonglow* away from the bridge.

Her father was right; she did love sailing, and was discovering that taking Bradley out on the boat rather than going to the theatre or restaurants did have one advantage: as long as he was the one handling the boat, she was free of his groping hands, something about their relationship that she was finding increasingly irritating, as it seemed impersonal, rather than affectionate touching. She looked at him; he was, she admitted, a very good-looking man, and had a physique that any woman should find most attractive, but looking at him now, clad only in his swimming trunks, she had come to the realization that there was little else about him that was appealing to her. She found it difficult to identify exactly what it was about him that failed to arouse her, or to consider him as one might a lifelong partner. The description of 'cardboard cut-out' came to her. Everything he said or did seemed mechanical, and she had come to the conclusion that she was now simply bored with him.

"I'm sorry, Ben. What did you say?"

"I said I'm getting hungry, my darling. How about you?"

"Good idea. Come to think of it I'm hungry now too, so let's find a convenient cove to moor in somewhere."

He pointed. "How about that little cove over there then? It looks nice and small and private. Wouldn't say no to us lingering there a bit after we've eaten either." He began to head the *Moonglow* towards the cove, but Diana shook her head.

"Sorry Ben, that one's off limits to me now. Couldn't bear to go in there. It's called Bass Cove, and it's where Finn and I first... well, you know. Have you ever been in there?"

Bradley shook his head. "No, I've never heard of it. As I told you, I don't know my way around this island at all."

"Strange, considering you grew up just over there, on the mainland, and know how to sail."

"Well, I never really had any reason to visit it, I guess. Besides, most of my sailing has been in the Caribbean. You and I must go there sometime, and I'll show you some real sailing!"

"How about this cove then, Ben?" Diana suggested sometime later. "Let's go in here instead, shall we? Sometimes the marsh gases from the nearby swamp make it so that you don't want to go in there, but the wind's blowing it all away from us today, so it should be fine."

Bradley pointed. "No. Look. There's already some boat moored in there. Let's find somewhere else where we can have our privacy."

"That boat looks as though it's been sitting there quite a while, though. Let's go and investigate, shall we, Ben? Who knows? Maybe it's a smuggler's lair," she laughed.

"All the more reason *not* to investigate. We don't want to drop in on people who might be up to no good."

"Oh, come on Ben. I was just joking about smugglers."

"Well, I'm not. I've heard that there are actually drug smugglers around this coast, and the last thing we want to do is drop in on them. You never know these days what can happen; there are some real weirdoes around."

Diana shrugged. "Okay."

Some hours later they were back at the McGuire dock, having eaten their lunch along the way.

Bradley looked at his watch. "I'm awfully sorry, Diana, my love, but I'm going to have to rush off." He stood up, then bent over to kiss the top of her head. "I promised to meet up with some friends, and hadn't realized how long this trip was going to take."

Diana smiled up at him. "No problem at all, Ben. You go ahead. I need to do some cleaning up around here anyway." She was relieved, and wondered yet again why he continued to want to be with her; if he was as relieved to leave her just now as she had been to see him go, then the next thing she hoped to hear from him was a call letting her know he had decided to end the relationship.

There was, at least, one positive aspect to their boat trips, though; she had learnt to enjoy sailing again.

CHAPTER 23

Finn woke to the sound of voices on deck, and feeling just as ill as when he had first woken up on the *Brandy X.* He tried to get off the bunk, but failed, and lay back, looking up at the companionway door. It was shut, which was unusual, and with the windows blacked out, it was completely dark and incredibly stuffy, the stench of rotting fish and bilge gases almost overwhelming him. There was the sound of popping beer cans, and a voice he recognized.

"You're late, Tiger," Tucker was complaining. "I timed that Mickey so he'd be out for the duration, so don't blame me if he comes to, and wonders why he's locked in the cabin in the dark."

"Who's Tiger?" Finn wondered in alarm. "And why am I not supposed to be able to hear them talking?"

"Well," the man answered. "He's got to find out sooner or later anyway, Gus. Although preferably later than sooner, so I hope you knocked him out good and proper. I dunno about you two, but every time I come on board this crate now, I keep thinking about us all here that morning, mopping up the guy's blood."

"Yeah, and I still get nauseated at the sight of him stretched out on the deck here, coughing up seawater, blood flowing out of that great gash in his arm." That was Harvey's voice.

Tiger coughed. "Yeah, well, that gash was your own doing, wasn't it, Dave? And if Gus and I hadn't arrived right then, he'd be dead, and I wouldn't be here now with a plan to put him to good use."

"About that arriving-in-time comment," Tucker interrupted. "There's something I need to tell you before you go any further, Tiger. He's started asking awkward questions, which I've done my best to field, but he's finally figured out that it wasn't a shark that bit him, and is now even suggesting that the two guys he noticed in the distance that morning, weren't fishermen at all, and that it was they who attacked him and Dave."

"You didn't let on that you and I were the ones in that boat, have you Gus?" Tiger's voice was urgent.

"Of course not, Tiger. I'm not that stupid," Tucker complained. "Anyway, you were saying something about putting him to good use. What good use? I feel badly for him, seeing him scrunched up on that bunk all the time, his feet pushed up against the bulwark because it's too short for him. He's a really nice guy too."

"Now stop that, Gus," Tiger warned him. "There's no way you can afford to get sorry for him, or too chummy with him either. We've no way of knowing yet how this is going to pan out, but whatever way it is, it isn't going to be a good one for him, so keep your distance, okay? Don't you start getting friendly, you hear?"

"I was only saying, Tiger."

"Well don't," Harvey agreed. "Like Tiger's been saying all along, things are complicated enough as it is, without you getting to feel sorry for him."

"What I can't figure out, Tiger," Tucker went on, "is why your dear uncle, Governor Brigham, had to go and consider hiring him to do the bridge inspection for the commission anyway?"

Finn's attempt to leap off the bunk failed, and he fell back onto the filthy mattress. This 'Tiger' guy was *Ben Bradley*? What the hell was going on here? He wanted to shout out and demand an explanation, but as the full extent of the danger he was facing began to sink in, decided against it; better to continue listening so he could at least be prepared for whatever it was they were planning to do with him.

"What was wrong with getting Dave and me to inspect the bridge, same as usual?" Tucker was arguing. "After all, we're the ones who've been doing all the annual inspections for Rollo Devine, and doctoring the reports for him, so he can submit them to the state, showing the bridge piers to be safe, when they're not, of course. All we'd have needed to do would have been to come up with another 'everything's just great' report for the commission, and everyone would have been happy, including your uncle, who says he doesn't want a new bridge built anyway!"

"For the umpteenth time, Gus," Bradley snapped. "I've been telling you, it's those '*Save our*

Bridge' people on Cautuxet island, who insist on having an independent company do it, 'cos they don't trust them up at the State House not to have a conflict of interest. It isn't as though my uncle was simply going to okay Westlake for the job, you know, without investigating him. He dragged me out to the golf course one day on the pretext of asking me how I was getting on after my divorce, then asked me to find out everything I could about Westlake. He knew I'd been in school with the McGuire girl, so suggested I go to that Cautuxet Island Yacht Club ball shindig, because he knew she and Westlake would be there. When I discovered the guy wouldn't be able to go back to work for the foreseeable future, I phoned my uncle Brigham right then and there from the ball, same as I called you two as well."

"So why did Governor Brigham then go ahead and let it be known that he'd be offering Westlake the contract if he knew he couldn't do it?" Tucker persisted.

"So as to look good to those *Save our Bridge* people, Gus. Showed he was happy to cooperate with them and find someone they'd approve of. He could then apologise afterwards, saying he knew nothing about Westlake being incapacitated, and would now be forced to find someone else at short notice, etcetera, etcetera. Oh, come on Gus. You of all people should know how the system works. Come to think of it; the way things are going, you and Dave might still end up with the contract after all."

"Yes, well. By the way, Tiger, how's it going with the McGuire girl?" Harvey asked. "She's not all hell bent on finding him, is she?"

"I suppose you could say pretty good, I guess. In fact, that's why I'm late. We were out on her sailboat this afternoon. She even suggested we come into this cove to have our picnic lunch, but I managed to persuade her it wasn't a good idea. Anyway, conveniently for us, and especially for me, she thinks he's dumped her, and is too proud to go after him. I've been taking her out a lot, but she sure is playing hard to get. Not to worry; it's become a challenge now, one I intend to win. I'll have it off with her if it's the last thing I do. After that, she can say goodbye to me too. She's not my type anyway."

"And there *he* was," Tucker said, "wondering why she hadn't come to fetch him, so I told him you'd phoned her, Dave, and that she'd told you he'd dumped her, and she didn't want to hear any more about him. Felt bad having to tell him that. The poor guy was really cut up about it."

Finn put his hand to his head. He felt so sick, he feared that, if he did not get up, he would faint. He raised his head, but that made him feel worse, and he lay back down, trying to keep his eyes open.

"Keep your voice down, Gus."

The bolt on the cabin door was being slid back, and Finn closed his eyes.

The door closed, and the bolt slid back in place. "Still out for the count. For the life of me, Tiger, I have to say I can't understand how come she's even still seeing you," Harvey commented. "Girls usually cotton on pretty quick that there's one thing you're after, and only one thing. No wonder you end up with a constant stream of one-nighters. You've got about as much genuine love and affection in you as a codfish."

There was a clattering of beer cans. "Damn you, Dave Harvey! Who gave you the right…"

"Oh! break it up you two," Tucker protested. "We've got enough problems without us falling out, and beating each other up. And keep it quiet if you don't want him to wake up and hear all this."

"Love and affection!" Tiger retorted. "You're a right old woman, Dave. Affection's something you feel towards a pet rabbit. And love? Well, that's a no-brainer. All you've got to do is say the words. I give women what they *really* want, in bed."

"You just don't get it, Tiger, do you?" Harvey persisted. "You've got a problem. There really *is* something missing in you. You can turn on the charm big time; I've seen you in action, but… but it's like it's all an act, and… and… Oh, forget it. I'm no psychiatrist. Anyway, it's getting late, and we're wasting time. Gus asked you how we could put him to good use, so what *are* we going to do with him then? We can't keep him here forever, and we sure can't let him go either. If we do, and he goes to the police, then we're all finished, Devine included. We've got to decide what we're going to do with him."

"As I said, he's getting antsy now too," Tucker added. "He's no fool, and I can't keep stringing him along anymore. What's more, I'm pretty sure he's beginning to distrust me, suspecting ulterior motives."

"If you two would stop prattling on like a couple of old women, and give me the chance to get a word in," Bradley grumbled, "I'll explain the plan I've come up with that'll take care of everything very nicely for all of us, including financially, providing you guys have got the guts to go through with it, although, at this point, I don't see you've got much option. What we need to do first, though, is to go over everything so far, and prepare my plan properly. Hand me another beer, Dave, will you?"

There was the sound of more popping beer cans.

"Okay," Bradley proceeded. "First let's go over why you got into this mess in the first place: Westlake calls you, Dave, and asks you to go spearfishing with him, but because you already knew all about him from when I phoned you from the Yacht Club ball that night, you guess that what he really wants to do is to take a look at the state of those bridge piers, so you call your boss, Rollo Devine, to ask him what you should do. Devine, as you said, goes into a panic at the thought of Westlake reporting the real state of the bridge piers to the authorities, and tells you to get rid of him one way or another.

"You were crazy not to have stopped this whole mess right there," Bradley went on. "There's a helluva difference between taking bribes from Devine to doctor the safety inspection reports for him, and outright murdering someone for him... I told you you were playing with fire when you took that first payoff from him to lie by producing a report declaring the bridge to be safe."

"Yeah? So, what would you have done?" Harvey snapped. "Let on to the state that three years after Devine had done a multimillion-dollar, shoddy repair job on those piers using substandard materials, all at taxpayers' expense, it was already falling apart?"

"No skin off your nose to have done just

that," Bradley argued.

"Yeah, well, you forget; we sort of owed him," Harvey explained.

"Yes, and if the state knew that that repair work Devine had assured them would last at least fifteen years, was starting to fall apart after just three," Tucker added, "They'd have had Devine by the short hairs, and that would've been the end of him."

Harvey gave a nervous sniff. "Besides, you don't know Devine. He threatened us, and I wouldn't mind betting we wouldn't have been the first to end up as part of the fancy foundation of some government housing construction job of his somewhere if we'd refused. I know; I've heard stories that some of his projects don't just have cement and steel in them. It's easy, you know, when you own a company like that."

Tucker let out a sigh. "Devine kept saying all we needed to do was to hang in for just a couple more years, then we could report the need for further major repairs without it looking suspicious. He said the public's got the memory of a goldfish, and would have forgotten all the hoopla and expense the last time."

"Yes, well, he could be right at that, but that doesn't help you any right now, does it?" Bradley argued.

"What's all this '*you*' business then, eh Tiger?" Harvey snapped. "You've not exactly been against enjoying some of the payoff money with us, have you now, eh? In fact, seems to me you've done darned well out of it, and as for giving us a lecture about getting ourselves in a bind, you ain't exactly lily-white yourself from what I hear around."

There were a few moments of silence before

Bradley continued. "Okay, after Devine ordered you to get rid of Westlake that night, Dave, and you called me in a panic, I was the one, if you will remember, who came up with the plan to drown him -- a pretty logical one too, I have to say, given Westlake's problem with his lungs and all that. After all, if he went diving against doctor's orders, no-one would think there was anything suspicious if he did drown, would they?"

Harvey sighed. "Yeah, but I wasn't to know he was going to turn around and fight like the devil when I went to put your plan into action, was I? And everything just went belly up after that, and that's all your doing, Gus. If you hadn't been so…"

"Yes, well," Bradley butted in. "Nothing we can do about that now, and the way things are, we're stuck with him, so, as I said in the beginning, that's why I'm here now with a plan to salvage things by putting him to good use." He took a deep breath. "Okay, it goes like this: we simply get Devine to pay ransom for him. If he wants Westlake out of the way, let him do it himself. He won't know who's holding him, and as you've already covered your ass, Dave, by telling him and the McGuires that Westlake never turned up that morning, you'll be off the hook, because neither Devine nor anyone else'll suspect you."

"Right then, let's get this over with," said Tucker. "I'm sick of fielding questions from him. Besides, it's harder for me than for the two of you; I've got to know him, and, like I said, he's a really nice guy…"

"Oh! You idiot, Gus! I warned you not to get

friendly with him!" Harvey shouted at Tucker.

"Well, *you* should have been the one here seeing to him then, instead of me, shouldn't you?" Tucker retorted.

"Humph!" Harvey snapped. "As I said, you're the reason we're stuck with him now, so all the more reason you're the one having to see to him, as you…"

"Dave, Gus, lay off bickering, will you? And you're going to have to continue fielding his questions for a while longer, Gus, because, having taken all this trouble to come up with a feasible plan," Bradley explained. "I've now discovered Devine's gone away on an extended summer holiday."

"Just our luck!" Tucker sighed. "Any idea when he'll be back?"

"Almost another month, I gather."

"Another month! You may not have noticed, Tiger, but he's getting stronger every day. Another month! I can't control him that long."

"Well, you're going to have to, Gus. There's no alternative that I can see, unless you can come up with a better plan. Anyway, look on the bright side. If this does all work out, and Devine pays a nice, hefty ransom for him, we could all end up doing quite well out of it as I said. He can't afford *not* to pay to get him silenced; there's no way he'll want to see Westlake free to go to the authorities."

"Devine's not the only one afraid to let the guy go to the authorities," Tucker pointed out. "It would be the end of us too after all we've done to him now!"

"There is *one* fly in the ointment though, and

I'm surprised one of you hasn't already mentioned it" Bradley remarked.

"And that is?" said Harvey.

"Well, Westlake has already seen you two, and me as well, at the yacht club ball, which is why, of course, I had to keep coming out here in the dark to give him those sedatives, so he couldn't recognize me. I suppose I could give him some more if he starts causing too much trouble."

Tucker shook his head. "Uh, Uh, not a good idea. You nearly ended up killing the poor sod the last time. Anyway, so what's this fly in the ointment then?"

"Well, when he's exchanged for the ransom, there's nothing to stop him from telling Devine who we are."

"Well, that's it, then!" Harvey exploded. "There's the whole bottom out of the plan right there! We're back in square one. What are we going to do with him now?"

"Wait, Dave. Hold your horses. I've thought this through, and have decided all we need to do is to take out some insurance," Bradley assured him.

"What sort of insurance?" Harvey scoffed. "What sort of insurance can you take out against the likes of Devine? Anyway, I can just see us going to an insurance company and saying: 'We're holding this guy for ransom, and he can recognize us, so we need to cover our asses in case… etcetera, etcetera.' That's crazy. No, I don't get it. We're shafted."

"Not that sort of insurance, you dope", Bradley explained. "No. We make out an affidavit, signed and sealed, and keep it in a bank vault, only to be opened in the event of any of us meeting an untimely death, except we'll make sure Devine has a copy too when we hand Westlake over to him. This will spell out the whole sorry saga, from the falsified safety reports, to Devine's order for Westlake to be killed, right down to Westlake's murder by Devine himself. Once Devine knows there's a copy in the bank, all ready to be opened if he comes after us, he'll be powerless to take any action at all against us. Good, eh?"

"I don't call it good," said Tucker. "But I suppose it would guarantee Devine couldn't come back at us; he couldn't afford to. What if he finds out who we are *before* we hand Westlake over to him, though?"

"Who's going to tell him? No-one. Westlake's the only one with that information, and by the time he's in Devine's hands, it won't matter, 'cos, as I said, we'll make sure Devine gets his copy of our insurance along with Westlake."

"You've got all the bases covered then," said Harvey.

"Exactly. Of course, Westlake may not think of it, although he's not stupid, so we have to expect he's going to try to somehow bargain his way out of being buried under six feet of cement in some housing project. Not that he'll succeed; we'll have already pulled the rug out from under his feet by telling Devine who we are with our insurance note in the bank. And anyway, what choice will Devine have but to kill him? None. None at all. He's a dead man walking at this point. There really is no other option, and I... My God!" Bradley leapt up. "What was that?

Westlake! What in hell's he done? I can't open the door. Here, help me out with it Gus."

The door shuddered, then flew open. Finn was lying on his back on the boards, staring up at them.

CHAPTER 24

Finn eased his legs out over the side of the bunk, one at a time. Even with no activity at all he was sweating, and the rotting mattress was damp beneath him. He stood up, and sweat trickled into his eyes and mouth. It was what he knew was called hereabouts 'HHH weather'-- hazy, hot and humid -- and it was all three. He glanced up as Tucker's huge frame appeared at the top of the companionway steps.

"Going to pull the door to. Some other boats around today, and we can't have you looking to attract attention by kicking up a fuss. This way they won't hear you if you do. Oh, and you can look after that arm of yours on your own now too, just in case you've got any ideas about trying to clobber me or something. And if you've got any other ideas, like escaping, forget them; I've got Dave here on board now as well, and, as you've already learnt, he'd as soon kill you as look at you."

"Where's my hold-all? All I've got to wear is what I'm standing up in."

"At the bottom of the bay, with a rock in it."

"Gus, stop chatting with him, and shut the door. How many times do we have to tell you not…"

"Oh, quit going on at me, Dave. I'm…" The door clicked shut.

Finn reached across and took a new bandage from the old washing-powder box, carefully peeling off the old dressing. The cut was wide, but appeared to be healing over at last, and apart from having no strength yet in his muscle where the cut was, and the crude, wide, ugly scar that would always remain, no other damage seemed to have been done. Even his lungs seemed to have suffered no lasting ill effects from Harvey's attempt to drown him all that time ago, although how long he had been their prisoner now he had no idea, his first days or weeks lost in a drugged haze. Everything considered, though, he could be in much worse shape physically, he decided.

After a while he leaned across and twisted the faucet over the little sink. The pump labored and banged, spurting out small gushes of rainbow-surfaced water. He took off his clothes, and slowly washed himself all over. There was nothing else to do, and this brief daily routine had become a ritual to look forward to. He had not shaved since before that first morning, leaving him with a scruffy beard, and this, together with his hair, now coarse and matted like an Old English sheepdog's, convinced him that he must look like some desert-island castaway.

Instead of drying himself after washing, he stood naked, letting the air and the occasional puff of air through a slit in the doorway cool his skin. In spite of this, it was barely minutes before the sweat beaded up on his body again, and as his jeans clung to his skin when he tried to pull them on, he spent most of his time in only his underpants.

One of the portholes had been cleaned of its black paint to allow some light in, and he bent down to peer through it. The salt-marsh, now the color of hay, lay off to one side. The cove was empty, and he lay down, his body clammy with a mixture of sweat and water that still had not evaporated. He stared at the once-white boards above his head. He knew every crack, every knot-hole, every nail and screw in this cell where even standing upright was impossible.

"Come on Westlake," he muttered. "*Do* something. You can't afford to lie around like this. Get some exercise."

But after a few minutes the heat and humidity proved too much, and he lay back down again, worrying that if he did not improve physically, and a chance to escape came along, he may not have the strength to take it.

Sunset finally came -- welcome in that it provided some relief from the stifling air -- and the dim, smoky light of the hurricane lantern, hanging from a chain above his head, cast swaying, brassy shadows around the cramped little cabin. As it swung, it illuminated the brown-stained planks of the deck beneath him, where water constantly seeped in between the caulking, then lit up the bunks' filthy and torn mattresses from which flakes of dry, crumbling, foam-cushioning dropped and disappeared between the gaps in the decking; and day and night, the air reeked of diesel fumes, burnt oil, stale beer and cigarettes, along with ancient bait lost, together with the crumbled bits of foam, between the planking, from which sludge constantly rose and fell in time with the rocking of the boat.

He put his hand behind his head. "Oh Diana, I miss you so much, and you trusted me. If only I could let you know I didn't let you down. What you must be thinking of me is torturing me, and now you'll most likely never know the truth."

CHAPTER 25

Diana was winding up the weights on the tall, mahogany long-case clock, when her father strode in, head high, and smiling.

He aimed, then tossed hat, mail and newspaper half way across the room into his armchair.

Diana turned to look at him. "You look happy tonight."

"Yes indeed, yes indeed!" He went straight to his liquor cabinet and raised his hands over it in his pianist-about-to-play attitude, then pulled out a bottle of bourbon.

"You want to make one for me too, please… vodka, that is." Diana reached up and set the clock key back on top of the hood, then picked up the letters and newspapers from the chair.

"Still nothing from him, I suppose," her father commented.

"No, but then, after all this time, I don't expect anything from him, if I ever did." She dropped everything back onto the chair, took her drink over to the window-seat, and sat down, gazing out at the seagulls lined up on the dock pilings.

Behind her, her father was muttering to himself as he went through his mail, and she turned to see him scrunch something up into a ball, and toss it into the fireplace.

"No. I don't want to go on a bargain cruise." He looked up. "Oh, by the way, Diana. I met with Moseley today, and Governor Brigham is still expecting us to host his grand fund-raising ball here after the Lillacray bash. Of course, I told him 'yes, no problem'; I'm only too glad to help him in any way I can. To be honest, it'll be great. For a while there, after all that fiasco with that young man of yours, I was afraid the Party would shove me out in the cold. I wonder where that young guy did go, anyway? He could have made things very awkward for me. It was embarrassing enough as it was."

"Aren't you conveniently forgetting that 'that young guy' you're referring to, Dad, saved your life not so very long ago, and almost lost his own doing it?"

"You're right, my dear. I shouldn't have said that. He did save my life, Moseley's too… You know, I can't wait to see all their faces when they see this place. I mean, just look at that view out there for starters. It'll make them sit up and take notice. It sure will. Yes, there'll be a lot of important people coming too, but there isn't a one that has a place to match this. Boy! At times like this, I wouldn't sell this place for anything!"

McGuire picked up another envelope, and turned it over. It was, Diana could see, a long, white business envelope with a company name imprinted along the edge, but even if she could read the name of the sender, she would not have bothered. After all, her father received many such letters.

He tore it open, after which he spent a considerable time going over the letter inside, before tossing the envelope into the fire. He then folded up the letter, put it in his pocket, and stood up. "Have to make a phone call," and he disappeared into the library, shutting the door behind him.

It was almost an hour before he came back and peered momentarily into the kitchen, where Diana was preparing supper, a supper which, when eventually served, he apologized for not eating, and left on his plate.

The rest of the evening passed with him being uncharacteristically quiet, sitting in his chair, occasionally drumming his fingers on the arms, followed by his getting up to go into the library where Diana could hear him on the phone, but was unable to hear what he was saying.

After he returned on one of these occasions, and he was not doing anything other than sitting in his chair, staring into space, it seemed to Diana like a good opportunity to bring up the subject for which he had earlier in the evening shown so much enthusiasm. "Dad, can we talk about this fundraiser for Governor Brigham's re-election then, we need to decide what…"

McGuire stood up. "Just a minute, my dear, I have to make another phone call. We'll discuss the fundraiser later, okay?"

"Dad? Is something wrong? You seem very

agitated this evening."

"Nothing I can't handle, my dear."

"Is there anything I can do to help?"

He shook his head. "No, but thank you, sweetheart. It's just business, although I think I may have to pop down to DC for a couple of days to sort it out. I'm not sure yet. I'll have to wait and see. Don't you worry, though. As I said, it's nothing I can't handle. It's just a bit of a pain to sort out, that's all."

CHAPTER 26

It was early afternoon, the air still, the *Brandy X* motionless. From a distance, Finn thought, she must even look like a painting on glass. With little else to do but sleep the time away, he had just woken up, and was lying, gazing, as usual, at the planks above him. It was quiet, too quiet. There was usually some conversation going on above, on deck, but even Tucker and Harvey were silent, and he wondered if they were still there.

He swung his legs out over the side of the bunk, and stood up, his bare feet avoiding a particular plank underfoot that always creaked when trodden on, like a Japanese nightingale board, a board that always let his captors know he was moving about. There was nothing he could do now without them checking on him.

He crept up the companionway steps, quietly negotiating each rung until he was able to peer out of the door. He looked around. Tucker and Harvey always slept up on deck, and had erected a tarpaulin cover over it to protect them from the heat and the rain. They were asleep.

He tiptoed out into the fresh air, and looked about for the gun Harvey always carried now; the tip of the barrel was sticking out from under his pillow, but too risky for him to make a dive for it, so he made his way aft until he was standing over the transom. Neither man had moved.

He climbed between the rails, and slid silently into the water. It was warm and still, with not even a ripple. His arm not up to the task of propelling him through the water, he went over on his back, and headed towards the marsh using only his legs, and trying not to make any splashing sounds. It was about three hundred yards to the shoreline, low tide, and a dark satin sheet of pure mud between the edge of the water and the dense reeds beyond gleamed in the sunlight like molten chocolate.

It was that time of year when tiny jellyfish congregate in New England waters like masses of colorless gooseberries, and making his way through them was like swimming through a soup of tapioca. At least they were not poisonous, unlike the Portuguese man-o'-war that sometimes invaded, its purple sails a warning of its presence.

He stopped to rest, and turned over to see how far he had come; the shore seemed as far away as ever, and he was already flagging. He swam on, stopping frequently, and had about another hundred yards to go when he heard the engine of Harvey's dinghy fire up.

He ducked down till only his eyes and the top of his head were visible, and watched. Both men were in the boat, coming towards him, and reaching the shore before they caught up with him was impossible. He was not willing to surrender yet, though. He might still have a chance to escape, and he had to take it; it could be the only one he would ever get, so he went over on his back again, and set off once more.

He had gone scarcely any distance when he heard the dinghy slow down. He turned to face them, his feet now able to touch the bottom, leaving him standing up to his waist in the water. For a few moments they stared at one another, then Harvey revved the engine, and aimed the dinghy straight at him. Unable to move out of its way in time, it hit him, knocking him backwards, and bringing the boat to a stop that stalled the motor.

Finn struggled to regain his feet, but by this time Tucker had flopped into the water, and immediately his huge arms were around his waist, trying to grab hold of him. He ducked, and slid his sweat- and water-covered body down and away from Tucker's grasping hands, and seeing Harvey struggling with the motor's starter cord, headed for the shore again, this time running as though in a nightmare, making little headway in the deep water, the gasps of Tucker's labored breathing so close he could almost feel them.

"Stop right there, Westlake, or I'll shoot." It was Harvey, but Finn kept going, judging that they would not risk killing him. The slimy silt squelched between his toes, and on shore the individual reeds had taken shape, no longer a mass of indistinguishable vegetation in the distance. He glanced over his shoulder. Tucker was standing, bent over, hands on his knees, shoulders heaving, out of breath.

Finn was making headway now, putting distance between them. Maybe he could still outrun them, but then, after a few sputters, the dinghy's motor revved up until it was almost screaming; Harvey was coming after him again, and the boat's shallow draft meant it could be almost ashore before running aground.

Finn put all his energy into his race against it, his breath coming in loud gasps, but with its engine running at full speed, the boat was skimming over the water, easily outrunning his labored wading. He had almost reached the shore, and was only up to his ankles when it crashed into the back of his knees, sending him sprawling into the muck, and grounding itself. He turned slowly over onto his back. Harvey was leaning over him, prodding him with the gun. "Get up! Get up, I said!"

Finn clambered to his feet.

"Damn you, Westlake! If you weren't soon going to make me rich, believe me, I'd kill you right now, and have done with it." Harvey, holding the gun by the barrel, raised his arm to hit Finn's head with the grip, but Finn swiped at it, sending the revolver flying off into a nearby bed of reeds, and with Harvey's attention diverted, Finn put his head down and butted him in the chest. Harvey stumbled and fell, giving Finn a moment in which to retrieve the gun, but Harvey reached out and grabbed hold of his ankles, bringing him down, then leapt on top of him, both men struggling to grab hold of the weapon.

The knife wound in Finn's arm had opened up and was bleeding again, but the adrenalin ensured he did not even feel it. The two men wrestled together in the mud, a battle that drew on all Finn's meager reserves of strength, and one that he lost, but not without first landing a heavy punch on the side of Harvey's head.

With Harvey in charge of the gun, but momentarily stunned by the blow, Finn headed towards a stand of trees at the edge of the swamp. He was no longer running, but staggering, and if he had previously wondered how he would fare if it were a race between him and Harvey, he now found out, because he had covered barely a few yards when the man was at his back, seizing hold of his legs once more, sending him crashing to the ground again.

Harvey dropped his knees onto Finn's back, pinning him down, then pulled his bad arm behind him, pushing it upwards, causing Finn to cry out, a cry drowned out by the sound of heavy scrambling that suddenly erupted in the nearby reeds.

Finn raised his head. "Help!" But it was only a large stag. Almost leaping over their heads, the terrified animal, snorting loudly, headed for a copse, and, in a series of enormous bounds, disappeared amongst the trees, but not before Harvey, in fear of the animal's flying feet, had raised his arms over his head to try to protect himself, giving Finn the chance, once again, to scramble to his feet. He had risen no further than his knees, when a large shadow came between him and the sun, and he glanced up just as Tucker's fist shot forward, slamming into his face.

When he awoke, he was lying on the deck of the *Brandy X*. Standing a few feet away were Harvey and Tucker. Each held a can of beer, taking no more notice of him than they would of a large fish they had just landed. He looked up at them, defeated, worse off now than he had been less than an hour before. He was exhausted, and, continuing to ignore him, they left him lying there.

Another hour passed before he recovered enough to haul himself to his feet and go back down to the cabin, where he collapsed onto his bunk. So much for his attempt to escape!

A curtain moved, a brief flutter, then another. Off in the distance, at the other end of the hallway, a door set up a faint banging, a gentle breeze pushing it, then letting go, making the latch tap against its plate. Diana turned over on her side and put a hand over her ear to shut out the noise, but could still hear it. She leaned over and looked at her bedside clock. It was three in the morning, and she had been awake for an hour or more already.

Ever since Finn had left, she had not been sleeping well, frequently waking at about two, and then unable to get back to sleep, her mind refusing to settle, going forever round and round over the same thing, like a windmill over which she had no control. How was it that she had been so wrong about Finn? When she compared the two men, he had been nothing like Eric, and now that she could look back on Eric more objectively, she could see that she had been so much in love with him that she had failed, or had been unwilling to see that her feelings towards him had not been reciprocated in the way Finn's appeared to have been. Finn had seemed so caring and affectionate, whereas Eric, she could see now, had always kept his distance emotionally. From that point of view, she thought, perhaps Eric had been more honest, in that Finn's displays of affection had to have been all a sham after all. "They say love is blind," she sighed, and turned over again.

The door down the hallway was still banging. It had to stop soon, or she would have to get up and shut it, and that would leave her even more awake.

When she could stand it no longer, she started to get out of bed, but then heard her father padding down the hallway; the constant tapping must have been bothering him too. A minute later she heard the guest-room window being closed, and a while later, her father going back to his room. Not long after, she finally fell asleep.

CHAPTER 27

It was late afternoon, and the northwest breeze that had dotted the bay with white caps for most of the day had dropped until it was almost calm, and Finn was sitting on the edge of his bunk, gazing out of the small porthole. It was tempting to give up trying to regain any sort of physical strength, his one attempt to escape having made him realize how very weak and out of shape he was.

Now too, since he had learnt what they planned to do with him, and there was no longer any necessity for any pretence on their part, his diet had deteriorated into one of heated canned food and water, something that was no help at all towards regaining his strength and building back his muscles. Perhaps they did that on purpose; he did not know. Whatever their intentions, the result was that he no longer had any visible muscle tone, and had lost so much weight, that his jeans, when he bothered to put them on, fell off him, his belt several notches too big, leaving him glad there was no mirror in which to see himself. There were even occasions now when he was tempted to give up altogether, and to wish they *had* left him to bleed to death that morning, and he wondered what had stopped them. After all, their initial plan had been to drown him, so why had they ended up not only preventing him from bleeding to death, but even going to considerable trouble to keep him alive? Why? He thought back to that devastating day, when he had overheard their plan to have this Rollo Devine kill him after handing him over to the man in exchange for a hefty ransom, and he remembered now the comment Harvey had made about it being all Tucker's fault that they were having to do this. Why? What was 'good ole boy' Tucker's part in this? There had to be even more about this trio of thugs, as he now considered them, that he had yet to learn. What was it? Not that it made any difference now though.

He sighed, straightened himself up, and massaged the crick out of his neck. While he had been gazing out of the porthole, a small sailboat, its mainsail and jib spread out on either side, running before whatever wind it could find, had been heading straight towards the *Brandy X*. He bent over again. It was still coming, and was already closer than any other boat had ever approached. Any minute now it would come about and head away again, as did any boat on entering the cove and encountering the pungent smell of the marsh gases. Instead, it dropped its sails, and he saw the splash as the anchor hit the water, and watched the boat swing around until it faced the current.

He turned as Harvey appeared at the entrance to the companionway, leaned in to take hold of the door, and pulled it shut.

He had hoped to attract the attention of the people in the other boat by shouting and yelling, but that would be useless now; they would never hear him from inside the closed cabin. The only other way would be to break the thick glass of the porthole, which was sealed shut. But if he did break it, it would have to be on the first try; Harvey and Tucker would hear him if he started chipping away at it.

It was so hot in the cabin now with the door closed, he could scarcely breathe, and every movement caused him to break out with more sweat. He searched for something with which to shatter the tough glass, looking in all the drawers, but could find nothing suitable. He looked around, but the only possible tool was the heavy metal chain attaching the hurricane lamp, swag-style, to the overhead planking. It was secured by two eye-screws.

He unhitched the lamp from the chain, and set it down on the bunk, but the chain itself was rusted into the eye-screws. His arm still had no strength in it, and neither chain nor eye-screws would budge when he tried to twist them with his left hand. He rummaged around some more, and found in one of the drawers a long-handled can-opener, which he stuck into the eye of one of the screws, using it as a lever, but it snapped in two under the pressure. He swore, and threw it onto the floor, where it slid down between the planks and disappeared. It had loosened the screw, though, and he was able to unscrew it until that part of the chain was free.

Now he had nothing with which to loosen the second screw, so he tugged and pulled at the chain, almost swinging from it. The wood began to splinter, and he gave it a final tug, putting all his weight behind it. Instead of the wood giving way, though, one of the links broke with a suddenness that left him sitting on the deck with about two feet of chain in his hand. He waited, expecting either Harvey or Tucker to appear as a result of the crash, but nothing happened.

Next, he practiced a few swings, trying to get the right angle without actually touching the glass. Being normally right-handed, he found it difficult to get the necessary coordination, but then, satisfied that this was the best he could do, he swung the chain at the half-inch-thick glass. Not only did it not break, it failed to even crack. All that showed for his effort was a small white star where the chain had chipped it. There was no chance to try again; Harvey was already standing in the doorway, waving his gun at him and shaking his head.

"Uh, uh! Don't even try it."

Finn glanced towards the porthole, wondering if the people on the other boat had heard anything. Harvey followed his eyes, a moment's distraction in which Finn hurled the chain at him, hitting him in the chest, causing him to lose his balance and slip down the companionway steps, dropping the gun. Finn rushed to grab it, but Harvey got to it first, picked it up and pushed it against Finn's stomach.

"Go on, Dave. Use it, why don't you? Just shoot me, and those people out there'll be sure to hear it."

"I don't have to kill you… just put you out of action long enough to get this ransom thing over."

"That's enough!" Tucker was standing at the

top of the companionway steps. "You, Finn, back off. Dave, use your head. You want the guy to die on us now? Believe me; I'm as sick of this as you are. I'm sick of this boat, this whole thing, but you shooting him now isn't going to solve anything."

He began climbing down the steps, and advanced towards Finn, fists raised. Finn backed up until he was against the for'ard bulkhead, and, his attention on Tucker, failed to see Harvey gather up the chain from the floor. It hit him on the side of his head, knocking him sideways, and dropping him to the deck. Harvey let out a roar, and raised the chain to hit him again, but Tucker grabbed it from him.

"I said that's enough, Dave."

Harvey, swearing, backed off. For a moment they stood there, then Harvey turned away and disappeared back on deck. Tucker followed, taking the gun and the chain with him, and shutting the door behind him. By the time Finn had recovered sufficiently to look out of the porthole again, the sailboat was gone.

Later that evening they came down again. They had welded a handcuff to either end of the chain, one end of which they snapped into an eye-screw in the for'ard bulkhead, the other, Harvey snapped onto his good wrist.

"That's it. It's your own stupid fault. You shouldn't have yanked the chain down from the ceiling in the first place, so now you don't have the lamp either."

As they went back up on deck, Tucker looked at Finn over his shoulder "I'll give you this; at least you had the guts to try." And they disappeared, leaving the door wide open.

CHAPTER 28

"I worked out that the best place for us to make the exchange is right here." Bradley poked his finger down on the survey map. "See, right in this inlet. I know this island like the back of my hand. It's quite a way off the main road, and hardly anyone visits it, so that's why I've picked it."

"What about all the details then?" Harvey asked. "Who does what? How do we know we're not going to get shot at by Devine and whatever goons he's got with him?"

Tucker stood up. "Hold it a minute, Dave. Let me shut the door here. No need for Westlake to have to hear all this."

Bradley put up his hand and shook his head. "No, leave it open, Gus. He can't go anywhere now he's tied up, and who cares what he hears anyway? So… to get back to the exchange. We've got to get it so we all know what we're doing and don't get shot at."

"Gus and me, we've never been right into that

cove, Tiger," Harvey pointed out. "Not much room to maneuver, is there? Bit of a tight squeeze. Hell! I've put pots down not far from those rocks. They're damned tricky too."

"You don't need to do much maneuvering, Dave. All you've got to do is to go straight in there, and put down the anchor. It'll be coming up for high tide. You then row him ashore, where I'll take over. That's all. After that you hightail it out of there pronto. That's all the two of you have to do. I've got the hard part; I've got to make sure it's all in place well before Devine shows up. That's why we've all got to get there early. Don't forget, either; I'm the one who has to make sure the trade goes without a hitch." He looked up. "Where are you off to now, Gus?"

"I'm going to shut the door whether you like it, or not, Tiger. We're arranging this guy's murder, in case you've forgotten; there's no call for us to torture him by forcing him to listen to how we go about doing it."

"Leave the door right where it is, Gus. I don't care how much we torture him. I've got every reason to hate his guts. He…"

"Why? What's he done to you, Tiger, that he hasn't done to the rest of us. In fact, he's caused Dave and me more…"

"Just shut up, Gus, will you? I've got my own reasons. If you…"

"Shut up both of you," Harvey sniffed. "Who cares *what* he's done at this stage? Let's get back to this ransom exchange deal, or we'll all be in it if it goes sour."

"Huh! You think Dave and me and

Westlake's going to make it ashore in that bathtub you call a dinghy, Tiger?"

"Quit it Gus, will you? You got cold feet already? All you do is gripe. That'll hold two, no trouble, and it needs only one of you to get him ashore. Do as I tell you, and everything'll go off just fine."

"Well I don't like this whole thing at all. It stinks, all of it."

"Oh, shut up, Gus! You think I like this any more than you do? So, unless you've got a better solution, as I said before, shut up."

"So, we doctored some reports. Is that any reason…"

Bradley glared at him. "If you're not careful, Gus, you're going to end up joining him. Are you with us, or aren't you? If not, you're finished anyway, because Devine'll see to it that you're punished, his way."

"Devine doesn't know I've got any part in this, other than doctoring the reports."

"Just hold it right there, and listen, Gus. You're up to your neck in it, same as Dave and me. You forget; right now, we have a man on our hands that Dave tried to murder, but that, as you know, didn't work out, and you both have been holding him hostage on this boat all this time, not knowing what to do with him, so I'm helping you out of your mess by coming up with this plan that, let's face it, is going to end up making us all pretty wealthy! Believe me, Gus! I'll say it yet again: if you've got a better way of solving the problem, let's hear it! And let me remind you; in case you didn't know, the punishment for kidnapping and holding any person hostage, or for ransom, is life imprisonment without eligibility for parole. I know, I've looked it up, and you're certainly guilty of that!"

"He's told me he won't say anything if we let him go."

"He may be willing to say nothing about what we've done to him, Gus, but you can bet he'll still feel duty bound to report the state of the bridge to the authorities, and we'll be back in square one."

"You realize he's listening to every word we say, don't you?"

"Like I already said, Gus, who cares whether he's listening, or not? I've every reason to hate Westlake, and I could care less what he hears. Anyway, it's now him or us, Gus. Make your choice, and make it now. We can't have you off in left field somewhere."

"Okay, okay. What time does this all take place then?"

"Right. We're all on board then. Trust me, Gus. It's the only way, and it's all set up already. Devine knows exactly when and where."

"So," said Harvey. "When and where?"

"A week next Friday. Seven in the evening. That's twelve days from now."

Harvey groaned. "Twelve days! Why so long?"

"Devine claims he can't get his hands on the cash before then." Bradley explained.

"Isn't that the day of that Lillacray fundraising thing?" Harvey asked.

"Yes, but never mind about that. Okay, that's

six o'clock, remember. As I said, I need to have Westlake safely on shore and ready for the exchange well before Devine gets there. I won't be able to come out here again before then, so this is it. Don't make a balls-up of it" Bradley stood up. "Right, see you at the rendezvous then. If you need anything in the meantime, you've got my number." He rummaged around in his pocket. "Uh, uh! what did I do with the key to my dinghy?"

"You went below to wash your hands earlier, remember? Maybe it dropped out of your pocket down there, or something," Tucker suggested.

Bradley started down the stairs into the cabin. "Yeah, maybe. I'll go check. Keep an eye on Westlake, will you, Dave?"

"Not to worry, Tiger," Harvey assured him. "He's shackled to that eye screw, remember?"

"Dammit. They're not down here. Hang on a minute, though. Maybe…" Bradley began turning out the contents of his pockets onto one of the bunks. "Ah! Got it! It was mixed up with all the other crap in my pocket. Thank God for… Heh! Damn you Westlake! He's just gone and kicked me in the stomach! You wait till I…"

"That handkerchief!" Finn shouted. "How did you get your hands on that handkerchief, Bradley?" He kicked out at him again with both feet, this time hitting him in the mouth, and knocking him backwards against the ladder, beyond his reach.

The noise brought Tucker skidding down the steps, almost falling over Bradley, who had slid to the floor. Tucker pulled him to his feet, and helped him to the sink, where he leaned over, grabbing it with both hands, spitting out blood.

Then Harvey came down, and Finn cried out as he grabbed hold of his bad arm and wrenched it behind his back, just as he had done that time when he had tried to escape.

Then all was quiet except for the sound of water dribbling down the drain, and Bradley's still labored breathing. Harvey released Finn's arm, and Bradley straightened himself, putting his hand on Tucker's shoulder in a gesture of thanks. Nothing was said, and no-one looked at Finn. The three went back on deck, and a few minutes later he heard Bradley leave.

Finn sat on the edge of his bunk, nursing his arm. The knife cut, still not yet fully healed, was bleeding yet again, and water was trickling down the companionway ladder; it had started to rain, cold and gray, out of the southeast.

CHAPTER 29

Diana had agreed to go to a movie with Bradley this evening, and she looked up at the long-case clock. It was ten minutes to six, plenty of time to take a shower and change before he arrived, but by half past seven he was already fifteen minutes late, which was unusual for him, so she went out onto the porch, and sat down, waiting for him.

The sailboats were heading back home now to their respective moorings after spending the day out on the bay, and she looked at the *Moonglow* tugging at her own mooring, her sails furled, their red covers glowing in the evening sunlight, and sighed. Usually, whenever she looked at the *Moonglow* these days, her thoughts turned to Finn, but this evening it made her think of her father instead, of how he had been behaving recently, and how it had been worrying her. It all seemed to have started the day he received that letter, and she had ended up asking him if anything was wrong, and he had told her it was nothing he couldn't handle. Ever since then he had seemed distracted, absent-minded even, and lately, she had even heard him on the phone, apologizing for not going out golfing with his friends, even when he had nothing else to prevent him from going. This was something she had never known him to do before, but then, on top of that, he had added to her concern by deciding to do something else he had never done before.

She had come down one morning to find him out on the porch, gazing out over the bay. He had turned when he heard her asking him why he wasn't already dressed in his business suit as usual on a weekday.

"You know what, Diana?" he had said. "I'm going to take the *Moonglow* out for a sail today."

"Oh! On the *Moonglow?* That's a change, Dad. You usually rent a fancy yacht for that sort of excursion. So, you're just taking a couple of your acquaintances out for a trip, then, are you? Would you like me to make some sandwiches? Will they be here soon? You haven't had breakfast yet, have you?"

"No to all those questions, Diana. No. I'm going out on my own."

"On your own! But Dad! You *never* do anything on your own! You're the most gregarious person I know."

"Yes. True. But I'm thinking it's time for me to go somewhere on my own for a change… somewhere where I can take stock, if you see what I mean. There's too much going on in my head right now, and I need to clear it out." He had turned to look out over the bay again. "And I think that going out alone, sailing, will be the way to do that."

And after that day, he had gone out on his own several times, but if any of it had cleared his head, it did not show, and yes, she was concerned about him, and what may have caused this… well, melancholia was the only way she could describe it.

It was certainly the letter that had started it. She wished now that she had had a chance to see the name of the company on the envelope. What had the letter said that could have had such an effect on him? As Finn had rightly noted that night at the yacht club ball, her father's social position meant a lot to him. Had something happened to tarnish that? If so, that would definitely hurt his pride severely, and could easily cause his current mood. Maybe he…

Her thoughts were interrupted by the sound of the doorbell ringing. It was nine o'clock, and she had even forgotten that she and Ben were supposed to be going to the movies.

"Ben! What on earth...?" She looked at his bruised chin and swollen lip with two ugly stitches in it. She put her hand on his arm, and led him into the living room. "Here, come on in."

"Car accident. Driver stopped suddenly."

"Come and sit down. Tell me what happened. You should have gone straight home. You could have called me. There was no need to... Can I get you anything?"

"Scotch. Straight."

"Was anyone else hurt?" She handed him the neat Scotch, and helped him remove his wet slicker.

He shook his head.

"Do you need anything else? Some food perhaps? No? Well let's go out on the porch, shall we?”

He followed, shoulders hunched, then switched on the small table-lamp and the radio, turning the dial until he found some bland background music.

Diana motioned him to a comfortable wicker chair, and stretched herself out on the wide rattan sofa, her hands behind her head. “Tell me more about the accident, that's if you can.”

“Banged my face on the dashboard, and one of my teeth went right through my lower lip. Hurt my stomach too. Sorry about the movie.” He got up and sat down next to her, lifting her legs sideways, making room for himself, and took her hand in his.

“Don't worry about the movie, Ben. You're lucky not to have been more seriously injured.”

He leaned across and switched off the lamp. The moon was bright enough to cast romantic shadows on the lawn, and he put his arm around her and smoothed her hair. “Nice music, eh, Diana? Diana, I love you.” He put his hand on her breast, and tried to undo the buttons on her blouse.

She put her hand over his and clutched it, pulling his hand away.

“Why? Why do you keep stopping me all the time? I need you, Diana. And you need me too. I know it.”

She let go of his hand, and he put it back on her breast. “Ben! No! You've just been in an accident, for heaven's sake, and just because I'm sorry you've been hurt, doesn't mean I…”

He moved closer, his hand inching up her thigh, caressing it.

"Stop it, Ben. Please."

"What the hell's wrong, Diana? What is it? Admit it. You love me, just as much as I love you. We love each other." He stood up and tried to pull her to her feet. "Come on. Let's go upstairs."

"Ben, I said 'no', and I'm sorry if this is probably not the best moment to have to say it, but I do really think we shouldn't see each other anymore. I'm sorry, but that's the way I feel. It... this is all wrong."

"Why is it all wrong? Even if you don't love me, what wrong with us just having sex anyway? It isn't as though you'd be making any sort of commitment. Anybody'd think you were some sort of Victorian spinster, the way you act. We *are* in the twenty-first century, you know. Just having sex doesn't have to mean anything more than kissing does, and even that you balk at.

"You keep on saying sorry" he went on. "Well, I'm sorry too. I want you so much, and one day, believe me, you *will* feel the same way about me. Right now, I know you still have feelings for... for him. But you just wait, Diana. I know I'm right. You *will* come to love me. I know you will." He put out his hand to touch her again, and she stood up.

"Ben, I don't want to discuss this anymore, especially right now. You're obviously suffering from the aftereffects of your accident, and I am sorry about that, but what you do need right now, more than anything, is to go home and try to get a good night's sleep."

"Oh well, seems we're going nowhere as usual, so I guess I might as well call it a night. As you say, I'll probably be better off with a good night's sleep anyway."

Diana fetched his slicker, and helped him put it on. "I hope you'll feel better soon, Ben."

At the front door, he leaned over and kissed her on the cheek. "I know you didn't mean it when you said we shouldn't see each other anymore. You're just going through a bad patch right now, and I understand that, but it'll be fine once you get that guy out of your system, and I'm very patient. That day will come; I know it will, my love." He put his hand in his pocket, and pulled out his keys, along with a handkerchief. "By the way, I've been meaning to give this back to you."

"Oh, thank you, Ben! I've been looking everywhere for it. Of course! I'd forgotten; I lent it to you the night you got something in your eye, didn't I? Thank you so much. I was really upset to think I might have lost it."

CHAPTER 30

Tucker had been on his hands and knees at the far end of the cabin for the previous hour, tinkering with the engine. His back to Finn during this time, he had said nothing except for occasionally swearing when his work was not going to his satisfaction.

"Gus?"

Tucker kept up his tinkering. "Yup?"

"There's something I'd like you to tell me. What you tell me now isn't going to make any difference as I'm never going to have the opportunity to pass it on, so there's no harm done in answering a question that's been puzzling me all this time. How was it that after Dave stabbed me once, he didn't just go ahead and finish me off? After all, that's what he had intended doing in the first place. Secondly, when you had me lying there on the deck that morning, why didn't you just leave me to bleed to death? And thirdly, what did Dave mean by saying it was all your fault? None of it makes sense, and you at least owe it to me to let me know what it was that made you all decide to first keep me alive, then to put me through this hell instead. It's hard for me to come to terms with the fact that seemingly civilized people could have such twisted minds, although I've heard that that is what psychopaths are like."

Tucker raised his head. "I don't need to explain anything to you."

Harvey appeared at the top of the companionway steps. "I heard that. There's a good reason why Gus doesn't want to enlighten you as to why we didn't just go ahead and kill you on the spot, but I'll be only too glad to explain it to you, after which, if Gus here doesn't clobber you for calling us psychopaths, I'll certainly be tempted to."

He came down the steps, leaned his back against the sink, out of Finn's reach, and took a deep breath. "We're not born sadists, you know."

"Well, congratulations on your achievement in becoming..."

"Sadists enjoy making life miserable for others; you don't think we enjoy doing this, do you?"

"Could have fooled me. Bradley in particular seems to be getting quite a kick out of his plan for having me buried in the foundations of this guy Devine's state building project, and you don't seem to be overly upset about digging a knife in me emotionally as well as physically."

"Do you want to hear this, or not? It's you that asked. In fact, I'm not upset either about telling you why we didn't kill you that morning." Harvey folded his arms, and stared at Finn. "You see, it was like this: after you forced me to knife you to stop you from strangling me, I did try to finish you off, but two other things that were happening at the same time stopped me. First, we were right next to the boat, but the tide was flowing real fast by that time, and I was trying to grab hold of the boat so as not to get swept away, and hold onto you at the same time. The last thing I wanted was for your corpse to end up being washed in by the tide somewhere, and then have the authorities start investigating what happened to you. Secondly, you were still flailing around and knocked the knife out of my hand, so I had nothing to kill you with anyway, and with you still alive, there was no way I could get you up onto the boat by myself. Fortunately, that's when Gus and Tiger turned up. As you heard already, they were the two men you'd seen in the distance earlier, but I'd let you think they were just other fishermen. What they were really doing, though, was waiting to come and help me load onto the boat what they were expecting to be your drowned body."

Tucker swung round, spanner in hand. "Heh! If you're going to answer his question, at least tell it as it really was." He faced Finn. "If you want the truth, what I expecting that morning was to go fishing for tautog along with Dave and Tiger and some stranger in town, who'd called Dave and asked him to be his diving buddy. No-one said a word to me about killing him."

"Yeah, well," Harvey conceded. "Tiger and I figured that, knowing you, it'd be better if, when you arrived and found he'd drowned, you'd assume it was an accident, and not cause a fuss." He shrugged. "But, as we all know, it didn't turn out like that, did it? What we had instead, was the guy bleeding to death with an obvious knife wound.”

“I still don’t understand,” Finn sighed “You could have simply left me to do just that, so, why didn’t you? Why did you go to the trouble of saving me? Surely it wasn’t so as to get a kick out of mentally and physically torturing me the way you have. I can’t believe even you would be so screwed up.”

Tucker pointed the spanner at Finn. “Huh! Us screwed up! You must be pretty screwed up yourself, to sit there, calmly listening to this like you’re just watching some third-rate TV thriller. Any normal person would be a gibbering idiot by now, knowing what’s going to happen to him.”

Finn glared at him. “You think I’m not terrified at the thought of what this Devine man is going to do to me? But if you’re hoping I’ll give you the added satisfaction of watching me fall apart and start begging, you’ve got the wrong man, so get on with it.”

Harvey adjusted his weight against the sink. “Well, I guess you could say that things not having turned out to be as simple as planned, the reason we didn’t kill you outright once we got you on board, or let you just bleed to death, was a mixture of logistics and natural panic at the turn of events; it wasn’t something we did every day, after all. And then there was old Gus here, thinking he was going for a morning’s fishing, and not knowing anything about what it was really all about. For him, the whole thing was such a shock, he went into orbit, and in the end, we were just going round in circles.” He shrugged. “And with Gus making threats about what he’d do if we didn’t keep you alive...”

Finn turned to Tucker, who had gone back to tinkering with the engine. "Well, the latest plan doesn't seem to be worrying you overmuch Gus, does it? It's still okay to have me murdered by someone else then, is it, as long as you're not the one to strike the fatal blow?"

"If we hadn't stopped you bleeding pretty fast, you'd have been dead anyway," Harvey went on when Tucker said nothing. "The trouble with Gus getting his knickers in a twist about you ending up dead with him being a party to your demise, though, was that he didn't give any thought to what we were going to do with you if we *did* keep you alive. Well, none of us had at that point, if it comes to that. The way it's turned out, though, I wish we *had* finished you off. Looking back, it would've been simple. We could've just taken you and buried you on land somewhere where no-one would even bother looking for you, everyone just thinking you'd hightailed it back to the UK. The way it's turned out, though, Gus is just as up to his neck in it now as the rest of us, so he can't do anything, but go along with the ransom plan."

Harvey heaved himself away from the sink, and started to leave. "So there, now you have it. Happy?" He disappeared onto the deck.

Finn watched Gus for a few minutes. He had his back turned towards him, still tinkering with the engine, his shirt halfway up his hairy back, his pants so low, Finn could see the divide between his buttocks.

"Gus?"

"Yeah, what?"

"It still isn't too late for you to go to the police, you know. Sure, you'll get a prison sentence, but you'll be able to plea bargain, which should cut down on your time spent inside. Do you really want to spend the rest of your life, knowing you not only deliberately sent a man to his death, but profited from it financially as well? Have you so little conscience? I don't think so."

Gus got up on his knees, and turned. "It isn't jail I'm afraid of; it's Rollo Devine. If I go to the police, and the whole story comes out about his worthless bridge repairs, our accepting bribes from him to falsify safety reports for him, his part in getting Dave to get rid of you, along with this whole ransom thing, my life wouldn't be worth zilch in jail, because Devine's the sort who always has cronies to do his dirty work for him, and I wouldn't last two minutes, and to me, my life is worth more than yours at this..."

Harvey's head appeared in the doorway. "Heh! Gus! Come here a minute. Your eyesight's better than mine. Isn't that Tiger heading this way? What's he doing? He said he wasn't coming back again now before we meet up for the ransom thing. Don't tell me it's all fallen through for some reason!"

Tucker followed Harvey onto the deck. "Guess we're about to find out." A few minutes later Finn heard the dinghy's engine putter to a stop.

"Heh! Tiger! What's up. Everything still on?"

"Help me up on board, Dave. No, the deal's still on. I just need to take care of some unfinished business."

Harvey peered into Bradley's face. "Gee! You look dreadful. Westlake really did a job on your face yesterday, didn't he? Stitches even. What are you all dressed up for? Had a night on the town?" He put out his arm to stop Bradley, but failed. "No! No Tiger! Don't go down there now and screw everything up by clobbering the guy just to get your own back. Only two more days, and then he's gone for good."

"No worry. I don't plan on clobbering him physically. I've just got something for him that he'll be delighted to have, won't you Westlake?" Bradley peered down into the cabin. "And you can sit back down. I've no intention of getting within your reach, nor even of smashing in that handsome face of yours at this point in our negotiations, much as I'm tempted. So, here, what about these for starters instead, eh?" He gave Finn an extravagant bow, and tossed some glossy magazines onto his bunk. "I've brought you a present… some fancy magazines for your lordship."

Finn glanced down at them, then looked back at him.

"Well, don't look so puzzled, my dear Finn Westlake. They're perfect for you: fine dining, luxury travel, ads for fancy skis and fancy vodka, and all that high-society crap." Bradley leant against the steps. "Well, you're the fancy gentleman, aren't you? So, I brought fancy magazines for the fancy gentleman. Aren't you going to look at them? Not that you're going to be able to take advantage of any of that stuff advertised, are you? Pity."

Finn shoved the magazines onto the floor, and lay back down on his bunk. "You're drunk."

"Yeah, well maybe I am, just a bit, but more with what you might call euphoria than with beer." Bradley settled himself down on one of the companionway steps, worrying the knot of his tie until it lay on his chest, too tight to slide. "And I'm sure you want to know why I'm feeling euphoric? No? Well, I'm going to tell you anyway. It's like this, I was getting sick of hearing from your darling Diana about how damned perfect you are, or 'were' I should say, shouldn't I? Have to say I was fed up hearing the sound of your wretched name: 'Finn' this, and 'Finn' that, so I brought these fancy magazines for the perfect gentleman. They cost me an arm and a leg too, but now you've got them all mucked up with bilge water. Ungrateful bastard, aren't you?" He picked some dirt out of his nail with a splinter of wood from the ladder. "Well, aren't you going to ask me about how I know so much about your dear, sweet Diana? No? Well, I'm going to tell you that anyway too. It's the real reason I'm here, to be honest. I want you to know that I've continued to keep my eye on her all this time to make sure she doesn't start getting too interested in your whereabouts. Anyway, as I'm sure your imagination has already figured out, it turned into far more than keeping an eye on her, if you see what I mean." He took in a deep, ostentatious breath, then blew the dirt off his nails. "She's quite a bit of all right, isn't she? Great tits and…"

Finn leapt up. "You son-of-a-bitch! Diana wouldn't touch *you* with a ten-foot pole!"

"Ah, well, that's what you'd like to think, isn't it? What I just *had* to come to let you know and to thank you so much for is that you ended up doing me a great favor by clobbering me yesterday. You see, after I'd spent the evening at the hospital, getting my face fixed up, I went round to see her, and told her how some idiot driver had crashed into me, causing me to hit the dashboard, etcetera, and boy! Did she ever get sympathetic! It was great having her all emotional and lovey-dovey about it, so what better time to seize the moment as they say. That bed where you and she used to have it off… My! What a night! Best lay around, I reckon, don't you? No wonder you fell for her." He stood up and made an obscene gesture to Finn, before turning to leave. "Looks like you've got a problem, buddy. You're going no place, and I've got your girl. So, thanks again for that."

"Damn you, Bradley, I'll kill you." Finn lashed out at him, but Bradley was already half way up the steps, and out of reach.

"Yeah, I believe you would, but then, you aren't going to get the chance, are you, buddy?" He laughed, and closed the door behind him.

CHAPTER 31

"Jan! How good to hear from you! How's life now you're right there, in Burgundy? Everything else still going well…?" And for the next half hour, Diana listened to Janice's latest news about how much she was enjoying life in Beaune, and visiting all the wonderful vineyards of Burgundy, how she was helping restaurants with selecting wines to complement their menus, and how she and her new beau, Jacques, were getting along, which was very well indeed…

"Me? At this point I'm not sure where I'm at anymore, Jan… totally confused, I guess you could call it…

"You're sure you really want to hear yet more about me and my love life, if you can even call it that? Okay, well, as I told you a while back, I've been dating Ben Bradley, the Governor's nephew, or rather, I should say, he's been dating me, although why, I still can't understand; I've been such a wet rag, and he even had to ask me to stop talking about Finn! He's good looking enough to find himself anyone he pleases, so with me being so unresponsive to his advances… and he certainly does do a lot in the way of advancing…

"Yes, I suppose that does sound sort of amusing, but it's not really. I mean, can you imagine any man wanting to go out with a woman who can't stop talking about her previous love interest?...

"So, you think he must be the sort of man to see getting into bed with me as a challenge, and that's why he's being so persistent? Well, yes, perhaps you're right…

"Yes, I know, Jan, as you asked me before: why *don't* I have sex with him? It may sound odd, but I actually don't want to. To be honest, I find his turning on the charm a turn-off, rather than a turn-on. Another thing too, he was in a car accident the other afternoon. He came here with a couple of stitches in his lip after cutting it on the dashboard, and it looked a bit of a mess, I have to agree. I was sympathetic, of course, but then he used that to come onto me! It was so inappropriate, and I felt insulted that he'd use my concern for him as a means to try to seduce me like that. And it isn't just that either, Jan. Somehow, whenever he tells me he loves me, which he does all the time, it sounds more like an official announcement than a sincere feeling. It's almost as though he's acting the part of a lover in a play, a part that he's learnt at some time, along with all the appropriate gestures, and whenever he wants a woman to have sex with him, or submit to him in some other way, he simply re-enacts the whole scene…

"You know, the more I think about it, talking

to you like this, there's never any true feeling behind his words at all; he isn't even a good actor. Finn was always giving me spontaneous hugs and light kisses -- at least, they felt like they were spontaneous. With Ben, it's always as though every move is choreographed with cold precision. And those pale blue eyes of his too; they might as well be glass for all the emotion they ever express. All in all, he seems more like a cardboard cut-out than a real person, and I really think now that that's what he is, Jan...

"Oh, you know something, Jan? You've no idea how good it always is for me to be able to unload on you like this. I do wish you weren't so far away, though ...

"You do too? Yes, I miss your company so very much as well, but at least we can Skype each other like this whenever we feel like it, which is something. It's great to able to sit and chat like this, isn't it? Almost as though we were enjoying our usual cup of coffee together over at Starbuck's...

"I'm sorry. I seem to be usurping all our time together this time, pouring out to you everything that's been churning around in my mind. I have to say, though, that your letting me prattle on like this has not only helped me clarify my thoughts, but it's given me a great sense of relief too...

"Why? Well it's true that I'd promised myself never to trust any man again, and not to get involved emotionally, but I *am* a normal woman after all, and I'd even begun to think that between Eric and Finn, and the way they treated me, they'd somehow killed off all my sexual urges as well. But I now realize that's wrong! *I'm* not the one with a problem! I truly ık *Ben* is! Underneath all that charm, he's cold, as though incapable of actually experiencing real love and affection at all, and you know something, Jan; I've made up my mind; if he won't end this weird relationship, then I'm going to, and I'm going to do it at the earliest opportunity! I just want him out of my life now. It's not going to be easy though. The last thing I can face right now is a load of animosity and recriminations. Maybe what I should do is to refrain from blaming him in any way, and accept full responsibility for the failure of the relationship myself. That way, he can leave the scene with his considerable ego intact…

"Yes, I *am* a scheming hussy, aren't I? But I do like your expression that I should try not to ruffle the peacock's feathers if at all possible. Oh! Changing the subject: I know what I wanted to ask you: are you coming home for Christmas? It's just that I was wondering if you could come to spend some time at our place, and bring Jacques with you, of course."

"Oh! Your Mum and Dad are going to Beaune to spend Christmas with you! Well, that's great. I'll miss seeing you though…

"Your father hasn't been well? I'm sorry to hear that, but you say he'll be well enough to make the trip to France. That's excellent. Oh, speaking of fathers, Jan, I have to say I've been quite worried about Dad lately too…

"Well, I can't put my finger on it exactly. He seems fine physically, but he's just not his usual, what you might call exuberant self, and he's even taken to going out on our sailboat all on his own! I've literally never seen him do that before. You know Dad --

always surrounded by either friends or business associates, or both, chatting away, but he seems to have clammed up, or something. I've asked him if there's anything wrong, but all he says is it's nothing he can't handle, whatever that means. It's been going on for a while now, though, and it would seem that whatever the problem is, it still hasn't gone away, and I think it's getting him down. I do wish he'd confide in me, but he's never discussed his business with me, so perhaps he feels it's something he can't start doing now, especially if it's something that's not going right for some reason. Oh well, there's nothing more I can do about it, so I guess I'll just have to wait until he's sorted it out. It *is* a bit depressing, though, seeing him like this. Perhaps I haven't helped any either, having been so upset myself by all the Finn situation.

"Oh! I'm looking at the clock here. He'll be home soon, so I need to start fixing supper, I guess. Where you are, it must be almost gone midnight already. Thanks so much for calling, Janice, though once again, I seem to have hogged the lion's share of our chat. Next time, I'll call you, and I promise to let you get a word in edgewise, okay?"

CHAPTER 32

The note on the kitchen table read: "*As I thought, I have to go to DC to sort things out. Back in time for Friday's fundraiser at Lillacray's, though. Meet me at airport will you, my dear. Usual flight. Dad.*"

"Oh, not Friday evening!" Whatever her father's problem was, it had to be very serious if he was willing to risk being late for, or even missing the Lillacray fundraiser. Even if his plane were on time, they would still most likely miss the start of it.

She sighed. Her father was not her only problem. Since talking to her friend, Janice, and deciding that she would end her unsatisfactory relationship with Bradley, she had been going over and over in her mind how and when she was going to do this. As they would be going out sailing together after lunch today, this, she was now determined, would be when she would finally be free of him. She would wait, however, until they were back at the mooring, before making her declaration.

As a result, that afternoon, her meticulously rehearsed words were now milling around in her brain the entire trip, and, knowing how it was going to end, making it hard for her to keep up the pretence that everything was normal.

Some hours later, just as the sun was sinking behind the houses on the mainland on the other side of the bay, they arrived back at the mooring, but instead of starting to gather up her things, Diana remained seated.

"Wait Ben. Sit down a minute for me, will you? I need to tell you someth..."

Bradley put up his hand. "Shh…Wait a minute. Listen! What's that?" He turned up the sound on the portable radio.

"*The National Weather Service has issued a preliminary hurricane watch for the New England area. The as-yet-unnamed hurricane is forming off Cape Hatteras, and its possible course could take it up the coast towards the area, arriving by Friday if it maintains its current direction and speed. Stay tuned for further information.*"

He switched off the radio. "Oh damn! *Just* what I need!" he exclaimed.

Diana nodded. "Well, it's just what none of us needs, is it? Uh, Ben, as I started to say: this is hard to explain, but you must be aware of how much I've appreciated your kindness in trying to cheer me up all this time, and, as I've said so many times already, I'm sorry to have been so unresponsive, and am frankly amazed that you haven't decided to leave me just as the others did." She sighed. "This is so hard to say, Ben, but I've been thinking a lot about this, and realize that with things being as they are, it really isn't a healthy relationship for either of us, and, as it's all my fault -- I accept that -- I'm going to be the one to end it, and to end it right here, right now.

"I want you to know it is has nothing at all to do with you not being a good, thoughtful and kind man. You have gone out of your way to make it work, but it isn't working, so it's time for us to go our separate ways, as they say, so...." She put out her hand to touch his arm. "I'm going to stay here on the boat for a while. This hasn't been easy to put into words, and I need to calm down a bit and clear my mind. I do hope you understand. You go on ahead now, and thank you for everything, Ben... *Ben*! What's the matter? Let go of me! Ben, please! What...?"

"No, Diana! No! I can't believe you're trying to do this to me! It can't end like this! I love you, and I'm not going, not now, not ever! I can't. Don't you see? Hasn't it been obvious? I adore you, and I'll adore you till I go to my grave! I thought you needed me too, but even if you don't, I need you, Diana -- desperately. I couldn't live without you now, and if you abandon me, there's no knowing what I'll do to myself. Do you want to be responsible for that? Think about it. How would you feel? You may feel bad about Westlake dumping you, but it's obvious you've never felt like doing away with yourself, which is what I'll risk doing to myself if you leave me. I've been keeping this to myself all this time, but now I need to tell you my true feelings for you, my dearest, darling Diana. You mustn't leave me. I love you way too much, my dearest one, and the thought of you not being a part of my life anymore is something I can't even contemplate. You mean everything to me, Diana. My life is worth nothing without you."

Diana's first inclination was to ask him from which movie he had taken this speech, but it had been such a shocking outburst, she was afraid of his response if she did. Could he even be capable of violence, of attacking her? His grip on her arms was painful enough to think he might well be.

"But Ben!"

"No, it's not going to happen. It can't happen. It's not an option. It's unthinkable."

He let go of her arms, and calmly picked up the picnic hamper. "Come on, my darling; let's think no more about it, shall we?" He pulled her to her feet. "Come on, Diana my love; you're obviously all upset now. Let me help you take these things back to the house."

CHAPTER 33

Finn could already feel its effects in the salt-marsh bay. A broad swell had arisen during the last few hours, and the anchor line of the *Brandy X* was chafing against the hull as her bow lifted and sank. The water had become a glaucus green, and heavy clouds of every shade from dark gray to almost black filled the sky. The rigging hummed, and ever since the National Weather Service had issued a hurricane watch a couple of days previously, the radio had been left on, and he had heard announcers constantly issuing further advisories, including small craft warnings for the area, and the *Brandy X* was in that category.

As usual, he lay on his reeking bunk. The old engine had just been fired up for the first time since he had been held captive there, and they were soon under way. It took only a few minutes to leave the calm of the cove that had been his home for how long now? He had no idea.

As soon as they came into the open water, the

seas began to hit the boat broadside, making her wallow. Further out it was almost worse, as the following sea boosted the old fishing vessel along in a series of great, rolling heaves, the waves pushing into her stern.

The cabin door had been shut soon after they had left the safety of the cove, and now, without any fresh air, the rolling and pitching of the boat, along with the stench of diesel fumes leaking into the cabin, made him seasick.

"Hi! Open the door. I'm suffocating down here." But the combined noise of the wind, the laboring engine and the waves drowned out his voice. He assumed the sickness would go once they landed, but he would need all his energy if he hoped to escape, and he had already lost his breakfast and his lunch. "Serve them right if I *am* suffocated before we get to their rendezvous. Devine isn't going to pay for my corpse."

Over the last weeks he had tried to create several escape scenarios, but as he knew nothing about where the exchange was to be made, it had been impossible to plan anything with any accuracy. The only constant was the need to try to stay in shape, and, unable to exercise for a long time now, having been shackled to the eye-screw, that had been impossible too.

It had been hard not to let panic take over, but if he had little else now, he did still have the willpower and determination to fight adversity, something his schooldays had taught him. All he needed was a chance to escape, but it had to come soon, and there was very little time left now. He peered out of the porthole, but all he could see through the salt-covered glass was the smoky gray outline of the coast in the distance.

He tried to think of Diana, but the thoughts brought no comfort. Bradley had said she talked about him all the time, even saying he was perfect, and if that were true, then it must surely mean she was still fond of him. On the other hand, there was Tucker, who had told him that she never wanted to see him again, but when he thought about this without his emotions getting in the way, he decided that Tucker was the one more likely to be lying, because he had had to come up with some reason why she had not come to visit him. That had to be it. What other excuse could he have used? That had been particularly cruel of Tucker, though, and had caused him so much anguish. Not that Bradley's alternative gave him any joy either, because Diana, regardless of how she still felt about him, must still be thinking he had walked out on her that day, that he had abandoned her, exactly as that Eric man had done -- although, again, if that were true, then it would be odd for her to still consider him perfect.

Then there was what Bradley had said about dating and sleeping with her. How much of that was true? The thought of her being with this man, being touched by him, fondled by him, filled him with revulsion, and he shuddered; and that she might even be being responsive to his advances and having sex with him was too depressing to even contemplate, and he tried to think of something positive. Right now, though, he could find nothing positive to think about; in all likelihood, he would even be dead by sundown, so what did any of it matter anymore?

He gazed out of the porthole; a jellyfish, decorated with four lavender rings, was floating past, undulating on its way. He turned away, and lay back down on the bunk again.

The tide had turned a couple of hours previously, and by now it was flowing swiftly up the bay, carrying the *Brandy X* with it, accelerating their journey, and when he looked out of the porthole some time later, he caught sight of the McGuire home about a half mile away off the starboard beam. What would Diana think if she knew he was so near to her? A short time after that, he noticed a dark shadow slide over the boat; they had just passed under the bridge, the cause of all his agonies, before heading round the top of the island.

The weather was worsening, and once around the tip, the force of the wind hit them head on. They were now in the dangerous and rocky waters off the shore of the island, and the boat pitched deeply, scooping up gallons of water, which cascaded along the foredeck and down into the cabin below, even though the door was still tightly latched.

He watched it slopping back and forth in between the wooden floor-planks, raising with it everything rotten that had lain below them in the bilges. He had been sick to his stomach several more times already, and the sight and smell added to his misery.

He lay down on his back again. He had nothing else to lose from his stomach, so the nausea now had a gnawing emptiness added to it. Now, too, the waves were no longer rollers, but breakers with high-pitched crests so steep that every time the boat troughed, her hull hit with a jarring crack, as though she were breaking in half. This slowed her progress, and when she finally came to a stop, he heard Harvey shouting to Tucker that it was nearly six o'clock.

The engine died, and the anchor splashed down into the water. Had he made his last journey ever? He did not even bother to look out of the porthole. Being so sick, combined with having to breathe the fumes from the engine, he was almost past caring what happened to him now.

In the relative calm of wherever it was they had come to a stop, and without the noise of the engine, he heard the radio announcing that the weather service had upgraded the hurricane watch for the area into a warning. It had turned on itself, and was now headed for the bay and Cautuxet Island, where it was expected to make landfall within a couple of hours, unless it picked up speed in the meantime, in which case it would arrive sooner.

The cabin door was unlocked, and Tucker's head appeared. "Come on then, Dave. We'd better get a move-on. We need to get him ashore before it gets any worse. You got the gun?"

"Yup."

"You'd better give it to me then, and take him in. That dinghy won't take me and Westlake together; I'm way too heavy. I'll cover you from here."

Harvey started to come down the steps. "Phew! Must be an exhaust leak down here, or something. It stinks of diesel."

"Heh! Westlake! Get up. It's time to move… Westlake!"

Finn opened his eyes.

"Dammit! Thought you'd snuffed it! Get up *now*! *Now*, I said!"

Tucker held the gun ready, while Harvey undid the handcuff from the eye-screw and slid it over Finn's other wrist, leaving him with both hands behind his back, with the length of chain separating them. He stood up slowly, but with the surf rising higher by the minute now, causing the boat to rock violently, and being lightheaded as well, Finn lost his balance, and collapsed back onto the bunk.

Harvey yanked him to his feet. "Come on, move it, will you? We need to get going." He waved his hand in the direction of the companionway, where Tucker, gun in one hand, was holding the door open with the other, allowing the fumes to escape.

"All right. Up top. I said move it, Westlake. *Move it*!" Harvey's voice was becoming hysterical.

It was another fifteen minutes before Finn was seated in the dinghy, having almost fallen overboard when he lost his balance again, and fell.

Once seated, he and Harvey set out, Finn facing back towards the *Brandy X* where Tucker stood, supporting himself against the rail, gun in hand. He turned briefly to look towards the shore to see if there was any chance of escaping, knowing that if he did try to make a run for it once on land it would be impossible for Tucker to hit him from the boat, the way she was tossing about. Given the man's attitude towards him all along, though, he wondered if he would shoot him anyway, but even if he did manage to escape, and Harvey were to come after him, it was unlikely that he would be able to outrun him in his present condition, which was much worse than when he had tried that other time. There was not much point thinking about it now though, because his glimpse towards the shore showed him that someone, presumably Bradley, was already there, waiting for his arrival, so there was no chance to escape anyway.

CHAPTER 34

Diana would not have seen the *Brandy X* plowing her way up the bay that afternoon because she was, at the time, taking a shower and washing her hair in readiness for the fundraising dinner at the Lillacray mansion. For herself, she would not mind missing the whole affair; she was only going as a companion for her father, whose political life was always so very active. Besides, she had already met Governor Brigham on several occasions, and had a profound dislike for the man.

She could already visualize the evening: Brigham, wearing a fixed smile, taking chummy grasps of shoulders here, giving hearty handshakes there, his eyes all the while flickering around the room, searching out the more politically- and financially-advantageous guests to be greeted. Then there would be all the political hangers-on, jockeying for position, while others gathered in small klatches in darkened corners, making secret deals the public would never hear about unless they somehow went sour.

She had listened to the hurricane reports earlier in the day, but had been comforted by the last one she had heard, which was predicting that it would most likely be heading out to sea. With this in mind, she had gone ahead with her plan to get herself ready for the Lillacray event before driving to the airport to pick up her father. She would then bring him back to the house, where he could make a quick change into his tux, and, with a bit of luck, he might not miss much of the fundraiser after all.

She blow-dried her hair, increasingly concerned that the problem that had been troubling him recently must be particularly serious to have led him to run the risk of missing such a politically and socially important event as this.

She put on her dove-grey dress, stopping as she put on her lip gloss to think of the last time she had worn it. She had worn her funky earrings that time too. Finn had always liked them, but now they were locked away in a small jewel box at the back of a drawer; she would never be able to wear them again. Tears came, and she brushed them away. How long would it ever take, before she could think of Finn without sadness and regret for what might have been? She stood in front of the big oval mirror in the living room, and could see him sitting there with his amiable grin and the big hole in his shoe, and felt lonely, the house, silent and empty.

When she was ready, she turned off all the lights except the small lamp in the living room, shut the front door behind her, and set out to fetch her father.

CHAPTER 35

Finn clambered out of the dinghy, struggling to keep his balance on the slippery stones, a problem made even more difficult, not only because he had not walked on solid ground for so long now, but also because his hands were tied behind his back. He looked up. The man was coming towards them, wearing a ski mask and waving a revolver in the air.

"Okay guys, phase one completed." It was Bradley, and he came down to the water's edge, pointing the gun at Finn. "You. Get over there, beyond that rock over there."

Finn looked about him and recognized now where he was. He was in Bass Cove, the little beach where he and Diana had first made love, and he stopped, a huge wave of sadness washing over him. If only she knew what was happening to him now in their secret cove! Now it had nothing to redeem it at all. Mean, choppy waves bit at the rock-strewn shore, all color absorbed by the rolling mass of slate-grey clouds threatening from above.

He felt Bradley's gun prodding him in his back. "Come on, Westlake, move it, will you? *Now*! I said." His voice was shrill with agitation.

Finn began picking his way over the sharp rocks and broken seashells. They cut into his bare feet like razor blades, and it took all his strength and concentration not to trip and fall over. What was it Diana had said about this place? That she loved it for its tranquility and peace? If tension could be translated into decibels now, every last rock would be screaming.

"Over here," Bradley was yelling at him. "Move it! I haven't got all day."

When they reached the rock, Bradley motioned him to sit down behind it, where he could not be seen by anyone entering the cove from the dirt road. Harvey joined them.

"Right. This part's over at least." Bradley looked at his watch. "And we're in plenty of time. Getting dark already, though. Hope this damn hurricane isn't going to screw everything up."

"It's the boat I'm worried about right now, Tiger. The bottom's mighty shaley out there, and she's sure as hell going to drag her anchor over it if we don't get her out of this place in the next few minutes, with the sea building up like this, and nothing for the Danforth to dig into. Those rocks are way too close already too, and it's gotten even wilder just in the time we've been here as well. Not sure she'll take it back out there in the bay either, if those seas get any rougher. Can't even hear the Devil's Candlestick bell buoy anymore over the roar of it all."

Finn looked down, his hands growing numb behind his back, his stomach aching with hunger and lingering nausea.

"I knew it!" Harvey, shouting above the noise of the storm, pointed towards the *Brandy X*. "She's dragging her anchor! She'll be up on those rocks if Tucker doesn't stop her. What the hell's he doing? What's going on?" He started running down the beach, slipping and tripping over the wet and slimy surface. "Damned engine! Gotta go," he yelled back at Bradley.

"No! I need you to help with Westlake here first."

But Harvey was already in the dinghy, struggling to get back to the *Brandy X* through the cove's now churning water.

Finn looked up at Bradley. "You keep waving that gun around like that, you're going to end up killing me anyway. Karma, wouldn't you say?" He then watched as Bradley tested the strength of the old Army-Corps-of-Engineers' ring set in the rock, his hope of ever getting out of this alive, vanishing. He knew that ring, of course; he had tested it himself that day. It would never give way if Bradley handcuffed him to it, and already, in the short time they had been here, the tide had advanced several feet, so if Bradley did shackle him to it, and something went wrong, and he was left there, his death would come by drowning after all.

His shoulders sagged. Being drowned, or being shot, what did it matter now? Either way, he would soon be dead, regardless of the manner in which his end came.

Bradley was yelling at him. "Get up I said."

Finn began to push himself up, his back

against the rock. He was stiff and wet, his leg muscles weak from lack of exercise, his hands aching with cold.

"Hurry up. Don't take all day."

Once standing, Bradley handed him a key attached to a long loop of string, tied to his belt. "You try anything, and I'll shoot you in the foot. Now, undo that right cuff."

His hands behind his back, and forced to feel, rather than see what he was doing, Finn fumbled to undo it, his hands so cold he could scarcely keep hold of the key, let alone manipulate it in the keyhole, but at last it was done, and Bradley snatched it from him.

"Now slip that cuff through that ring there and snap it shut. Now! Do it!" He pointed the gun at Finn's feet. "Hurry! Damn you, Westlake! Don't stand there looking at me like that! Do it, I said!"

When Finn still stood there, he clouted him with the gun butt, knocking him backwards against the rock, then used the opportunity to grab hold of the loose cuff himself, and snap it into the ring.

"Okay, now stay there."

Where did Bradley think he was going? Handcuffed to that ring, he was going nowhere, and hidden behind the rock, he could see nothing of what might be happening up on the beach either, nor could he hear anything above the roar of the now hurricane-force wind.

CHAPTER 36

It was a little over thirty minutes before Diana's car was parked in the short-term parking lot at the airport. Her father's plane was almost due, and after locking the Mercedes, she went into the big concourse to await its arrival. Feeling a little ridiculous in her formal party-dress, she wandered around the bookstall for a few minutes, then glanced up at the screen where take-offs and arrivals were listed. Right next to her father's flight from DC, it said, 'CANCELLED'.

She scanned the other flights, but the next possible time of arrival for him would mean another hour's wait, not long enough to drive home, then come back. The only thing to do was to find somewhere to sit and be patient. As for the fund-raising dinner, well, they most likely would not get there now until it was nearly over. She found a vacant seat, and sat down.

The minutes passed as various flight arrivals were announced, and she watched the passengers emerge to be hugged and kissed by eager relatives clustered around the exit doors.

It was a long wait, and she wondered again what sort of business urgency it was that had led to father finding it necessary to go to DC on this particular day, and risk missing an important political event such as tonight's fundraiser. As she had been surmising all along, it had to be something to do with one of the many deals he was always negotiating, but, as the most he had been willing to say to her about it was that it was nothing he couldn't handle, she simply had to leave it at that, and hope that his mission to DC had been successful.

She gave up thinking about it, and looked again at the overhead screen, where the arrival of the next possible flight for him had just been announced, and she watched from her seat, waiting for him to appear.

A short time later the passengers began emerging, a small trickle at first, followed by the main body, and she stood up, raising herself on her toes to try to see over the heads of the waiting crowd, which dwindled until all the passengers had come and gone, leaving no-one. It was the last flight in or out that night because of the weather. All the screen showed now were cancellations.

She looked around, expecting to see him walking up to her from some other quarter, but there was no sign of him. Maybe she had made a mistake; maybe he had caught an earlier flight, and taken a taxi home. They could even have passed each other on the bridge.

She tried phoning him, but his phone was switched off, and for a few minutes she lingered in the concourse, not sure what to do next. There was no point in staying at the airport any longer, though, as there were no more planes to meet, so she went back to the car. There was nothing else to do but go home.

CHAPTER 37

There was a small rock right next to Finn, and he stood on it, allowing him to peer over the top of the big, flat one to which he was attached. He peered out into the gloom, barely able to distinguish Tucker and Harvey clambering around on board the *Brandy X*.

She was pitching badly now, and had to be bottoming out on the shale. She was also much closer to the rocks than when they had first put the anchor down. There was no sound of her engine either; it was either being drowned out by the roar of the wind and the waves, or had failed somehow. Given how close she was to the rocks, he guessed it was the engine, in which case it would not be long before she was smashed to bits, throwing her crew into what was now a maelstrom.

Given his own situation, he found it odd that he was even bothering to think about what might happen to Harvey and Tucker, and turned away, glancing in the other direction. Bradley was standing at the water's edge, also looking out at the foundering

Brandy X. He followed his gaze. She was even closer to the rocks now, and certainly past the point where they would be able to extricate her and get her out of the cove, and even if they could, there was little hope of their making it safely back to Brickton harbor now. Although barely visible in the increasing murkiness and the fog of spray thrown up by the breakers beyond the cove, the white caps flying atop the heaving sea out there told him that that was a situation in which a small boat like the *Brandy X* could never survive even if she did manage to get out of the cove, and he stood down from his little rock.

At first, he had hoped that, left alone with Bradley, he might have a better chance of escaping, although that no longer seemed possible. If Bradley could see the situation becoming too risky for him, his only option would be to forget about the ransom money altogether, and leave him to drown. It would be the only safe thing for him to do. Thus far, no-one, apart from Harvey and Tucker, knew of his part in all this, and he would not be able to say anything without implicating himself, so could still safely walk away from the ransom deal if it became too dangerous for him to go ahead with it.

Finn stood on the little rock again, and looked around, but saw nothing anywhere to raise his spirits. The sky, an eerie shade of greenish black, loomed over him like the vault of a dank cavern, and the rain that had started to spatter in his face a few minutes earlier, was now whipping at him in a steady, crosswise downpour. He cupped his free hand above his eyes, and peered out towards the *Brandy X*. She was nothing more now than a dark blur, almost merging with the rocks, and it had to be only minutes before she crashed into them.

He was turning to look back towards the shore again, when he caught sight of another dark image, this one in the surf, not far away. It was the dinghy, and, at first, he assumed it had broken free, but then, as it came nearer, he could make out someone struggling to row it towards him, and he wondered who it was, Harvey, or Tucker. Whichever it was, he was having great trouble keeping it afloat, the waves constantly splashing over the gunwales, threatening to flood it. He strained to see, peering at it, but still could not tell who it was.

He wiped his eyes. The rain was so heavy now, beating straight into his face, he had trouble keeping them open, and when he looked again, the dinghy had disappeared, and whoever it was who had been in it, was floundering towards him, up to his chest, the breaking surf first hurling him towards the shore, then sucking him backwards when it receded. At the same time, he was struggling to hold one hand high above his head, where the waves could not reach it, as though trying to protect something he was carrying.

Finn closed his eyes. The object being held in the air had to be Harvey's gun, and the man holding it, Harvey. For whatever reason, the ransom deal was off, and he was going to be killed, right here, right now. He took a deep breath, and waited for the end, but when no shot came, opened his eyes again to see that it was Tucker, not Harvey, and he was near enough now to hear what he was shouting at him.

"…key… handcuffs…"

Finn glanced over to see where Bradley was. He was standing close by, at the water's edge. Feet apart, arms straight out in front of him, he was bracing himself, his gun held steady by both hands like a marksman, and aimed directly at Tucker.

"Watch out Gus! Ben's…"

There was a sharp report as the gun went off, and Tucker, now barely a few feet in front of him, staggered and fell face down into the churning surf; and Finn recoiled as his limp body, spread-eagled on the surface, began slowly undulating with the rise and fall of the waves. The next wave pushed it onto the shale at his feet, where it lingered for a few seconds, before being lifted again by the next, and dragged back again into the surf.

He looked away. Bradley was hurrying back up towards where the path met the beach.

CHAPTER 38

Diana stood in the middle of the living room; it seemed the safest place to be. She was frightened now. Ever since she had arrived home, the wind had been buffeting the house, hurling at it torrents of rain, which cascaded down the window panes. Their old frames sucked and gurgled, and water was trickling over the sills and down the inside walls. A short while before, she had cupped her hands to the panes, and peered outside. She had never seen the waters of the bay like this before. Great, white-capped rollers were thundering straight up along the shore, not gently towards the beach as the waves normally did, and as they roared past the house, they obliterated both beach and a large section of the lawn. The *Moonglow* was already gone, and she had watched as the dock, appearing and disappearing as the waves rolled over it, had slowly leaned over, sliding sideways, the huge pilings wrenched up by the careening breakers. Then, like pieces from a child's set of building blocks, the whole dock had suddenly split apart, the great timbers flying like matchsticks into the air, to be swallowed up by the darkness.

That was when she had retreated to the center of the living room, scared of the sea's cataclysmic power and of where it would attack next.

She looked at the French ormolu clock on the mantelpiece, its sharp bell piercing the roar of the storm. At that moment, a stunning blast of howling air slammed into the house, which shuddered, and all the lights went out.

She began to make her way out of the living room, bumping into chairs in her panic, and crying out when she cracked her shins against the low, glass coffee table, terrified that at any second, another gust of wind would tear the roof from the house, or bring the waves surging in over the porch. She stood for a moment, rubbing her leg and willing herself to remain calm, while taking cautious steps towards the door in the dark, but almost immediately, something crashed through a window behind her, and hurtled across the room, smashing into the big oval mirror above the fireplace. It shattered, the pieces crashing to the floor. Then, before she could recover from this shock, the living room door, barely inches away, and blown by the sudden inrush of air from the broken window, slammed shut in her face.

She grabbed hold of the handle and tugged at it, her cries drowned by the blasting of the wind and rain through the gaping window frame. The sodden drapes stretched out into the room, flapping and snapping like evil black witches struggling to grasp hold of, and envelop her, and she hurried into the hallway, using all her strength first to open the door, then to hold it open. As soon as she had gone through it, it slammed shut behind her, making the walls shudder.

Once in what she hoped was the greater security of the hallway, she stood for a few seconds, trying to calm herself and adjust her eyes to the darkness there, but knowing now that she would have to leave the house and go out into the storm to reach higher ground, her home no longer a sanctuary.

She groped her way towards the hall closet, feeling more lonely and vulnerable than ever before, and, reaching up, passed her hand over the shelf above the coat rack, all the time crying to herself, "Oh, please let it be here! Please!" but found only gloves, a scarf and her father's fishing hat. Behind her, the living-room door rattled and shook under the pressure of the wind behind it. She dropped down onto her knees and felt around the closet floor, but here all she could find were her father's boots. Then, in the corner her hand touched what she was searching for -- the high-intensity camping-lamp.

She fumbled for the switch, her fingers shaking so much she could not even find it at first. Then it seemed it was either stuck or the batteries had gone flat, because it refused to light, but when she shook it, it finally came on, and its stark light cast a cold harsh glare on the hallway, creating leaping black demons of the shadows as it swung in her hand. Even so, it afforded her some semblance of security, removing as it did that primitive fear of total darkness, and she headed for the front door, fearing at any second that the sea would wash both house and her into the bay.

She pulled open the front door, and hesitated, knowing that the only possible shelter would be the tiny studio up by the road, and to get there, she would have to face the wind, the rain, falling trees and chunks of debris flying through the air as lethal missiles – and there was no guarantee even that it would still be there if and when she arrived. It was a risk she was going to have to take.

CHAPTER 39

Ever since Bradley had turned his back on him, walking away from the murder he had just committed, Finn, now in a dark fog of spray, had seen nothing at all. He had heard nothing either, except for the ever-increasing roar of the wind and crashing tide, which had risen until the water was breaking against his knees, bringing with it Tucker's corpse, and causing him to retch painfully, his empty stomach no longer having anything to offer.

He had wondered all along if the big man would be able to go through with the ransom, and now he had given his own life trying to save his, killed by his friend! How could a man like Bradley appear so charming and charismatic, yet be so evil? And Diana? If she had indeed been dating him as he claimed, surely she must have sensed something sinister beneath that handsome exterior. He gave a sardonic laugh. What did any of it matter now? He himself was going to die, probably within the hour, and here he was, agonizing over Diana. Did other people, facing death, entertain such totally irrelevant thoughts too?

The minutes went by with still no sign of Bradley or Devine, and the water continued to rise until it was almost up to his waist, the bigger waves now washing right over his head. Tucker's body surged into his chest, and, retching yet again, he reached out with his free hand to push it away. And still no-one came. Maybe something had happened to Bradley, and in that case, the best solution for Devine would be to simply leave him to drown.

His ears picked out the roar of a tidal surge. It was even louder than the hurricane, and he turned his back to the sea, bracing himself against the rock, taking in a deep breath, waiting for the impact. The immense breaker slammed into him, then retreated, lifting him off his feet, twisting his body, and dragging him backwards with such violence that it wrenched his arm out of its socket. His body went rigid with the pain, and he closed his eyes. When he opened them again, Tucker's body had vanished.

Certain now that he had been left to drown, and desperate to save his life, he tried to free himself, regardless of how much it hurt, and pulled against the iron ring, his cries lost in the wind, but it was secure, as was the chain. He thought of gruesome tales of men who had hacked off a foot or a hand to save themselves in similar circumstances, but he had nothing with which to do even that, and, his body twisting and turning in the rising surf, he gave up.

Although it made no difference now, he went over in his mind the time since Harvey had nearly killed him that morning when they had gone out to the bridge together. Had he in any way been soft? Had he ignored chances to escape, or, since then, failed to plan one properly? Had he allowed himself to be led to this, without doing enough to stop it?

While the waves continued to break over his head, his mind scanned the last weeks of his capture, looking for some hidden weakness on his part. Had he faced everything *that* passively? Cursing himself now he was facing death, he berated himself for having allowed this to happen to him, refusing to concede that, for the first weeks, he had been physically incapable of escaping, or of putting up any sort of fight, and after that, it had always been two or three with a gun against him. He ignored all his efforts to build up his strength and his futile attempts to escape, and gave himself no credit for the reality of the last few weeks in which exercise was impossible, and he condemned himself for what had happened to him.

He had no use for weak, gutless men, and was still allowing himself no excuses, when he noticed three strong shafts of light shining out over the surf. Two were stationary, the other moving back and forth over the water, as though searching for something.

His foot found his small rock again, and when he stood on it, he could see that the two stationary lights were headlights; the third, hand-held up on dry land, was trained on a man struggling to reach him through the surf, presumably prevented from being washed away by being attached by rope to something on land. The beam of the flashlight coming from the shore proved that there had to be at least one other person with this man, but how many more might be hidden there, waiting to make sure he would not succeed if he tried to escape?

CHAPTER 40

The wind knocked Diana down almost at once, and she grasped at some branches with one hand, holding high the precious source of light with the other. Whimpering and drenched, her sodden dress clinging to her knees, she half crawled, half pulled herself up the lawn. Not far ahead there was a long-drawn-out, agonized groan as the great roots of one of the tall trees bordering the driveway, gave up and lost their hold on the earth, bringing it crashing down. Flying twigs lashed her face like whips, and she hung onto the old blueberry bushes, a tenuous hold that barely prevented her from being carried away along with the twigs.

Knees raw, her dress ripped, it took her over a half hour to reach the door of the still-standing studio, and it was several more minutes before she was able to release the catch. Then it flew open, the sudden rush of air sending old bits of paper and cardboard whirling round the room. Once inside she strained to shut it again, leaning hard against it until the latch finally caught and held.

She stood there for a few moments, recovering her breath and welcoming the solid comfort of the sturdy walls and the relief of having made it this far with no injuries apart from some scratches caused by flying twigs. She put the lamp down on the table and looked about her. Compared with the house at least, the danger here was minimal. The wide avenue of tall trees, about a hundred feet away on the windward side, and their broad undergrowth of evergreens shielded the studio from the full blast of the storm, as did the stand of big rhododendrons almost encircling it, and it would take an immense tidal surge for the waves to reach this far.

She slumped down onto the wooden chair. It was where Finn had been sitting that day when they had been looking for some snorkeling equipment, the dreadful day he thought he had found something wrong with the bridge. She put the flat of her hand on the table, touching the place where his head had rested that morning, then kissed the spot, but Finn was long-since gone.

After a while she switched off the lamp to conserve the batteries, and from then on sat, shivering in her wet clothes and the increasing darkness howling about her, flinching when twigs and branches, hurled against the windows, threatened to shatter them.

Once, she got up to look outside, and, after wiping one of the dusty panes with a piece of old newspaper, cupped her hands against it, peering out into the darkness. The hurricane was still at its height, and it would not be safe for her to leave the safety of the studio until the dead-calm eye of the storm arrived.

Only then could she make her way back to the house, assuming it was still there.

Maybe she would not have to wait too long for the wind to abate, and, sitting back down on the wooden chair, she rested her head on the table, just as Finn had done that morning, and waited, exhausted, wondering if her father too had become caught up in the hurricane. She was not too worried about him though; he had probably been forced to stay in DC until planes to Davenport started flying again. She did wish he had phoned to let her know, though. Maybe he had tried, but there was no connection because of the storm. She dozed off, then shrieked, sending the old wooden chair flying backwards when the door suddenly flew open, showering her with a hail of flying leaves, twigs and raindrops. In its wake was Bradley, and he was clutching a briefcase and a heavy-duty flashlight.

"Ben!"

He stood there, hesitating momentarily as though uncertain what to do next. "*Diana*! What on earth are you doing in here?"

"Oh Ben! You frightened the life out of me, and I could ask the same thing of you: what are *you* doing here? Well, don't just stand there. Come on in, and for goodness sake shut the door, or it'll soon be as bad in here as it is outside." She switched on her own lantern, and watched as he put the briefcase down on the floor.

"You told me you were going out fishing today, and I've been thinking about you out there in this. What happened? I don't understand. Where have you come from now, and how did you get here? And why here to the studio? Oh no! Don't tell me you went down to the house, and it's been washed away!"

"Diana! You've no idea how glad I am to have found you, my love. I... I've been so worried about you. I... had to make sure you were alright, and... and... I was on my way down to the house to look for you, but it was so dangerous, with falling trees and all, I thought to take refuge here till it calmed down a bit."

"You came all the way over from the mainland in this to check on me?"

"Yes, well... You know how much I love you, my darling. How could I possibly *not* come to see if you were alright?"

Diana pointed to the briefcase. "What have you got in there then? Don't tell me you've even thought to bring me a thermos of wonderfully hot tea as well!"

"Uh... no. I'm afraid I didn't think of that. Sorry. No. It's like this." He perched himself on the edge of the table. "As you can imagine, although we did go out fishing, when we heard the hurricane warning, we hightailed it back to Brickton, and... and... because I was going to be driving back up to Davenport to my uncle's, one of my friends asked me to do a favor for him, and hand deliver some very important documents to him. Then... then... it was while I was driving back up there that I decided to make a detour and come over here first to see if you were alright... Anyway, that's what's in the briefcase, and I brought it in here with me because I was afraid to leave it out in the car, which I left parked up on the road. So, you see, nothing so exciting as a thermos of hot tea, I'm sorry. Anyway…"

Diana held up her hand. "Just a minute, Ben. Before you go any further, why don't you take off your slicker? It's soaking, and you'll be much more comfortable without it."

"Well my darling, what I was just about to say is that I'm sorry, but this has to be a very short visit. I, uh, just wanted to check you're alright, but I'm afraid it's not possible for me to stay with you, much as I'd like to." He stood up, picked up the briefcase, and patted it. "I promised to get these documents delivered to Governor Brigham tonight. He was very insistent, so I can't let him down. You understand, don't you, my love?" He bent over to kiss her, dripping water over her.

"But you can't possibly leave right now, Ben! You could get killed! I'm amazed you've even made it this far! Wait at least until we get into the calm eye of the hurricane. Those documents can't be *that* important, surely! No-one can possibly expect you to deliver anything in this!"

Bradley shook his head, switched on his flashlight, and grabbed hold of the door latch. "No. I'm sorry, Diana, but I really do have to go. I must get back to the mainland tonight, but as soon as I get these things delivered, I'll come back to be with you, okay?"

Diana put her hands to her head, shaking it. "I still can't believe you're doing this, Ben. It's absolutely crazy. It's just as dangerous as when you got here, and you're expecting to drive over the bridge in this too!"

"Don't worry, my darling. I'll be fine. You take care now too, okay?" He lifted the latch; the door flew open, and he disappeared out into the storm.

Diana shut the door, and sat down again at the table, still shaking her head in disbelief. "That man just has to be crazy," she said to herself, and began thinking yet again about Bradley's reaction to her failed attempt to end their relationship that day. It had not only startled her; it had frightened her, especially as he had continued since then to behave as though it had never taken place. Surely he could not be so much in love with her that he felt he could not go on living without her. He did come all the way over from the mainland through the storm tonight to check to see if she was alright, though, which had to mean something, even though, looking at his brief visit in retrospect, his words and actions had sounded uncharacteristically awkward, as though he had been caught unawares, and, without a set script from which to quote, was having to adlib for a change.

It was not as though he normally behaved towards her either in such a way that would give her the impression that he was really *that* much in love with her, his dramatic outburst that day seeming to be just that, drama, and when she had called Janice afterwards to tell her about his reaction, although she had never met Ben, she had been blunt, accusing him of emotional blackmail and of being melodramatic, and encouraged her to be firm and end the relationship as soon as possible.

Since then, however, the appropriate moment in which to do this had not arisen, and tonight certainly was not it, and she sighed, folded her arms on the table, and, resting her head on them, waited for the brief respite the eye of the hurricane would offer.

CHAPTER 41

The man pushed Finn into the front passenger seat of a luxury sedan, and slammed the door on him, before climbing into the driver's seat.

"Okay, boss! Mission accomplished!"

"Yeah, and a right mess he's making of my Beamer too. We should've brought the pickup, and dumped him in the back. He stinks." There was a snort of disgust, and Finn felt the barrel of a revolver being shoved into the back of his neck. "This piece of garbage sure ain't worth messing up my car for."

Finn sat there, eyes closed, shivering with cold and shock, and wondering why he had not already been killed. His hands, once more behind his back, added to the agonizing pain in his shoulder, and he hunched forward to take the pressure off it. In response, he received another sharp prod in the neck, and he stifled a gasp, determined not to give this Rollo Devine any more satisfaction than he was sure he was already enjoying – determined too to concentrate his mind on a way to escape, and not to simply give up and dwell on the horror of what faced him if he failed.

For a while they drove in silence, making their way down the muddy track towards the road. It had become a quagmire, and the car slithered from side to side, the driver fighting to keep it moving forward. Once they reached the hard surface, the high wall of dense scrub afforded some protection from the hurricane-force winds, but the wipers were almost useless against the solid sheet of water hitting the windshield. Inside the car, the moisture-laden air condensed against the windows, steaming them up and slowing their progress even further.

Devine leaned forward, and Finn could feel his breath against his cheek. "Well now, Westlake, it's good to meet you at last. Too bad our visit will be a brief one. You should've taken McGuire's advice that night."

"As you, above all people, should know, Devine, if you think you're driving back home to the mainland over that bridge in this, you're crazy; you'll be lucky if it's even still there."

"I'm not interested in your opinion, so you can keep your mouth shut. First of all, I…"

"Think of all those exposed rods in the pilings, Devine, all that rotten cement breaking apart under the pressure of this wind and tide thundering against those piers, tearing them apart, everything caving in. Heh! Maybe even while we're half way over it, taking us with it. That would take care of all of us nicely, wouldn't it? But no, my bet is that it's a gonner already. Then what are you going to do with me, eh? Stuck here on the island? Think about that. Not going to be so easy to get rid of me then, is it? It's not like I'm some dead cat you can simply throw in the bushes without anyone noticing. What will you do? Knock on someone's door and ask to borrow a shovel so you can bury me in their front yard? Of course, you could always stuff my corpse in the trunk, but then, with no way to get back to the mainland, I'm going to get pretty stinky, aren't I?"

"Shut your mouth, I said."

"Just creating the upcoming scenario for you, Devine, that's all." Finn looked at the driver out of the corner of his eye. All his attention was concentrated on the road. They were driving right into the wind now, and the wild gusts caused the car to alternately surge forward, then slow down, interfering with his pressure on the gas pedal, and making it veer from one side of the road to the other. Several times they found themselves driving axle deep through streams rushing across it, and once or twice, the engine faltered too, threatening to stall.

After another period of silence, Finn could see the entrance to the driveway leading to the Lillacray estate not far ahead. It was in darkness, with no sign of any fundraiser party taking place. Guests had obviously done the wise thing, and either stayed at home, or headed back there early.

Devine instructed the driver to turn left, and they drove along a road heading in the direction of the bridge, but which, as Finn already knew, would not actually take them to it; they were on the wrong road. He said nothing; the longer they remained on the island, the greater chance he had of finding a way to escape.

Devine prodded his driver on the shoulder. "I

can see the bridge lights, Stan. Can't be too far now."
He gave Finn a prod too. "See Westlake. Got it wrong,
didn't you? The bridge *is* still there"

Finn felt Devine's body pressing against the
back of his seat. "Have fun, do you, Devine, playing
with people's lives? Gives you a buzz of excitement
and a warped delight in your power over them, does
it? You're nothing but a greedy, amoral, self-serving,
unprincipled crook, not to mention upcoming
murderer, who doesn't give a damn about other
people's lives. Yes, a cheap thug, that's what you
really are, and chances are you'll get what you deserve
in the end."

"Who cares what you think, Westlake? I sure
don't. Besides, everyone's crooked in their own way. I
know; I see 'em in action every day. All I do is make
sure I get my share. No-one pulls a fast one on Rollo
Devine either. No sir! And no-one gets away with
even trying. Huh! Let me tell you a thing or two,
college boy. You don't know nothing! You think your
generous host, Mr. Bigwig Chester McGuire, the big
fish in a kids' paddling pool, is on the up and up?" He
gave a triumphant cackle. "You're deluded, kid, and as
you already know what I intend to do with you, so
won't be around to tell tales, it doesn't matter what I
let you in on, so let me enlighten you."

Finn felt him change position behind him, but
the gun was still against his neck.

"So, as I said, let me enlighten you. McGuire
and I go back quite a way. Yes sir. Quite a way, and
he doesn't even know I know *all* about him, and where
he's come up from. Everything! I don't have friends in
the right place for nothing, and when he blew into

town way back when, I was told to watch out for him. McGuire isn't even his real name. Huh! You didn't know that, did you, college boy? No, his real name is Dwayne Sanderson, and he did time in Oregon for defrauding some people of their life savings in some pyramid scheme involving check kiting."

Finn shifted in his seat, trying to ease the pain in his shoulder. "Figures then that the two of you are buddies – birds of a feather, and all that."

"Yeah, well, people like him have the gift of the gab, and can turn on the charm, and that's what makes him capable of gaining people's confidence and trust. It also makes him useful to people like me. He's worked hard on ingratiating himself with people in authority, so he can use his influence with them to do what you might call 'favors' for his friends. He manages to stay on the right side of the law now, though… just." Devine laughed. "Yep. A right old bullshit artist is our McGuire. I bet he told you all about his great wealth, and I bet you believed him, like everyone else does. He even boasts about being a graduate of Harvard Business School! In actual fact, he never made it past eighth grade! And the properties he does own, if you don't count what he owes the bank: the one in Florida, and the lumber mill; they were inherited by his wife, and both of them he's used as collateral for big loans. I have to say I really get a kick out of it, though, when I hear him giving his spiel to people, knowing he hasn't any idea that I know it's all a load of bull."

"There's only one thing at all that interests me here: does Diana know all this about her father?"

"His daughter? Naah. What he did was before

he was even married. His wife was a local girl, who fell for his charms not long after he got here, and married him. She came from a wealthy family, and never knew anything about his past. Her father gave them quite a handsome sum as a wedding present too – another sucker to his charms. No, I think that daughter of his is probably the only human being he genuinely cares about, and I know for a fact, he keeps her well shielded from anything he thinks might cause her any harm.

"Anyway, as I was saying: take that heap on the waterfront there that he's so proud of -- that mansion of his? Well, it isn't his at all; it's mine. Yup, mine. Technically, I sold him that place not long after he came here – a cosy deal between him and me, no awkward paperwork involved, except for the deeds, that is. They say it's his estate, but we both know that in reality, it still belongs to me. The deal between us, see, was that I gave him a no-down-payment, one-percent mortgage on that property, so he pays me peanuts every month for it, in return for which he uses his influence with the state to get me the cream of their contracts. It worked well too, until you came on the scene, that is, and stupidly decided to do your public duty, and raise everyone's consciousness about the state of the bridge piers. I think that's what they like to call it anyway: 'raising consciousness'. I call it sticking your nose into other people's business.

"When McGuire as he called himself turned up here, he was borderline broke; couldn't afford anything, not even a down payment. Couldn't have afforded a real mortgage through a bank neither, and spent the bit he did manage to scrounge on impressing everyone. I recognized his talents, though, and the useful connections he'd built with state, so that's why I was willing to make that hand-shake deal between the two of us."

Finn shifted his hands behind his back. He expected Devine to react, but although he still held the gun to his neck, he seemed not to have noticed.

"Yeah. So, as I said, the deal was that in exchange for that token mortgage interest, he'd use his blarney and his influence to make sure I got as many of the nice fat state contracts as possible -- you know, public housing, bridge maintenance and repairs, etcetera -- anything that the state wants built or fixed using taxpayer money. That sort of thing."

Sensing that Devine's attention was now on regaling him with the details of his relationship with McGuire, Finn used the opportunity to move again, then every time the car surged forward, or came to a sudden stop, he inched his hands further under him, working the chain under his buttocks until it was under his knees, each move of his shoulder requiring him to hold his breath to stop himself from crying out.

"It's worked well for both of us for a good many years now," Devine continued. "I scratch his back; he-scratches-mine type of deal. Then, as I said, you had to breeze into town and stick your nose in where it wasn't wanted.

"I'll have you know too that when McGuire phoned me that night, telling me what you'd found, I went to great lengths to impress on him that, however he went about it, he had to stop you from going to the authorities. I even had to exert a bit of pressure on him, and remind him where his loyalties lay, you might say, so as to get my message across.

"Too bad he crossed me like that anyway by going against what I told him he had to do, and let you go ahead, 'cos the result, as far as I'm concerned, is that you can blame him for what's about to happen to you. As I said, no-one gets away with crossing old Rollo Devine here. It was McGuire's fault, and if he thought he was going to get away with it, he had another thing coming. Oh yes indeed!" He tittered. "Too bad for him that the guy he chose to go down with you the next morning, just happened to be one of my own men, and he twigged right away that your story about going after fish was a load of bull, and that what you really were after was a look at those piers; so, when he called me to say you were on the phone, asking him to be your diving buddy the next day, I told him to say 'yes', but to make sure you never made it back to land.

Devine sighed. "Then it looked like the problem had gone away, when he called me later to say you'd never turned up for him after all that morning. We assumed then that you'd had a change of heart and conveniently scarpered, but then, out of the blue, I get this ransom note, demanding a heap of money in exchange for you, alive, and at that point I made sure it wasn't me, but McGuire who was going to pay it. So, as I said, you can thank him."

All the time Devine was talking, Finn concentrated on trying to get his hands to the front of him. The length of the chain made this possible, but what he found almost impossible was to bear in silence the excruciating pain every time he moved. Thus far, he was lucky, as neither man paid any attention to his movements, the driver staring into the darkness, concentrating on the road, Devine too busy venting his wrath on McGuire. He even gave Finn the impression that he was relieved to get it all off his chest, using him as a father confessor who would be conveniently buried along with all he had told him.

He poked Finn in the neck again. "Well, don't you want to know how I'm gonna be getting the money from him to pay for you? No? Well, I'm gonna tell you anyway. I sent him a letter calling in the mortgage. Yup, that's what I did... the whole mortgage! And that property, located as it is on the shore of the most desirable bit of real estate in the state, don't come cheap, I can tell you." He laughed. "O boy! I never ain't seen a guy grovel like old McGuire there. Well, yes, I have, several times in fact, but this was different; he's a pompous old fool. He kept calling me back the evening he received that letter, and it was fun listening to him begging me not to ruin him, but ruin him I have. Boy! Have I ever! Bankrupt. That's what he'll be now, and without that fancy home of his, all his cronies will see the emperor really ain't got no clothes, not a rag to his name, and they'll drop him like a hot potato. Yup, those so-called friends of his only stick to him 'cos of what he can do for them, and because they believe he's the high-society gent he's painted himself to be, and without either of those assets to recommend him, he'll be of no interest to anyone. Come to think of it, it was a good excuse to call in that mortgage anyhow. I've got the state in the palm of my hand now anyway, so don't need him anymore -- can get my own contracts, so I guess you can say I've got the best of both worlds."

The chain was almost behind Finn's knees now, making him lean quite far forward, but with the attentions of both the driver and Devine elsewhere, they still had not noticed what he was doing. Devine, though, appeared now to have come to the end of his confession, and Finn needed to keep him distracted. "How come you're bothering to drive me alive to wherever you plan to bury me? Why didn't you just shoot me, and get it over with?"

Devine gave a chuckle. "Call it vanity. You didn't think I was going to let some upstart young structural engineer with his fancy degree go to his grave thinking that ignorant old country-boy, Rollo Devine here, could so easily be conned, did you? Besides, I figured you'd want to know that that fatherly, genial host of yours ain't nothing more than a social-climbing has-been, in hock to me for everything he 'holds so dear', as you might say.

"As I said, all that man has to his name is that lumber mill up in Maine, and that pad in Sarasota that he inherited from his wife, and the bank's got them as collateral. I'm the only one that knows that. He loves to give the impression that he owns some fancy offshore property as well, complete with fancy income to match his fancy home, and all those posh cronies of his go for it, of course. Now that he's got to come up with the cash to pay me what he owes on that property, though, he'll be bankrupt because he's got nothing left, and all those so-called friends of his will, like I said, abandon him like rats from a sinking ship." He gave another titter. "Can't wait to sit back and watch the stampede. Oh… and in case you're thinking he can go to some lawyer and claim the deeds say it's his, he knows he can't do that, 'cos he also knows what happens to folks who cross me – and it ain't nice. Oh… and also, before you go mentioning that old Stan here is listening in to all this too, I'd like you to know that he and I go back to childhood, and Stan's a whole lot more than my driver." He patted the man on the shoulder again. "We both know where each of us is coming from, and are beholden to each other. Yeah, I guess that's what you'd call it: beholden."

"You needn't have wasted your time telling me all this. I'm not the slightest bit impressed. To me you're still nothing more than a two-bit criminal. No, let me correct that; you are something more, because you get a kick out of what you do to others, which shows you also have a screw loose in that twisted brain of yours. So, you murder me too; what do you get out of that? Another notch on your gun barrel and another buzz of excitement? A cheap thrill?"

"I'll show you what's on my gun barrel, Westlake, your blood." But at that moment the big car bounced into a deep rut, its springs, not meant for driving on country lanes, bottoming out, and the intended blow missed Finn altogether.

"Hell! That was a bad one, Rollo. Are you sure this is the right road. Seems mighty bumpy to me."

"I can still see the lights on the bridge, Stan. They're definitely closer than they were. No, we're fine. Won't be far now. By the way, Finn Westlake, I won't forget what you just said about me, and, as I explained to you, no-one gets away with making a fool of me. Yeah, you're right; I *am* going to kill you, but now you can amuse yourself contemplating what I plan to do to you before I complete the job. And, by the way, I don't know yet who all has been hiding you away all this time, but you can't tell me they haven't let some names slip or shown their faces, so, while I'm at it, you might as well know I intend getting that out of you as well before I finish you off. Happy now, Westlake? You're finished. Heh! Stan! Get that? He's Finn-ished. A good one that, eh?"

"Bit slow off the mark thinking that one up, weren't you, Devine? But then, being a thug and being intelligent are two different things, aren't they? And you don't strike me as being the brightest kid on the block." Finn leaned forward to avoid the expected blow, but it didn't come, Devine being more concerned now about his car, and wincing at each loud clunk as the springs continued to bottom out on the increasingly bumpy road.

Then the road disappeared altogether; they had come to the end, and the driver stopped. Ahead of them the headlights lit up massive, white-crested waves rolling past one of the northern arms of the island, and between them and the bridge not far off to their left, lay an impassable salt marsh.

The hurricane was blowing now in savage gusts that slammed into the side of the car, causing the heavy vehicle to rock violently on this exposed point. The driver backed it up, with several anxious moments as the rear wheels spun in the mud, before turning it around, then driving all the way back along the deserted track, eventually coming to the entrance to the Lillacray estate again, where the road was now almost blocked by the remains of cars, yard furniture, and other debris from the mansion, tossed there by a tidal surge. The driver inched around the accumulated junk, and a few hundred yards further on, the road curved off to their right, and they were once again heading in the direction of the bridge.

"I can't see the bridge anymore, Stan. All the lights have gone out!"

Stan said nothing, and Finn watched him. His face almost touching the windshield, his attention was directed on the road, peering through the curtain of rain, and trying to make his way in the blackness, the headlights now so covered with mud, their light little more than a dim glow.

Devine leaned forward. "I think all the power's out. I can't see any lights anywhere now."

It was impossible to see more than a few yards in front, and because of the continuous build-up of mist on the inside of the windshield, the driver had to keep wiping it with his hand, and was almost half way across the road junction before realizing he had missed the turn-off to the bridge, and was within feet of plowing into a hedge. He swung the car violently to the left at the last moment, and Finn, who was not wearing a seat belt, could not hide a loud gasp when his shoulder slammed into the door.

Now the wind was hitting them broadside again. The gusts came in tremendous surges, causing the car to rock, making steering treacherous. The driver continued to lean well forward, flinching and jerking his head backwards when flying branches whipped against the windshield, then slid away into the night. Twigs and leaves, caught in the wipers, slid back and forth, their constant scraping barely audible above the roaring wind and hammering rain.

There was a bend in the road. The wind was coming at them from behind now, trying to propel the car before it, but being a heavy vehicle, it fared better than any standard-sized car would have done under these circumstances. The driver pushed his glasses up off his nose and wiped his eyes, then leaned forward over the steering wheel again, watching out for fallen trees, and they all flinched when heavy debris smashed against the windshield, threatening to shatter it.

They continued to drive in silence, seeming to make little headway. Then, not far ahead, a faint white light appeared. It was a small sign, reflecting the dim light of the headlights, and shuddering at the top of its slender pole.

Devine's arm shot past Finn's ear, finger pointing. "It's the sign to the bridge. It's pointing to the left. We must be almost at the road junction, and the bridge has to be only a few hundred yards from there."

A large sheet of white plastic flew out of the night and into the windshield, for a moment blocking out everything, before disappearing over the top of the roof. The driver braked instinctively, shooting Finn forward, his head almost hitting the dashboard. As he recovered himself, he slipped his hands down behind his ankles, pulled the chain under his feet, and, all within seconds, his hands were in front of him, the chain, hanging down between his knees, hidden; and although still shivering, he was also soaking in sweat from the agonizing pain in his shoulder.

With his hands now in front of him, there was, for the first time, a real chance to escape. They were getting near to the bridge now, though, so if he were going to get out of the car, it had to be before they reached it.

The driver was no problem, but there was still the gun Devine continued to poke against his neck every now and then. Finn could hear him breathing loudly too, hyperventilating, and the thought suddenly occurred to him that the real reason Devine had not killed him already had to be because it was not a gun after all that he had been poking into him! He leaned his head back gently, until the cold barrel touched his neck, and now that he could feel it properly, realized it felt different, not quite the same shape as the hollow bore of a gun barrel. It felt more solid, like the end of some sort of metal tool. He leaned forward again, and Devine did nothing.

The car was going downhill now, so they had to be nearing the entrance to the bridge. Gun or not, Finn, with nothing to lose now, raised his left arm, and his injured right one as high as it would go, and, letting out a howl of pain, swung the chain over the driver's head, pulled back sharply, and yanked the man's neck towards him.

There was no shot, and although he could hear Devine gasping at him, and felt him trying to hit him with whatever it was he was holding, there was no shot.

The driver, choking and trying without success to steer the car with one hand, tore at the chain with the other, but Finn held on. The car, now out of control, began to speed up, rolling down the hill towards the bridge, and in one quick move, Finn raised the chain back over the driver's head, then released his door catch, allowing the door to fly open.

He looked down. The bridge was very close now, the car heading erratically towards it with no chance of remaining on the road long enough to end up on it.

"By the way, Devine, be sure to read the contents of that envelope you were given along with me; it'll tell you exactly who was holding me all this time."

He fell rather than jumped, landing on his dislocated shoulder on the soft, muddy grass roadside, and the momentum of his fall rolled him over several times before he came to rest in a water-filled ditch. As he came to a stop, a volcanic flame of fire erupted from below the embankment next to the bridge.

He raised his head as another fiery blast lit up the sky, and in its momentary brilliance, he caught a glimpse of the bridge -- the whole center section was a void.

CHAPTER 42

Finn lay in the water in the ditch, in too much pain to appreciate that he was free at last, albeit in the middle of a hurricane, on what appeared to be a deserted island, and he lingered there, too weary to fight the exhaustion overtaking him. The only light from any direction came from Devine's car, which burned with a steady orange glow that gradually faded, then disappeared, leaving him in complete darkness.

Although it was as wet out of the ditch as it was in it, he knew he needed to get moving, and he roused himself sufficiently to clamber up onto his knees, then out onto the grass verge, where he sat down on the edge of the road, cradling his one arm in the other in an attempt to relieve the pain. All about him the wind continued to roar, boosted every now and then by wild gusts that sounded like jet airplanes taking off; the rain deluged him as though coming from a fireman's hose, taking away his breath, and every now and then a loud report, like a gunshot, cut through the general noise -- a tree trunk shattering under the strain.

He almost wished he had stayed in the water in the bottom of the ditch. It had been calmer there, but he did not go back. Instead, he sat on the edge of the road, too tired to even think. His body ached all over, and his shoulder was beyond anything he had ever suffered before, and still remained conscious.

He began to shiver again. Although the night was warm, sitting motionless in the rain was like lying in a swimming pool without swimming, and the cool water was draining away his body heat. He would have to move if only to keep warm. To give in and lie there was a temptation almost too strong to resist, but he was afraid that if he submitted to it, and passed out, he might never wake up, and Devine would have had his revenge after all, even though he could not possibly be alive now to appreciate it.

Finn had spent enough time on the island with Diana to know his way around, and to work out that he was now about a mile away from her home. Would she even be there in this storm? Was she alright? He had to find out, and he pulled himself to his feet, turned away from the bridge, and began heading back towards the T-junction.

He had gone only a short distance when, needing to rest already, he sank down onto the grass verge, head bent, but looked up when he saw the headlights of a car approaching. He staggered to his feet, and went out into the center of the road. The force of the wind made it difficult for him to keep his balance, but he managed to stand there, waiting for the car to slow down, confident that he was clearly visible, the beam from the headlights being strong enough to light up his once-white shirt. Instead of stopping, however, the driver kept up his speed, and, showing no sign of slowing down, merely moved over to the side of the road to avoid hitting him.

Finn tried to back up out of the way, but stumbled and went sprawling right into the path of the car, which swerved at the last moment, missing him by inches.

The car, a large, white, vintage Cadillac, went into an uncontrolled skid, and as Finn scrambled to his feet, he could see it slew around, before hydroplaning sideways for some distance down the road, where it came to a stop, its headlights angled downwards into the ditch where he had been lying only minutes previously.

The car had not crashed, nor had it behaved in any way likely to injure its occupants, and almost immediately the headlights began to rock, as though the driver were trying to back it out. After a few failed attempts, however, the rocking stopped, and the lights switched off, leaving the car in the ditch.

For a few minutes Finn waited, expecting someone to come to see if he was alright, but no one did, and, his need to reach the McGuire home foremost in his thoughts now, he got up and began making his way again towards it.

Even for a fit person, the strain of battling against the storm would have been a good test of stamina, but for him, hampered by exhaustion, pain, and lack of food and water, the strain was such that, even after the first hundred yards, his breath was coming in gasps, his muscles trembling with fatigue.

The gale was relentless, and he had to fight

his way along the road, often stumbling after leaning into a gust, only to find the wall of air had evaporated, causing him to fall into nothingness. Several times he lost track of the road altogether when he floundered into rushing streams, often tumbling into ditches knee-deep in water, and stumbling into hedges or old field-stone dry-walls. He had to take frequent rests, and on one of these, passed out, waking later to find himself lying in the middle of the road. It even felt comfortable, and no bed could have been more inviting, tempting him to lie there and sleep in peace.

He pushed himself to his feet again, not knowing how far he had come, or remembering even if he had passed the T-junction. Judging from the wind direction, though, it must mean he had turned the corner, and was close to the McGuire home now, and, head down, he plowed ahead.

He could see her. She was standing at the front door, waiting for him, smiling, happy, her arms open, ready to hold him in their gentle warmth, but then she vanished, and he was lying with his head resting against a clump of wet grass.

Once again, he got up and started off, finding it ever harder to stay alert. What if Diana *had* fallen in love with someone else? Maybe even with Bradley, the only man he had ever come to hate. What about the lace handkerchief? How had it come to be in his pocket? The possibility that she might have fallen in love with this man, and may even have forgotten about him altogether, produced now an agony of its own, a mental one to add to his physical ones, and he let out a huge, primeval cry of despair that vanished into the storm.

CHAPTER 43

It was not warm and gentle arms, but a scream that greeted Finn when the studio door, giving way when he fell against it, flew open. For a moment he stood there, swaying, forcing his eyes to stay open, blinking into the bright light of the lantern. He shuffled sideways until his feet found the wall, and leaned back against it for support. His eyes wanted to close, to allow sleep to take away the pain and the trembling of his limbs. The backs of his knees quivered as they had when, as a child, he had stood on the edge of a high cliff and looked down.

Now too, the floor seemed a long way away, the room starting to spin, and he let his head roll back to find the comfort of the supporting wall, and to stop himself pitching forward into the abyss; and he leaned against it, knees sagging, head lolling uncontrollably to one side.

He could see Diana. She was backed up against the far wall, staring at him, and clutching a hammer.

"Sorry." He could barely hear his voice, which sounded more like a croak. "Didn't... mean... to frighten..." He shuffled his feet, trying to keep his balance. "Diana? Diana?"

"*F-i-n-n*?" She took a hesitant step towards him, leaning forward and peering into his face, still holding the hammer.

"Yes... I've come... saw light..." He shook his head. There was so much he wanted to say, and was trying to say, but the words refused to come out. Not being able to say what he wanted struck him as funny, and he laughed. It was a short, hysterical laugh, a bark almost. He looked up at the roof -- must look upwards. When he looked down, the floor drew him towards it, and he felt himself pitching forward as though falling off the cliff.

"*Finn*!" Diana dropped the hammer, and put her arms out towards him.

It was so tempting to let himself go, to fall forwards into the sanctuary of their embrace. If he did, though, maybe she would evaporate into nothingness again, just as she had earlier. The floor was heaving like the deck of the *Brandy X*, and he had to keep adjusting his feet to stop falling over, but his knees buckled, and he pushed his back against the wall again to stop himself from collapsing.

Diana was putting her arms around him. This time he felt their warmth; she was real, and he let his head rest on her shoulder.

"Oh Finn! What on earth has happened to you? Where have you been? What have they done to you?" She held him close.

"I... I wanted... wanted to come... love

you… couldn't…" His voice trailed off again; his eyes began to close, and his body sagged against her, but then jerked up again when he lost his balance and began to fall.

"Finn, darling, let yourself go. It's okay. I'm here." She held him under his arms, supporting him, and, giving in to his quivering knees, he subsided slowly to the floor, coming to rest with his back against the wall.

She smoothed his hair, and he raised his head. "Hold me, Diana… Just… just hold me… Please… Please hold me." He smelled her familiar perfume, felt her hair against his cheek, and wanted to put out his arms to pull her towards him, but had no strength left to do anything, and, finally overcome, he slid sideways, his head coming to rest on the floor.

Diana closed the studio door, then sat down next to him, passing her hand lightly over his bare feet, his swollen wrists and hands. She stared at the chain, at his dripping hair and beard, and cried, remembering his eyes just before he had passed out -- faded and hollow, haunted. She smoothed his cheek. "Love you so much too, Finn." She smoothed his hair again. It was long and matted, and while struggling to recover from the shock of Finn's astounding reappearance, she carefully plucked away the bits of debris caught in it. "Come along, Diana," she said aloud. "He's in need of your practical help more than anything else right now, so get your head together. Think."

First, she needed to find something with which to remove the handcuffs. She had heard that they were not complicated, not being intended to be worn for long periods, and, having seen characters in movies use bits of bent wire to undo them, she looked around for something that might fit the purpose. She pulled one of the cardboard boxes from the shelf, and searched through it, eventually finding a coil of wire used for staking plants. Next, she found a pliers with a small cutting edge, and snipped off about four inches. It was quite stiff, which was good, and she used the pliers to bend it, not knowing what shape would be best, but creating a small hook on the end. She took it over to where he was lying on his side, one arm out in front of him, the other beneath him.

She knelt down and took the hand lying in front of him. It was sticky with blood, mostly drying, and she was relieved not to see any sign of ongoing bleeding. She put his hand on her lap, then set about removing the handcuff. To her surprise, it did not take as long as she had expected, not even knowing when she started, whether she would be able to open it at all. She did have to experiment a bit with the shape of the wire, though, before it popped open, allowing her to remove it from his wrist.

His other hand was more difficult to get at as he was lying on it, and when she tried to move him over onto his back, he groaned. The other lock was not as easy either, and she spent the next half hour fiddling with it until it finally gave way.

Her next task was to try to locate the source of the bleeding. She undid his shirt, pulling it gently back off his shoulder. Here she found a great deal of swelling and bruising around it, and she spread her hand over it. It felt very warm, and a hard knob protruded from under the skin.

"Poor Finn, my darling, you must be hurting so much. What on earth has happened to you, my love?" She bent over and kissed him, then moved his shirt down his arm, flinching when she found the knife wound. She held up the lantern to see it more clearly. It was not inflamed, as though infected, so that was something, but it had been bleeding recently. It still was, slightly. More tears came as she studied him. He was so bruised, battered and scratched, and she cuddled up to him as close as she could, waiting for the eye of the hurricane to arrive.

A short time later the roaring of the wind stopped, and Diana pulled open the door and looked out. Apart from the plop of water from the trees dripping onto puddles, it was quiet, and a silent, eerie mist floated up from the sodden ground, glowing where shafts of pale yellow from the rising sun created an almost magical fairyland scene -- a miraculous transformation from what she had experienced just a few hours earlier.

She stepped outside, her feet sinking at once into the debris-covered mud, then glanced up the driveway leading to the road. A huge tree was lying across it, blocking the way, so even though she would have liked to have taken Finn over to the hospital on the mainland, it would be impossible for any vehicle to enter or leave the property until the way was cleared, which could take days.

She could not leave him where he was until then, though, and turned to look at him. He was still asleep, or unconscious, so she decided to see if she could fetch her car, and take him down to the house, assuming both were still there, and the driveway leading to it, passable. She would need to hurry, though; it would not do for him to wake up while she was gone, and, in his confused state, wander off. There was also the backside of the hurricane to consider, and that could come at any moment.

CHAPTER 44

It was past mid day. The hurricane had passed without causing any further damage, and Finn was still asleep. It had taken a great effort on both their parts to get him down to the still-standing house, but once there, he had collapsed onto the sofa bed in the library right next to the front door, where she had left him to sleep while surveying the damage caused by the storm.

The *Moonglow* was gone, of course, as was the dock, which left no sign that it had ever even been there. The whole shoreline of the property had changed shape as well, several yards of it washed away, leaving the house much nearer to the bay than it had been before. The part of the house itself that had received the most damage was the living room, which was a shambles, although still appearing to be structurally sound.

On the floor beneath the fireplace was a metal garbage-can lid, surrounded by the shattered remains of the big oval mirror it had hit when it smashed through the window. The drapes were ruined, and the carpet sodden and littered with grit, bits of seaweed and shells, deposited there by the remains of a huge wave. The porch screen was ripped, and parts of it missing as well. Considering the violence of the hurricane, however, she was relieved to be able to acknowledge that the damage could have been very much worse.

She was on her way back to check on Finn in the library, when she heard the sound of a chainsaw coming from up the road somewhere. She rushed out, eventually working her way past the fallen tree to the end of the driveway, where she found a crew working to open up the road. They were almost at the beginning of her driveway, and she shouted to them.

The man switched off his saw, and cupped his hand to his ear. "What?"

"I need you to clear my driveway, please. Can you?"

"Sorry, Miss McGuire, but we have to take care of the roads before we can start on private driveways."

"No! You have to, please. I need to get an ambulance here to take my friend to hospital. He's been hurt."

The man put down his saw, came running over, and after hearing about Finn's injuries, took out his phone and dialed 911. After a fairly lengthy call, in which he made a few exclamations of surprise, he switched it off and returned it to his pocket.

"Unfortunately, Miss McGuire, the ambulance is stranded over on the other side of the bay, on the mainland, because the bridge is down, so it can't get here. The paramedics are stuck there with it, but the police say they'll be over as soon as they can. They've got a couple of other emergencies to deal with at the moment, so they'll be over right after they've taken care of them. They said they were coming up to see you anyway, but hadn't yet been able to get through to you by phone or road; but don't worry, Miss, we'll get it all cleared for you now, so they can get to you."

"Thank you so much." Diana walked back down to the house, then busied herself with cleaning up the living room as best she could, and wondering what she had in the house for them to eat. There being no electricity, everything in the fridge was warming up fast, and already the milk was starting to turn. There was some hamburger that needed to be used as soon as possible, and as the barbeque and the gas cylinder, which had been sitting on the porch, seemed to have survived the storm, at least they would have something for dinner tonight.

Finn looked up and saw a plain white ceiling. He blinked, expecting oozing brown pustules to appear. His gaze moved over to the walls, but instead of grubby little portholes with water beyond, there was a large, mullioned window opening out onto green grass, with shrubs and trees in the distance. The air smelled of he did not know what. Maybe it was simply that there was no smell of diesel fumes and bilge, and everything was still, the only sound that of a bee buzzing around somewhere beyond the open window.

Where was he? What day was it? He remembered seeing Diana in the studio, but nothing after that. Had it all been a hallucination? He dragged himself up, and sat on the side of the bed, nursing his arm, looking down at the floor; a colorful Persian rug over polished wood boards lay beneath his feet.

The door opened; it was Diana, and he smiled at her. "Wondered where I was."

She sat down next to him, put her arm round him, and, gently pushing his hair back off his face, gave him a kiss. "Well, you're safe at home here with me once more, Finn, and I'm not going to let you out of my sight again either, now I've got you back. Oh, my darling! I'm so relieved you've woken up at last. I've been so worried about you."

Finn took her hand, and squeezed it. "You'll never know how much I've missed you, Diana. It's been killing me, thinking that you'd believe I'd walked out on you. I'd never, ever…"

"Aaah, Finn, my darling, I'm so sorry… Yes, I did try very hard to forget you, because I *did* believe you'd walked out on me. Even so, I still couldn't stop thinking about you constantly, and of our time together. I've been so very, very sad, and missing you terribly. And now, to see you like this, so battered and bruised…"

"I'd never, ever have treated you like that, Diana. I'd never have walked out on you like that, and knowing what you must have been thinking of me all this time, and fearing too that you'd never learn the truth." His voice caught, and he paused. "It's… it's been pure hell." He leaned over and kissed her. "Oh

Diana, my love. I do love you. I want you to know that. I love you so very much.”

They kissed each other, then Finn smiled. “I wish I could… we could… I want you… want for us to make love, right now… to hold you close…” He tried to put his arms round her, and yelped. “Oh hell!! Not good… Dammit!” He grinned. “Well, that was a pretty romantic declaration, wasn’t it?”

Diana put her arms around him instead, and kissed him again, smiling. “Ah Finn, I’m so happy to see that, despite everything else that’s happened to you, your sense of humor has survived. And you must know that I love you too, my darling. I’ve loved you all the time, and now we have all the time in the world to be happily back together again.” She sat back and looked at him. “But first we must concentrate on getting you all mended and back to normal, yes, my darling?”

He nodded, and smiled back. “You’re right, although I’m finding it hard to believe that we *are* actually together again. I keep expecting you to disappear, and discover this is all in my head. I honestly thought I’d lost you forever, and that I’d never see you again.”

“Is there anything I *can* do to make you feel better, my dear? You do look terrible, and I can’t get you to hospital, or even phone to ask for help right now, so we’re on our own for the time being, I’m afraid, although the police have promised to come as soon as they can to see if they can be of help in any way.”

“Well now, going from the erotically sublime thought of our making exquisite love together, to the passion-killing mundane, you haven't got any painkillers by any chance, have you?"

"Let me go take a look. I think I've got some Tylenol somewhere. Will that do?"

"I'll take anything right now."

"Wait here a minute, then, sweetheart." At the door, she turned and blew him a kiss. "Oh, you've no idea how happy I am to be able to look at you now, and to say your name to your face again, Finn." And she left the room repeating it over and over.

She brought him the Tylenol and a couple of cookies to take with it. "How about you sit over there in Dad's old recliner. You might find it more comfortable than this hard sofa-bed, and I'll get you something to put at your back... How's that?" she asked him once he was resettled.

"How did I get here?"

"You don't remember? I brought you down from the studio in the car."

"I don't remember anything after I landed up there..."

"Just as well, perhaps. Getting you this far was quite a struggle for both of us one way or another."

"What day is it? I've lost track."

"It's Saturday, and last night was the hurricane, when you turned up at the studio, and it's now just gone noon."

She sat down on the arm of the chair, and smoothed the only part of his cheek not covered by a straggly beard. "I have to say you're absolutely filthy, my love; your hair is full of tangles; your beard looks as though you haven't shaved since I last saw you, and you smell of seaweed and stale sweat. I don't know if you've seen yourself lately, but I don't think you'd even recognize yourself... Has the painkiller helped at all? I looked at your shoulder while you were asleep. I don't know much about these things, but I think it's dislocated. It's all very swollen and bruised."

"It got dislocated earlier, then I landed on it when I fell out of the car; maybe I did something more to it then. I don't know."

"Fell out of the car? I'm so very anxious to find out what on earth has been happening to you all this time. Whatever it was, it must have been horrendous. Right now, though, it's more important to get you seen to. There's plenty of time now for you to tell me everything."

She stood up, fetched a chair, sat down in front of him, and put her hand on his knee. "I do so wish I could get you to hospital, my love, but the bridge is down. When I looked out of the window a while back, I could see the whole center span has disappeared, so you were right after all, Finn, when you said you thought a high wind and tide could bring it down. I do hope no-one was on it when it went, though. My phone battery's flat as well, and I think the landlines must be down too as nothing's working."

She stood up. "By the way, when did you last have anything to eat or drink?"

"If today is Saturday, then it would be Thursday evening. I had food after that, but lost it all to seasickness and diesel fumes."

"Seasickness and diesel fumes? Falling out of cars?" She shook her head. "No. All that can wait. As I said, we need to see to you first, although I'm afraid

I don't have much to offer in the way of food at the moment. Will bread and cheese do? And I can open a can of ham."

Finn nodded. "Thanks. That would be good. All right if I stay here while you get it?"

"Of course. Better if you do. Oh, by the way, before I go, I wanted to tell you that when I was talking to the men clearing the road earlier, they told me the police were having to deal with a rather nasty situation caused by the hurricane. Remember that little cove I took you to that beautiful day when we first made love? Bass Cove? Well, they told me it seems there was a horrible accident there in the storm last night. A fishing boat went in there for shelter apparently, but somehow ended up smashed to smithereens on the rocks. They think there must have been at least two people on board, but so far haven't found them. They're presuming they were drowned though. That's terrible, isn't it? Poor men! They couldn't possibly have survived in those seas. What they too must have gone through! I hope the end came for them without too much suffering…"

Finn looked up at her, but said nothing.

"Well, I guess I'd better get you those sandwiches, hadn't I?"

However, when she returned with them, he only picked at them. "Sorry. I can't manage any more right now. Later perhaps."

"I know you're not alright by any means, Finn, my love, but you're not feeling worse are you? No new aches or pains anywhere, or anything? You're not going to pass out on me again, are you, darling? You look as though you…"

"No. I'm okay."

"But you've hardly eaten anything, sweetheart, and you must be starving. Oh, I do so wish I could do something to help you. How about I help you clean up a bit? Do you think that might make you feel better?"

"A shower would be nice."

By the end of an hour she had helped him take a shower, and he was now wearing a pair of grey sweat-pants belonging to her father. They were a bit short, and way too big, but at least they were clean and dry. She had found him a T-shirt as well, but had failed to put it on without hurting him, and as he was not well enough to have her spend time trying to cut and tidy up his hair and beard, they remained long and full of tangles, leaving him still looking, as she told him, like some wild man of the woods.

"I'd really like to sit outside on the porch if that's possible. Is it? It's so long since I've been out in the fresh air."

"Yes, of course, my darling. I'd brought in the cushion from the couch on the porch before the storm, so that's nice and dry for you, and the sun is shining right in there at the moment."

Once outside, he sank down onto the couch, staring out over the bay a while, before stretching himself out and falling into a fitful sleep. He remembered Diana bringing out a camp bed at some point, and it was the following morning when he finally woke.

<h1 style="text-align:center">CHAPTER 45</h1>

"Hi Joe, Gene! Come on in, won't you? Sorry the living room in here is a bit of a mess, but come in anyway. I guess we were lucky, though; at least the house is still here. Sit down, won't you?"

"No. No thank you, Miss McGuire. We can't stay. There's too much going on right now." The two local policemen stood to attention, twisting their caps around in their hands.

"You're here to see what you can do to help my friend, yes? He's just outside there, on the porch. I don't know what's happened to him altogether, but he's not well at all, and looks dreadful."

Well, we'll do our best, but we're not paramedics, so can't do too much to help on that score. But first, Miss McGuire, we're sorry, but why we've really called is because we've some very sad news for you. We'd have come earlier, but…"

"Oh? No-one's been hurt in the hurricane, have they?"

"No, Miss McGuire. Uh… well, not in the

hurricane, but we're terribly sorry to have to tell you that your father's been fatally injured."

"*My father*! Oh no! Fatally injured? He's dead? How? What happened? Not in the hurricane? Oh dear! Poor Dad!" She collapsed onto the sofa. "Oh no! His plane must have crashed? Where? When?"

"Yesterday, Miss McGuire. No, it wasn't a plane crash. There was a fire at a lumber mill in Maine. Apparently, he owns it? No-one could get near the site until early this morning, and even then, only just inside the perimeter. It was near there that they discovered your father's remains."

"At his mill in Maine? No. No, I'm sorry, but it couldn't be him. It has to be someone else. My father's in Washington. I took him to the airport myself only a few days ago, although he wasn't on the plane when I went to pick him up at the airport last evening. I don't understand. What makes you think it's him? Are you even sure it's him? It can't be. You're saying someone's already identified him then?"

"I'm afraid it wasn't possible to identify his body, Miss McGuire. It was too badly burnt, but one of the mill workers recognized his metal belt-buckle, which was still intact -- a particular one from the Civil War, we understand."

"Well yes, he does always wear a rather rare, Civil-War belt-buckle, but I still don't understand what he might have been doing up at the mill. He must have left DC and gone straight up to Maine for some reason. I don't know. I wonder why he didn't let me know, although with the hurricane and everything..." She put her head in her hands. "Oh, I don't know. Oh dear! This is terrible!"

"We're afraid that's not all, Miss McGuire. We also have reason to believe, uh… We're real sorry to have to tell you this, but we have reason to believe he was murdered."

Diana looked up in horror. "*Murdered*! Why? Why would anyone want to murder my father? How do you know he was murdered?" She shook her head. "Oh! I can't believe all this. It's… it's more than I can take in. I don't know what to say."

"We found definite clues leading the police to come to that conclusion. There was a paper trail leading to the mill, which had been set on fire deliberately, and…"

Diana stood up, and began walking towards the door to the porch. "I'm… I'm sorry to interrupt, Joe, but before you go any further, I want my friend to hear all this. I can't take all this, and need his support. Come out here onto the porch, will you please, where he can hear…"

She led the two policemen out of the living room onto the porch, where Finn was still lying, stretched out on the couch. "Darling, these men here have come with some dreadful, dreadful news. They say… They say Dad's been killed. *Murdered*!"

Finn tried to sit up, but lay back down, grimacing and clutching his shoulder. "Murdered!" He reached out and took Diana's hand, looking up at the two policemen, and, as Diana had done, asked: "When? Where? How?"

"Well Sir, first of all, let us say, we're right sorry you've been injured, and we'll do what we can to get help to you as soon as possible," Joe said. He then repeated what he had told Diana, then shrugged, putting out his hands, showing they were empty. "And that, I'm afraid Sir, is all we know at this time, Sir, except that the trail leads to someone by the name of Finn Westlake, and there's a warrant..."

"*Finn Westlake*!" Diana shrieked.

"Yes, Ma'am. Why? Do you know...?"

Finn let go of Diana's hand, and pointed to his chest. "*Me*! *I'm* Finn Westlake! What on earth could possibly make them think *I* murdered him?"

Diana put her hand on Finn's shoulder, and shook her head vigorously. "Uh! Uh! No! Absolutely not! That's just plain ridiculous! Absolutely ridiculous! Impossible in fact. Besides, Finn would never..."

Gene pointed his finger at Finn. "*You're* Finn Westlake?"

"Yes, I am, and I can most certainly assure you I haven't murdered Mr. McGuire. I haven't even seen him since the night after the yacht club ball at the beginning of the season, back in early June."

The two officers began fumbling for their handcuffs. "I'm sorry, Miss McGuire," Joe announced, his sympathetic tone gone. "But this man will have to come with us. As I started to say, there's a warrant out for his arrest for arson and for the murder of Mr. McGuire, and I should warn you, Westlake, that you have the right to remain silent. Anything you say..."

Finn shook his head. "No! No! Wait a minute! You can't think..."

"Stand up," Gene ordered him.

Diana moved to stand between them. "No,

Gene. I tell you; it's impossible. This is totally ridiculous. Finn was here last night."

"What time did he arrive, Miss McGuire?"

"Around midnight I think it was. Right in the middle of the hurricane."

"And where were you before that, eh, Westlake?"

"I was trying to find my way here in the hurricane, and got injured in the process."

"That injury of yours could well be as a result of a struggle with Mr. McGuire. Anyway, although we're not at liberty to tell you precisely what was found at the scene, what we *can* say for sure is that this paper trail, in the form of certain documents, has led to you."

"Documents! What sort of documents? The only documents I have are my passport, credit cards and driver's license, and they're all upstairs in the guest room, where I left them, back in June."

"They've been up *there* all the time? Oh Finn! I didn't know. Wait, and I'll fetch them. Where are they?"

"Yes. Please do. I can prove I have absolutely nothing to do with Mr. McGuire's death. They're in the vase on the table beneath the window. I dropped them in there for safe keeping, along with my phone the morning I left here to look at the bridge foundations. Besides, if I'd done everything you say I've done, would I be daft enough to leave behind such an obvious trail of evidence, such as that?"

"You were probably in such a hurry to get out of there, you dropped them by mistake, and didn't even realize it," Gene scoffed.

There was an awkward silence while Diana went to look for Finn's documents, and after what appeared to him an extraordinarily long time, she returned, breathless. "Finn? They're not there. The vase is empty."

"Not there? Are you sure, Diana? They have to be there! I know I left them there. I don't understand."

Gene held out the cuffs. "Okay Westlake. Nice try. Now get up. Now, I said, or I'll yank you up from there."

Finn hauled himself up, and stood there, swaying.

Diana stood in front of him for the second time. "No! No! I tell you; this is all wrong. You can't do this."

"I must ask you to move out of the way, Miss McGuire. Interfering with the police in the course of carrying out their lawful duty is an offence. Now, Westlake, put your hands behind your back, towards me."

"No! Please. I can't."

"Right. We've better things to do than stand around waiting for you, and like I started to say before, you have the right to remain silent..." He thrust his arm forward around Finn's waist and, jerking his arm backwards, seized hold of his other hand, at which Finn slumped to the floor.

When he opened his eyes, Diana was kneeling at his side. "...shoulder's dislocated," she was telling the policemen, "as well as suffering from other injuries. He tried to tell you, but you wouldn't listen, would you, Gene? Couldn't wait, could you?

Why do you think I tried to get hold of the ambulance? If you'd taken the trouble to look, you could have seen he's got something very wrong with his shoulder. Look at it! What are you? Blind?"

"Oh? And how do you suggest that happened then, Miss McGuire? As I already said, that could have happened during a struggle with your father."

"I can't suggest how it happened," Diana snapped. "Because I don't know how it happened; he hasn't had the chance to tell me yet. All I do know is that he was like that when he arrived in the middle of the hurricane. You can't take him in like this. He's ill. Can't you see? Anyway, for heaven's sake, think! There *has* to be a reasonable explanation for this. He couldn't have done it. I know him. Do you even know *when* my father died?"

"As we said, the mill went up yesterday, but your father could have been killed well before that, and the mill set on fire later to cover up the murder."

"Think, though! How could Finn possibly have got back here in the state he's in? And on foot yet, without any of the documents of his that you say you have? It doesn't add up at all. Use your common sense, for heaven's sake! Besides, as I said, I know him. He'd never murder anyone. And don't you think when he heard you coming, he'd have tried to escape? He even sat there and *told* you who he was! It's obvious my father's death was as much of a shock to him as it was to me!"

"Huh, the state he's in, I'm not surprised he didn't try to escape," Gene scoffed. "By the looks of him I'd say he couldn't have gotten ten feet, let alone run away. What else could he do, but stay put, eh?

Besides, who's to say he didn't get into this state *after* killing your father, and after getting back here to the island? No, sorry Miss McGuire, but your excuses for him just don't hold up, and he's going to have to come with us. There's a warrant out for him, so we're duty bound to take him in anyway; it's the law. Besides that, it's obvious he needs to go to hospital, if nothing else, and for that we're going to have to call in the HEMS as there's no other access to the mainland at the moment, other than by boat, and I'll agree he doesn't look up to that right now."

The two officers set Finn down on the sofa in the living room, then put a call into the Helicopter Emergency Medical Service, giving the location of the McGuire property, and letting it be known there was plenty of open space on the front lawn for the chopper to land. "They'll be here within the hour, and there's no call for you to put on your coat, Ms. McGuire. He's a murder suspect, and you can't go with him."

CHAPTER 46

Outside, the two policemen were still standing on the lawn looking out for the helicopter, while Finn lay stretched out on the sofa in the living room, eyes closed, Diana sitting next to him, holding his hand.

"Just a minute, sweetheart. I'm sure I just heard someone knocking on the front door. I'll be right back." She patted his hand, and left the room.

Seconds later Finn heard the front door opening.

"*Ben*! How did you manage to back get here? Come on in."

"The sea'd calmed down enough for me to use my dinghy. I'd intended tying it up to your dock, but saw it was gone, so I've run it up onto the beach down the road. What's wrong, Diana? Has something happened? You look exhausted. I wish now I hadn't left you. I should have stayed, but I had to deliver..."

"I'm sorry, Ben. Come on in here to the living room." Diana held out her hand, inviting

Bradley to enter. "Everything's a mess, and... and... I don't know where to start. I'm in complete turmoil. Just this last hour the police arrived with the most horrible news, that..." She hesitated as Bradley hung back. "Well, no need to stand there in the doorway, Ben. Yes, it *is* a mess in the living room here, but don't let that stop you. Do come on in, please. I need to tell you that..."

Bradley entered the room, then stopped again, and Diana turned to look at him.

"Ben? Are you all right? You don't look good at all. Don't you pass out me as well! Come. Sit down here in Dad's old armchair, and I'll get you some whisky. You look like you've seen a ghost."

Bradley took the glass, and, sitting down, casually crossed his legs and downed the whisky. "Ah, that's good! Thank you, darling. Your father always has good Scotch. Whew! That's much better. Must have been the aftermath of the hurricane finally catching up with me."

"I'm not surprised. You must have had a nightmare journey back to Davenport last night. At least some color's coming back into your face now. You had me worried there. I thought you were having a heart attack, or something. But Ben, I..."

Bradley held out his hand for another whisky. "No. I'm fine now, thanks my darling. About the police, then: what's happened? But first, I do have to ask: you said things were in a turmoil, so who's that taking up your sofa? Is it about him? Is he the cause of your turmoil? I must say, he looks a right mess, poor guy. Was he washed up on your beach in the storm, or something? He does look to be pretty much out of it, I must say. Did the police bring him here?"

"No, no. It wasn't anything to do with him. At least, to start with, it wasn't. It was about my father. He's been murdered!"

"*Murdered!* When? Where?"

"Well, I don't know where to start. You see, that's the other thing that's happened. Right after you left, Finn turned up looking like this! This is Finn! He's come back!"

"*Finn*! Finn Westlake? After all this time? What the hell's happened to him?"

"I don't know. He hasn't been able to tell me yet. He's been out of it most of the time since he got here. Whatever *has* happened to him, though, and wherever he's been, he's obviously had a terrible time, and he hadn't walked out on me after all!"

"He hadn't? How do you know?"

"It turned out he'd left all his documents: driver's license, passport, credit cards, everything, up in the guest room, hidden in a vase. I didn't know they were there, and he obviously couldn't have walked out on me without them! But that's not all, though. It's all so horrible, and I don't know what to do. My poor Dad's dead, and the police are waiting for a helicopter to take Finn to jail, because they say they found documents belonging to him near the scene!"

"It's all right Diana, my love. I'm here now. I'll look after you. What's he supposed to have done then?"

"I can't believe it. Apparently, there's an arrest warrant out for him for Dad's murder! I've tried to tell them that's ridiculous, but they won't listen to me. I know Finn couldn't have murdered him; he wouldn't murder anyone!"

"Do you happen to have some more of that Scotch? All this is a bit overwhelming. Come on, my love. Come and sit here, with me." Bradley patted the arm of the chair. "People can change, you know, Diana. After all, how well did you know the guy in the first place? Really know him, I mean? There has to be another whole side to him that you never discovered. Come here," he repeated, but Diana sat down on the sofa next to Finn instead, and put her hand on his arm.

"Finn. Wake up, darling. Look who's here. Remember Ben Bradley? You met him that night at the yacht club ball. I've been telling him how you came back here during the storm."

Finn pushed himself slowly to a sitting position, grunting with pain, and pointed at Bradley. "You! You murdering bastard!"

"Finn! What on earth's the matter? This is Ben Bradley! Surely you remember him!"

"Remember him! I'll never forget him! He's the one who held me prisoner all this time! He's the one who gave me sedatives that nearly killed me. He's the one who tried to exchange me for ransom, so I could be murdered! He's the one who did this to me! *Remember him*! His damned face is imprinted on my brain forever!"

"I'm sorry, Diana, but obviously something really serious has happened to the poor guy's brain during his absence. He's definitely got a screw loose! And I wouldn't be at all surprised if the police have got it right; I'm beginning to think now that he's more than capable of having murdered your father."

"But that's not possible! I'm sure he couldn't

have done it. Finn would never do anything like that!"

Bradley shook his head. "Diana, my love, would you have *ever* imagined the Finn you knew -- the one I was delighted to meet that time at the yacht club ball -- *ever* producing a ridiculous outburst like the one you've just witnessed? I'm sure you wouldn't. He's certainly not the same Finn Westlake *I* talked to that night!" He squeezed himself down on the sofa next to Diana, and put his arm around her.

"Get your filthy hands off her, Bradley. You're not fit to be within a hundred miles of her."

"I think you'll find you're very much mistaken there, my friend. Diana and I got together right after you left to go wherever it is you've been."

Diana leapt up. "I'm sorry, but I can't take any more of this. I'm going out." The front door slammed behind her.

One of the officers put his head around the living room door. "Everything all right in here? We heard some shouting, and thought our prisoner here might be acting up, so what's going on, eh?" He looked at Finn. "You making trouble, buddy? Ah! There's the chopper coming." He took hold of Finn, and yanked him to his feet. "Now you stand there a minute, while I go help Joe get them landed, and don't you try kicking up a fuss just because I can't put cuffs on you, Westlake." He turned to Bradley. "You Sir, I recognize you, don't I? Mr. Bradley, isn't it? Governor Brigham's nephew?"

"Yes indeed. Don't worry, officer, I'll keep an eye on him till you get back."

"Thank you, Sir."

Bradley waited until he was out of hearing,

then stood up. "I don't know how the hell you got yourself out of this, Westlake, but I'll get you one way or another. There's no way you can pin anything on me, as you well know. Who knows? With luck, they'll make this murder rap stick. In the meantime, as you can see, Diana and I are in love, and have been ever since you did your disappearing act. We've been sleeping together for weeks, up in that guest room of yours, no less."

Finn let out a roar, and launched himself at Bradley, butting him in the stomach, knocking him backwards over the glass-topped coffee table, smashing it, and landing on top of him. Bradley pushed him off, grabbed hold of him, pulled him up, and, blood coming from a cut above his eye, aimed his fist at Finn's dislocated shoulder, giving it a bone-crunching punch. This he followed with a hefty shove, sending Finn reeling back onto the sofa.

The officer re-appeared, along with a paramedic. "Right. All's ready. Heh! What's happened here?"

"He decided to attack me, officer. The man's a maniac."

Diana came rushing back in. "What was that crash? I could even hear it from… My God! What's happened? Ben?"

Bradley wiped the blood from his cut. "He attacked me. The psycho attacked me! Don't worry my love, I'm all right, but the idiot needs locking up."

"Diana! Diana! You know I love you. Don't believe anything Bradley tells you; he's a liar and a murderer!" And Finn was carried out to the chopper.

"Diana! You absolutely must know the guy

was insane when he started up swearing at me like that! He's even called me a murderer! And then, on top of that, despite being on his last legs, he went and butted me like an enraged bull! For what? What the hell got into him? If he'd been a dog, I'd have said he'd come down with rabies!"

His shoe crunched on a piece of glass from the broken coffee table. "Sorry about the table, but I couldn't avoid it. Good job I didn't do some real damage to myself. I've a good mind to sue him for assault and battery as well, the maniac!"

"I'm sorry, Ben, but I don't know what to say anymore. Obviously, the idea of you doing everything he accused you of does not make sense. On the other hand, Finn definitely suffered from some terrible trauma of some sort. *Someone* had done *something* to him; there's no doubt about that. He gave every impression of having suffered from mental as well as physical abuse, maybe enough even to make him lose his mind, poor Finn!"

"Poor Finn be damned! That's what I'm trying to tell you: no matter the cause, the guy belongs in a loony bin, and if he murdered your father as well, then that's certainly where he belongs. Ask yourself: whatever reason would he have for killing your poor father? That's what I want to know."

"That's what I keep saying: he *wouldn't* have had a reason. Oh, I don't know. I honestly don't know, although I'm sure he couldn't have killed Dad anyway; he wouldn't have had the time, or even the wherewithal to go anywhere without his identification and credit cards, etcetera, let alone get to Maine and back."

"Yes, but you say the police claim they found his documents at the scene," Bradley argued. "So it's Westlake's word against theirs, and they would certainly have no reason to claim that if it weren't true, would they? And you've no proof at all that he did actually leave them there, do you?"

"No, I guess not."

Bradley shrugged. "There then. I rest my case."

"Even so, I think I'll need to go see him wherever they've taken him. Maybe he'll have calmed down, and be more rational I need to talk to him, to find out what's going on."

"Go to see him! I give up, Diana. I can't believe you want to visit a prison to see this guy after all this, especially with him just accused of murdering your own father! You can't be thinking straight yourself. You're just crazy about him. You always have been! Maybe you should get away from here for a while until this whole thing has been settled, and the idiot's safely locked up in a padded cell, where he belongs. Right now, you obviously can't view him objectively. You need to be able to stand back and see him for what he really is.

"I tell you what! I've a great idea! Why don't you and I go away together? If it's a question of money now when your father's finances need sorting out, I'll pay. In fact, I insist on paying anyway. I can afford it. Why don't we take off for some exotic place in the Indian Ocean, or wherever? We could have a great time, just the two of us."

"No. But thank you for the offer, Ben. That's very generous of you, but I can't simply take off on holiday like that when my father's just been murdered, nor can I leave Finn without anyone to support him, no matter what. He has no-one to help him through this new ordeal. He shouldn't have to bear it all alone. Having seen what we've seen, I doubt very much that he can cope alone with this second blow to hit him. No. I can't let him do that."

"Right. I think you're crazy, but then who am I to say what you should, or shouldn't do? I should warn you, though; in my own opinion, he's nothing more than a slippery, smooth-talking psychopath. These types can persude you into doing anything, you know! All I ask is that you be on your guard with this nutcase, and not be led into doing something you'll regret."

CHAPTER 47

Finn gazed out of the window at the remains of the bridge, and gave a deep sigh as the helicopter flew low across the bay. The paramedic accompanying him ignored him; he was taking care of the prisoner physically, but there was none of the usual friendly, comforting banter afforded to victims they were transporting. This one had a police escort. He had been arrested for murder, and he certainly looked the part with his matted hair and straggly beard, and, after injecting him with morphine to ease the pain, the man chatted to the policeman instead, leaving him to his ongoing physical agonies and his new mental ones.

The flight was short, only fifteen minutes, and within a half hour of leaving the McGuire home he was lying on a gurney in a corridor, waiting to be attended to, his escort standing guard over him. Six hours after that, he was in a special police unit, dislocated shoulder and broken arm taken care of. His hair had also been cut, and his beard shaved off, allowing for a more accurate mug shot of him to be taken.

He lay on the narrow cot, gazing up at yet another white ceiling, this one dotted with harsh, fluorescent strip-lights. He thought he had already been through the most daunting experience he was ever likely to face, but now he was being accused of murder. Not only was he being accused of murder, but he could see no way of proving his innocence. His only alibis were Ben Bradley and Dave Harvey, if the latter had managed to escape the wrecking of the *Brandy X*, and there was no way they were going to admit that he had ever been with either of them.

From what the police had intimated, they had not yet discovered Tucker's body yet either, and, as of now, he could not see how Bradley could ever be linked to his murder.

Who would ever believe he had been kidnapped and held for ransom on that boat for all those weeks, the prisoner of those men, one of whom was definitely dead, another most likely dead as well? No-one. Who would believe Devine was the one who had paid ransom money for him? That man had to be dead too, along with his driver; surviving that huge explosion when the car's gas tank blew up at the bottom of the embankment below the bridge entrance would have been impossible. And who would ever believe him if he claimed it was Bradley who had blackmailed Devine and killed Tucker? No-one.

He thought too of how his documents had led the police to accuse him. As he had told them, the only documents he had were those he had left in the vase in the bedroom, and they had vanished. They had to be the ones the police had found, and unless Bradley had taken them, which, given the circumstances of McGuire's death and his own knowledge of Bradley's whereabouts during the given time-frame, was impossible, there was only one other person who could have taken them, and that was McGuire; and the only reason he would have taken them would have been because he himself had intended to set fire to his mill and lay the blame on him; and the only reason McGuire would have done that would have been to claim the insurance on the mill so as to pay off Devine, and stop him from repossessing his mansion. But how could he, Finn Westlake, ever prove any of it? He could not. It was his word against McGuire's, and McGuire was dead. Lying there, he almost wished he were dead too. At best, he faced the rest of his life in prison, a bleak future indeed. Maybe even, this state still had the death penalty.

After a few days, he was moved to a regular prison cell in the state penitentiary, bail not allowed, and kept in isolation for his own safety, not being in a position to fight back if attacked by other inmates. Except that the floor did not heave up and down, he might just as well have been back on the *Brandy X*, and with nothing to do, and not even Tucker to talk to, his mind switched constantly back and forth between his legal situation and his personal one. He wished now that he had not allowed Bradley to provoke him like that. The man had definitely achieved his aim too, because Diana must surely question his sanity now, having seen what he had done to him for no apparent reason.

He was sure Bradley was lying when he

claimed they were in love and were sleeping together, and thought again about the few hours he had spent with Diana after arriving at the studio, and reminded himself again how many times she had told him after that that she loved him, and Diana was not the sort to say that just to please him.

On the other hand, Bradley was capable of turning on the charm like a cowboy-builder selling you a new patio. He gave a sardonic laugh. "Probably what he actually does in his spare time." And how quickly he had recovered his composure after coming into the living room and seeing his former prisoner lying there on the sofa! The shock must have been immense, yet he scarcely missed a beat, creating a scene of concerned innocence for himself as calmly as though the script had been learnt in preparation for the event. Surely Diana could see through the act though! But while both he and Bradley knew Bradley was lying, Diana did not, and if his – to her inexplicable -- attack on the man had resulted in her no longer loving him after all, he did not think he would be able to go on without falling even deeper into his new pit of despair, and giving up altogether.

He went over everything that had brought him into this situation, and how a few, seemingly minor occurrences, had changed the course of his life: if he had not happened to have left early for his office that morning back in March, and if he had not decided, because he was early, to take the scenic route along the riverbank; if he had not gone spear-fishing that Sunday morning and seen the condition of the bridge foundations; if Diana had had some reason to look in that vase. What a difference it all would have made!

CHAPTER 48

Finn was still dressed in McGuire's sweatpants, along with a new, dark-green T-shirt with 'CELTICS' and a white shamrock emblazoned on the front. He had also been provided with a pair of cheap flip-flops, and this was how he would be greeting Diana when she arrived to see him.

"Westlake! Booth number six." He walked up to the bullet-proof glass window, and sat down.

"I'm so sorry I'm late, sweetheart. Now that there's no bridge to cross, they're transporting everyone to and from the island on one of the old summer tourist boats, which they've brought in to stand in as a makeshift ferry."

She put her hand up to the glass. "Oh Finn, my darling, I can't bear to see you sitting there looking so lost, especially when I think of that strong man with the lovely amiable smile I met at the airport all that time ago, his old hat perched on the back of his head, striding towards me -- the man who had saved two men's lives. If only I could put my arms around you to comfort you. I'm devastated at the thought of what has brought you to this, my darling. How are they treating you? Well, I hope."

"Okay, I guess."

"Have you any idea how your case is progressing. Have you managed to retain a good lawyer?"

"I've found someone. I don't know how good he is. As far as the case is going, they told me they're doing forensic work on the car I supposedly rented using my driver's license and credit card... Have you had your father's funeral yet?"

"No, they're not releasing his remains until they've finished their investigations. Oh dear, Finn. I don't know what to say or do. This whole thing is so horrendous." She started to cry. "And poor Dad. What a horrific death he must have had, being consumed by fire like that! I do hope he didn't suffer too much."

Finn put his hand up to the glass to touch hers. "You're going to miss him too, I know. The two of you were pretty close; I could see that, and with your mother gone as well... Please don't cry, darling. I'm so very sorry, and feel so utterly useless too, being stuck in here, unable to help you."

"What *I'm* going through is nothing compared with what *you*'ve been through, and are still going through, my darling, but, you're right, I'm feeling sad for myself too right now; and I don't have the will either, to even start trying to sort out whatever needs to be done now Dad's gone."

"I know, and I wish more than anything that I could hold you, and be there for you." He sighed. "Instead, all I *can* do right now, is to try to persuade you that I was telling the truth when I said that Ben Bradley was a liar and a murderer. I wasn't ranting, you know, and I've not lost my mind."

"If you're so sure, my love, why don't you use this opportunity now to bring it to the attention of the authorities? Get him arrested?"

"That's the problem; I can't. I've thought it all through, and I can't prove anything yet, but I swear, I'll be his nemesis yet. If I get out of here, I'll not give up till he's behind bars. You do believe me, don't you Diana? You know I'd never lie to you."

"I do so much want to believe you, my dear, but, at the same time, I can't imagine Ben being such an evil monster as that. Is there anything you can give me to hold onto? I love you so much, but you already know that, don't you? I want more than anything to believe you. Think back. Is there anything, anything at all, that happened to you during the time you say he kept you prisoner, that I can link up with Ben? Is there anything that he said, or that happened, that I'd recognize, and that you wouldn't know about, unless you were with him?"

"Well, yes, maybe I can. For starters, you know you told me about that boat being wrecked in Bass Cove during the hurricane? That boat, you'll find, was called the *Brandy X*, the boat I was kept on all that time, and I can tell you now, that when they find the bodies of the two men, they'll discover one of them was shot, and he was shot by Bradley, because I saw him do it. The problem is that I have no proof that he shot him, and if I say anything now, I could very well be accused of having shot the man myself. No-one would believe me if I told them Bradley did it, and as you're looking for proof that I'm telling the truth, that isn't going to help my argument either, is it? You'd still have no proof that Bradley was guilty of murder.

"I've been wracking my brains, but without any success so far, looking for real proof that he held me prisoner. He was obviously pretty savvy about keeping his other life a secret from you.

"Heh! Wait a minute, though. There *is* one thing! Yes! Just a week or so ago, it would have been, or round about that time, not long before the hurricane. I'd pretty much lost track of time by then. Did you happen to see him with a very swollen lip with two stitches in it?"

"Yes! As a matter of fact, I did. He came to me right after it happened. He'd been in a car crash, and his face had hit the dashboard. Why? Isn't that what happened?"

"Not only is that not what happened, but how would I even know about it, if I'd not been with him at the time? Think about that."

"Well, yes. You obviously wouldn't have known anything about it if you hadn't seen each other since the yacht club ball, as he's claiming."

"I'll go one step further. Remember that crochet-edged handkerchief I bought for you at that antique store?"

She nodded.

"Do you still have it, or did you give it to Bradley for some reason?"

"Yes, he got something in his eye one evening, and I lent it to him, and he forgot to give it back."

"That was no car accident he had, Diana. He came out regularly to the *Brandy X*, where he and the other two men were holding me prisoner, but he never stayed overnight as the other two did. On this particular occasion, he was getting ready to go home, but couldn't find the key to his dinghy. He came down to the cabin, where they kept me chained up, and turned everything, including that handkerchief, out of his pockets and onto one of the bunks. When I saw it lying there I just lost it, and kicked him first in the stomach, then in the mouth, and his tooth went through his lip. That's where he got that swollen lip. I gave it to him!"

"Oh Finn! Guess what! There's something else. He gave that handkerchief back to me that same night, the night you say you kicked him." She held out her hand again, and laid it flat against the glass. "And they kept you chained up too? Oh Finn, my darling! How could they do such a thing? And Ben Bradley was in on this too?" She shuddered. "And I've been dating this man! Oh, this is just horrible, so disgusting!" She shuddered again.

Finn raised his hand, putting it up against hers. "There's another thing as well. Remember the man who was supposed to act as my diving buddy that morning? Dave Harvey? Well, it was he who tried to first drown me when we were diving by the bridge, then gave me the cut on my arm when I fought back; and the *Brandy X*, where, as I said, I was held prisoner, belonged to him and his buddy, Gus Tucker. It was Gus Tucker that Bradley shot, and if and when they find the body, I'm telling you, it'll be Gus Tucker's, and, as I said, it'll have a bullet hole in it.

Believe me now?"

"Yes, yes, I do, and it's making me feel not only sick to my stomach, but scared as well, knowing now that all the time Ben's been going out with me, he's known exactly where you were and how desperately I missed you, yet telling me what a bastard you were for walking out on me! Oh Finn! To think that I've been going out with this man! It makes me really frightened, knowing now that he's a cold-blooded murderer as well! And to think of those hands of his touching me…" She gave another shudder.

"What am I going to do now, though, Finn? If he suspects I know the truth, what's he going to do? There's no knowing with someone like that. How can I get rid of him without letting on? Are you sure you can't bring some lawsuit against him from here? Get him arrested before he can do any more harm to anyone, including me?"

"Please don't cry Diana. I hate to see you cry, and no, desperate as I am to see him behind bars, I can't do or say anything yet. Apart from not having any hard evidence to back up my accusations, I still need to prove that I didn't murder your father. I know it'll be hard for you, my darling, but can you possibly bear to string him along for the time being? Pretend nothing has changed in your relationship? I know that that's going need all your willpower, but obviously I didn't kill your father, and I'm sure -- at least, I hope I'm sure -- that the evidence will prove that. Once that's taken care of, I hope I'll still have the stamina left to take on Bradley. He's cunning though, with some powerful connections to boot, but with luck I can come up with a way to get him convicted; he deserves it. You do still love me, don't you, Diana? I love you so very much, and I need you desperately."

Diana kissed her fingers, then pressed them against the glass again. "Yes, sweetheart. Of course I do. I'll always love you, and I know it's a question you're probably afraid to ask now, but you once asked me if you had reason to be jealous of Ben. I want you to know the answer is still, 'no'. Whatever he may have told you to the contrary is not true. It might seem impossible, given the time we've been dating, but it's been a strange relationship that I've actually tried to end several times, and when you and I are back together again, I'll spell it out for you. A lot of that strangeness is now making sense to me too, now that I know what sort of person he really is behind all that charm."

"Thank you for telling me. You're right; it was a question I was afraid to ask, and, on top of everything else, it's been driving me nuts, not knowing."

"Oh Finn! I've been meaning to tell you: something that went a long way towards reinforcing my belief that you'd dumped me was that Dave Harvey called me the day after you disappeared. He told me he was furious with you because you hadn't turned up the previous day, especially as he'd given up his Sunday to go diving with you."

Finn nodded. "Yes, I heard he'd done that; it was all a part of their plan to make you think I'd walked out on you."

"Sadly, it worked too." Diana placed her hands on the ledge in front of her. "Now, I'm looking at the clock behind you, and we're running out of time, so let's think positive here. Where my father's concerned, at least, I'm sure things will all work out well for you there. I must say I do feel in better spirits now than when I arrived. As you no doubt rightly guessed, I hadn't known what to think, especially after you went after Ben like that."

"Yep. Lost it big time, didn't I? All that pent-up anger… Just couldn't stop myself. Didn't do myself any favors, I know. Anyway, back to thinking positive: just knowing you love me and believe in me makes the world of difference to how I feel, and to how I can cope with all this. Thank you so much for coming, Diana. I know you wouldn't have done that if you didn't love me."

"How's your shoulder by the way?"

"Well, I did do quite a job on it one way or another, and Bradley punching me on it didn't help either. In fact, it was in such a mess up there, they ended up having to do some risky surgery on it that could result in putting an end to my career. They say it'll take time, so it'll be quite a while before I know if that's the case. I'll just have to hope all goes well with it."

"I'm, so sorry, Finn. There's that cut that Harvey gave you too. How exactly did you get that?"

"Well that's a long story, and Bradley's all a part of it, but I can hear the warden coming, so it'll have to wait; this isn't the place to tell it anyway. You *will* come and see me whenever you can, won't you? I need to see you. Better not let Bradley know though. He may get suspicious. Say you're coming into Davenport to go shopping, or something."

Finn felt the warden's hand on his back. "Come along. Time's up."

They both stood up, and Diana lingered, watching him being taken back to his cell. Finn turned briefly, and blew her a kiss.

CHAPTER 49

Diana looked at Finn through the bullet-proof glass of the prison's visitors' room. "Finn! I don't know if you've heard this news already, but it's just as you said; that man, Tucker, he's been found! And, you were right, of course. He *was* shot!"

"I told you so. They still haven't found Harvey then?"

"No, but Ben came around last evening, and told me he's been reading up on the case in the newspaper, because he'd known the two men slightly, and he believes that, drowned or not, Harvey was probably the one who shot Tucker."

"Yes, he would, although I'm a bit surprised he admitted to even knowing them. Re Tucker, though: I'd have thought that given that they would both have ended their lives in the same place, tides and currents would have washed up Harvey's body in the same place as Tucker's, so maybe he didn't drown after all. If so, I wonder where he is."

"I'm thinking now that when you get out of

here, Finn, as I'm sure you will before long, you're going to have not only Ben to deal with, but maybe this Harvey guy too, given his own involvement in this, and that he's already tried to kill you once."

Finn sighed. "I can't believe this dreadful spider's web I've got myself into, and I still haven't been able yet to tell you the whole story, so you're hearing only bits of it piecemeal. If and when I do get out of here, though, I'll tell you everything, from the moment I stormed off to bed that night, to when I arrived back at the studio all that time later.

"Even if I do get out of here, though, and manage to get Bradley indicted for kidnapping me, I'd still not be out of the woods, because I wouldn't trust him not to use whatever connections he has to try to find some other way of getting rid of me. After all, he had no compunction at all about shooting a man who wasn't just an acquaintance, but his friend; and now, given everything you've told me about his behavior towards you as well, I truly believe he's a psychopath; he certainly seems to tick all the right boxes."

Diana nodded. "Odd you should say that. That's what he said *you* were."

"Well, maybe he's already been diagnosed as one himself, so knows what it is to be one."

"Scary."

"Yes, well, watch out for him. His next move could be to tell you he can make a killing for you on the stock market with whatever you inherit from your father, and that would be the last you'd see of it."

"I'm finding it difficult to hide how I feel about him now, Finn. I'm sure he's noticed a change in my attitude towards him. Still, he's always known

I've not stopped loving you, so maybe he'll put it down to your having come back. You don't think he'll decide that if he can't have me, then you won't either, do you? He's already asked me to go away with him to somewhere exotic, and pretty much everything he says to me now I see as having some sinister motive. I really am scared of him."

"Well, until I'm out of here, just take care, Diana, and make an effort not to be alone with him anywhere isolated if you can. Tell you what! Why don't you use this opportunity to get the house redecorated after all the storm damage? That way, you'll have people around during the day, at least. Also, perhaps the best thing regarding your relationship with me will be to pretend you've decided I'm a nutcase after all, and have washed your hands of me. Then, if and when I'm exonerated, you can say you've heard I've taken off, and gone back to the UK."

"What? You mean hide yourself away whenever he comes visiting? Yes, I suppose you could do that. That way you could keep an eye on me at the same time, and be there in case he does try something. I'd certainly feel a lot safer, knowing you're around, that's for sure, but you can't hide away forever, can you?"

"I have to be honest and say that the more I think about it, the more I can expect that as long as he knows I'm alive, he *is* going to try to silence me, so I *will* need to keep out of sight until I find a way of having him locked up, not only for what he did to me, but for murdering Tucker as well. I'm thinking, too, that it's good that I'm being kept in isolation here, because I wouldn't put it past him to put out a contract on me, if he thought someone could get at me to kill me. There's a lot on both of our plates right now, isn't there, my love?"

CHAPTER 50

Diana had just arrived at the penitentiary to pick up Finn, all charges having been dropped. As they were walking towards the car she stopped, turned to him, and put her hands up to her ears. "Look! See! I can wear these earrings again! I never thought I could. After you disappeared, I put them away at the back of a drawer; I couldn't bear to look at them, because they reminded me of you."

He drew her towards him, and kissed each ear. "I think I actually fell in love with you right then and there in the Sarasota hospital that time. You were wearing them, and I remember thinking all you needed was a matching spoon to hang from your nose," he teased.

"Well, at least I'd have looked different, I suppose, although, if I had, I imagine the last thing you'd have done would have been to find me attractive with me looking like that! You'd have thought I was a junkie," Diana laughed.

"No. I'd have found you attractive, no matter

what." He put his arm round her and kissed her. "Thank you, my darling Diana. Thank you so much for standing by me, and believing me; I'll never forget it."

Diana rummaged for her car keys, held them up, and gave him a sly look. "Well, you looked so miserable, Mr. Finn Westlake, what else could I *possibly* do?"

"Well, I only looked that way because I knew you'd fall for it, didn't I?" He opened the car door for her. "Come on; get in, Miss Diana McGuire."

On the way home, he told her how Harvey had tried to drown him on the morning of his disappearance, and everything that had happened to him afterwards.

"I'd written you a note too, telling you how much you meant to me. I meant to put it under your door before I left, but then I fell asleep, and when I woke, realized I was late. It wasn't until I was on board the *Brandy X* with Harvey that I discovered I still had it in my pocket."

"And I forgot to tell you: I found that note, and have been treasuring it. I keep it under my pillow, even though it's pretty messed up after all this time."

"You found it? When? Where?"

"After they carted you off in the helicopter, I went to put your clothes, such as they were, in the wash, but out of habit, checked the pockets first. I found it in the back pocket of your jeans. After that, I sat down and cried."

He leaned across and kissed her. "I was tempted to throw it overboard, but couldn't; it was the only connection to you I had left. I think we should frame it, don't you?"

"Yes, we should at that. It's the most precious note I've ever received, or rather, *not* received."

"You know, not having anything else to do in jail, I decided to spend the time writing out everything I just told you, a sort of diary for which I dredged up every detail I could remember, no matter how seemingly trivial. It wasn't easy, because I had to do it left-handed, but I did it. I wrote down everything, right from the beginning, from when I saved your father and Moseley from that plane wreck, and then I put it all in a big envelope, and got my attorney to put a dated seal on it, to be opened if and when necessary."

"Necessary?"

"Well, I was thinking that if the worst happens, and Bradley does have me killed, then what I've written and sealed in the envelope will nail him as my murderer -- or thinking more optimistically -- when I finally manage to get him into court, I don't want anyone accusing me of inventing anything after the fact to suit my own purposes. I don't know, but you never know how things are going to turn out, and I wanted every detail I could remember down in black and white, and notarized, just in case."

They were half way across the bay now, the old summer-cruise ship chugging along slowly, the fall breeze blowing into their faces. It felt fresh and clean, and they got out of the car and went to lean over the rail, looking over towards what was left of the bridge.

"Given all the other news you've been telling me about, Finn, I still haven't found out the details of why they dropped the case against you for murdering Dad."

"Well, that in itself is quite a complicated story too, one way and another, but I'll try to explain it, so here goes:

"My lawyer told me that when the car found outside the lumber-mill gates hadn't been returned to the rental company on time, and they'd failed to get in touch with the man who'd rented it, namely me, they contacted the police to ask if there were any reports regarding where it might be. They were told it was being impounded as evidence in a murder enquiry, but would be returned as soon as they'd obtained whatever forensic evidence they could from it.

"Seems they were stymied for quite a while. What had led them to me initially, of course, were my passport, driver's license and VISA credit card, which they'd found lying together on the ground next to the car, and as that officer, Gene, said when they arrested me, they thought I must have been in such a hurry, I didn't even notice I'd dropped them.

"The forensic team had then searched for fingerprint and DNA evidence, and this is where their case against me started to become unstuck. I'd been fingerprinted right after they hauled me in, and they'd taken a blood sample at the same time so as to get my DNA, but then, when they went to match these up with whatever they'd found inside the car itself, they couldn't find any sign that I'd ever been in it, nor could they find any evidence, of course, that I'd kept a body in the trunk.

"What they did find were some receipts in the glove compartment, though, which were for items recently bought using my credit card, items that included some clothing which they found on the back seat, still with their labels attached, but when they looked at them closely, they realized they would have been way too large and too short for someone of my height and build."

The ferry drew up alongside the pier, and they climbed back in the car, ready to disembark.

"Let's hope Ben isn't waiting for me when we get back," Diana sighed. "I never know these days when he's going to drop by. It's like he's waiting for me to let something slip, which will let him know I'm privy to some concrete, incriminating evidence against him. How he'd react if he saw you, I don't know. Who knows? Maybe he carries a gun hidden under his jacket, just in case he does."

Finn nodded. "Better drop me off at the studio then, and I'll wait there while you check the coast is clear. I do feel a real coward trying to avoid him like this, but common sense tells me that with my arm still in an immovable cast like this, there's no way I could get the better of him if he decided to attack me, much as I'd like to floor him. And, of course, having used a gun once already, to kill Tucker, I'm sure he'd have no trouble adding me to the list."

"Ridiculous, isn't it that we have to go to these lengths to protect ourselves, but, like you, Finn, I certainly don't trust him now, knowing what he's capable of. You do need to try to work out some way of getting him arrested soon, though, don't you, darling?"

"True. Give me a few days to get my head back together, though; I know there has to be some way of nailing him; I just haven't been able to figure it out yet."

"You didn't finish telling me how they failed in the end to indict you for Dad's murder."

"Oh yes. Well, then they studied all the other receipts they'd found, and tracked the use of my credit card, discovering that I'd supposedly rented the car at the Hertz Rental office at Logan airport, in Boston, two days before the mill fire.

"The second time my card had been used was at the Holiday Inn in Freeport, in Maine, that same night, and the last time at the L.L. Bean store there. That's where the clothes came from, and with none of my DNA or fingerprints to be found on them, they went back to the car, which, being a rental car, of course had a multitude of fingerprints in it, all of which they had tested, of course, looking for mine among them. I don't know where they got your father's fingerprints and DNA from, but..."

"I know where they got them; they contacted me asking for any object that Dad had used, and which would be likely to have his fingerprints on it and, preferably, his DNA as well. I gave them his electric razor, which he hadn't taken with him. They also wanted a photo of him, but wouldn't tell me what they wanted everything for."

"Ah, well then, now we know, because that's how they were able to identify as your father's both the prints as well as the saliva they found on a crushed-up beer can lodged under the driver's seat.

"Seems they couldn't make sense of it at all now. Why would I have rented the car, but then given it to your father to drive, without ever getting into it myself?" Finn began to laugh. "And if I hadn't driven it myself, then how had I got to the mill, unless I was driving a separate car? But there were no other new tire tracks at the scene, so now they wondered, finally, how I managed to get from Maine to Cautuxet Island by midnight on the night of the hurricane." He laughed again. "I must have given them quite a headache trying to sort that lot out!

"Anyway, armed with what little evidence they did have of my involvement in the murder, the police then went to the various locations at which I'd supposedly used my credit card, and this is what saved me, because they discovered that neither the woman at the Hertz counter, nor the person on duty at the Holiday Inn on the night in question recognized my mug shot. Then they showed these people the photo of your father, and they confirmed that he was the man they'd served! Unfortunately, the photo of me on my driver's license was a bit messed up after I'd accidentally left in my pants' pocket, and put it through the washing machine and dryer, so I guess the person renting out the car didn't look at it closely enough to realize my face didn't match your father's.

"Anyway, they then, finally, decided to take into account your local policemen's evidence that I'd claimed I'd left all those documents in that vase in the bedroom, and that someone must have taken them. With that as well, their whole case against me fell apart as they came to the conclusion that it had to be your father himself who'd stolen them."

"My father!"

"Well, unfortunately yes. The rest is not funny at all I'm afraid, Diana, because it implicates your father in a rather nasty fraud attempt. Armed with their findings, they concluded that the reason your father had taken my documents and used them was most likely in an attempt to defraud his insurance company and frame me for it, but that he had failed to get out of the compound in time after setting the fire, so had perished in the flames. They said it was something to do with the location of his body indicating that he had become trapped inside the high, chain-link fence when a stack of timber fell on him.”

"I don't understand. Yes, it does appear obvious from the evidence that that's what happened, but why would Dad have done such a thing? And to try to put the blame on you too. That's dreadful," Diana sighed. "This is a case of: the good news is, and the bad news is, isn't it? And I'm not trying to be flippant either. Here I am, elated that you've been set free, but at the same time discover that my father did something terrible, although I have to ask it again: why? Why would Dad ever have done anything like that? Why would he even have needed to? And to realize too that, after he'd found your documents, he had to have known something bad must have happened to you, but didn't report it. My own father, doing something like that! It's horrendous. What could possibly have driven him to do it?"

"I can explain that too, but just let's get home now; it's not a subject I feel like going into at the moment, except to say that there's no way your father would have known where to look for those documents, so his finding them has to have been fortuitous, not a deliberate attempt to steal them. Secondly, when he did find them, he would have immediately concluded that I was dead. Why he would have come to this conclusion is something I'll have to explain later. It's complicated, and I just don't want to have to think about it right now."

CHAPTER 51

Several days had passed since Finn's arrival back at the McGuire mansion, and Bradley had visited on one of them, forcing him to retire to the guest room for the duration, and, apart from having to face his unfinished business with the man, Finn had, for the first time in months, the chance to enjoy his freedom, and begin to feel civilized again.

For Diana, though, he could see the situation was very different, it being obvious that Bradley's visits had become very stressful for her now that she knew what sort of man he really was, and what he was capable of.

"I think I'm starting to get paranoid about him now, Finn. I'm expecting him to suddenly leap out from somewhere, waving a gun, or to find some more sneaky way of getting rid of me, because he thinks I might know too much. At least he believes you've returned to the UK, so doesn't seem that concerned about you anymore. When it comes to what he thinks of me, though, I keep looking for hidden meanings in everything he says. While he was here yesterday he asked me out again to the *Poulet Noir*. I put him off, and told him I'd let him know today, as I wasn't sure whether I had something else I needed to do.

"That reminds me; I need to call him and give some excuse for not going, and sound all natural about it. Goodness knows, it isn't as though I haven't become a pro at finding excuses to refuse him. When I think, too, how guilty I used to feel for putting him off so consistently, but, as you've said, he's a charmer, and he certainly did his best to try to get me to put you out of my mind. He never succeeded though. As I told you before, I even told him several times that we should stop seeing each other, but on the last occasion, you should have heard him! He went all melodramatic on me, and even threatened to commit suicide if I left him! I realize now, though, that it was, and still is, all a conquest issue. It's almost as though he has a bet with someone that he'll get me into bed with him, and, seeing that it was you that he saw as being the one preventing him from winning his bet, makes his attitude towards you understandable now; he must absolutely hate you!" And she leaned over and put her arms round Finn's neck.

He reached up and held her hand to his lips. "And there was I too, wondering what I'd done to make his attitude towards me become quite so bitter. I can see now, though, that the more you refused him, the more he got to loathe me. In fact, right now I can't imagine any two men who can possibly hate each other more! Oh, let's forget about Bradley, shall we?

He put out his arm. "Come here. I wish I

could give you a proper hug, my darling Diana. I can't wait to get back to normal. I'd hoped another few weeks would do it; now I'm not so sure. They say it'll be another month yet before I even get to start using my arm again, and that it's still going to take considerably longer for me to get full use of it back, if ever. Oh well, come on; at least it doesn't stop us from doing what matters most, does it?"

And they went up to the bedroom, where he discovered all over again what a beautiful body she had, and how well she knew how to arouse him and satisfy him more than any woman he had ever known -- and yes, he had been honest with her about that too.

Finn propped himself up on his elbow. "By the way, to get back to the unpleasant subject of Bradley again, didn't you say you have to phone and put him off? That was well over an hour ago, so maybe you should do that soon, and get it over with."

"Oh yes, I totally forgot about him! You're right. I'll call him right now. Get it over with, as you say."

"And while you're doing that, I'm going to lock myself away in the library, and put my brain to work on anything that I can use to bring him to justice. I'm mentally, if not physically up to doing that now."

Diana opened the door to the library, phone in hand.

"What did…?" Finn started.

She put her finger to her lips, and pointed to the phone. She mouthed "Ben" to him, and switched on the speaker so that Finn could hear.

Bradley's voice echoed in the small room.

"Who was that? Who've you got there with you?"

"Oh, sorry Ben… uh… It's the man come to check on the furnace. It's been acting up." She turned her head away from the phone, as though talking to someone else. "It's in the basement. First door on the left down there."

Finn grinned. "Thanks, honey."

"*Honey*! Bit familiar, isn't he?"

"I'm sorry to have interrupted you Ben. He's gone now. What was it you were saying about our relationship?"

"Yes, well, as I was saying, you were right. Our relationship is going nowhere, and I know you've lost your father and two other partners in a row, and I'm sorry, but I'm going to have to call it quits as well. I just can't take it anymore. As you can imagine, with you being so unresponsive, and talking about that maniac, Westlake, all the time, it's not been easy to remain faithful to you -- impossible, in fact -- and all the time we've been going out, I've been dating several other women on and off as a result, and…"

"Oh Ben! Please! You don't have to explain. As I've said so many times before, I don't know how you've remained with me for so long, given the way I've been..." She paused, and gave Finn a wicked look. "Still, I have to say that having told you that I finally realized you were right about Finn being a nutcase, and that I was perhaps now ready to have a proper relationship with you."

Finn raised his eyebrows, and shook his head. "Don't push it!" he mouthed at her.

"Too little, too late, I'm afraid, Diana. I know it means that you'll now have been dumped three times in a row, but maybe perhaps it also means it's time to look to yourself to see what's gone wrong with your relationships, instead of blaming us guys all the time. After all, we can only tolerate so much rejection, and a woman that constantly refuses to have… well… and I know you kept on and on about Westlake, but if you were with him and that Eric guy like you've been with me, then I'm not surprised you're now left without anyone. At the rate you're going, you're going to end up a lonely old spinster rattling around in that mausoleum of yours that you call home. Anyway, I guess that's all I have to say, and I'm out of here, so I'll just say, goodbye, and wish you luck, and take a hint from me: you're just going to have to change your attitude towards men, or you're going nowhere." The phone went dead.

"Wow! That's put me in my place, hasn't it?"

Finn stood up and took her hand. "Come on, you lonely old spinster, you; let's go celebrate again. We could show Bradley a thing or two, couldn't we?"

"Finn?"

"Hmm?"

"Wake up. I think I've remembered when Dad might have found your documents."

"What? It's three o'clock in the morning? What are you doing, being awake now?"

"Thinking about you as usual, my darling,

and I suddenly remembered being awake at this time one night back in the summer. It was a really hot and humid night, and I was lying on top of the sheets, too hot to sleep, and being so sad that you were gone, and then a breeze came up, and I heard the door to the guest room banging. It was one of those Chinese torture-like sounds, and I couldn't sleep because of it. I was just getting up to shut it, when I heard Dad going down there. It must have bothered him too. I heard him shut the guest-room window, which was causing the door to bang, but it was quite a while before he went back to bed afterwards, and I'm thinking now that that must have been when he found your things."

"Oh? What makes you think that?"

"Well, it could be that, in the dark, he knocked the vase off the cabinet while reaching across it to close the window. The carpet in there would have stopped the vase from breaking, but maybe everything fell out, and that's how he found them. I still can't fathom why he did what he did with them, though."

"You're probably right. That vase fell off the cabinet when I touched it too." Finn propped himself up on his elbow, and yawned. "Well, now I'm awake, I guess this is as good a time as any to explain why your father did what he did with my documents, although it's not something I'm going to get any pleasure from at all, and the reason I know all this is because Devine, believing I would never be alive to repeat what he told me, took it upon himself to tell me everything while he had me in his car that night.

"Remember you said how horrendous it was that your father hadn't gone to the police when he found my documents, and you couldn't understand why he hadn't, or even why he needed the insurance money in the first place? Well, as you already knew, of course, your father and Rollo Devine were good friends, but what you would not have known is that they had a strong and pretty dodgy business relationship as well, so when your father phoned Devine that night to ask him about the bridge…"

Finn then went on to relate to Diana everything Devine had told him, omitting the details of her father's early criminal career and name change before he met and married her mother, this being something he felt she did not need to know now, if ever.

"To your father's credit, I think he honestly believed that I was wrong about the bridge. If he had at all suspected I was right, he would never have called Devine in the first place. Then, after Devine told him to tell me to mind my own business and that he would sue me if I accused him of being a crook, I suspect that your father was actually quite relieved when he thought I'd walked out on you, and was no longer a potential problem.

"That said, it would have been an immense shock to him when he found my documents. This because he would have known, as well as anybody, what Devine was capable of, and would have immediately concluded that what had really happened to me was that Devine had taken it into his own hands to make sure I was silenced, and that my body was, by then, lying under six feet of concrete somewhere. And the reason he didn't go to the police, I am sure, would have been because -- again knowing what Devine was capable of -- he would be in fear that if he did, he too would meet the same end. Then, when Devine called in the mortgage, your father decided that if I were already dead, he had nothing to lose by having me blamed for the mill fire.”

Diana gave a hesitant nod. “You know, Finn, I’m thinking now that all this was the reason Dad started to behave very much out of character round about that time, and to lose his usual rather exuberant personality. He wasn’t his usual, gregarious self at all, and even started going out sailing alone on the *Moonglow*, saying he had a lot on his plate, and needed to be able to go somewhere where he could think clearly. In fact, I even told my friend, Janice, that I was worried about him.”

“Yes,” Finn agreed. “He certainly did have a lot on his plate. There he was, threatened by Devine if he didn’t come up with ransom money; then finding all my documents, leading him to believe I had been murdered by Devine; afraid to go to the police for fear of what Devine might do to him, and battling with his conscience about whether to use my documents to frame me if he were to set fire to the lumber mill for the insurance. Yes indeed. He did have a lot on his plate. No wonder he behaved abnormally!”

“It’s all horribly sordid, though, isn’t it? I find it so hard to believe Dad was involved in something like this.”

“Well yes, it has to come as a shock to learn that the father you loved wasn’t quite what you thought he was. Look at it this way, though; if nothing else, one good thing has come out of it. The deeds say this house is your father’s, free and clear of all debt, and as it appears he made you sole beneficiary of everything in his will, that makes you a pretty wealthy woman property-wise at least, although it's extraordinarily sad, of course, that it had to come about this way."

"Yes. Very. I hardly know what to think or say at this point. It all leaves me with such mixed emotions."

CHAPTER 52

Diana and Finn were sitting out on the lawn in the sun. Fall had arrived, crisp copper leaves falling around them like paper coins. Finn's arm was almost back to normal, and he was capable of doing most things that did not require putting too much strain on it.

He looked at his watch, and stood up. "Fancy a vodka and tonic and some nibbles?"

"Yes, but let me get it. You'll need me to carry it."

"No, it'll be fine, unless you were intending me to bring the kitchen sink out as well."

He went into the kitchen, where he spent some time putting everything together, and was making his way out again through the porch door when he heard Diana exclaim in an unusually loud voice: "*Ben*! What brings you here?" but it was too late for Finn to retreat, because by this time he was negotiating the first step down onto the lawn, and, concentrating on what he was carrying, had not seen

Bradley arrive, so was in full view, both hands holding a tray containing the two vodka tonics, two half-empty bottles of tonic for top-ups, and a dish of pretzel sticks.

He hesitated, his foot poised on the first step, and caused one of the bottles to first wobble, then tip over, clunking down onto the tray, and sending its fizzing contents down his chinos. He looked up to see Bradley striding up the lawn towards him. "What the hell?"

Finn dumped the tray on the step behind him, then stood, watching the loudly cursing Bradley advancing on him, with Diana in pursuit. She grabbed hold of him. "No, Ben! No!"

He turned and shook her off. "Where the hell has *he* come from then? You lying bitch! You told me he'd gone back to England. He swung his arm, hitting her on the side of her face with the back of his hand, knocking her to the ground, then stepped over her, his eyes on Finn, who was striding towards him. "I'll deal with you later," Bradley yelled at her. "But first I'm going to deal with him. Yeah, you, Westlake! I sure *am* going to deal with you, and I mean big time."

The two men advanced on each other, and when Bradley put out his arm to seize hold of Finn, Finn grabbed it, swinging him round, and before Bradley could regain his balance, hit him on the chin with his fist, knocking him off his feet.

"Get up, Bradley. Get up! Now! Damn you for hitting Diana like that! Get up and fight, you twisted, murdering psycho! I'm not safely shackled to anything now, you miserable coward, and your uncle and the police aren't here to protect you either, so stand up and let's see what you're really made of, eh?" Finn stood, waiting, staring down at him.

Diana stood up, wiping blood from her cheek. "No Finn, no! Let it go. Please! I don't want you hurt anymore. Please, let it go." She turned to Bradley, who was clambering to his feet. "Ben. Whatever it was that you came here for, I don't want to know. Go away. You said you were ready to get out of my life, so just go. Get lost. Finn being here is none of your business, so leave us alone."

Finn stood, watching Bradley. "No, he's not going away, Diana. He's not going anywhere till I've finished with him, so please stay out of this. In fact, you can call the police. I want him arrested for assaulting you."

Bradley, his eyes fixed on Finn's face, took off his jacket, and dropped it on the lawn. "Yes, you bitch, why don't you go call the cops? Yes, you do that. Your perfect Finn here has already attacked me once, haven't you, dear, beloved Finn, darling? I'll tell them you assaulted me yet again, and when Diana tried to protect me, you hit her too. Of course, you'll try to protect him by lying to the police, and saying I did it, won't you Diana dearest, but given his history of violence towards me, they won't believe you, and this time, I'll see you, Finny boy, locked up for the rest of your natural."

He raised his fists and put on an exaggerated boxing stance, dancing around, feinting punches. "Yeah, Diana, darling, jump to it then. Go call the police, why don't you? Tell them to bring an ambulance too. Your beloved Finn's going to need..." The next instant he was stretched out, unconscious, on the lawn, having failed again to see Finn's fist coming.

Finn turned away, walked over to the steps, and sat down.

Diana ran after him. "Are you all right, Finn? You haven't hurt your arm again, have you?"

"I've no idea, but even if I have, it was well worth it. Can't tell you how long I've been waiting to do that."

Diana called the police, then pointed towards Bradley. "He's coming round. What are we going to do with him till they get here?"

"I'll show you exactly what we're going to do with him," and by the time Bradley was fully conscious, Finn had attached him to the flagpole using the handcuffs, with chain still attached, that Diana had removed from his own wrists on the night of the hurricane.

"And now let's enjoy our vodka tonics, shall we?" Finn raised his glass to Bradley. "Cheers. I'm sure you recognize the handcuffs, Bradley. After all, you yourself used them to shackle me to that rock in Bass Cove. Come to think of it, you're the only one with the key too, so…"

Bradley sat up, then got to his feet, swaying slightly, and spitting out blood. "You know you can't get me to go down for that or anything else! Just you wait, though. You've broken my nose, and knocked out one of my teeth. I'll see you locked up in the worst pen in the whole country. I know the right people too, and I'll make sure the only way you'll ever come out is in a pine box; I guarantee it."

"But before you manage to do that, Bradley, I'm going to get you locked up for life for kidnapping and holding me hostage for all that time, then exchanging me for ransom."

"You haven't a hope in hell of ever pinning any of that on me. Nobody's ever going to believe you."

"I wouldn't be too sure about that. Ah! The police, I believe."

Gene and Joe skidded into the driveway, siren blaring, and Diana and Finn went to greet them.

"It's Ben Bradley," Diana explained as they led them round to where their prisoner was still chained to the flagpole. "He arrived here earlier, and when he saw Finn, he turned on me, and hit me on the side of my face. Look." She turned to Joe and showed him where her cheek, still bleeding, was swelling up and turning into a large bruise.

"Officer! Officer!" Bradley shouted. "Don't you believe a word she's saying." He nodded his head towards Finn. "It's that maniac, Westlake, again. I came here to see Diana, and he flew at me, and knocked me down, and when she tried to come to my rescue, he hit her as well. I'd never lay a finger on her. I love her, and wouldn't hurt her for the world." He turned towards Diana. "I know you love him, my darling, but you can't protect him any longer."

Gene and Joe looked at Finn, then at each other. "Miss McGuire," Gene remarked. "I do have to say it does seem odd that Mr. Westlake appears to be the only one not to have sustained any injury here, and I have to assume that Mr. Bradley's obvious injuries were not caused by you. What Mr. Bradley says, therefore, would seem to support his argument that Mr. Westlake is the aggressor here, not Mr. Bradley, wouldn't you agree? And in view of what appears to be the case, would you care to change your version of events? Lying to the police is a punishable offence, as I'm sure you are already aware."

"No, Gene. I assure you; I told you the truth."

Joe went over to where Bradley was shackled to the flagpole. He rattled the cuffs, then turned towards Finn, eyebrows raised into a question mark.

"I'm sorry, officer, but you'll have to pick the lock, I'm afraid; I don't have the key."

"I'd also like to know, Sir, where you even got these handcuffs, and why there appears to be a length of heavy chain attached to them. Mr. Bradley's argument appears to be carrying more weight by the minute. No innocent citizen would be in the possession of something like this." He started to take out his own handcuffs. "Under the circumstances, Sir, I…"

"Wait!" Diana said. "Wait! I can prove that what we said is true. Right there!" She pointed. "That's a CCTV camera, right next to the porch door. See it? I had it installed after my father died, and was all alone here. There's one attached to the wall on the other side of the house too."

"And it's switched on?" Gene asked.

"Yes, twenty-four-seven."

CHAPTER 53

Finn and Diana were curled up together on the sofa. They had turned on the television earlier so as to watch the late-night news from the local station, but their attention was elsewhere, being otherwise occupied, their clothes scattered on the floor beside them.

"*… As was mentioned last week, the body of Gus Tucker, one of the partners in the 'Stateside Underwater Engineering Company' was found washed up on a small beach on Cautuxet Island. It was first believed that he and his business partner, David Harvey, had drowned after their boat, the Brandy X, had dragged her mooring, and foundered on the rocks in Bass Cove, on the island.*

"*It was later discovered, however, that Tucker had not drowned, as previously thought, but had been shot, killed by a bullet that had pierced his heart, killing him instantly. Harvey's body has still not yet been recovered, and it is now believed he may have escaped, and a warrant has been issued for his arrest.*

"The case has today taken on a new twist, tests on the bullet that killed Tucker indicating that it was fired from a very rare Ruger Speed six variant 9mm Parabellum, and police are asking anyone with any knowledge about where such a gun might have come from, to contact them... Now, here's John Godsall with the weather..."

Finn leaned across Diana, picked up the remote, and switched off the TV. "Well, that bit of news was a passion killer, I have to say. How about a goodnight glass of wine instead?"

"Good idea."

He retrieved a bottle of her favorite Pinot Grigio from the fridge, and the two of them sat side by side, back on the sofa again, contemplating the latest news about Tucker.

"So, our Ben Bradley was using a rare gun, was he?" Finn leapt up off the sofa. "That's it! I've got him! *Yes! I've got him Diana!"* He raised his glass high in the air, spilling most of the wine over himself in the doing.

"How? How have you got him?"

"I *know* where he got that gun!" He sat down again. "The problem, though, will be to prove it."

"Wait a minute, Finn. Let's not get too excited yet. You've got to think this through carefully. First of all, how do you know where he got it from?"

"Poor old Gus Tucker. He gave me the information himself, although unwittingly, of course. He actually told me how to nail the man who'd end up murdering him! Extraordinary!"

"How and when did he give you the information?"

"Well, he used to like to come down into the cabin and chat to me. He'd talk about all sorts of things, and on this one occasion he'd been telling me something about eBay, which reminded him of a story about Governor Brigham. This is weird beyond. He told me that Governor Brigham has a collection of rare handguns, but likes to tell everyone they're repros he picked up, including the display case, for a song, on eBay. Tucker said he does that for security reasons, telling people the only reason he bought them was because they went with the décor.

"Now the thing is, as we know, Bradley spends most of his time living with his uncle since his divorce, because he told us so that night at the yacht club ball. He'd have access to those guns, and would know they're for real. I bet my life on it that that Ruger is a part of Brigham's collection! I've got him, Diana! I've got him! I'm sure I have. Where else could he have got it? Yup. I bet he borrowed it for the ransom exchange, but then ended up using it on Tucker, which obviously wasn't a part of his plan at all. It was just that poor old Tucker decided he couldn't go through with it, knowing I was going to be killed, and Bradley considered the ransom money more important than his friend."

"I hate to play Devil's advocate here, Finn, but wouldn't Governor Brigham have noticed the gun missing from its display case?"

"Not if Ben replaced it temporarily with a reproduction one. Didn't you tell me he left you in the middle of the hurricane, saying he had some documents he needed to deliver urgently to his uncle, Governor Brigham, back on the mainland? That urgent delivery, Diana, my love, wasn't documents at all, but the real gun, which he needed to return to the display case before Brigham *did* notice! He must have been on completely on edge, worrying that he mightn't be able to get back to the mainland that night. Okay! So, the police want to know where that rare Ruger might have come from. Well, tomorrow they're going to find out, because I'm going to tell them!"

CHAPTER 54

Gene and Joe, the island's two police officers, were once again in the McGuire living room, this time seated side by side on the sofa. Suspended between their knees, their hats rotated in a series of jerks, tweaked along by nervous fingers, and although tempted, Finn refrained from showing any satisfaction with their new respect towards him.

"Can I get some coffee for you, gentlemen." Diana stood poised, the perfect hostess.

They looked at each other.

"This is going to take quite a while, so you might as well," she urged them, and receiving nods and murmurs of thanks, disappeared into the kitchen.

Finn excused himself for a minute, and returned carrying a bottle of sparkling water. He held it up. "As Miss McGuire said, what I have to tell you is going to take quite a while, so I'm going to need this." He sat down opposite them in McGuire's old chair, and started to take the top off, but failed – an aftereffect of his fight with Bradley.

Joe leapt up. "Let me help you with that, Sir. How is your arm anyway? Coming along, I trust." He handed Finn the opened bottle.

"Thanks. I don't know yet, and won't know if any permanent damage has been done until the physiotherapist gets to work on it some more. It's taken quite a beating one way and another, as you know." He looked across at Gene, who was studying his fingernails.

"Good job Miss McGuire had that CCTV installed," Joe remarked, "otherwise you'd have had some difficulty explaining that it was Bradley, not you, that did the assaulting, especially after your attack on him that day we arrested you."

"Yes, luck was on my side for once. By the way, has he been charged with assaulting Miss McGuire yet?"

"No. A decision has been made not to go ahead with the charges in this case, it being considered as just a lovers' tiff, and, without any audio, impossible to judge what it might have been about otherwise."

Diana returned with the coffee, then sat down on the arm of Finn's chair. "Right, gentlemen, let's get started, shall we?"

For the next hour Finn told his whole story, beginning on the day when he rescued Diana's father and Sebastian Moseley from the plane wreck in the river.

"Moseley!" Gene exclaimed. "You rescued him as well?"

Finn savored their growing respect.

"And that's it," he ended at last. "And I know

you're looking for Harvey, alive or dead, but wherever he's got to, I assure you that, while he did try to drown me, he didn't shoot Tucker; Bradley did."

Joe twirled his hat some more. "Too bad Governor Brigham's involved. It makes it much more of a delicate situation, if you see what I mean. We can't simply rush off and get a search warrant to go over Governor Brigham's home. He's not going to be happy at all with any sort of negative publicity now with the elections coming up either, and him hoping to get back into office. It's going to be tricky."

"So, you've told us this story." Gene twirled his hat some more. "You must admit it's a pretty wild story, though. How can you prove any of it is true? Tucker's dead, so are Devine and his driver – in case you didn't know -- and Harvey and Bradley would get you laughed out of court with it."

"Well, for starters, I've just told you where to find the murder weapon. Secondly, as the center span of the bridge has collapsed, you can have someone go in and prove I was right about the foundations being dangerous, so I was right in saying the reports had to be being faked. Also, how would I have known it was Devine's car that blew up if I hadn't been in it a just few seconds before it happened? And how would I even know Governor Brigham has a collection of rare guns?"

"It's still all based on your version of events, though. How do we know you haven't conveniently altered parts of it to suit your own ends? For example, it's all public knowledge now, anyway, that it was Devine's car that blew up."

"Yes, but I can even tell you where he was

sitting in the car, and that was right behind the front passenger seat, and I know that, because I'd been the one *in* that front passenger seat. Forensics will be able to corroborate that, and obviously I'm not psychic, so couldn't possibly know where Devine was sitting, unless I'd been there."

"Well, who's to say it wasn't you who shot Tucker then?"

"If I'd killed Tucker, would I be stupid enough to raise my head above the parapet now, and suggest you go to Governor Brigham's home, above all places, to find out if one of his rare handguns had been used in the murder I'd committed? Or even if I wasn't virtually a hundred percent sure you'd find the murder weapon there? And there's absolutely no way I could have stolen it myself as the place must be littered with security, but Bradley lives there; it would have been easy for him."

"What I don't understand," said Joe, "is why you didn't come out with all this when we arrested you that day, or while you were in the pen. Why wait till now? It makes it look as though you're hiding something, or have some self-serving motive here."

"The only self-serving motive I have is to nail the bastard who made my life hell for three months, and maybe left me physically unable to carry on with my career. Anyway, think back, Joe. The day you arrested me, apart from the bad shape I was in, even if I'd started then to try to tell you where I'd actually been, and what had happened to me, can you see yourselves, either of you, letting me even finish my story, let alone believe me? You wouldn't even believe me when I told you where I'd left all my documents, and the reason I've waited is simply because, although I knew Bradley shot Tucker, I'd no way of proving it till yesterday. I could easily have ended up being accused myself. Even now, Gene, you've suggested that I might have conveniently altered things to suit my own purposes, and murdered Tucker myself."

"There's something else too," Diana said, and she told them about the time Bradley had come to the house, sporting a thick lip with two stitches in it. "There's no way Mr. Westlake would have known about that if, as Ben told me, he received that injury in a car crash."

"That's something else you can check, then, as well," Finn added. "I can't remember the date on which that happened; I'd lost all track of time by then, but Miss McGuire will remember. If Bradley had been in an accident as he claims, there'd be a police report on it, and even if he wasn't in his own car at the time, his name would be listed as one of the occupants and one of the injured. Go check on that. I can assure you, you won't find any such report, because he wasn't in any car accident; I kicked him in the face, as I told you in my story. I'd go one step further: Bradley won't know you know how he got that injury. Question him, and I bet he repeats the car-accident story. He can't tell you I did it, because then he'd incriminate himself by having to tell you when and where I did it."

"I've thought of something else too," said Diana. "The night of the hurricane, when Ben breezed in and found me in the studio, he was carrying a briefcase, and I'm thinking now that what it contained was the ransom money as well as the gun!"

"Can you describe the case to us, Miss McGuire," Joe asked her.

Diana gave him the description, then suggested they check his apartment in Davenport, as the briefcase could be there. "Maybe the money's still in it!"

Gene nodded. "Yes, that we could do."

"Heh! Wait a minute!" said Diana. "Something else has just occurred to me too. He'd originally told me he was going out fishing with his friends that evening, and that was why he wouldn't be able to accept my father's invitation to accompany us to the Lillacray fundraiser. So when he suddenly turned up at the studio with that briefcase in the middle of the hurricane, I was astounded, and asked him what brought him there. He said that although they did go out fishing, when they heard the hurricane warning they went back to Brickton, and because he was going to be driving back up to Davenport to his uncle's, one of his friends asked him to do a favor for him, and hand deliver some very important documents to Governor Brigham. He then went on to say that he was so worried about me, that he decided to come over here first to see if I was alright. It was all very convoluted, and he was very hesitant while explaining it too, something I put down to his anxiety about my welfare. We were in the middle of a hurricane too, of course, so it didn't occur to me to question why he would have come to the studio looking for me, and not the house, especially as the place was in complete darkness. It's not a question I've thought to ask till now either, but now I know what he had really been doing that night, I think I can answer it. Yes. That's why he came to the studio! I'm sure of it! He went there, and not to the house, because he intended to hide the ransom money in there! Of course! That has to be it! It had nothing to do with me at all, and that's why he seemed so surprised to see me there!"

"My turn to play Devil's advocate, Diana," Finn said. "That studio is completely surrounded by rhododendrons, and invisible from the driveway. How would he even have known how to find it?"

"He came up with me one day to find something for the "*Moonglow*" and the more I think of it now, the more I'm convinced he fully intended to hide the ransom money there, rather than find somewhere safe to hide it back on the mainland. I mean, can you think of anywhere better to hide it? I'm the only one who ever goes up there, and that only rarely; as you say, Finn, it's hidden from the road; isn't locked, and with all those old boxes full of all sorts of stuff stacked up on the shelves, no-one else would even think of looking for it there.

"On top of that, it would have provided easy access for him anytime he wanted to dip into it without being seen! No wonder he looked so taken aback when he flung open the door and saw me there! I totally ruined his plan, forcing him to take it all home with him, so I'm thinking there's even more reason to suspect that it's now hidden away in his apartment somewhere, don't you? As I say, no wonder he was shocked to find me there! His being there had nothing to do with me at all!

"What he *had* been doing that evening, of course, had nothing to do with fishing or any documents at all either, nor had he even been on the mainland at any time. What he *had* been doing was exchanging poor Mr. Westlake for ransom in Bass Cove, before being hell bent on making it back to Davenport asap afterwards, money safely stashed away, and gun ready to be returned to its rightful place in his uncle's display case! No wonder he was in such a rush to leave! It's a miracle he did actually make it back across the bridge before it came down! He must have been one of the last, if not *the* last, to have done that."

"Well, I guess all that makes sense, Miss McGuire, but let's come back to that later. Right now, Sir, what interests me is what suddenly made you decide you *did* have proof of Bradley's guilt. You said something about having found out yesterday. How was that?" Gene wanted to know.

"Yesterday's late-night news, when they said the forensic evidence showed that Tucker had been killed by a bullet from a rare Ruger. It was then I remembered Tucker himself telling me while I was on the boat, that Governor Brigham had this collection of rare handguns, but liked to tell everyone they were repros... something about buying the whole lot on eBay."

The two men nodded. "Yes, we've heard that story too," said Gene.

"Well then. And the rest of what we've told you is true as well."

"We still need reasonable cause to go searching Governor Brigham's home, though," said Joe. "But maybe he'd be amenable if the state police asked if they might take a quiet look at his collection - - no publicity. I can't imagine he'd have any objection to that. After all, the last thing he'd expect would be that one of his rare collector-guns had been used in a murder, especially if there were no signs of the display case being tampered with… and from what you're telling us, it would seem that Bradley would have pretty-much free access to anything in his uncle's house, so would know where to find the key."

"What about his fingerprints, though. I bet they're all over the place. They wouldn't prove anything, even on the gun. I'm sure he would have handled them all in the presence of Governor Brigham before now," said Gene.

"It wouldn't be his fingerprints you'd be looking at, though," Finn said. "Forensics has the bullet, so they'd be able to tell if that was the particular gun used, wouldn't they?"

Joe nodded. "Yes." He stood up, followed by Gene. "Well, the police did say they wanted anyone who might know where that gun came from to contact them, and you've done that; it's now up to us to follow the lead, I guess." He went towards the door. "We'll let you know what happens, okay?"

"Oh! Be sure to see if you can find that briefcase as well" Diana added. "That should help prove what we've told you too."

They nodded, then thanked her for the coffee, put on their hats, and left.

Finn smiled. "I hate to be crude, but let's stand back now, and watch the shit hit the fan, shall we?"

CHAPTER 55

Finn walked over to the window. A squirrel was hanging upside down, front legs stretched out in a frantic effort to reach the bird feeder. For a while he watched it dangling from the branch, reaching down so far that it seemed perilously close to losing its grip, then, leaving it to its struggles, he sat down next to Diana on the sofa, putting his arm around her.

"You know, now the dust has settled a bit, and I'm having time to think objectively, I'm imagining Bradley's state of mind that night: desperate to get back to Governor Brigham's mansion so as to return the gun, only to find when he got there, that he had to put it back still loaded, because he couldn't remove the clip! He must have been scared stiff to have had to return it to the display case like that, and realizing that the only way he was going to be able to get the clip out, would be with the proper tool, which he didn't have. Thank goodness, he wasn't able to find one before the police inspector arrived. Things could have turned out very differently for me if he hadn't found it with the clip still in it. I'd like to have seen Governor Brigham's face too, when tests proved his nephew's fingerprints were all over that clip, and that the bullet that killed Tucker came from the empty cartridge case in it."

Diana put her arms around him. "Well, my darling, we can both finally relax. It's all over. You're free, and Ben Bradley will spend the rest of his life in prison for kidnapping and holding you for ransom. Thank goodness too that they did find the briefcase with most of the ransom money still in it. That definitely had to be the clincher, didn't it? And I agree, it's good to be able to see the funny side of it now, but pretty unnerving and nail-biting for us too while his trial was ongoing, wasn't it?"

"Yes, not something I'd want to go through ever again, but all the evidence you and I were able to provide, along with the briefcase with much of the ransom money still in it… Thank God you suggested they look for that in his apartment. I wouldn't have thought of that. It all paid off, though, and with the verdict reached in record time as well." Finn sighed. "I'm still wondering, though, why, with all the evidence given about the Ruger, they haven't charged him with Tucker's murder as well. There seems to be what you might call a disturbing silence where that's concerned, and I'm suspicious as to what that silence indicates. There's Harvey too. They would surely have found his body by now if he'd drowned, don't you think? I have to believe he's still alive, and that loose end has me worried as well Something tells me it's still too early to celebrate: I'm not out of the woods yet."

"I think the police are pretty sure Harvey's on the run somewhere as well, otherwise they wouldn't have a warrant out for his arrest. Presumably they're assuming he killed Tucker, don't you think?"

"Well, wherever he is, he knows I'm the chief witness against him regarding his attempt to drown me, as well as everything else he did to me, and I have to say, that does make me nervous; he was perfectly willing to kill me once, so I wouldn't put it past him to have another go at silencing me."

"I honestly don't think he'd try, though, Finn. It would surely be too obvious who your murderer was."

Finn got up and grabbed her hand. "Oh, come on. Let's go out for a celebratory dinner somewhere. We can't have us calmly discussing my murder like this, not yet anyway. Bit premature. Come to think of it, let's go out of state somewhere to eat; the celebrity status we've both achieved here locally as a result of all the press and TV coverage because of Governor Brigham's involvement is getting to me."

Diana laughed. "Not to the *Poulet Noir* then, I gather."

CHAPTER 56

Finn gave a big sigh. He was standing in front of the window again, this time looking out at where the rest of the old bridge was already in the process of being demolished.

"Apart from meeting you, Diana, this has been the worst time of my life, and it's almost more than I can take to have my fears confirmed that it's still not over. Maybe, even, the worst is still to come, and I've reached the stage when I'm not sure I have the stamina to cope with this latest development, especially as, for the first time in ages, I'd stupidly allowed myself to relax, managing to convince myself that it was all behind me, and turning a blind eye to those niggling loose ends as I'd called them. I should have known there was good reason why Bradley hadn't been accused of Tucker's murder. Well, now I know."

He went over to where Diana was standing on a stool in front of the long case clock, winding it up, and looked up at her. "Just think, it's scarcely any time since we were able to joke about Governor Brigham finding out that it was his gun that had killed Tucker But now…"

Diana turned and put her arms around him, giving him a silent hug, and he laid his head on her shoulder.

"I know it's all very well for me to tell you not to worry, Finn, because we have no idea how it's going to end, but I do truly believe Ben's clutching at straws."

Finn raised his head, and kissed her cheek. "Then I'm just going to have to deal with this new assault, aren't I? And there's no way I could do it without you. I do love you very much, you know. I just wish I knew what evidence they've come up with that gives them sufficient cause to take seriously Bradley's claim that I, not he, was the one who actually shot Tucker. I'd have thought that, given everything that came up during his trial, it would have been obvious that he had shot the man as well. I only wish that Harvey hadn't managed to remain on the run until after Bradley's kidnapping trial was over. Maybe now he's facing trial for his own part in all this, though, he can be persuaded to turn state's evidence in return for a plea bargain; he should be able to prove that Bradley was the one that shot Tucker, unless, of course, he claims it was too dark for him to see who fired the gun. Oh, I don't know. I guess I'll find out at the preliminary hearing tomorrow."

"Well, I said I'd find out today what grounds they had for considering I might actually be responsible for Tucker's murder, but I have to admit I wasn't prepared for what Bradley claims happened. How on earth did he manage to come up with a scenario claiming that, yes, he had borrowed the Ruger purely for protection, but that I had escaped from Devine while still in Bass Cove, had hidden in the bushes, and then jumped him from behind, grabbed the gun from him, knocked him out, used it to kill Tucker, then put it back in his hand so as to make it look like he shot him. It's ludicrous! I mean, if his theory were correct, Tucker would still be on the boat, where I couldn't have shot him even if I'd wanted to. And where was Devine too? He wouldn't have simply driven off and left me still alive there, would he? None of it holds water. It's ridiculous."

He sighed. "I'd really hoped the judge would have acknowledged all the holes in the case, and thrown it out right there and then, finding insufficient evidence to constitute probable cause to indict me. I can't see why he didn't. Instead, he's still insisting on pursuing 'more of the facts', as he calls them."

"I have to say, Finn, that if it were anyone but Governor Brigham's nephew, I'm sure they wouldn't be allowed to take up court time like this with such a flimsy case! His version of what happened is, as you say, ridiculous. You know something else? I'm beginning to wonder if it *is* actually Ben who's decided to put you through the mill like this, knowing he can't possibly win. I know he's devious, but I really don't think he's bright enough to come up with all this on his own."

"What do you mean?"

"Well, maybe the powers-that-be up there in the State House aren't too happy with you for having threatened to blow the whistle on the state of the bridge, even though they can now throw all the blame for its condition on the conveniently-dead Rollo Devine" Diana argued. "And why would Ben bother anyway? He's already serving a life sentence without parole, and this state doesn't have the death sentence, so why would he want to cause himself even more grief by going through the process of testifying against you? And, come to think of it, why does he have Governor Brigham's own attorney – that abominable little Stephen Green -- representing him if Governor Brigham's claiming he's disowned his nephew now as a result of his conviction for kidnapping you? Who's paying for that fancy service, eh? Not Ben himself, especially as the police relieved him of the ransom money."

"I don't know, but it all comes down to the same thing; I'm still being put through the wringer to satisfy someone, and where Bradley's concerned, I imagine his eagerness to make my life as mentally and financially miserable as possible, far outweighs any grief it might cause him. And yes, you're right; I can't see any ordinary citizen being allowed to use the courts like this, purely out of revenge. And as for Green, the attorney, I don't know. As you say, first he's Governor Brigham's lawyer, now Bradley's. I think you're right; something's definitely going on here, and it makes me very nervous as to whether I'm going to have a fair hearing, which could mean my fate could all hang on Harvey's ability and willingness to say he saw Bradley kill Tucker."

"Well, if you're wondering who's really providing the weight behind this case against you, I'd say that, given what's happened now to Brigham's rating in the polls as a result of all the trouble you've caused him, I wouldn't mind betting on exactly who's behind it, wouldn't you agree, darling?"

Finn let out another big sigh, sat down, and picked up the day's edition of *The Davenport Daily News* from the new coffee table.

"Heh! Diana! Listen. It says here: '*TARRED WITH THE SAME BRUSH: GOVERNOR BRIGHAM SLIPS FURTHER IN POLLS. Readers of The Daily News will already be fully aware of the recent, extraordinary court case, which our newspaper has followed and detailed in full, in which Benjamin Bradley, Governor Brigham's nephew, received a life sentence, having been found guilty of kidnapping, holding hostage and exchanging diver engineer Finn Westlake for ransom, an event that has led to revelations of crooked dealings up at the State House regarding the issuing of state contracts.*

'*Even though there is no indication that Governor Brigham himself was in any way involved, the latest polls show that, previously considered a shoo-in, he is now facing an increasingly strong challenge from his opponent, Cuthbert Stillwater.*

"'*When interviewed about his improved chances of winning the governorship in the upcoming elections, Mr. Stillwater was anxious to point out that Governor Brigham, having claimed the replacement of the old island bridge to now be a top priority, has yet again bypassed normal contract-issuing procedures, and already awarded a contract to build a new bridge in a new location, starting on the Honeydale Farms land at the southern end of the island.*

"'Mr. Stillwater went on to say that, given the new evidence regarding the questionable issuing of state contracts, he would, if elected, take it upon himself to call for an investigation into this new contract, including also the – in his opinion – questionable rationale for relocating the bridge to the southern end of the island.

"'When contacted, Mrs. Charles Lillacray, President of the Cautuxet Island Save our Bridge committee, expressed enthusiasm for Mr. Stillwater's promise if elected. Acting Commodore of the prestigious Cautuxet Island Yacht Club, Mr. Benedict Southern (standing in for former Commodore Mr. Chester McGuire, deceased) concurred with Mrs. Lillacray's comments."

Finn looked up at Diana. "Huh! Yes. And I wonder who *did* receive that nice little contract for the new bridge from Brigham, and what the real reason is for relocating it too. Boy! Am I ever getting cynical these days!"

CHAPTER 57

It was the second day of the hearing, and as the new case had raised the general public's interest even higher, the press was well represented, several being from the more sensational newspapers, one of which had already headlined its column with: "BRITISH ENGINEER NOT SO INNOCENT?" and proposing that Finn had, not surprisingly, "lost it", and killed one of his kidnappers in revenge. Another had noted that a number of young ladies, having seen photos of the suspect in a popular magazine, had declared their love for him on Facebook, and had offered to marry him and have his children, should he end up being jailed for the rest of his life.

Bradley's attorney, Stephen Green, gave Finn an imperious stare. "My client, Mr. Bradley, has testified that you were obviously able to break away from Mr. Devine's custody immediately after the exchange was made, because, while he himself was still in Bass Cove, you took him completely by surprise by coming up behind and attacking him, just as you viciously attacked him the day you were arrested on suspicion of murdering Ms. McGuire's father." He paused, and looked at the judge, allowing time for his statement to sink in. "You don't deny you attacked Mr. Bradley on that particular occasion, do you, Mr. Westlake?"

"No."

"Well then." He paused again. "Now, on the day in question -- the day Mr. Tucker was shot and murdered -- as I say, you escaped from Mr. Devine's custody, and seized the Ruger from Mr. Bradley in a surprise attack from the rear, in which you knocked him out. When he came to, Mr. Tucker was lying dead on the beach, shot in the heart, and you had disappeared, having first laid the gun back in Mr. Bradley's hand, so as to implicate him in the shooting. Do you deny any of this, Mr. Westlake?"

"Yes, I do deny it. None of what Bradley claims, took place. First of all, if he was attacked from behind, in the dark, in the middle of a hurricane, how did he know it was me? Anyway, if I did have a gun, and planned on shooting anyone, I'd have had a much greater reason to kill Bradley himself than I would Gus Tucker, who, in the end, tried to save my life by rowing ashore to bring me a key to the handcuff that shackled me to that rock. Bradley saw him coming to help me, and shot him before he could reach me. I was still handcuffed to that rock when Tucker died right at my feet, the key lost in the surf.

"Secondly: Bradley himself has testified that the exchange took place at just after seven o'clock, so how would it have been possible for me to have escaped from Devine immediately after the exchange had been made, do everything Bradley claims I did, and then witness Devine's car explode over four miles away, at the entrance to the bridge, in the middle of the hurricane, less than half an hour later? It all would have been impossible, especially given my physical state at the time, something to which the hospital, I am sure, will attest."

"We have only your word for it that you witnessed Mr. Devine's tragic accident, Mr. Westlake. You could have read the details about it in the newspapers."

"No, I couldn't, because I was in police custody, accused of murdering Mr. McGuire before that news became public, and I had no access to the news."

"But you've had plenty of time since then to read up about it, and use it now to try to mislead the court."

"If necessary, Sir, I can provide written proof of exactly what I knew, or didn't know while I was still in jail. That information is in a sealed and dated envelope in the possession of my attorney. Anyway, Mr. Green, Sir, you yourself can testify as to where I was just a few minutes after Mr. Devine's car blew up."

There was a gasp from all present in the court. Mr. Green pointed a finger at his own chest, eyebrows raised in mock shock. "*I* can?"

"Yes Sir, you can."

Mr. Green looked around at all those present, including reporters, a smirk on his face.

The judge leaned across his desk. "Mr. Westlake, this court is not here to provide you with the opportunity to display your own warped sense of humour, and waste the court's the time."

"Sir, I am most certainly not joking, and furthermore, I request that Mr. Green be put under oath before he replies to my statement."

The judge called the two lawyers to the bench, and minutes later Mr. Green took his place in the dock, where he gave everyone a confident smile, while taking the oath.

Finn's lawyer stood up. "Mr. Green, Sir. Could you please remind the court where you were just after 7:30 p.m., on the night of the hurricane?"

"Yes, indeed I can. I was stuck in a ditch on Cautuxet Island, along with Governor Brigham, Mr. Moseley, Director of our State Department of Transportation, and Mr. Francisco, Governor Brigham's campaign manager." He smiled around at everyone. "A pretty good alibi, wouldn't you say?"

The whole court laughed.

"Order!" the judge called, and banged his gavel.

"Right, Mr. Green, Sir," Finn's lawyer continued. "And would you care to repeat to the court now, under oath, of course, exactly how you came to be in the ditch. Please explain to us how a so-called 'providential gust of wind' affected the car."

Mr. Green coughed. Other than that, the silence continued, everyone's attention now turned from laughing at Finn, to watching Governor Brigham's attorney.

"Mr. Green?"

The silence continued.

"Well, perhaps you'll allow me to tell the

court how you came to be in the ditch, Mr. Green, Sir, and then you can contradict me if I am wrong. First, I assume you will agree that you yourself, Governor Brigham, Mr. Moseley, and Governor Brigham's campaign manager, Mr. Francisco, were, at the time, in the antique white Cadillac Eldorado belonging to Mr. Lillacray, whose fundraiser for Governor Brigham you had just attended, and in whose car you tried to escape back to the mainland, when your helicopter failed to pick you up due to weather conditions. That is true, is it not?"

Mr. Green nodded.

"I take that as a yes then, Sir. Now, to come to that so-called providential gust of wind I mentioned a minute ago." He paused, surveyed the court, and raised a copy of the *Davenport Daily News*. "If I may quote from this recent issue of our newspaper ..." He turned to the page with a dramatic flourish. "I quote, ladies and gentlemen:

"*'Governor Brigham, hot on the campaign trail, made more urgent now following his recent decline in the polls, concluded last Saturday's rally with a reference to his miraculous escape on the night of the hurricane. As mentioned in an earlier edition of this newspaper, his helicopter grounded on account of the storm, he, along with Department of Transportation Director, Sebastian Moseley, attorney Stephen Green and Campaign Manager Eugene Francisco, were attempting to leave a fund-raising dinner they'd attended at the Lillacray estate on the island, when a providential gust of wind forced the vintage white Cadillac Eldorado he had borrowed from his host's garage, into a ditch. If it hadn't,*

Governor Brigham told reporters, they would have attempted to cross the bridge, only to end up at the bottom of the bay! 'That providential gust of wind saved our lives!' Governor Brigham was quoted as declaring'

"Would you deny, Sir, that it wasn't a wind of any sort that forced the Cadillac into the ditch? It was, rather, that the driver of your car -- and we can call him if necessary to corroborate the facts -- without making any attempt to stop, moved over so as to bypass an unfortunate individual who was standing in the middle of the road, trying to attract your attention, and in obvious need of help. Was it not, then, right as the car was about to pass this individual, that the said individual collapsed onto the road, right in the Cadillac's path, forcing the driver to swerve to avoid running over him? Would you also deny, Sir, that it was as a result of this swerve, that the car then went out of control, and hydroplaned down the road a number of yards, before coming to rest in the ditch?"

He carefully folded the newspaper, and laid it down in front of him. "I should like to suggest to you Mr. Green, Sir, that it wasn't a wind of any description that saved your lives that night; it was the unfortunate gentleman that you swerved to avoid running over!" He paused again. "I should also like to ask you, Sir, and please remember; you are still under oath, if, at any time, any of the occupants of that car, went to see if the man they left lying in the road was injured? I shall submit, Sir, that the answer is, as you already know, 'No'."

He turned to the judge. "That unfortunate individual, Judge, was my client, Mr. Westlake here --

and just to remind you: as Mr. Westlake has stated, his entire record of the event is in this signed, sealed and dated envelope." He waved it in the air. "Signed, sealed and dated well before Governor Brigham made his statement regarding that 'providential gust of wind'.

There was no stopping the pandemonium that ensued, or the amazing speed at which the court emptied, reporters rushing off to return to their desks.

EPILOG

A log shifted in the fireplace, sending a shower of sparks up the huge chimney, and lighting the room with orange fingers that danced around, creating leaping shadows on the walls. Off in the corner, a newsreader on the TV was giving the evening report. Diana and Finn were lying on the sofa, arms round each other, admiring his renewed diving certification, which had just arrived in the mail.

"Can't wait to get back to work now. Sitting around doing nothing like this hasn't been good for me, or you either when I start getting antsy. Can't have you wanting to divorce me because I'm a complete nuisance, being under your feet all day, can I?"

"Don't worry, my darling. That's never going to happen. You can be under my feet or any other part of me as much as you like; I'll never fall out of love with you."

Finn laughed. "Ah, what a wicked woman you are!" He edged forward off the sofa until he was on the rug in front of the fire. He pulled her down gently on top of him, her face close to his. She smelled of 'Fidji', and began to undo the buttons on his shirt, bending over and kissing his chest as each button was opened. "You have such a beautiful body, Finn; I do so love every bit of it." She kissed his chest again, then undid the buckle on his belt, and slid her hand down...

"Our newly-elected governor, Governor Stillwater, stated today that, as a result of the recent investigation into the replacement of the old Cautuxet Island Bridge, a new contract will be awarded following standard procedures, and that the new bridge will simply replace the old one, in the same location. Save our Bridge's Mrs. Lillacray..."

Finn's arm reached out, searching for the remote.

THE END